AMY TAN is the author of *The Joy Luck Club, The Hundred Secret Senses, The Bonesetter's Daughter, Saving Fish from Drowning,* books for children, and the recent memoir. __ was a co-pr... *Joy Luck Cl...* ...umerous magazi... ...translated into more than t... ...

Amy Tan h... ... ...er's degree in linguistics, and has worked as a language sp...alist concerned with children with learning disabilities. She lives with her husband in San Francisco and New York.

Praise for *The Kitchen God's Wife*:

'Once again this wonderful novel has extended experience. There is something dizzyingly elemental about Tan's storytelling; it melds the rich simplicities of fairytales with a delicate lyrical style'

*Sunday Times*

'Tan is a prodigal with her talent ... she weaves [a] dazzling web of unfamiliar colours, smells, tastes and landscapes'

*Sunday Telegraph*

'It is [her] sharp eye for the double vision, the tragi-comedy of cultural splitting, which lifts this novel out of the timeless space of the family saga and places it firmly inside a living tradition'

*Independent*

'With a pen that strokes simplicity out of the tangle, Amy Tan proves herself, once again, a wonderful novelist'  *Mail on Sunday*

'Amy Tan writes with passion and humour, making East and West mutually more comprehensible'  *Daily Mail*

'Ms Tan also manages, even within often tragic circumstances, to illuminate the nobility of friendship and the necessity of humour'

*New York Times Book Review*

BY THE SAME AUTHOR

*The Joy Luck Club*
*The Hundred Secret Senses*
*The Bonesetter's Daughter*
*Saving Fish from Drowning*

Non-fiction
*The Opposite of Fate*

For children
*The Moon Lady*
*The Chinese Siamese Cat*

# AMY TAN

# *The Kitchen God's Wife*

**HARPER PERENNIAL**
London, New York, Toronto and Sydney

This edition produced for The Book People Ltd,
Hall Wood Avenue, Haydock, St Helens, WA11 9UL

Harper Perennial
An imprint of HarperCollins*Publishers*
77–85 Fulham Palace Road
Hammersmith, London W6 8JB

www.harperperennial.co.uk

This edition published by Harper Perennial 2008
1

First published in Great Britain by HarperCollins*Publishers* 1991

A catalogue record for this book is available from the British Library

This novel is a work of fiction. Any references to historical events: to real
people, living or dead; or to real locales are intended only to give the fiction
a sense of reality and authenticity. Other names, characters, places and incidents
either are the product of the author's imagination or are used fictitiously, and
their resemblance, if any, to real-life counterparts is entirely coincidental.

ISBN 978-0-00-781541-8

Set in Times

Printed and bound in Great Britain by Clays Ltd, St Ives plc

**Mixed Sources**

Product group from well-managed
forests and other controlled sources
www.fsc.org  Cert no. SW-COC-1806
© 1996 Forest Stewardship Council

FSC is a non-profit international organisation established to promote the
responsible management of the world's forests. Products carrying the FSC
label are independently certified to assure consumers that they come
from forests that are managed to meet the social, economic and
ecological needs of present and future generations.

Find out more about HarperCollins and the environment at
**www.harpercollins.co.uk/green**

To my mother, Daisy Tan,
and her happy memories of
my father, John (1914–1968),
and my brother Peter (1950–1967)
with love and respect

*I am grateful to the other mothers of this book:*
*Sandra Dijkstra, Molly Giles, and Faith Sale.*
*As a writer, I feel lucky to have your wisdom and advice.*
*As a friend, I feel blessed. And thanks always to*
*Robert Foothorap, Gretchen Schields, and Lou DeMattei*
*for warmth, humor, and Chinese take-out food—*
*essential ingredients for writing this book.*

# I

# THE SHOP
# OF THE GODS

Whenever my mother talks to me, she begins the conversation as if we were already in the middle of an argument.

"Pearl-ah, have to go, no choice," my mother said when she phoned last week. After several minutes I learned the reason for her call: Auntie Helen was inviting the whole family to my cousin Bao-bao's engagement party.

"The whole family" means the Kwongs and the Louies. The Kwongs are Auntie Helen, Uncle Henry, Mary, Frank, and Bao-bao. And these days "the Louies" really refers only to my mother and me, since my father is dead and my brother, Samuel, lives in New Jersey. We've been known as "the whole family" for as long as I can remember, even though the Kwongs aren't related to us by blood, just by marriage; Auntie Helen's first husband was my mother's brother, who died long before I was born.

And then there's my cousin Bao-bao, whose real name is Roger. Everyone in the family has been calling him Bao-bao ever since he was a baby, which is what *bao-bao* means, "precious baby." Later, we kept calling him that because he was the crybaby who always wailed the minute my aunt and uncle walked in the door, claiming we other kids had been picking on him. And even though he's now thirty-one years old, we still think of him as Bao-bao—and we're still picking on him.

"Bao-bao? How can he have an engagement party?" I said. "This will be his third marriage."

"*Fourth* engagement!" my mother said. "Last one he didn't marry, broken off after we already sent a gift. Of course, Helen is not calling it engagement party. She is saying this is a big reunion for Mary."

"Mary is coming?" I asked. Mary and I have a history that goes beyond being cousins. She's married to Doug Cheu, who went to medical school with my husband, Phil Brandt, and in fact, she was the one who introduced us to each other sixteen years ago.

"Mary is coming, husband and children, too," my mother said. "Flying from Los Angeles next week. No time to get a special discount. *Full*-price tickets, can you imagine?"

"Next week?" I said, searching for excuses. "It's kind of late notice to change our plans. We're supposed to—"

"Auntie Helen already counted you in. Big banquet dinner at Water Dragon Restaurant—five tables. If you don't come she is one-half table short."

I pictured Auntie Helen, who is already quite short and round, shrinking to the size of a table leg. "Who else is coming?"

"Lots of big, *important* people," my mother answered, saying the word "important" as if to refer to people she didn't like. "Of course, she is also telling people Bao-bao will be there with his new fiancée. And then everybody asks, 'Fiancée? Bao-bao has a new fiancée?' Then Helen, she says, 'Oh, I forgot. This is supposed to be a big surprise announcement. Promise not to tell.' "

My mother sniffed. "She lets everyone know that way. So now you have to bring a gift, also a surprise. Last time what did you buy?"

"For Bao-bao and that college girl? I don't know, maybe a candy dish."

"After they broke up, did he send it back?"

"Probably not. I don't remember."

"You see! That's how the Kwongs are. This time don't spend so much."

Two days before the dinner I got another phone call from my mother.

"Now it is too late to do anything about it," she said, as if whatever it was were my fault. And then she told me Grand Auntie

Du was dead at age ninety-seven. This news did come to me as a surprise; I thought she had already died years ago.

"She left you nice things," my mother said. "You can come get it this weekend."

Grand Auntie Du was actually Helen's blood relative, her father's half sister, or some such thing. I remember, however, it was my mother who had always helped take care of Grand Auntie. She carried out her garbage every week. She kept the old lady from subscribing to magazines every time she got a sweepstakes notice with her name printed next to the words "One Million Dollars." She petitioned Medi-Cal over and over again to pay for Grand Auntie's herbal medicines.

For years my mother used to complain to me how she did these things—not Helen. "Helen, *she* doesn't even offer," my mother would say. And then one day—this was maybe ten years ago—I cut my mother off. I said, "Why don't you just tell Auntie Helen what's bothering you and stop complaining?" This was what Phil had suggested I say, a perfectly reasonable way to get my mother to realize what was making her miserable so she could finally take positive action.

But when I said that, my mother looked at me with a blank face and absolute silence. And after that, she did stop complaining to me. In fact, she stopped talking to me for about two months. And when we did start talking again, there was no mention of Grand Auntie Du ever again. I guess that's why I came to think that Grand Auntie had already died long ago.

"What was it?" I asked when I heard the news, trying to sound quiet and shocked. "A stroke?"

"A bus," my mother said.

Apparently, Grand Auntie Du had been in vigorous health, right up to the end. She was riding the One California bus when it lurched to the side to avoid what my mother described as a "hotrod with crazy teenagers" running a stop sign. Grand Auntie pitched forward and fell in the aisle. My mother had gone right away to visit her at the hospital, of course. The doctors couldn't find anything wrong, besides the usual bumps and bruises. But Grand Auntie said she couldn't wait for the doctors to find out what she already knew. So she made my mother write down her will, who should get the thirty-year-old nubby sofa, her black-and-white TV set, that sort of thing.

Late that night, she died of an undetected concussion. Helen had been planning to visit the next day, too late.

"Bao-bao Roger said we should sue, one million dollars," my mother reported. "Can you imagine? That kind of thinking. When we found out Grand Auntie died, he didn't cry, only wants to make money off her dead body! Hnh! Why should I tell him she left him two lamps? Maybe I will forget to tell him."

My mother paused. "She was a good lady. Fourteen wreaths already." And then she whispered: "Of course, we are giving everyone twenty-percent discount."

My mother and Auntie Helen co-own Ding Ho Flower Shop on Ross Alley in Chinatown. They got the idea of starting the business about twenty-five years ago, right after my father died and Auntie Helen was fired from her job. I suppose, in some way, the flower shop became the dream that would replace the disasters.

My mother had used the money donated by the First Chinese Baptist Church, where my father had served as an assistant pastor. And Auntie Helen used the money she had saved from her job at another flower shop, which was where she learned the business. That was also the place that had fired her. For being "too honest," is what Auntie Helen revealed to us as the reason. Although my mother suspected it was because Auntie Helen always urged her customers to buy the cheapest bouquets to save money.

"Sometimes I regret that I ever married into a Chinese family," Phil said when he heard we had to go to San Francisco, a hundred miles round-trip from our house in San Jose, made worse by weekend football traffic. Although he's become genuinely fond of my mother over the fifteen years we've been married, he's still exasperated by her demands. And a weekend with the extended family is definitely not his preferred way to spend his days off from the hospital.

"Are you sure we have to go?" he said absently. He was busy playing with a new software program he had just loaded onto his laptop computer. He pressed a key. "Hotcha!" he exclaimed to the screen, and clapped his hands. Phil is forty-three years old, and with his wiry gray hair he usually strikes most people as reserved and dignified. At that moment, however, he had the pure intensity of a little boy playing with a toy battleship.

I pretended to be equally busy, perusing the help-wanted section. Three months ago, I took a position as a speech and language clinician with the local school district. And while I was basically happy with the job, I secretly worried that I had missed a better opportunity. My mother had put those thoughts in my head. Right after I announced I had been chosen over two other candidates for the same position, she said, "Two? Only two people wanted that job?"

And now Phil looked up from his computer, concerned. And I knew what he was thinking, about my "medical condition," as we called it, the multiple sclerosis, which thus far had left me not debilitated but easily fatigued. "It'll be a stressful weekend," he said. "Besides, I thought you couldn't stand your cousin Bao-bao. Not to mention the fact that Mary will be there. God, what a dingbat."

"Um."

"So can't you get out of it?"

"Um-nh."

He sighed. And that was the end of the discussion. Over the years that we've been married, we've learned to sidestep the subject of my family, my duty. It was once the biggest source of our arguments. When we were first married, Phil used to say that I was driven by blind devotion to fear and guilt. I would counter that he was selfish, that the things one had to do in life sometimes had nothing to do with what was fun or convenient. And then he would say the only reason we had to go was that I had been manipulated into thinking I had no choice, and that I was doing the same thing to him. And then our first baby, Tessa, came along, and a year later my illness was diagnosed. The shape of our arguments changed. We no longer fought self-righteously over philosophical differences concerning individual choice, perhaps because Phil developed a sense of duty toward the baby, as well as to me, or at least to my medical condition. So the whole issue of individual choice became tricky, a burden to keep up, until it fell away, along with smoking cigarettes, eating veal, and wearing ivory.

These days, we tend to argue about smaller, more specific issues—for example, my giving in to Tessa's demands to watch another half-hour of television, and not our different attitudes toward discipline as a whole. And in the end, we almost always agree—

perhaps too readily, because we already know the outcome of most disagreements.

It's a smoother life, as easy as we can make it. Although it bothers me from time to time. In fact, sometimes I wish we could go back to the old days when Phil would argue and I would defend my position and convince at least myself that I was right. Whereas nowadays—today, for instance—I'm not really sure why I still give in to my family obligations. While I would never admit this to Phil, I've come to resent the duty. I'm not looking forward to seeing the Kwongs, especially Mary. And whenever I'm with my mother, I feel as though I have to spend the whole time avoiding land mines.

So maybe it was guilt toward Phil or anger toward myself that made me do this: I waited until the next day to tell Phil we'd have to stay overnight—to attend Grand Auntie Du's funeral as well.

For the dreaded weekend, Phil and I had decided to come into the city early to get settled and perhaps take the girls to the zoo. The day before, we had had a polite argument with my mother over where we would stay.

"That's very kind of you, Winnie," Phil reasoned with my mother over the phone. "But we've already made reservations at a hotel." I listened on the other line, glad that I had suggested he call and make the excuses.

"What hotel?" my mother asked.

"The TraveLodge," Phil lied. We were actually booked at the Hyatt.

"Ai, too much money!" my mother concluded. "Why waste money that way? You can stay at my house, plenty of rooms."

And Phil had declined gracefully. "No, no, really. It's too much trouble. Really."

"Trouble for who?" my mother said.

So now Phil is getting the girls settled in the room that once belonged to my younger brother. This is where they always stay whenever Phil and I go away for a medical convention. Actually, sometimes we just *say* it's a medical convention, and then we go back home and do all the household chores we aren't able to finish when the children are around.

Phil has decided that Tessa, who is eight, will sleep on the twin bed, and three-year-old Cleo will get the hideaway cot.

"It's my turn for the bed," says Cleo. "Ha-bu said."

"But Cleo," reasons Tessa, "you *like* the cot."

"Ha-bu!" Cleo calls for my mother to rescue her. "Ha-bu!"

Phil and I are staying in my old room, still crammed with its old-fashioned furniture. I haven't stayed here since I've been married. Except for the fact that everything is a bit too clean, the room looks the same as when I was a teenager: the double bed with its heavy legs and frame, the dressing table with the round mirror and inlay of ash, oak, burl, and mother-of-pearl. It's funny how I used to hate that table. Now it actually looks quite nice, art deco. I wonder if my mother would let me have it.

I notice that she has placed my old Chinese slippers under the bed, the ones with a hole at each of the big toes; nothing ever thrown away, in case it's needed again twenty years later. And Tessa and Cleo must have been rummaging around in the closet, scavenging through boxes of old toys and junk. Scattered near the slippers are doll clothes, a rhinestone tiara, and a pink plastic jewelry case with the words "My Secret Treasures" on top. They have even rehung the ridiculous Hollywood-style star on the door, the one I made in the sixth grade, spelling out my name, P-E-A-R-L, in pop-beads.

"Gosh," Phil says in a goofy voice. "This sure beats the hell out of staying at the TraveLodge." I slap his thigh. He pats the mismatched set of guest towels lying on the bed. The towels were a Christmas gift from the Kwongs right after our family moved from Chinatown to the Richmond district, which meant they had to be thirty years old.

And now Tessa and Cleo race into our room, clamoring that they're ready to go to the zoo. Phil is going to take them, while I go to Ding Ho Flower Shop to help out. My mother didn't exactly ask me to help, but she did say in a terse voice that Auntie Helen was leaving the shop early to get ready for the big dinner—in spite of the fact there was so much to do at the shop and Grand Auntie's funeral service was the very next day. And then she reminded me that Grand Auntie was always very proud of me—in our family "proud" is as close as we get to saying "love." And she suggested that maybe I should come by early to pick out a nice wreath.

"I should be back at five-thirty," I tell Phil.

"I wanna see African elephants," says Tessa, plopping down on our bed. And then she counts on her fingers: "And koala bears and a spiny anteater and a humpback whale." I have always wondered where she picked up this trait of listing things—from Phil? from me? from the television?

"Say 'Please,' " Phil reminds her, "and I don't think they have whales at the zoo."

I turn to Cleo. I sometimes worry she will become too passive in the shadow of her confident big sister. "And what do you want to see?" I ask her gently. She looks at her feet, searching for an answer.

"Dingbats," she finally says.

As I turn down Ross Alley, everything around me immediately becomes muted in tone. It is no longer the glaring afternoon sun and noisy Chinatown sidewalks filled with people doing their Saturday grocery shopping. The alley sounds are softer, quickly absorbed, and the light is hazy, almost greenish in cast.

On the right-hand side of the street is the same old barbershop, run by Al Fook, who I notice still uses electric clippers to shear his customers' sideburns. Across the street are the same trade and family associations, including a place that will send ancestor memorials back to China for a fee. And farther down the street is the shopfront of a fortune-teller. A hand-written sign taped to the window claims to have "the best lucky numbers, the best fortune advice," but the sign taped to the door says: "Out of Business."

As I walk past the door, a yellow pull-shade rustles. And suddenly a little girl appears, her hands pressed to the glass. She stares at me with a somber expression. I wave, but she does not wave back. She looks at me as if I don't belong here, which is how I feel.

And now I'm at Sam Fook Trading Company, a few doors down from the flower shop. It contains shelves full of good-luck charms and porcelain and wooden statues of lucky gods, hundreds of them. I've called this place the Shop of the Gods ever since I can remember. It also sells the kind of stuff people get for Buddhist funerals—spirit money, paper jewelry, incense, and the like.

"Hey, Pearl!" It's Mr. Hong, the owner, waving me to come in. When I first met him, I thought his name was Sam Fook, like the shop. I found out later that *sam fook* means "triple blessing" in old Cantonese, and according to my mother—or rather, her Hong

Kong customers—*sam fook* sounds like a joke, like saying "the Three Stooges."

"I told him he should change the name," my mother had said. "Luckier that way. But he says he has too much business already."

"Hey, Pearl," Mr. Hong says when I walk in the door, "I got some things for your mother here, for the funeral tomorrow. You take it to her, okay?"

"Okay." He hands me a soft bundle.

I guess this means Grand Auntie's funeral will be Buddhist. Although she attended the First Chinese Baptist Church for a number of years, both she and my mother stopped going right after my father died. In any case, I don't think Grand Auntie ever gave up her other beliefs, which weren't exactly Buddhist, just all the superstitious rituals concerning attracting good luck and avoiding bad. On those occasions when I did go up to her apartment, I used to play with her altar, a miniature red temple containing a framed picture of a Chinese god. In front of that was an imitation-brass urn filled with burnt incense sticks, and on the side were offerings of oranges, Lucky Strike cigarettes, and an airline mini-bottle of Johnnie Walker Red whiskey. It was like a Chinese version of a Christmas crèche.

And now I come to the flower shop itself. It is the bottom floor of a three-story brick building. The shop is about the size of a one-car garage and looks both sad and familiar. The front has a chipped red-bordered door covered with rusted burglarproof mesh. A plate-glass window says "Ding Ho Flower Shop" in English and Chinese. But it's easy to miss, because the place sits back slightly and always looks dark and closed, as it does today.

So the location my mother and Auntie Helen picked isn't exactly bustling. Yet they seem to have done all right. In a way, it's remarkable. After all these years, they've done almost nothing to keep up with the times or make the place more attractive. I open the door and bells jangle. I'm instantly engulfed in the pungent smell of gardenias, a scent I've always associated with funeral parlors. The place is dimly lit, with only one fluorescent tube hanging over the cash register—and that's where my mother is, standing on a small footstool so she can see out over the counter, with dime-store reading glasses perched on her nose.

She is talking on the telephone in rapid Chinese and waves impatiently for me to come in and wait. Her hair is pulled straight back into a bun, not a strand ever out of place. The bun today has been made to look thicker with the addition of a false swatch of hair, a "horse's tail," she calls it, for wearing only on important occasions.

Actually, now I can tell—by the shrillness of her pitch and the predominance of negative "vuh-vuh-vuh" sounds—that she's arguing in Shanghainese, and not just plain Mandarin. This is serious. Most likely it's with a neighborhood supplier, to judge from the way she's punching in numbers on a portable calculator, then reading aloud the printed results in harsh tones, as if they were penal codes. She pushes the "No Sale" button on the cash register, and when the drawer pops forward, she pulls out a folded receipt, snaps it open with a jerk of her wrist, then reads numbers from that as well.

"Vuh! Vuh! Vuh!" she insists.

The cash register is used to store only odds and ends, or what my mother calls "ends and odds and evens." The register is broken. When my mother and Auntie Helen first bought the store and its fixtures, they found out soon enough that anytime the sales transaction added up to anything with a 9 in it, the whole register froze up. But they decided to keep the cash register anyway, "for stick-em-up," is how my mother explained it to me. If they were ever robbed, which has yet to happen, the robber would get only four dollars and a pile of pennies, all the money that is kept in the till. The real money is stashed underneath the counter, in a teapot with a spout that's been twice broken and glued back on. And the kettle sits on a hot plate that's missing a plug. I guess the idea is that no one would ever rob the store for a cup of cold tea.

I once told my mother and Auntie Helen that a robber would never believe that the shop had only four dollars to its name. I thought they should put at least twenty in the cash register to make the ruse seem more plausible. But my mother thought twenty dollars was too much to give a robber. And Auntie Helen said she would "worry sick" about losing that much money—so what good would the trick be then?

At the time, I considered giving them the twenty dollars myself to prove my point. But then I thought, What's the point? And as I look around the shop now, I realize maybe they were right. Who would ever consider robbing this place for more than getaway bus fare? No, this place is burglarproof just the way it is.

The shop has the same dull gray concrete floor of twenty-five years ago, now polished shiny with wear. The counter is covered with the same contact paper, green-and-white bamboo lattice on the sides and wood grain on the top. Even the phone my mother is using is the same old black model with a rotary dial and a fabric cord that doesn't coil or stretch. And over the years, the lime-colored walls have become faded and splotched, then cracked from the '89 earthquake. So now the place has the look of spidery decay and leaf mold.

"*Hau, hau,*" I now hear my mother saying. She seems to have reached some sort of agreement with the supplier. Finally she bangs the phone down. Although we have not seen each other since Christmas, almost a month ago, we do none of the casual hugs and kisses Phil and I exchange when we see his parents and friends. Instead, my mother walks out from around the counter, muttering, "Can you imagine? That man is cheating me! Tried to charge me for extra-rush delivery." She points to a box containing supplies of wire, clear cellophane, and sheets of green wax paper. "This is not my fault he forgot to come last week."

"How much extra?" I ask.

"Three dollars!" she exclaims. I never cease to be amazed by the amount of emotional turmoil my mother will go through for a few dollars.

"Why don't you just forget it? It's only three dollars—"

"I'm not concerned about money!" she fumes. "He's cheating me. This is not right. Last month, he tried to add another kind of extra charge too." I can tell she's about to launch into a blow-by-blow of last month's fight, when two well-dressed women with blond hair peer through the door.

"Are you open? Do any of you speak English?" one of them says in a Texas drawl.

My mother's face instantly cheers, and she nods, waving them in. "Come, come," she calls.

"Oh, we don't want to bother y'all," one of the ladies says. "If you might could just tell us where the fortune cookie factory is?"

Before I can answer, my mother tightens her face, shakes her head, and says, "Don't understand. Don't speak English."

"Why did you say that?" I ask when the two ladies retreat back into the alley. "I didn't know you hated tourists that much."

"Not tourists," she says. "That woman with the cookie factory, once she was mean to me. Why should I send her any good business?"

"How's business here?" I say, trying to steer the conversation away from what will surely become a tirade about the cookie woman down the street.

"Awful!" she says, and points to her inventory around the shop. "So busy—busy myself to death with this much business. You look, only this morning I had to make all these myself."

And I look. There are no modern arrangements of bent twigs or baskets of exotica with Latinate-drooping names. My mother opens the glass door to a refrigerator unit that once housed bottles of soda pop and beer.

"You see?" she says, and shows me a shelf with boutonnieres and corsages made out of carnations, neatly lined in rows according to color: white, pink, and red. No doubt we'll have to wear some of these tonight.

"And this," she continues. The second shelf is chock-full of milk-glass vases, each containing only a single rosebud, a fern frond, and a meager sprinkling of baby's breath. This is the type of floral arrangement you give to hospital patients who go in for exploratory surgery, when you don't know yet whether the person will be there for very long. My father received a lot of those when he first went into the hospital and later right before he died. "Very popular," my mother says.

"This, too, I had to make," she says, and points to the bottom shelf, which holds half a dozen small table sprays. "Some for tonight. Some for a retirement dinner," my mother explains, and perhaps because I don't look sufficiently impressed, she adds, "For assistant manager at Wells Fargo."

She walks me around to view her handiwork in other parts of the shop. Lining the walls are large funeral wreaths, propped on easels. "Ah?" my mother says, waiting for my opinion. I've always found wreaths hideously sad, like decorative lifesavers thrown out too late.

"Very pretty," I say.

And now she steers me toward her real pride and joy. At the

front of the shop, the only place that gets filtered daylight for a few hours a day, are her "long-lasting bargains," as she calls them—philodendrons, rubber plants, chicken-feet bushes, and miniature tangerine trees. These are festooned with red banners, congratulating this business or that for its new store opening.

My mother has always been very proud of those red banners. She doesn't write the typical congratulatory sayings, like "Good Luck" or "Prosperity and Long Life." All the sayings, written in gold Chinese characters, are of her own inspiration, her thoughts about life and death, luck and hope: "First-Class Life for Your First Baby," "Double-Happiness Wedding Triples Family Fortunes," "Money Smells Good in Your New Restaurant Business," "Health Returns Fast, Always Hoping."

My mother claims these banners are the reasons why Ding Ho Flower Shop has had success flowing through its door all these years. By success, I suppose she means that the same people over the last twenty-five years keep coming back. Only now it's less and less for shy brides and giddy grooms, and more and more for the sick, the old, and the dead.

She smiles mischievously, then tugs my elbow. "Now I show you the wreath I made for you."

I'm alarmed, and then I realize what she's talking about. She opens the door to the back of the shop. It's dark as a vault inside and I can't make out anything except the dense odor of funeral flowers. My mother is groping for the piece of string that snaps on the light. Finally the room is lit by the glare of a naked bulb that swings back and forth on a cord suspended from the high ceiling. And what I now see is horrifyingly beautiful—row after row of gleaming wreaths, all white gardenias and yellow chrysanthemums, red banners hanging down from their easels, looking like identically dressed heavenly attendants.

I am stunned by how much hard work this represents. I imagine my mother's small hands with their parchmentlike skin, furiously pulling out stray leaves, tucking in sharp ends of wire, inserting each flower into its proper place.

"This one." She points to a wreath in the middle of the first row. It looks the same as the others. "This one is yours. I wrote the wishes myself."

"What does it say?" I ask.

Her finger moves slowly down the red banner, as she reads in a formal Chinese I can't understand. And then she translates: "Farewell, Grand Auntie, heaven is lucky. From your favorite niece, Pearl Louie Brandt, and husband."

"Oh, I almost forgot." I hand her the bundle from Sam Fook's. "Mr. Hong said to give you this."

My mother snips the ribbon and opens the package. Inside are a dozen or so bundles of spirit money, money Grand Auntie can supposedly use to bribe her way along to Chinese heaven.

"I didn't know you believed in that stuff," I say.

"What's to believe," my mother says testily. "This is respect." And then she says softly, "I got one hundred million dollars. Ai! She was a good lady."

"Here we go," I say, and take a deep breath as we climb the stairs to the banquet room.

"Pearl! Phil! There you are." It's my cousin Mary. I haven't seen her in the two years since she and Doug moved to Los Angeles. We wait for Mary to move her way through the banquet crowd. She rushes toward us and gives me a kiss, then rubs my cheek and laughs over the extra blush she's added.

"You look terrific!" she tells me, and then she looks at Phil. "Really, both of you. Just sensational."

Mary must now be forty-one, about half a year older than I am. She's wearing heavy makeup and false eyelashes, and her hair is a confusing mass of curls and mousse. A silver-fox stole keeps slipping off her shoulders. As she pushes it up for the third time, she laughs and says, "Doug gave me this old thing for Christmas, what a bother." I wonder why she does bother, now that we're inside the restaurant. But that's Mary, the oldest child of the two families, so it's always seemed important to her to look the most successful.

"Jennifer and Michael," she calls, and snaps her fingers. "Come here and say hello to your auntie and uncle." She pulls her two teenage children over to her side, and gives them each a squeeze. "Come on, what do you say?" They stare at us with sullen faces, and each of them grunts and gives a small nod.

Jennifer has grown plump, while her eyes, lined in black, look small and hard. The top part of her hair is teased up in pointy spikes, with the rest falling limply down to the middle of her back. She looks as if she had been electrocuted. And Michael's face— it's starting to push out into sharp angles and his chin is covered with pimples. They're no longer cute, and I wonder if this will happen to Tessa and Cleo, if I will think this about them as well.

"You see how they are," Mary says apologetically. "Jennifer just got her first nylons and high heels for Christmas. She's so proud, no longer Mommy's little girl."

"Oh, Mother!" Jennifer wails, then struggles away from her mother's grasp and disappears into the crowd. Michael follows her.

"See how Michael's almost as tall as Doug?" Mary says, proudly watching her son as he ambles away. "He's on the junior varsity track team, and his coach says he's their best runner. I don't know where he got his height or his athletic ability—certainly not from me. Whenever I go for a jog, I come back a cripple," Mary says, laughing. And then, realizing what she's just said, she suddenly drops her smile, and searches the crowd: "Oh, there's Doug's parents. I better go say hello."

Phil squeezes my hand, and even though we say nothing, he knows I'm mad. "Just forget it," he says.

"I would," I shoot back, "if she could. She *always* does this."

When Phil and I married, it was Mary and Doug who were our matron of honor and best man, since they had introduced us. They were the first people we confided in when we found out I was pregnant with Tessa. And about seven years ago, Mary was the one who pushed me into aerobics when I complained I felt tired all the time. And later, when I had what seemed like a strange weakness in my right leg, Phil suggested I see Doug, who at the time was an orthopedist at a sports medicine clinic.

Months later, Doug told me the problem seemed to be something else, and right away I panicked and thought he meant bone cancer. He assured me he just meant he wasn't smart enough to figure it out himself. So he sent me to see his old college drinking buddy, the best neurologist at San Francisco Medical Center. After what seemed like a year of tests—after I persuaded myself the fatigue was caused by smoking and the weakness in my leg was sciatica left over from my pregnancy—the drinking buddy told me I had multiple sclerosis.

Mary had cried hysterically, then tried to console me, which made it all seem worse. For a while, she dropped by with casserole dishes from "terrific recipes" she "just happened to find," until I told her to stop. And later, she made a big show of telling me how Doug's friend had assured her that my case was really "quite mild," as if she were talking about the weather, that my life expectancy was not changed, that at age seventy I could be swinging a golf club and still hitting par, although I would have to be careful not to stress myself either physically or emotionally.

"So really, everything's normal," she said a bit too cheerfully, "except that Phil has to treat you nicer. And what could be wrong with that?"

"I don't play golf," was all I told her.

"I'll teach you," she said cheerily.

Of course, Mary was only trying to be kind. I admit that it was more my fault that our friendship became strained. I never told her directly how much her gestures of sympathy offended me. So of course she couldn't have known that I did not need someone to comfort me. I did not want to be coddled by casseroles. Kindness was compensation. Kindness was a reminder that my life had changed, was always changing, that people thought I should just accept all this and become strong or brave, more enlightened, more peaceful. I wanted nothing to do with that. Instead, I wanted to live my life with the same focus as most people—to worry about my children's education, but not whether I would be around to see them graduate, to rejoice that I had lost five pounds, and not be fearful that my muscle mass was eroding away. I wanted what had become impossible: I wanted to forget.

I was furious that Doug and his drinking-buddy friend had discussed my medical condition with Mary. If they had told her that, then they must have also told her this: that with this disease, no prognosis could be made. I could be in remission for ten, twenty, thirty, or forty years. Or the disease could suddenly take off tomorrow and roll downhill, faster and faster, and at the bottom, I would be left sitting in a wheelchair, or worse.

I know Mary was aware of this, because I would often catch her looking at me from the corner of her eye whenever we passed someone who was disabled. One time she laughed nervously when she tried to park her car in a space that turned out to be a handi-capped zone. "Oops!" she said, backing out fast. "We certainly don't need that."

In the beginning, Phil and I vowed to lead as normal a life to-gether as possible. "As normal as possible"—it was like a mean-ingless chant. If I accidentally tripped over a toy left on the floor, I would spend ten minutes apologizing to Tessa for yelling at her, then another hour debating whether a "normal" person would have stumbled over the same thing. Once, when we went to the beach for the express purpose of forgetting about all of this, I was filled with morbid thoughts instead. I watched the waves eating away at the shore, and I wondered aloud to Phil whether I would one day be left as limp as seaweed, or stiff like a crab.

Meanwhile Phil would read his old textbooks and every medical article he could find on the subject. And then he would become depressed that his own medical training offered no better under-standing of a disease that could be described only as "without known etiology," "extremely variable," "unpredictable," and "without specific treatment." He attended medical conferences on neuro-logical disorders. He once took me to an MS support group, but we turned right around as soon as we saw the wheelchairs. He would perform what he called "weekly safety checks," testing my reflexes, monitoring the strength of my limbs. We even moved to a house with a swimming pool, so I could do daily muscle training. We did not mention to each other the fact that the house was one-story and had few steps and wide hallways that could someday be made wheelchair-accessible, if necessary.

We talked in code, as though we belonged to a secret cult, search-ing for a cure, or a pattern of symptoms we could watch for, some kind of salvation from constant worry. And eventually we learned not to talk about the future, either the grim possibilities or the vague hopes. We did not dwell on the past, whether it had been a virus or genetics that had caused this to happen. We concerned ourselves with the here and now, small victories over the mundane irritations of life—getting Tessa potty-trained, correcting a mistake on our charge-card bill, discovering why the car sputtered whenever we put it into third gear. Those became our constants, the things we could isolate and control in a life of unknown variables.

So I can't really blame Phil for pretending that everything is normal. I wanted that more than he did. And now I can't tell him what I really feel, what it's like. All I know is that I wake up each morning in a panic, terrified that something might have changed while I slept. And there are days when I become obsessed if I lose something, a button, thinking my life won't be normal until I find it again. There are days when I think Phil is the most inconsiderate man in the world, simply because he forgot to buy one item on the grocery list. There are days when I organize my underwear drawer by color, as if this might make some kind of difference. Those are the bad days.

On the good days, I remember that I am lucky—lucky by a new standard. In the last seven years, I have had only one major "flare-up," which now means I lose my balance easily, especially when I'm upset or in a hurry. But I can still walk. I still take out the garbage. And sometimes I actually *can* forget, for a few hours, or almost the entire day. Of course, the worst part is when I remember once again—often in unexpected ways—that I am living in a limbo land called remission.

That delicate balance always threatens to go out of kilter when I see my mother. Because that's when it hits me the hardest: I have this terrible disease and I've never told her.

I meant to tell her. There were several times when I planned to do exactly that. When I was first diagnosed, I said, "Ma, you know that slight problem with my leg I told you about. Well, thank God, it turned out *not* to be cancer, but—"

And right away, she told me about a customer of hers who had just died of cancer, how long he had suffered, how many wreaths the family had ordered. "Long time ago I saw that mole growing on his face," she said. "I told him, Go see a doctor. No problem, he said, age spot—didn't do anything about it. By the time he died, his nose and cheek—all eaten away!" And then she warned me sternly, "That's why you have to be careful."

When Cleo was born, without complications on my part or hers, I again started to tell my mother. But she interrupted me, this time to lament how my father was not there to see his grandchildren. And then she went into her usual endless monologue about my father getting a fate he didn't deserve.

My father had died of stomach cancer when I was fourteen. And for years, my mother would search in her mind for the causes, as if she could still undo the disaster by finding the reason why it had occurred in the first place.

"He was such a good man," my mother would lament. "So why did he die?" And sometimes she cited God's will as the reason, only she gave it a different twist. She said it must have been because my father was a minister. "He listened to everyone else's troubles," she said. "He swallowed them until he made himself sick. Ai! *Ying-gai* find him another job."

*Ying-gai* was what my mother always said when she meant, I should have. *Ying-gai* meant she should have altered the direction of fate, she should have prevented disaster. To me, *ying-gai* meant my mother lived a life of regrets that never faded with time.

If anything, the regrets grew as she searched for more reasons underlying my father's death. One time she cited her own version of environmental causes—that the electrician had been sick at the time he rewired our kitchen. "He built that sickness right into our house," she declared. "It's true. I just found out the electrician died—of cancer, too. *Ying-gai* pick somebody else."

And there was also this superstition, what I came to think of as her theory of the Nine Bad Fates. She said she had once heard that a person is destined to die if eight bad things happen. If you don't recognize the eight ahead of time and prevent them, the ninth one is always fatal. And then she would ruminate over what the eight bad things might have been, how she should have been sharp enough to detect them in time.

To this day it drives me crazy, listening to her various hypotheses, the way religion, medicine, and superstition all merge with her own beliefs. She puts no faith in other people's logic—to her, logic is a sneaky excuse for tragedies, mistakes, and accidents. And according to my mother, *nothing* is an accident. She's like a Chinese version of Freud, or worse. Everything has a reason. Everything could have been prevented. The last time I was at her house, for example, I knocked over a framed picture of my father and broke the glass. My mother picked up the shards and moaned, "Why did this happen?" I thought it was a rhetorical question at first, but then she said to me, "Do you know?"

"It was an accident," I said. "My elbow bumped into it." And of course, her question had sent my mind racing, wondering if my clumsiness was a symptom of deterioration.

"Why this picture?" she muttered to herself.

So I never told my mother. At first I didn't want to hear her theories on my illness, what caused this to happen, how she should have done this or that to prevent it. I did not want her to remind me.

And now that so much time has gone by, the fact that I still haven't told her makes the illness seem ten times worse. I am always reminded, whenever I see her, whenever I hear her voice.

Mary knows that, and that's why I still get mad at her—not because she trips over herself to avoid talking about my medical condition. I'm mad because she told *her* mother, my Auntie Helen.

"I had to tell her," she explained to me in an offhand sort of way. "She was always saying to me, Tell Pearl to visit her mother more often, only a one-hour drive. Tell Pearl she should ask her mother to move in with her, less lonely for her mother that way. Finally, I told my mother I couldn't tell you those things. And she asked why not." Mary shrugged. "You know my mother. I couldn't lie to her. Of course, I made her *swear* not to tell your mother, that you were going to tell her yourself."

"I can drive," I told Mary. "And that's not the reason why I haven't asked my mother to live with me." And then I glared at her. "How could you do this?"

"She won't say anything," Mary said. "I made her promise." And then she added a bit defiantly, "Besides, you should have told your mother a long time ago."

Mary and I didn't exactly have a fight, but things definitely chilled between us after that. She already knew that was about the worst possible thing she could have done to me. Because she had done it once before, nine years ago, when I confided to her that I was pregnant. My first pregnancy had ended in a miscarriage early on, and my mother had gone on and on about how much coffee I drank, how it was my jogging that did it, how Phil should make sure I ate more. So when I became pregnant again, I decided to wait, to tell my mother when I was in my fourth month or so. But in the third month, I made the mistake of confiding in Mary. And Mary slipped this news to her mother. And Auntie Helen didn't exactly tell my mother. But when my mother proudly announced my pregnancy to the Kwongs, Auntie Helen immediately showed my mother the little yellow sweater she had already hand-knit for the baby.

I didn't stop hearing the laments from my mother, even after Tessa was born. "Why could you tell the Kwongs, not your own mother?" she'd complain. When she stewed over it and became really angry, she accused me of making her look like a fool: "Hnh! Auntie Helen was pretending to be so surprised, so innocent. 'Oh, I didn't knit the sweater for Pearl's baby,' she said, 'I made it just in case.' "

So far, Auntie Helen had kept the news about my medical condition to herself. But this didn't stop her from treating me like an invalid. When I used to go to her house, she would tell me to sit down right away, while she went to find me a pillow for my back. She would rub her palm up and down my arm, asking me how I was, telling me how she had always thought of me as a daughter. And then she would sigh and confess some bit of bad news, as if to balance out what she already knew about me.

"Your poor Uncle Henry, he almost got laid off last month," she would say. "So many budget cuts now. Who knows what's going to happen? Don't tell your mother. I don't want her to worry over us."

And then *I* would worry that Auntie Helen would think her little confessions were payment in kind, that she would take them as license to accidentally slip and tell my mother: "Oh, Winnie, I thought you knew about your daughter's tragedy."

And so I dreaded the day my mother would call and ask me a hundred different ways, "Why did Auntie Helen know? Why did you never tell me? Why didn't you let me prevent this from happening to you?"

And then what answer could I give?

At the dinner, we've been seated at the "kids' table," only now the "kids" are in their thirties and forties. The real kids—Tessa and Cleo—are seated with my mother.

Phil is the only non-Chinese tonight, although that wasn't the case at past family events. Bao-bao's two former wives were what

Auntie Helen called "Americans," as if she were referring to a racial group. She must be thrilled that Bao-bao's bride-to-be is a girl named Mimi Wong, who is not only Chinese but from a well-to-do family that owns three travel agencies.

"She looks Japanese," my mother had said when we first arrived and had been introduced to Mimi. I don't know why she said that. To me, Mimi looks just plain weird, as well as awfully young. I guess that she is around twenty, although it may be her dyed orange hair and pierced nose that makes her seem so young. I heard that she was training to be a hairstylist at a trendy salon called Oliphant's. My mother heard that what Mimi did mostly was wash people's hair and sweep up loose clippings.

Bao-bao has changed his looks since the last time I saw him. His hair is slicked back with pomade. He has on a black T-shirt underneath an iridescent sharkskin suit. Each time he introduces Mimi to the guests, I allow myself to stare at her pierced nose. I wonder what happens when she has a cold.

"How's my favorite cuz?" Bao-bao says to me from across the table, then gives me a toast with his upraised champagne glass. "Lookin' good. I like the hair, short, nice. Mimi, what do you think of Pearl's haircut? Nice, huh?" He has a knack for handing out compliments like party favors, one for everybody. I wonder sometimes if I would have liked him better if I didn't already know so much about him.

"Hey, Phil, bro'," Bao-bao calls, pouring more champagne. "You put on a few pounds, I see. The good life's been good. Maybe you're ready for that new system I told you about. A lot of decibels for the dollar." Bao-bao sells stereos and TVs at The Good Guys. He's very good at convincing people that their ears and eyes are refined enough to tell the difference between a standard model and its five-hundred-dollar upgrade. Phil once said that if Bao-bao were turned loose, he could sell Bibles to the Shiites.

Behind us, at the "grownups' table," is a man named Loy Fong, "Uncle Loy." He turns around and offers a toast of ginger ale in a plastic glass. "So convenient for Mimi," he says. "All she has to do is add a *k* to her name to get a husband! 'Wong' to 'Kwong,' get it?" He laughs the loudest at his own joke, then turns back around to repeat the joke to the others at his table. Next to him is his wife, Edna. These people have been going to the same church for years, but they're not really that close to either the Kwongs or my family. I think they were invited because Edna Fong is in charge of ordering flowers for the sanctuary, and she's always bought them from Ding Ho, twenty percent off, of course.

Auntie Helen is sitting at the same table as Loy and Edna Fong. For this special occasion, she has on a baby-pink sateen Chinese dress, which is too tight for her plump body and already creased at her lap and above her round stomach. Every time she reaches over to pour more tea, her dress strains at the armpits, and I wonder which seam is going to rip first. Her thin hair has been newly permed, perhaps with the mistaken notion that it would look fuller. Instead her hair looks deep-fried, exposing her scalp underneath.

My mother is seated directly across from Auntie Helen. She is wearing a new blue dress she made herself—in fact, designed herself, she told me, "no pattern necessary." The dress is a simple A-line with pouffy princess sleeves. It makes my mother's thin body look waiflike.

"Such a pretty silk," Edna Fong says to her.

"Polyester," my mother proudly informs her. "Machine washable." Cleo slips off her chair and climbs up onto my mother's lap. "Ha-bu," she says, "I want to eat with chopsticks."

My mother spins the lazy Susan around and dips her chopsticks into the appetizer plate. "This is jellyfish," my mother explains, and dangles the quivering strand in front of Cleo's mouth. I watch my daughter open her mouth wide like a baby bird, and my mother drops the morsel in.

"See, you like it!" my mother proclaims as Cleo chomps and smiles. "When your mother was a little girl, she said it tasted just like rubber bands!"

"Don't tell me that!" Cleo suddenly shrieks and then wails, the half-eaten jellyfish dribbling out from her pouting lips.

"Don't cry, don't cry," Auntie Helen says soothingly from across the table. "Look, here's some fragrant beef, ah? Yum-yummy, tastes like McDonald hamburgers. Take it, you like."

And Cleo, still full of indignant sobs, reaches over for the slice of beef and gobbles it down. My mother's mouth is shut tight. She looks away.

And I feel so bad for her, that she's been betrayed by her memory and my childhood fondness for rubbery-tasting things. I think about a child's capacity to hurt her mother in ways she cannot ever imagine.

The evening turns out to be much worse than I expected. Throughout the dinner I watch my mother and Auntie Helen getting on each other's nerves. They argue in Chinese over whether the pork is too salty, whether the chicken is overcooked, whether the Happy Family dish used too many water chestnuts to cut down on the ration of scallops. I see Phil trying to make polite conversation with my cousin Frank, who is chain-smoking, something Phil hates with a passion. I see old family friends who are not really friends making toasts to a bride-and-groom-to-be who will surely be divorced in two years' time. I smile woodenly and listen to Mary and Doug chatting to me as if we were still the best of friends.

Mostly I see my mother sitting one table away, and I feel as lonely as I imagine her to be. I think of the enormous distance that separates us and makes us unable to share the most important matters of our life. How did this happen?

And suddenly everything—the flower arrangements on the plastic-topped tables, my mother's memories of my childhood, the whole family—everything feels like a sham, and also sad and true. All these meaningless gestures, old misunderstandings, and painful secrets, why do we keep them up? I feel as if I were suffocating, and want to run away.

A hand taps my shoulder. It's Auntie Helen.

"Not too tired?" she whispers.

I shake my head.

"Then come help me cut the cake. Otherwise I have to pay the restaurant extra." And of course, I wonder what secret she's about to confess now.

In the kitchen, Auntie Helen cuts a white sheet cake into little squares and puts each piece on a paper plate. She licks whipped cream off her fingers, stuffs a falling strawberry back into its spongy center.

"Best cake in San Francisco," she says. "Mary got it from Sun Chee Bakery on Clement. You know the place?"

I shake my head and keep adding a plastic fork to each plate.

"Maybe you know something else, then," she says sternly. "About my own sickness?" She stops cutting, and looks at me, waiting for me to answer. I am surprised by her sudden change in tone, because I honestly don't know what she's talking about.

"Doesn't matter," she answers tartly, and goes back to cutting more cake. "I already know."

And standing in the kitchen like that, she tells me how she had to go to the doctor two months ago. She had fallen down her front steps on a rainy day and hit her head against the rail. And my mother, who was with her at the time, had taken her to the hospital. They took X rays: no broken bones, no concussion, not like Auntie Du, lucky for her. Instead they found a little dark spot on her skull, did more tests.

"And that's how I knew," she says, tapping her head, sounding triumphant. "God touched his finger there and told me, Time to go. I have a brain tumor."

I gasp, and Auntie Helen quickly adds, "Of course, the doctors did more tests later to make sure. Then they told me it is *benign.*" She says this word as if she were calling out a bingo slot, B nine. "They said no problem, no need to operate."

I sigh, and she continues, "Your mother said, Lucky you, nothing wrong. My children, your Uncle Henry, they all said, Now you will live forever. But what do you think they are really saying?"

I shake my head.

"You look. Why does Bao-bao suddenly say he is getting married? Why does Mary say she is flying home, bringing the whole family? Let's have a reunion, she says. And Frank, he got a haircut before I had to ask twice." She smiles. "Even your mother. Today she said at the shop, Go, go, you are busy with your son's party. I can make the wreaths. Why are you shaking your head? This is true!"

Her face becomes more serious. "I said to myself, Eh, why this big change, everyone so nice to me? Why so sudden? My children now respect me, why? They come to see me, why? Mary calls me Mommy again. Your mother wants to do all the work. You know why? They know. They all know I'm dying. They won't say, but I think it must be very fast."

I'm putting the plates on a tray. "Oh, Auntie Helen, I'm sure there's nothing wrong. If they said it's benign, it means it's—"

She holds up her hand. "No need to pretend with me. I'm not scared. I'm not a young woman anymore. Almost seventy-three."

35

"I'm not pretending," I insist. "You're not going to die."

"Everyone wants to keep this news from me, okay. They want to be nice before I die, okay. I can pretend too that I don't know."

I am starting to feel confused. I don't know whether Auntie Helen is really sick, or only imagining something bad out of her children's good intentions. It does strike me as strange, though, what she said about everyone's sudden change of character. It would be just like the Kwongs to pass around a secret and then pretend nobody knows a thing.

"Don't worry for me," she says, and pats my hand. "I am not telling you this so you have to worry. I only want to tell you so you understand why I can no longer keep your secret."

"What secret?"

She sighs deeply. "Pearl-ah, this is too much burden for me. It makes my heart and shoulders heavy that your mother does not know. How can I fly to heaven when this is weighing me down? No, you must tell your mother, Pearl. Tell her about your multiple neurosis."

I am too stunned to laugh or correct her mistake. "This is the right thing," Auntie Helen says with conviction. "If you cannot tell her, then I must tell her myself—before the Chinese New Year." She looks at me with a determined face.

And now I want to shake her, tell her to stop playing this game. "Auntie Helen, you know I can't tell my mother that. You know how she is."

"Of course," she says. "For fifty years I've been knowing your mother. That's why I know this is the right time to tell her."

"Why should I tell her now? She'll only be angry that we kept it a secret."

She frowns. "You are only concerned your mother will be angry with you? Tst! Tst! So selfish."

"No, I mean, there's no reason to tell her now. I'm fine."

"You think you can hide this until she dies? Maybe she lives to be a hundred. Then what do you do, ah?"

"It's not that. I just don't want her to worry."

"This is her right to worry," says Auntie Helen. "She is your mother."

"But she shouldn't have to worry about something that isn't really a problem."

36

"That's why you should tell her now. No more problem after that."

"But then she'll wonder why we kept this a secret from her. She'll think it's worse than it is."

"Maybe she has secrets too." She smiles, then laughs at what must be a private joke. "Your mother, oh yes, plenty of secrets!"

I feel I am in a nightmare, arguing with someone who can't hear me. Maybe Auntie Helen is right and she does have a brain tumor. Maybe it's eaten away at her brain and she's gone crazy. "All right," I finally say. "But you can't be the one who tells her. I will."

Auntie Helen looks at me suspiciously. "This is a promise?"

"Promise," I whisper, and even I don't know if I'm lying.

She rubs my shoulder, plucks at the fabric of my green wool dress. "This is a good color for you, Pearl. Anh! No more talking now. Let's go back." She hoists the tray of cakes.

"I can carry that," I say tersely. She hesitates, ready to argue. And then, perhaps in deference to her own illness, she lets me.

After the dinner, we are back at my mother's house. The girls have done their usual segue of giggling, then fighting, then wailing, and have finally fallen asleep. I had considered asking my mother about Auntie Helen's brain tumor but decided it was not the best time to have one subject lead into another. I'm exhausted. So after declining my mother's offers of tea, instant coffee, and orange juice, I stand up and yawn. "I'm going to bed," I say. Phil offers my mother a good-night kiss, which she cautiously accepts with a stiff upturned cheek. And at last we have escaped to our room.

"Did you bring your toothbrush?" my mother calls to us through our closed door. "Brush your teeth already?"

"Got 'em!" Phil calls back. "They're brushed."

"Enough blankets, enough towels?"

"Plenty," he says. He rolls his eyes at me. "Good night!" he calls, and turns off the light. It is quiet for about five seconds.

"Too cold? Heater can be turned up."

"Ma, we're fine," I say with a little too much irritation. And then I say, more gently this time, "Don't worry. Go to bed."

I hold my breath. There is only silence. And finally, I hear her slippers slowly padding down the hallway, each soft shuffle breaking my heart.

# 2

# GRAND AUNTIE DU'S
# FUNERAL

My mother left the house two hours ago with Auntie Helen so they could decorate the funeral parlor. And now Phil and I are going to be late for Grand Auntie's service, thanks to a spat between Tessa and Cleo that resulted in eggs over easy being flung onto Phil's only good shirt and tie. While we searched for replacements along Clement Street, Phil suggested that we shouldn't bring the girls to the funeral.

"They might be disruptive," he said. "And they might not appreciate seeing someone who is D-E-A-D."

Tessa grinned and said in a singsong voice, "Daddy's saying a naughty word."

"Maybe I could wait with them outside in the car," said Phil.

"They'll be fine," I assured him. "I already asked my mother if it's closed-casket and she said it is. And I've explained to the girls it's like that time we went to Steve and Joanne's wedding—grownup time. Isn't that right, girls?"

"We got cake after," said Cleo.

"All right," said Phil. "But after the service, let's make the usual excuses and go home."

"Of course."

At twenty minutes after two, the four of us walk into the reception area of the funeral parlor. My cousin Frank hands us black armbands to wear. As I put mine on, I feel somewhat guilty, this pretense of grief. I realize now that I knew almost nothing about Grand Auntie Du, except that she smelled like moth-balls and was always trying to feed me old Chinese candies and sugared beef jerky, pulled out of dusty tins stored on top of her refrigerator.

Bao-bao is there to greet us as well. He's smiling broadly. "Hey, man, glad to see you guys finally decided to make it." He hands each of us a piece of foil-wrapped candy and a small red envelope of lucky money.

"What are we supposed to do with these?" Phil whispers. "Offer them to Grand Auntie Du?" He pulls out a quarter from the lucky-money envelope.

"How should I know?" I whisper back. "I've never been to a Buddhist funeral, or whatever this is."

"My mom says it's like insurance in case you pick up bad vibes here," says Bao-bao. "You eat the candy for luck. You can buy more luck later with the money."

"I'm gonna eat mine now," announces Tessa.

Cleo waves her candy for me to unwrap. "Mommy, me too, me too!"

Phil flips his quarter. "Say, if I buy chewing gum with this, will my luck last longer?"

We turn toward the main parlor. Suddenly we are blinded by the glare of a spotlight. I'm surprised to see Tessa is now walking down the aisle in the manner of a coquettish bride. And Cleo—she's preening and blowing kisses like a movie star. I can't believe it: Uncle Henry is standing in the middle of the aisle—videotaping the funeral! Who's going to watch this later?

Through the haze of the incense-blurred light, I can barely see my mother. She's gesturing for us to come sit with her in the second row. Phil corrals the girls. As the camera continues to roll, we walk quickly down the aisle, past what must be only a dozen or so mourn-ers—Mary, Doug, and their children, some people from the church, all Chinese. I also see several old ladies I've never met before. They look like recent immigrants, to judge from their undyed cropped hair and old-style brown padded jackets.

As we slide into our seats, Auntie Helen turns around in the front row. She squeezes my hand, and I see she has tears in her eyes. My mother is dry-eyed. "Why so late?" she asks crossly. "I told them to wait until you came."

Suddenly Cleo starts laughing and points. "Daddy, there's a lady sleeping up there! And her dinner's on fire!" Tessa is staring too, only her eyes are big, her mouth dropped open.

And then I see it too—God!—Grand Auntie Du lying in her casket, with glasses perched on her emotionless waxy face. In front of the casket is a long, low table overflowing with food—what looks like a nine-course Chinese dinner, as well as an odd assortment of mangoes, oranges, and a carved watermelon. This must be Grand Auntie's farewell provisions for trudging off to heaven. The smoke of a dozen burning incense sticks overlaps and swirls up around the casket, her ethereal stairway to the next world.

Phil is staring at me, waiting for an explanation. "This has to be a mistake," I whisper to him, and then turn to my mother, trying to keep my voice calm. "I thought you decided on closed-casket," I say slowly.

She nods. "You like? Clothes, I chose for her, all new. Casket, I also helped decide this. Not the best wood, but almost the best. Before she is buried, we take the jewelry off, of course."

"But I thought you said the lid would be down."

My mother frowns. "I didn't say that. How can you see her that way?"

"But—"

"Do we have to eat here?" Tessa asks fearfully. She squirms down low in her seat. "I'm not hungry," she whispers. I squeeze her hand.

"Tell that lady to wake up," Cleo squeals, giggling. "Tell her she can't sleep at the dinner table. It's not nice!"

Tessa slaps Cleo's leg. "Shut up, Cleo, she's not sleeping. She's dead, like Bootie the cat."

And Cleo's bottom lip turns down, dangerously low. "Don't tell me that!" she shouts, and then pushes Tessa's shoulder. I am trying to think of what I can say to comfort the girls, but—too late—they are pushing each other, crying and shouting, "Stop it!" "You stop!" "You started it!" My mother is watching this, waiting to see how I will handle it. But I feel paralyzed, helpless, not knowing what to do.

Phil stands up to lead both of the girls out. "I'll get them some ice cream over on Columbus. I'll be back in an hour."

"Make it forty-five," I whisper. "No more than that. I'll meet you out front."

"Daddy, can I have a chocolate and a rocky road?" asks Cleo.

"And sprinkles on top?" adds Tessa.

I'm relieved to think this may be all the damage that will remain, a ruined appetite and sticky hands. Over on the other side of the pews, Mary's son, Michael, is snickering. As I throw him a scowl, I notice something else: Uncle Henry still has the videocamera going.

After Phil and the girls leave, I try to regain my composure. I look ahead to avoid glaring at my mother or Uncle Henry. No use arguing, I tell myself. What's done is done.

In front of the pews is a large picture of Grand Auntie. It looks like a blown-up version of a passport photo taken fifty years ago. She's not exactly young, but she must have had most of her teeth back then. I look at Grand Auntie in her casket. Her mouth looks caved in, her thin face like that of a wizened bird. She is so still, yet I feel we are all waiting for something to happen, for Grand Auntie suddenly to transform and manifest herself as a ghost.

It reminds me of a time when I was five years old, that age when anything was possible if you could just imagine it. I had stared at the flickering eyes of a carved pumpkin, waiting for goblins to fly out. The longer I waited, the more convinced I became that it would happen. To this day, I can still vividly remember the laughing ghost that finally poured out of the pumpkin's mouth. My mother had come rushing into the room when I screamed. I was babbling tearfully that I had seen a ghost. And instead of comforting me, or pooh-poohing that it was just my imagination, she had said, "Where?" and then searched the room.

Of course, my father later assured me that the only ghost was the Holy Ghost, and He would never try to scare me. And then he demonstrated in a scientific way that what I must have seen were smoky fumes created when the candle inside the pumpkin burned too low and extinguished itself. I was not comforted by his answer, because my mother had then stared at me, as if I had betrayed her and made her look like a fool. That's how things were. She was always trying to suppress certain beliefs that did not coincide with my father's Christian ones, but sometimes they popped out anyway.

"The *jiao-zi*, I made them," my mother is now telling me. "Grand Auntie always said I made the best-tasting." I nod and admire the steamed dumplings on the banquet table. She really does make the best ones, and I think it's a pity that these are just for show.

"Auntie Helen made the chicken and green peppers dish," she says, and after I nod, she adds, "Very dry-looking." And I nod again, wondering if Grand Auntie is appreciating this culinary post-mortem in her honor. I scan the other dishes and see they have even added the cake left over from last night.

Above the casket, a white banner made out of ten feet of butcher paper is stuck to the wall with masking tape. The banner is covered with large black characters, and the whole thing ends with an exclamation point, just like political billboard slogans I once saw in magazine photos of China.

"What does that say?" I ask my mother quietly.

" 'Hope that your next life is long and prosperous.' Nothing too special," my mother replies. "I didn't write it. This is from people with the Kwong family association. Maybe Helen gave them a donation."

I see all the wreaths perched on their easels. I search for mine, and I'm about to ask my mother where it is, when Uncle Henry turns the spotlight on again and starts filming Grand Auntie Du, lying at center stage. He waves to someone at stage left.

The next moment, I hear hollow wooden knocking sounds, followed by a persistent *ding-ding-ding*, as if someone were impatiently ringing for the bellhop in a hotel lobby. These sounds are joined by two voices, chanting a tune that seems to consist of the same four notes and syllables. It repeats so many times I'm sure it's a record that has become stuck.

But now, emerging from the left alcove are two Buddhist monks with shaved heads, dressed in saffron-colored robes. The older, larger monk lights a long stick of incense, bows three times to the body, then places the incense in the burner and backs away, bowing again. The younger monk is sounding the wooden clapper. Then they both begin walking down the aisle slowly, chanting, "Ami-, Ami-, Amitaba, Amitaba." As the older monk passes by, I see one cheek is flattened, and the ear on the same side is badly misshapen.

"He must have been in a terrible car accident," I whisper to my mother.

"Cultural Revolution," she says.

The smaller monk, I can see now, is not a monk at all, but a woman, a nun with three or four small scabs on her skull.

"She must have been in the Cultural Revolution too," I tell my mother.

My mother looks. "Too young. Flea bites, maybe," she concludes.

"Amitaba, Amitaba," they drone. And now the old ladies in the old-style jackets begin moaning and wailing, waving their arms up and down, overcome with grief, it seems. Uncle Henry turns the camera toward them.

"Are they Grand Auntie's good friends?" I ask my mother.

She frowns. "Not friends, maybe Chinese people from Vietnam. They came early, later saw we didn't have too many people to mourn Grand Auntie. So they talked to Auntie Helen, she gave them a few dollars. And now they're doing the old custom, crying out loud and acting like they don't want the dead person to leave so fast. This is how you show respect."

I nod. Respect.

"Maybe these ladies can do two or three funerals every day," my mother adds, "earn a few dollars. Good living that way. Better than cleaning house."

"Um," I answer. I don't know if my mother has said this to be disdainful or simply to state a matter of fact.

The wooden clapper and the bell sound again, faster and faster. Suddenly the white paper banner tears away from the wall, and the family association wishes for lucky and long life spiral down and land draped across Grand Auntie's chest like a beauty pageant banner. My mother and several of the older women jump up and cry, "Ai-ya!" Mary's son shouts, "Perfect landing!" and laughs hysterically. The monk and nun continue chanting with no change of expression. But my mother is furious. "How bad!" she mutters. She gets up and walks out of the room.

In a few minutes, she comes back with a young Caucasian man with thinning blond hair. He is wearing a black suit, so he must be with the funeral parlor. I can tell my mother is still scolding him, as she points to the disaster-ridden banner. People are murmuring

43

loudly throughout the room. The old ladies are still wailing and bowing stiffly; the monk and nun keep chanting.

The blond man walks quickly to the front, my mother follows. He bows three times to Grand Auntie Du, then moves her casket, which glides forward easily on wheels. After another bow, the man ceremoniously plucks the banner off Grand Auntie's chest and carries it in both arms as if it were holy vestments. As he tapes the banner back up, my mother is fuming, "That corner, put more tape there! More there, too. How can you let her luck fall down like that!"

Once he has finished, the man pushes the casket back in place and bows three times to the body, once to my mother, who huffs in return, then quickly retreats. Did he bow to show genuine respect, I wonder, or has he learned to do this only for his Chinese customers?

Now Frank is passing out lit sticks of incense to everyone. I look around, trying to figure out what to do. One by one, we each get up and join the monk and nun, everyone chanting, "Amitaba! Amitaba!"

We are circling the coffin 'round and 'round, I don't know how many times. I feel silly, taking part in a ritual that makes no sense to me. It reminds me of that time I went with some friends to the Zen center. I was the only Asian-looking person there. And I was also the only one who kept turning around, wondering impatiently when the monk would come and the sermon would begin, not realizing until I'd been there for twenty minutes that all the others weren't quietly waiting, they were meditating.

My mother is now bowing to Grand Auntie. She puts her incense in the burner, then murmurs softly, "Ai! Ai!" The others follow suit, some crying, the Vietnamese ladies wailing loudly. Now it is my turn to bow. And I feel guilty. It's the same guilt I've felt before—when my father baptized me and I did not believe I was saved forever, when I took Communion and did not believe the grape juice was the blood of Christ, when I prayed along with others that a miracle would cure my father, when I already felt he had died long before.

Suddenly a sob bursts from my chest and surprises everyone, even me. I panic and try to hold back, but everything collapses. My heart is breaking, bitter anger is pouring out and I can't stop it.

My mother's eyes are also wet. She smiles at me through her tears. And she knows this grief is not for Grand Auntie Du but for my father. Because she has been waiting for me to cry for such a long, long time, for more than twenty-five years, ever since the day of my father's funeral.

I was fourteen, full of anger and cynicism. My mother, brother, and I were sitting by ourselves in an alcove, a half-hour before the service was supposed to begin. And my mother was scolding me, because I refused to go up to the casket to see my father's body.

"Samuel said good-bye. Samuel is crying," she said.

I did not want to mourn the man in the casket, this sick person who had been thin and listless, who moaned and became helpless, who in the end searched constantly for my mother with fearful eyes. He was so unlike what my father had once been: charming and lively, strong, kind, always generous with his laughter, the one who knew exactly what to do when things went wrong. And in my father's eyes, I had been perfect, his "perfect Pearl," and not the irritation I always seemed to be with my mother.

My mother blew her nose. "What kind of daughter cannot cry for her own father?"

"That man in there is not my father," I said sullenly.

Right then my mother jumped up and slapped my face. "That bad!" she shouted. I was shocked. It was the first time she had ever struck me.

"Ai-ya! If you can't cry, I make you cry." And she slapped me again and again. "Cry! Cry!" she wailed crazily. But I sat there still as a stone.

Finally, realizing what she had done, my mother bit the back of her hand and mumbled something in Chinese. She took my brother by the hand, and they left me.

So there I sat, angry, of course, and also victorious, although over what, I didn't know. And perhaps because I didn't know, I found myself walking over to the casket. I was breathing hard, telling myself, I'm right, she's wrong. And I was so determined not to cry that I never considered I would feel anything whatsoever.

But then I saw him, colorless and thin. And he was not resting peacefully with God. His face was stern, as if still locked in his last moment of pain.

I took so many small breaths, trying to hold back, trying not to cry, that I began to hyperventilate. I ran out of the room, out into the fresh air, gasping and gulping. I ran down Columbus, toward the bay, ignoring the tourists who stared at my angry, tear-streaked face. And in the end, I missed the funeral.

In a way, this is how it's been with my mother and me ever since. We both won and we both lost, and I'm still not sure what our battle was. My mother speaks constantly of my father and his tragedy, although never of the funeral itself. And until this day, I have never cried in front of my mother or spoken of my feelings for my father.

Instead, I have tried to keep my own private memories of him— a certain smile, a coat he wore, the passion he exuded when he stood at the pulpit. But then I always end up realizing that what I am remembering are just images from photos. And in fact, what I do remember most vividly are those times when he was ill. "Pearl," he would call weakly from his bed, "do you want help with your homework?" And I would shake my head. "Pearl," he would call from the sofa, "come help me sit up." And I would pretend I didn't hear him.

Even to this day I have nightmares about my father. In my dreams, he is always hidden in a hospital, in one of a hundred rooms with a hundred cots filled with sick people. I am wandering down long hallways, looking for him. And to do so, I must look at every face, every illness, every possible horror that can happen to one's body and mind. And each time I see it is not my father, I shake with relief.

I have had many variations of this dream. In fact, I had one just recently. In this version, I have gone to the hospital for a checkup, to see if the multiple sclerosis has advanced. Without explanation, a doctor puts me in a ward with terminally ill patients. And I'm shouting, "You can't treat me this way! You have to explain!" I shout and shout and shout, but nobody comes.

And that's when I see him. He is sitting in front of me, on a dirty cot, in soiled bedclothes. He is old and pathetically thin, his hair now white and patchy after years of waiting and neglect. I sit next to him and whisper, "Daddy?" He looks up with those helpless searching eyes. And when he sees me, he gives a small startled cry—then cries and cries, so happy!—so happy I have finally come to take him home.

Grand Auntie's memorial service is finally over. We are all standing outside and the bay wind has already started to blow, cutting through our thin jackets and causing skirts to whip up. My eyes are stinging and I feel completely drained.

My mother stands quietly next to me, peering at me every now and then. I know she wants to talk about what happened, not about all the disasters at the funeral, but why I cried.

"All right?" my mother asks gently.

"Fine," I say, and try to look as normal as possible. "Phil and the girls should be here any minute." My mother pulls a balled-up Kleenex from her sweater sleeve and hands it to me without a word, pointing to her own eye to indicate I've smudged my mascara.

Right then, Bao-bao comes up. "Boy, that was sure weird," he says. "But I guess that's the kind of funeral the old lady wanted. She always was a bit *you-know*," and he taps his finger twice to the side of his head.

My mother frowns. "What is *you-know*?"

Bao-bao grins sheepishly. "You know, uh, different, unusual—a *great* lady!" He looks at me and shrugs. And then relief springs to his face. "Whoa! There's Mimi with the car. Gotta run. You guys going to the cemetery?"

I shake my head. My mother looks at me, surprised.

Bao-bao walks over to a shiny black Camaro, and Mimi slides over so he can drive. "I don't got a choice. Mom roped me into being one of the pallbearers." He flexes his arm. "Good thing I've been pumping iron." He turns the radio way up and flexes his arm faster in rhythm with the vibrating music. "Well, nice seeing you again, Pearl. Catch you later, Auntie." The car rumbles off.

And now I hear Auntie Helen calling from behind. "Pearl! Pearl!" She waddles over, dabbing a tissue to her eyes at the same time. "You going to the cemetery? Nice buffet afterward, our house. Lots of good food. Your mother made the potstickers. I made a good chicken dish. Mary and Doug will be there. You come."

"We can't. Tomorrow's a work day, and it's a long drive."

"Oh, you kids," she says, and throws her hands up in mock frustration, "always too busy! Well, you come visit me soon. No invitation needed. You come, so we can talk."

"Okay," I lie.

"Winnie-ah!" Auntie Helen now calls loudly to my mother, even though they are standing only five feet apart. "You come with us to the cemetery. Henry is getting the car now."

"Pearl is taking me home," my mother answers, and I stand there, trying to figure out how she manages to catch me every time.

Auntie Helen walks up to my mother, a worried look on her face. She asks her quickly in Chinese: Not coming? Are you feeling sick?

I can't understand all the Mandarin words, only the gist of them. It seems my mother doesn't want anyone to worry, nothing is wrong, only a little discomfort here—and she points to her chest—because something-something has been bothering her. She mentions something-something about the banner falling down, and how her whole body has been aching ever since.

Auntie Helen rubs my mother's back. She tells my mother she can visit Auntie Du when something-something is more quiet, not running around all over the place. And then Auntie Helen laughs and tells my mother that Auntie Du will wait, of course she will wait for her visit, she has no choice. And my mother jokes back that maybe Auntie Du has already become mad-to-death about what happened today and has flown off to something-something place where she doesn't have to do something-something anymore with such a crazy family.

They are laughing hysterically now, laughing so hard that tears sprout from their eyes and they are barely able to catch their breath. My mother covers her mouth with her hand, giggling like a school-girl.

Uncle Henry drives the car up, and as Auntie Helen climbs in, she sternly reminds my mother to drink plenty of hot tea. They take off, beeping the horn twice.

"Aren't you feeling well?" I ask my mother.

"Ah?"

"You told Auntie Helen you couldn't go to the cemetery because you were sick."

"I didn't say sick. I only said I didn't want to go. I did my duty. I sent Auntie Du to heaven. Now it's Helen's duty to put her inside the ground."

That's not what they said. And although I'm not sure I understood most of their conversation, apparently there's a lot I don't know about my mother and Auntie Helen.

As we drive across town to my mother's house, Phil drops hints: "I hope we're on the freeway before the weekend rush hour to get back home."

My mother is making small talk. She tells me that Bao-bao may lose his job soon. This gossip she heard at the dinner from Uncle Loy, who heard it from his son. She tells me that Frank is now working the day shift as a security guard, but he is breaking Auntie Helen's heart, spending all his extra time and money at a pool hall on Geary Street.

As we get closer to her house, she points to a place on Clement Street, Happy Super, where she always does her grocery shopping. It's one of the typical Asian markets in the neighborhood, people standing outside, pinching and poking through piles of fruits and vegetables, hundred-pound bags of rice stacked like giant bricks against the window.

"Tofu, how much do you pay?" asks my mother, and I can tell she's eager to outdo me with a better price, to tell me how I can save twenty or thirty cents at her store.

But I can't even oblige her with a guess. "I don't know. I've never bought tofu."

"Oh." She looks disappointed. And then she brightens. "Four rolls of toilet paper, how much?"

"One sixty-nine," I answer right away.

"You see!" she says. "My place, only ninety-nine cents. Good brands, too. Next time, I buy you some. You can pay me back."

We turn left onto Eighth Avenue and head toward Anza. Auntie Helen and Uncle Henry live one block up, on Ninth. The houses in this area all look the same to me, variations of two-story row houses built in the twenties, differing mostly in what color they are painted and whether the front has been modernized in stucco, asbestos shingles, or aluminum siding. Phil pulls into my mother's driveway. The front of her place is Day-Glo pink, the unfortunate result of her being talked into a special deal by a longtime customer, a painting contractor. And because the outside is bumpy stucco, the whole effect looks like Pepto-Bismol poured over cottage cheese. Amazingly enough, of all the things my mother complains about, the color of the house is not one of them. She actually thinks it's pretty.

"When will I see you again?" she asks me as she climbs out of the car.

"Oh, soon," I say.

"Soon like Auntie Helen's soon?" she says.

"No, *soon*. Really."

She pauses, looking as if she doesn't believe me. "Oh, anyway, I will see you at Bao-bao's wedding next month."

"What? The wedding is next month? I didn't hear that."

"Very fast," my mother says, nodding. "Edna Fong from our church said she heard this from her daughter. Mimi washes her hair at that beauty shop. Mimi told Edna Fong's daughter they are in a big hurry to get married. And Edna Fong said to me, Maybe because something else is hurrying to come out. Auntie Helen doesn't know this yet. Don't tell her."

So there goes Auntie Helen's theory about Bao-bao's getting married because she's going to die soon. Something's growing all right, but it's not a tumor in Auntie Helen's head.

My mother climbs out of the car. She turns back and gives Tessa a cheek to kiss, then Cleo. My mother is not the cheek-kissing type, but she knows we have taught the girls to do this with Phil's parents.

"Bye-bye, Ha-bu!" they each say. "We love you."

"Next time you come," my mother says to the girls, "I make potstickers. And you can eat moon cakes for Chinese New Year's." She takes a tissue out of her sleeve and wipes Cleo's nose. She pats Tessa's knee. "Okay?"

"Okay!" they shout.

We all watch my mother walk up the steps to her front door, all of us waving the whole time. Once she's safe inside, we wave once more as she peers out the window, and then we take off.

"Whew!" Phil sighs. "Home." And I too sigh with relief. It's been a difficult weekend, but we survived.

"Mommy?" Tessa says at the first stop sign.

"Yes, sweetie."

"Mommy," she whispers. "I have to go to the bathroom."

"Me too," says Cleo. "I have to go oo-oo *real* bad."

My mother is standing outside the house when we return.

"I tried to chase you, but you were too fast," she says as soon as I get out of the car. "And then I knew you would remember and come back." Tessa and Cleo are already racing up the stairs.

"Remember what?"

"Grand Auntie's farewell gift. Remember? Two three days ago I told you not to forget. Yesterday I said, Don't forget. You forgot?"

"No, no," I say. "Where is it?"

"In back, in the laundry room," she says. "Very heavy, though. Better ask your husband to carry it." I can just imagine what it must be: the old vinyl ottoman Grand Auntie used to rest her feet on, or perhaps the set of chip-proof Melmac dishes. As we wait for Phil to come back with the girls, my mother hands me a cup of tea, waving off my protests. "Already made. If you can't drink it, I only have to throw it away."

I take a few quick sips. "This is really good." And I mean it. I have never tasted tea like this. It is smooth, pungent, and instantly addicting.

"This is from Grand Auntie," my mother explains. "A few years ago she bought it for herself. One hundred dollars a pound."

"You're kidding." I take another sip. It tastes even better.

"She told me, 'If I buy myself the cheap tea, then I am saying my whole life has not been worth something better.' So she decided to buy herself the best tea, so she could drink it and feel like a rich person inside."

I laugh.

My mother looks encouraged by my laughter. "But then she thought, If I buy just a little, then I am saying my lifetime is almost over. So she bought enough tea for another lifetime. Three pounds! Can you imagine?"

"That's three hundred dollars!" I exclaim. Grand Auntie was the most frugal person I knew. "Remember how she used to keep all the boxes of See's candies we gave her for Christmas, telling us they were too good to eat? And then one year, she gave a box back to us for Thanksgiving or something. Only it was so old—"

My mother was nodding, already laughing.

"—all the candies were white with mold!"

"Bugs, too!" my mother adds.

"So she left you the tea in her will?" I say.

"Already gave it to me a few months ago. She was thinking she was going to die soon. She didn't say, but she started to give things away, good things, not just junk. And one time we were visiting, drinking tea. I said, 'Ah, good tea!' same as always. This time, Grand Auntie went to her kitchen, brought back the tea. She told me, '*Syau ning*, you take this tea now.' That's what she called me, *syau ning*, 'little person,' from the old days when we first knew each other.

"I said, 'No, no! I wasn't saying this to hint.' And she said, '*Syau ning*, you take this now so I can see how happy you are to receive it while I am still alive. Some things can't wait until I'm dead.' How could I refuse? Of course, every time I came to visit, I brought back her tea."

Phil returns with Cleo, Tessa is right behind. And now I am actually sorry we have to leave.

"We better hit the road," says Phil. I put the teacup down.

"Don't forget," my mother says to Phil. "Grand Auntie's present in the laundry room."

"A present?" Cleo says. "Do I have a present too?"

Phil throws me a look of surprise.

"Remember?" I lie. "I told you—what Grand Auntie left us in her will."

He shrugs, and we all follow my mother to the back.

"Of course it's just old things," says my mother. She turns on the light, and then I see it, sitting on the clothes dryer. It is the altar for Grand Auntie's good-luck god, the Chinese crèche.

"Wow!" Tessa exclaims. "A Chinese dollhouse."

"I can't see! I can't see!" Cleo says, and Phil lifts the altar off the dryer and carries it into the kitchen.

The altar is about the size of a small upturned drawer, painted in red lacquer. In a way, it resembles a miniature stage for a Chinese play. There are two ornate columns in front, as well as two ceremonial electric candles made out of gold and red plastic and topped by red Christmas tree bulbs for flames. Running down the sides are wooden panels decorated with gold Chinese characters.

"What does that say?" I ask my mother.

She traces her finger down one, then the other. "*Jye shiang ru yi.* This first word is 'luck,' this other is another kind of luck, and these two mean 'all that you wish.' All kinds of luck, all that you wish."

"And who is this on the inside, this man in the picture frame?" The picture is almost cartoonlike. The man is rather large and is seated in regal splendor, holding a quill in one hand, a tablet in the other. He has two long whiskers, shaped like smooth, tapered black whips.

"Oh, this we call Kitchen God. To my way of thinking, he was not too important. Not like Buddha, not like Kwan Yin, goddess of mercy—not that high level, not even the same level as the Money God. Maybe he was like a store manager, important, but still many, many bosses above him."

Phil chuckles at my mother's Americanized explanation of the hierarchy of Chinese deities. I wonder if that's how she really thinks of them, or if she's used this metaphor for our benefit.

"What's a kitchen god?" says Tessa. "Can I have one?"

"He is only a story," answers my mother.

"A story!" exclaims Cleo. "I want one."

My mother's face brightens. She pats Cleo's head. "You want another story from Ha-bu? Last night, you did not get enough stories?"

"When we get home," Phil says to Cleo. "Ha-bu is too tired to tell you a story now."

But my mother acts as if she has not heard Phil's excuses. "It is a very simple story," she says to Cleo in a soothing voice, "how he became Kitchen God. It is this way."

And as my mother begins, I am struck by a familiar feeling, as if I am Cleo, again three years old, still eager to believe everything my mother has to say.

•

"In China long time ago," I hear my mother say, "there was a rich farmer named Zhang, such a lucky man. Fish jumped in his river, pigs grazed his land, ducks flew around his yard as thick as clouds. And that was because he was blessed with a hardworking wife named Guo. She caught his fish and herded his pigs. She fattened his ducks, doubled all his riches, year after year. Zhang had everything he could ask for—from the water, the earth, and the heavens above.

"But Zhang was not satisfied. He wanted to play with a pretty, carefree woman named Lady Li. One day he brought this pretty woman home to his house, made his good wife cook for her. When Lady Li later chased his wife out of the house, Zhang did not run out and call to her, 'Come back, my good wife, come back.'

"Now he and Lady Li were free to swim in each other's arms. They threw money away like dirty water. They slaughtered ducks just to eat a plate of their tongues. And in two years' time, all of Zhang's land was empty, and so was his heart. His money was gone, and so was pretty Lady Li, run off with another man.

"Zhang became a beggar, so poor he wore more patches than whole cloth on his pants. He crawled from the gate of one household to another, crying, 'Give me your moldy grain!'

"One day, he fell over and faced the sky, ready to die. He fainted, dreaming of eating the winter clouds blowing above him. When he opened his eyes again, he found the clouds had turned to smoke. At first he was afraid he had fallen down into a place far below the earth. But when he sat up, he saw he was in a kitchen, near a warm fireplace. The girl tending the fire explained that the lady of the house had taken pity on him—she always did this, with all kinds of people, poor or old, sick or in trouble.

" 'What a good lady!' cried Zhang. 'Where is she, so I can thank her?' The girl pointed to the window, and the man saw a woman walking up the path. Ai-ya! That lady was none other than his good wife Guo!

"Zhang began leaping about the kitchen looking for some place to hide, then jumped into the kitchen fireplace just as his wife walked in the room.

"Good Wife Guo poured out many tears to try to put the fire

out. No use! Zhang was burning with shame and, of course, because of the hot roaring fire below. She watched her husband's ashes fly up to heaven in three puffs of smoke. Wah!

"In heaven, the Jade Emperor heard the whole story from his new arrival. 'For having the courage to admit you were wrong,' the Emperor declared, 'I make you Kitchen God, watching over everyone's behavior. Every year, you let me know who deserves good luck, who deserves bad.'

"From then on, people in China knew Kitchen God was watching them. From his corner in every house and every shop, he saw all kinds of good and bad habits spill out: generosity or greediness, a harmonious nature or a complaining one. And once a year, seven days before the new year, Kitchen God flew back up the fireplace to report whose fate deserved to be changed, better for worse, or worse for better."

"The end!" shouts Cleo, completely satisfied.

"Sounds like Santa Claus," says Phil cheerfully.

"Hnh!" my mother huffs in a tone that implies Phil is stupid beyond words. "He is not Santa Claus. More like a spy—FBI agent, CIA, Mafia, worse than IRS, that kind of person! And he does not give *you* gifts, you must give *him* things. All year long you have to show him respect—give him tea and oranges. When Chinese New Year's time comes, you must give him even better things—maybe whiskey to drink, cigarettes to smoke, candy to eat, that kind of thing. You are hoping all the time his tongue will be sweet, his head a little drunk, so when he has his meeting with the big boss, maybe he reports good things about you. This family has been good, you hope he says. Please give them good luck next year."

"Well, that's a pretty inexpensive way to get some luck," I say. "Cheaper than the lottery."

"No!" my mother exclaims, and startles us all. "You never know. Sometimes he is in a bad mood. Sometimes he says, I don't like this family, give them bad luck. Then you're in trouble, nothing you can do about it. Why should I want that kind of person to judge me, a man who cheated his wife? His wife was the good one, not him."

"Then why did Grand Auntie keep him?" I ask.

My mother frowns, considering this. "It is this way, I think. Once you get started, you are afraid to stop. Grand Auntie worshipped him since she was a little girl. Her family started it many generations before, in China."

"Great!" says Phil. "So now she passes along this curse to us. Thanks, Grand Auntie, but no thanks." He looks at his watch and I can tell he's impatient to go.

"It was Grand Auntie's gift to you," my mother says to me in a mournful voice. "How could she know this was not so good? She only wanted to leave you something good, her best things."

"Maybe the girls can use the altar as a dollhouse," I suggest. Tessa nods, Cleo follows suit. My mother stares at the altar, not saying anything.

"I'm thinking about it this way," she finally announces, her mouth set in an expression of thoughtfulness. "You take this altar. I can find you another kind of lucky god to put inside, not this one." She removes the picture of the Kitchen God. "This one, I take it. Grand Auntie will understand. This kind of luck, you don't want. Then you don't have to worry."

"Deal!" Phil says right away. "Let's pack 'er up."

But now I'm worried. "Are you sure?" I ask my mother. She's already stuffing the plastic candlesticks into a used paper bag. I'm not exactly superstitious. I've always been the kind who hates getting chain letters—Mary used to send them to me all the time. And while I never sent the duplicate letters out as instructed, I never threw the originals away either.

Phil is carrying the altar. Tessa has the bag of candlesticks. My mother has taken Cleo back upstairs to find a plastic neon bracelet she left in the bathroom. And now my mother comes back with Cleo and hands me a heavy grocery sack, the usual care package, what feels like oranges and Chinese candy, that sort of thing.

"Grand Auntie's tea, I gave you some," my mother says. "Don't need to use too much. Just keep adding water. The flavor always comes back."

Fifteen minutes after leaving my mother's home, the girls fall asleep. Phil has chosen to take the 280 freeway, which has less traffic and longer stretches between speed traps. We are still thirty-five miles from home.

"We're not really keeping that altar thing?" Phil says. It is more a statement than a question.

"Um."

"It sure is ugly," he adds. "Although I suppose we could let the girls play with it for a while, until they get tired of it."

"Um." I look out the car window, thinking about my mother, what kind of good-luck god she will get for me. We rush past freeway signs and Sunday drivers in the slow lane. I look at the speedometer. We're going nearly eighty miles an hour.

"What's the rush?" I say.

Phil slows down, then asks, "Do we have anything to snack on?"

And now I remember the care package my mother gave us. It is stowed at my feet. I look in the bag. Inside are a few tangerines, a roll of toilet paper, a canister of Grand Auntie's tea, and the picture of my father that I accidentally knocked over last month. The glass has been replaced.

I quickly hand Phil a tangerine, then turn back toward the window so he does not see my tears. I watch the landscape we are drifting by: the reservoir, the rolling foothills, the same houses I've passed a hundred times without ever wondering who lives inside. Mile after mile, all of it familiar, yet not, this distance that separates us, me from my mother.

# 3

# WHEN FISH ARE
# THREE DAYS OLD

Helen thinks all her decisions are always right, but really, she is only lucky. For over fifty years I have seen this happen, how her foolish thinking turns into good fortune. It was like that at lunch yesterday. ·"Winnie-ah," she said, "have more chicken." I told Helen I did not want to eat any more funeral leftovers—five days was enough. So we went shopping at Happy Super, deciding what new things to eat for last night's dinner.

Helen picked out a flat fish, pom-pom fish, she called it, only a dollar sixty-nine a pound, bargain bin.

And I said, "This kind of bargain you don't want. Look at his eye, shrunken in and cloudy-looking. That fish is already three days old."

But Helen stared at that fish eye and said she saw nothing wrong. So I picked up that fish and felt its body slide between my fingers, a fish that had slipped away from life long time ago. Helen said it was a good sign—a juicy, tender fish!

So I smelled that fish for her. I told her how all the sweetness of its meat had risen to the skin and turned stinky-sour in the air. She put that fish to her nose and said, "That's a good pom-pom smell."

She bought that three-day-old fish, the dinner I ate at her house last night. And when she served it, her husband poked out a fish cheek, popped it in his mouth, and praised its taste; then their son

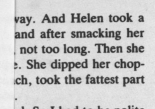

vay. And Helen took a
and after smacking her
not too long. Then she
e. She dipped her chop-
ch, took the fattest part
.

ed. So I had to be polite

vas sweet. It was tender.
d to think, Maybe Helen
ed that fish. But then I
at's when I remembered
rt, even though she was
n pretty, she has always
had luck pour onto her plate, even ....om the mouth of a three-
day-old fish.

I am not the same way. I was born with good luck. But over the
years, my luck—just like my prettiness—dried out, then carved
lines on my face so I would not forget.

I cannot explain exactly how this happened, these changes in my
life. If I try to say what happened, my story would not flow forward
like a river from the beginning to the end, everything connected,
the lake to the sea. If my life had been that way, one thing leading
to another, then I could look back and I would know the lessons
of my life: the fate that was given me, the choices I took, the
mistakes that are mine. And perhaps I would still have time to
change my luck.

Helen always tells me, "Why do you think about those old things?
Useless to regret. You cannot change the past." She doesn't remember. She and I have changed the past many times, for many
reasons. And sometimes she changes it for me and does not even
know what she has done.

It is like that pom-pom fish Helen bought. Now it is swimming
backward into my memory. Because once, many years ago, I bought
a special fish for my husband, for Jimmy Louie. Oh, how I loved
him! The fish was swimming in a tank when I saw it, caught from
the ocean just that morning, so it was still angry. Its body was
gleaming with red-orange scales, and when it flashed its tail to turn
around in that small tank, the scales swimming now the other way

looked pale golden. I told the butcher to wrap that fish live, not in newspaper but in clean, white paper. And as I carried that fish home on the bus, I was so proud, feeling it thrash and knock its head, then its tail. I imagined how sweet this fish would taste in Jimmy's mouth, how my husband would know this was a special fish, a lucky fish, and that I had good news to give him.

Let me tell you, that fish never stopped fighting me. Before I killed it, it puffed its gills out, spouted bubbles from its mouth to make me think it was poisonous. And even after I gutted it, it jumped up and down in the pan and threw itself on the floor, flopping all around as I chased it with a hammer. And after I cooked it, it still found a way to fight me. Jimmy ate only one bite before a little bone swam down his throat and got stuck, so that each time he swallowed he thought that fish was biting him from the inside out, all night long.

Later, in the hospital, the doctors operated to remove the fish bone. And even though Jimmy could not talk, I knew by his worried face that he was thinking about the cost of the fish-bone operation, the cost of the bed, the cost of the medicines that made him sleep. That's when I remembered my good news, the reason why I had bought that expensive fish. I had found a job, I told him, making noodles for Hang Ah Bakery. My extra money would now be enough, more than enough, to pay off the hospital in less than one year. And after I told him this, Jimmy squeezed his eyes and tears came out. He moved his mouth; no words came out of his wounded throat. But I could see what he was saying, what he wanted to shout: "Lucky for us! How lucky for us!"

So my luck is not like Helen's. It is not like other people's, people who brag how their bad luck turned good. No, I'll tell you how it is with other people, how it is with me. It is like that girl I once knew in Shanghai, the schoolmate who went to the same Christian school as me. She came from a rich family like mine. She was almost as pretty as me. Around the same time I married my first husband, she had a wedding contract to a rich banking family. But after the summer, her face became marked forever with smallpox, and that contract disappeared. I pitied that girl because she had lost her face two ways.

Many years later I met her again, when Jimmy and I moved to

Fresno. She was married to an American Chinese man who owned a grocery store, selling soda pop, potato chips, cigarettes, everything at high prices. That's how I met her again, at the checkout counter. I was buying ice cream on a stick. She cried, "Sister, sister, remember me!" But she didn't give me a discount. After I paid her, she told me how her husband was honest, very kind, very nice, and as she said this, she pushed her many jade bracelets up her arm so they would fall back down and clink together like rich music. She was smiling so big all her pock marks looked like the happy dimples she now wore.

But later she dropped her smile and whispered to me, "You remember that son from the banking family in Shanghai?" And she told me, with sincere sadness, not bitter at all—that's how good life had been to her—that the family had lost all its banks when the Communists took over. Then later, their son, the same who had refused to marry her, jumped off the tower of a building the family once owned along the Huangpu River, and even his wife, the pretty one that he did marry, was too scared to go and claim his body. "Lucky he didn't marry me," said my friend.

I have never had luck like that. I refused to marry a good man, a man named Lin, for my first husband. I married the wrong one instead, a man named Wen. Both of them came from the same island where I had lived ever since I was six years old. This was in the old-fashioned countryside, in a little place surrounded by water, the river and the sea, so no new ideas could easily come in.

The man I should have married was from a family with not very much money, but educated and with good manners. When I was sixteen by my Chinese age, I refused his family's offer without ever meeting their son. This was because I listened to Old Aunt, the way she announced the family's offer at the dinner table, in front of New Aunt and Uncle, my cousins, and visiting family friends.

"That family, Lin," she began, and then sniffed her nose, "hnh! Wants to climb into our family on Weili's wedding skirt." With those words, I could see this boy, a boy I had never met, looking like a big ugly lizard, crawling up my leg at night. And then Old Aunt turned to me at the dinner table and asked, "Weiwei-ah, do you want to make a marriage with this family?"

She said this in a way that sounded as if she were asking, "Do you want to jump in the river?" which is what Old Aunt always threatened to do when she was unhappy with her husband. "I'd rather use these two feet to jump in the river!" she would shout. "I'd rather use these two hands to hang myself!" And then she would turn to Uncle and her voice would be even more shrill. "Which would you rather I do? Come on, you decide!"

My uncle was the one who later used his two feet and his two hands to kill himself. When the Communists came in 1949, he was too scared to run away, too scared to stay. He became so confused he walked with his own two feet all the way to the port at the north edge of the island, and there he sat down to think about his choices. Two fishermen later said that when a truck loaded with little crabs drove down the dark road to the port, they saw my uncle stand up, run in front of the truck, waving both hands: Go back, go back.

So peculiar, the fishermen said, as if he were now in command of the whole world, as if he really could have stopped that truck before it ran him over. After he was killed, Old Aunt started to believe that the dead tree in our courtyard was her husband, still too lazy to move and help get her out of one bad situation after another.

So that was the kind of family I had. What advice could they give me? If I had not lost my mother so young, I would not have listened to Old Aunt. And maybe I would have married that boy Lin when I was young. Maybe I would have learned to love him after we married. And maybe we would have had difficulties in life, just like everyone, but not the kind that would make me hate myself and think that my own heart was my worst enemy.

I met this same man Lin for the first time twenty years later, when I had already been living in the United States for five years. I was a grown woman then, now called Winnie Louie, married to Jimmy Louie. Pearl was more than four, Samuel almost three. And even though we were poor, I believed my life was full, just as a Christian lady once explained it for me. "A full bowl of rice is as much as you can ask for," she said.

I believed that was true. How could I not? Jimmy was the minister of our church in Fresno, the same one that paid him fifty dollars a week and gave us a little house to live in. So I believed I should not ask for more. I believed this until the day a man named Lin showed up at our same church and saved my life.

Of course, there were many Lins in China, even many Lins in

our church, so I thought nothing of this at first, that he might be that boy I refused to marry. He had just moved into the area, and people were whispering: "He's a doctor, lives in Tulare, with a big swimming pool. Married to a former general's daughter who speaks beautiful Chinese, Peking accent, just like an opera star."

That Sunday, when he and his wife visited our church, we were all standing in the hot morning sun. Everyone was curious about them, the doctor, his high-class wife. Jimmy and I were at the bottom of the church steps, greeting everybody. My husband was speaking in English, the common language among all the different Chinese dialects of our church: "Pleased to see you, pleased to meet you, please come again." Over and over he said those words, all those phrases I practiced at night but still could not say. So I would only nod and smile, pretending to be shy. Every Sunday was the same way. Only, that Sunday turned out to be very hot, and I could not take off my sweater because a little moth had eaten a hole in the right shoulder of my dress.

I nodded to the doctor and his wife. And after they stepped away, I saw other church people moving over to the Lins and introducing themselves: "Gladys Wong," "Mavis Chew," "George Po," "Murray Yang," "Irene Wing"—all of them saying just their names, too shy, I thought, to say more than two words to a big, important doctor.

I was thinking about these little things, not really thinking, just letting words float in and out of my mind, because I was sleepy. My mouth felt heavy, my face hot and itchy. As I scratched at my cheek, the doctor saw me and scratched his neck, nodded and laughed, then said to me, *"Ding-ngin."* Itchy.

When he said that word, *ding-ngin*, I felt as if I were dreaming. How strange, I thought, he knows that same local island expression from my childhood. And then I was remembering that time when I first heard that expression.

I was six and it was the first summer after my father had sent me to live on the island. Day and night, little invisible fleas bit me all over my tender thighs. And soon I was in terrible misery: scratching, scratching, not able to stop even one second. Both hands moved quickly up and down my legs, and I cried in front of everyone, *"Yangsele!"* which in common Mandarin means "itching to death!"

Everyone roared with laughter, and Old Aunt quickly slapped

my hands to make me stop. "How can you say this!" The next day an older cousin told me that local island people say *ding-ngin* when they want to talk about itching, and that *yangsele* means something completely different. I did not know how different until more than ten years later, on the night before my wedding to the wrong man. That's when I heard my boy cousins whispering to one another: "*Yangsele!* She's itching for sex. Her bottom can't wait to be stung by a man."

That hot day at the church in Fresno, when I heard this word *ding-ngin* again, I remembered how innocent I once was. And then I came out of that memory, and I felt my face burning, from anger, from shame, I didn't know which. The more I thought about that memory, the more feverish my mind and body became.

And then Dr. Lin was touching my elbow, asking me, "Are you ill?"

I could not answer him, only watch his face: the way he squeezed his eyebrows up, then jerked his chin twice, letting me know he was anxious to hear my answer. His face!—that squeezing-jerking expression on Lin's face was the same one that the Lin father had, that everybody in that family had, an expression Old Aunt once described as "that Lin long-face look, like a horse nudging you for sweets in your pocket."

Seeing that same face on Lin made me think everything had melted together—my past, my life today, my first husband, my second husband, Lin. That's how confused I was. So I did not know who was shouting, "Heat stroke! Poisoned by too much sun." I did not know why they were taking off my sweater, lifting me up, and carrying me inside the church.

My husband later told me, as I lay wet in his arms, that he had once baptized me to save my soul. And now, he said, both laughing and crying, the doctor had baptized me to save my life. I was still confused, so I could only murmur a bad excuse, "I thought I saw a ghost."

And then I realized we were not alone. Lin was there, his wife, other people from the church—everyone watching me! Right away my senses came back. I was embarrassed, knowing everyone had seen me in that dress with a big hole eaten away by a moth.

I never told Jimmy, That man Lin was the one I could have married instead of marrying that other man first, then you second.

I only told him about that "itchy" word, the language Lin and I
shared from long time ago. So of course, Jimmy was proud to inform
Lin the next Sunday that I was from the same place in China, the
one on Tsungming Island, the place we called the Mouth of the
River. I wanted to claim back my husband's words, to explain that
I was perhaps mistaken, that it was another island. Because I
thought Lin would say in front of everyone, "Hey, aren't you that
girl who refused my family?"

But Lin only smiled and said, "We're both from a long time ago,
eh, little sister?"

Maybe he was being polite. He had very good manners. Or maybe
he never wanted to marry me either. His wife was very beautiful.
Or maybe he was not the Lin boy I was supposed to marry. After
all, I had heard there were other sons in that family. I never found
out. I was scared to find out. What would I gain by knowing this?

So I did not ask further questions. Still, from that day on, I began
to look at everything in my life two ways, the way it happened, the
way it did not.

Late at night, when my husband and children were sleeping, I
would think to myself, Of course, I do not regret marrying Jimmy
Louie. I love my husband. I waited five years to marry him. I came
to this country to live with him. I was willing, more than willing.
It was a true love, not just the devotion that comes from feeding
a husband and raising his children. I was not thinking about Lin,
his wife's pretty clothes, or their swimming pool. Who wants those
things? I said to myself.

But then later and later at night, I thought about it this way:
How I was sorry I did not marry Lin. Because if I had, I would not
have married that other man. I would not have become the kind
of wife who prayed the Japanese would kill her husband. I would
not have become the kind of mother who could not grieve when
her children died. I would not have poisoned my mind thinking of
ways to escape my marriage, only to bite my flesh every day that
I did not. And I would not have regretted that I had so little left
to give my second husband and that I could be only grateful, never
completely happy.

After Jimmy died, I could not help myself from thinking, If I
had married Lin, I would not have met Jimmy Louie, married him,
now be always missing him. My eyes and ears would not be always

searching for Jimmy, searching for nothing, my skin waiting to be touched by no one. I would not be feeling this kind of pain that has no cure. If I had married Lin, I would not even know Jimmy. And then I would not be always missing someone whose name I did not even know.

And now, just recently, I have been thinking about this again. If I had married Lin, I would still be married to Lin. Helen would not know my worst secrets. And I would have no reason to let her boss me around. I know this, because Helen told me last night, during that fish dinner, that a man named Lin, a widower who used to live in Fresno, just joined our church in San Francisco.

"He's a doctor," she said, "but he only put a five-dollar bill in the offering tray."

And Helen, who saw my astonished face and thinks she knows everything, said to me, "Yes, can you imagine? What kind of man is that?"

I didn't say to Helen: I could have married that man, a good man. I didn't say, Was it fate that I did not? Or was it because I didn't know I had a choice? And I didn't admit to her: Maybe I made a mistake, such a simple mistake, saying no to one, yes to another, like choosing fish in a tank. How can you know which one is good, which is bad, until you have tasted it?

Even if I told her, she wouldn't understand. Our thinking is too different. Her head is still back in China. It's like this: When she bought that fish for dinner, I said to her, "Ai, do you know what happens when fish are three days old?"

And right away she said, "They swim out to sea."

For nearly forty years, I have told people Helen is my sister-in-law. But she is not.

I have told people she is the wife of my brother, Kun, the one who was killed during the war. This is not the truth.

But I did not say this to deceive anyone. The truth was too complicated to tell. No one would understand even if I could explain it all.

That brother I said was killed? In truth, he was only my half brother—related not even by blood, just by marriage. He was the son of my father's second wife, the one who died before my mother took her place. So we were never close with that part of the family.

And this half brother Kun did not die in the war. He died before the war, his head chopped off in Changsha for selling three bolts of cloth to the revolutionaries. This was in 4638 by the Chinese calendar, a Horse year, when people stamped their feet and became reckless. By the Western calendar, I don't know. Maybe it was 1929, maybe 1930 or 1931, in any case, before I met Helen.

But if I said these things, then I would have to explain that my half brother was not really a revolutionary. That in truth, he protested—with angry foot-stomping at first, then finally desperate cries on his knees—telling them he did not know his late-night customers were revolutionaries, bragging that he cheated them by charging them a ridiculously high price, laughing that the cloth was of poor quality. The Kuomintang killed him anyway, as a lesson that others could profit by.

But how could I ever reveal this?—that a member of my family meant to cheat his customers. No, all I could say was, Many people were being killed at that time, for any little thing. No one needs to know that we all saw the danger, that my half brother was being foolishly greedy.

Even his real wife thought this. She never wanted to go to Changsha in the first place. But if somebody asked me where she is, I couldn't say. After her husband died, she wrote and told us what had happened. But after that we heard no more about her, only that there was a flood where she lived and so many bloated bodies that people along the shore had to flee inland to escape the stink. So maybe that sister-in-law also drowned and floated down the river and out to sea. Or perhaps she changed her name, maybe even changed her mind and became a Communist, and today is living somewhere in China with a different name.

If I said all this, people might think that was the end of the story of my half brother. And I would have to lie to agree: He is dead. His real wife is gone. There's no more to the story, no surprise happy ending. And for several years that truly was the end of him.

Oh. sometimes within our family we told a tale about a bull howling at the crescent moon, thinking it was his own horn caught up there. And everyone knew who we were talking about: the fool who climbed all the way up to the sky, thinking he could pluck down a star, only to fall and leave behind his life. We did not mention Kun's name. It was dangerous to know anyone who had rubbed shoulders with the Marxists. It didn't matter that Kun was already dead and not really even a revolutionary.

But then my half brother went on to have many other lives. When the Japanese took over Shanghai in 1937, my uncle pretended to welcome them to his textile shop. "My own nephew was educated in Japan, now lives in Changsha, married to a Japanese girl."

And then my half brother took on another life. When the Japanese lost in 1945 and the Kuomintang came back, my uncle said, "My poor nephew, Kun, he was a Kuomintang hero. Died in Changsha."

And when the Communists took over in 1949, the first story came back. Only by then Uncle was dead. So it was Old Aunt who said that my half brother Kun was a big revolutionary hero! "Gave good-quality cloth to the underground students—at no cost, of course, except to his own life."

When I came to this new country, I thought I could finally forget about this half brother Kun, who had died so many times, in so many ways. It was too confusing to explain over and over again: who was related to whom, which half brother by which marriage, what year this happened according to the Chinese or the Western calendar, what happened to that sister-in-law, why we changed our minds so often about the Japanese, the Kuomintang, and the Communists.

How could I explain such a story to the immigration authorities. They wouldn't understand! They knew only one kind of government. They were always asking me all kinds of confusing questions: "Why does it say you are born in 1918 on this paper and 1919 on this one?" "Why do you have no papers for marriage, no papers for divorce?" "Did you contract worms in China or in another country?"

When I came to this country, I told myself: I can think a new way. Now I can forget my tragedies, put all my secrets behind a door that will never be opened, never seen by American eyes. I was thinking my past was closed forever and all I had to remember was to call Formosa "China," to shrink all of China into one little island I had never seen before.

I was thinking, Nobody can chase me here. I could hide mistakes, my regrets, all my sorrows. I could change my fate.

Oh, I was not the only one who put away old things to suit new circumstances. People from our church, that schoolmate with the pock-mark face, Lin and his wife, even Helen—they all left something behind. Old debts and bad beginnings. Elderly mothers and sick fathers, arranged first wives and too many children, superstitions and Chinese calendar destinies.

Even I was scared my old life would catch up with me. But then China turned off the light, closed the door, told everyone to be quiet. All those people there became like ghosts. We could not see them. We could not hear them. So I thought I really could forget everything. Nobody could get out to remind me.

But then Helen wanted to come from Formosa. I had to let her come. She told me I had a debt from many years before, now I had to pay her back. So I told the U.S. immigration officials in 1953 that Helen was my sister, born to one of my father's other five wives. And once she was here, I couldn't tell our church friends that my father had five wives. How could I say that? I was the wife of a minister.

So I said that Helen was my sister-in-law from long time ago, once married to my brother Kun, a big Kuomintang hero who died during the war. Too bad.

I could not use the real story why Helen should come here, why I had to sponsor her. That was even more complicated to explain.

I have told this story about Helen being married to my brother so many times even Helen believes it now. She tells people who ask about those old days: "Oh, I had a big, big Western wedding. Winnie was my maid of honor. Too bad he died so young." She says this even though she has been a citizen for many years and nobody can send her back.

And Helen has told stories about me, so many times, I sometimes believe they are true. That Jimmy was my first and only husband. That she introduced him to me in Shanghai. She was a witness at my wedding, a big, big Chinese wedding.

No one would believe me now if I said Helen is not my sister-in-law. She is not related by blood, not even by marriage. She is not someone I chose as my friend. Sometimes I do not even enjoy her company. I do not agree with her opinions. I do not admire her character. And yet we are closer perhaps than sisters, related by fate, joined by debts. I have kept her secrets. She has kept mine. And we have a kind of loyalty that has no word in this country.

So you can imagine my anger when Helen told me in her kitchen, right after that fish dinner, that she has decided to let all my secrets out.

# 4

# LONG, LONG DISTANCE

Here is how she told me.

After that fish dinner, Henry went into the living room to watch TV and sleep on the sofa. Helen was still in the kitchen, cooking water for tea. And I was sitting in the dining room. Actually, it is not really a dining room, but part of the kitchen, separated by a thin plastic screen. But because Helen could not see me, she was shouting, as if she were calling long-distance, bragging about her Bao-bao getting married in three weeks.

Bao-bao this, and Bao-bao that, was what she was saying. She sounded just like those TV shows that brag, Win this, win that, every week the same thing.

Her son is thirty-one years old and she still calls him baby. But maybe Helen is right. Her Bao-bao is still a baby, so spoiled and impatient he can't even wait for a bus. One time his car was broken down, and he called me, so nice and polite: "Oh, Auntie, I haven't seen you for a long time. Oh, Auntie, how is your health? Good, good. Oh, Auntie, please let me borrow your car for an important job interview."

When he returned my car three days later, I saw his character scattered inside and out—a bump on my bumper, Coca-Cola cans on the floor, no gas. And he didn't even get that job.

So I wasn't listening to Helen praising Bao-bao. I was remembering how mad I was about my car. And because I had never complained, remembering made me mad all over again. I was thinking, My son, he isn't like that. Samuel does not say polite words as an excuse to borrow something. And he doesn't have to borrow Helen's car to go for an interview. He already has a good job, in New Jersey, a senior benefits administrator, analyzing sick leave, sick pay, who is really sick, who is only fooling around.

Helen came in the room with our tea, still talking loud as if I were far away. Now she was talking about Mary. "Did I tell you? Mary called me a few days ago, told me she and Doug are going to Hawaii—again! This is already their fourth time. I said, 'You already saw it. You don't need to go again.' And she said, 'Nobody goes to Hawaii because they *need* to. You go because you *don't* need to.' "

Helen gave me my tea. "I told my daughter, 'What kind of thinking is this? I don't need to go to Hawaii, I don't go. I want to go to China, I also don't go!' " Helen laughed to herself. "That daughter of mine!" she said. "Oh! Did I tell you? She called me again, late last night, after ten." Helen waved her hands, so disgusted. "Scared me to death almost! I said to her, 'What's wrong? Someone is sick? Car accident? Doug lost his job?' And she said, 'No, no, no. I just wanted to call.' " Helen smiled. "What do you think? Why did she call? Tell me."

"She is a good daughter," I said.

Helen shook her head, "This time she said she was calling for no reason. No reason! This is not a reason to call."

Helen poured me more tea. "Of course, it wasn't her idea, not entirely. She saw a TV commercial for a phone company, a daughter calling a mother for no reason. I said to my daughter, 'Now you're calling long-distance, no reason? Don't talk too long, then, too expensive.' And she said, 'It's okay. After eight o'clock, it's cheaper.'

"So I told her, 'Don't be fooled. They say all kinds of lies on television. Maybe it's only cheaper if you talk faster. Who knows what their meaning is.'

"She said, 'Oh, Mommy, the cost doesn't matter.'

"I said, 'Wah! Doesn't matter? How can you say cost doesn't matter? You want to waste ten dollars? Don't give it to the phone company, then. Send it to me instead.' "

In my mind, I could hear Helen arguing with her daughter, wasting money to argue about not wasting money. Helen doesn't have any sense.

Helen sighed. "Finally I convinced her, and she hung up." She looked at me, smiled real big, and went back to speaking Chinese. "See, she still listens to me. She knows her mother is still right." She took a noisy sip of tea. "So, have you heard from Pearl this week? Does she call and waste long-distance money, too?"

When Helen asked me that, I knew she was not looking for an answer. She knows my daughter and I do not talk too often. Pearl does not call me for no reason. Of course, she calls me to say she is bringing Tessa and Cleo for baby-sitting. She calls me to say, Can you bring the Chinese stuffing for Thanksgiving? And she calls to warn me. Last week, for example, she called me to say she and her family could not stay overnight at my house. Actually, she did not call me herself, her husband called. But I knew she told him to call. I knew she was listening on the other line.

"Pearl doesn't live long distance," I reminded Helen.

"San Jose is still long-distance," she argued. "Fifty miles away. Different area code."

"But she is not long, long distance," I said.

Helen would not give up. "Long-distance enough! You still have to pay extra every minute. You still can't talk too much."

"Maybe we should not talk too much either," I said. "Henry is asleep." And I pointed to her tired husband, lying on the sofa, his mouth wide open. "Maybe I better go home."

"Henry, get up!" Helen shouted, and then pushed her husband's shoulder, until one frowning eye popped open, then two feet were pushing along the floor, moving slowly to his bed.

After Henry left, Helen said to me, "So now maybe I have some good news to tell you." She smiled.

"What kind of good news?"

She smiled again. She sipped her tea. She took her Kleenex out of her sleeve and wiped her nose. She sipped her tea again and smiled again. Why does she make everything like a Buddhist ceremony?

"Now you no longer have to hide," she said at last.

"I am not hiding. I am here."

"No, no, all your life you have been hiding. Now you can come out." She jumped up and found her purse, a big bag, then dug her hand inside. I could tell she was in a big hurry to find something. She pulled out an orange and put that on the table, then two bags of airline peanuts, restaurant toothpicks, her extra wallet for tricking robbers. She turned the purse sideways and spilled out all sorts of other junk in case a war breaks out and we have to run away like the old days: two short candles, her American naturalization papers in a plastic pouch, her Chinese passport from forty years ago, one small motel soap, one washcloth, one pair each of knee-high stockings and nylon panties, still brand-new. And then she pulled out more things: her *pochai* stomach pills, her potion for coughs, her tiger-bone pads for aches, her good-luck Goddess of Mercy charm if her other remedies do not work.

"Where is it?" she said, sorting through everything over and over again, until she finally pulled out from a side pocket what she had been chasing for along the bottom of her purse. It was a letter, the kind that looks like a sheet of paper but when you fold it, it becomes an envelope, stamp and everything already on it. She waved it in her hand.

"It's in here," she said with a big proud look on her face. "That man!"

And then I became alarmed for Helen. Lately she has been acting senile. Lately she has been forgetting many things. Lately she does not make sense. Maybe it is because of that fall on her stairs two months ago, the one that now makes her think she is going to die.

"How can you put a man in an envelope?" I asked her carefully.

"What?"

"You said you put a man in the envelope."

"Anh! I didn't say this. I said my good news is in here. And my good news is this: That man is dead. Betty Wan from Hong Kong told me, here in this letter. She went to Shanghai recently. You remember her. 'Beautiful Betty,' we called her during wartime. Although maybe she's not so beautiful anymore." Helen laughed. "Do you remember that sewing machine I gave her? She made a good business for herself later on, now owns a clothing shop in Kowloon."

Lately Helen's mind wanders everywhere, like a cow following grass wherever its mouth goes.

"It was a jewelry store she started," I reminded her. "A store in Kowloon, in the Ambassador Hotel arcade."

Helen shook her head. "A clothing shop," she said. "Ladies' things, all discount." I did not argue. I did not tell her how she always remembers things wrong, always better than what really happened. She does not remember: I was the one who gave Beautiful Betty the sewing machine.

"What man is dead?" I finally asked, pointing to the letter.

"Oh, yes, that man." And then she sighed, pretended she was exasperated with me. "That man, *that man*. You know the one. How can you not guess?" And then she leaned over and whispered: "That bad man."

My breath stopped. I could see him, that bad man, Wen Fu, my first husband, the one I told Helen to never mention: "Never say his name, never tell anyone."

I could see his thick hair, his tricky eyebrows, his smooth, lying face, his clever mouth. I had not seen him for over forty years. And now, just to hear Helen mention his name, I could feel his breath on my neck, remember him laughing and telling me he had finally found me and would drag me back, no choice.

"Don't be scared. It's true, he's gone," said Helen. "Read it yourself."

I took the letter from her hands. I read it. I found out: Forty years later and Wen Fu was still laughing in my face. Because the letter did not say he died twenty, thirty, forty years ago. He died last month, on Christmas Day.

I slapped the letter. "Can you imagine?" I said to Helen. "Even to the end, he found a way to make me miserable forever! Died on Christmas!"

"What does it matter when he died?" said Helen. She was poking her mouth with a toothpick, raising one corner of her mouth so she looked as if she were smiling. "He's dead, can't come get you anymore, that's what matters."

"Already got me!" I cried. "Already in my mind! Now I will always be thinking of him on Christmas. How can I sing 'Silent Night,' 'Joy to the World,' when I want to shout and say, So glad he is dead! Wrong thought, wrong day."

"Then you should sweep your floors, sweep him out of your mind," she said, throwing her hand out—as if it were so easy!

And I knew she was talking about the Chinese new year coming up soon, about that old saying: Sweep away last year's dust and all bad feelings.

What does Helen know about sweeping? If you looked at her kitchen floor, you would see—dust balls as big as mice, black smudges polished smooth in every corner, twenty years' worth, all the disappointments she thinks I can't see.

"That's what I was thinking," said Helen. "We should sweep all the lies out of our life. Tell everyone our true situation, how we met."

"What are you saying?"

"Why should I go to my grave with all those lies? That I am your sister-in-law, married to your half brother, a man I never met. And my birthdate is wrong. You made me one year younger. Now when I die, my long life is cut short one year early."

"What kind of nonsense are you saying?"

"I am saying now that Wen Fu is dead, I want to correct everything before it's too late. No more secrets, no more lying."

A bad feeling was moving in my stomach. Why was she talking this way? She wanted to expose everything!—my past, my marriage to Wen Fu, everything I had worked so hard to forget.

"How can you do that?" I scolded her. "You want to tell my secrets, just like that? We made a promise—*never* to tell."

"That was a long time ago," argued Helen. "Of course, we couldn't say anything then. You were afraid. You thought Wen Fu would still chase you. And we both needed a way to get into this country. So it made sense back then. But now—"

"This is a secret."

"What does it matter now? Wen Fu is dead," said Helen. "He can't come get you. We can't be deported. It matters more to tell the truth, not to go to the next world with so many lies. How can I face my first husband in heaven, when all these years I have been saying I was married to your brother? How can I have a tombstone that says I was born in 1919? Everyone will laugh at me behind my dead back, saying I was so old I could not even remember how old I really was."

"Then you tell everyone your things, just don't tell them about mine," I said.

Helen frowned. "How can I do that? Then I have to make up

more lies, how we met, why I know you. You are asking me to talk to the devil. If you don't tell, I must—before the new year."

"You are asking me to bring disaster into my life. If you tell your children, then my children will know too."

"Then you should tell them yourself," said Helen. "They are grownups now, not children anymore. They'll understand. Maybe they'll be happy to know something about their mother's background. Hard life in China, that's very popular now, nothing shameful in that."

"You don't know what shameful is!" I said.

We argued like that, back and forth, back and forth. But after a while, I knew it was useless. It was like her pom-pom fish and her long-distance money. Helen thinks she's always right. How could I argue with someone who makes no sense? I was shaking mad.

When she went to put more water on for tea, I told her it was already too late. I picked up the groceries I had bought at Happy Super that afternoon, then put on my coat.

"Wait a little," Helen said. "Henry can drive you. Safer that way."

Every time I come to her house she says that. Every time she says that I know what she really means. Thirty years ago, Jimmy and I moved out of Chinatown and bought our house on Eighth Avenue between Geary and Anza. And for two years Helen said to me, "That part of town, not too safe. That part of town—oh!—we could not move there." Then after Jimmy died—guess what?—she and Henry bought a bigger house one block from my place, on Ninth, a higher-number street. "Now we can take care of you," she said. "Safer that way." But I knew she was just using me as her excuse.

Last night I said the same thing I always say. "Don't bother, I can walk by myself. Good exercise."

"Too dangerous," she insisted. But I knew she already didn't mean it. She was whispering, so she would not wake up her husband. "You should be more careful," she said.

"Wah, you think someone wants to rob me for my tangerines, for one can of bamboo shoots?"

She grabbed the plastic bag from my hand. "Then I will help you carry this," she said. "Too heavy for you."

I grabbed back my bag. "Don't do polite words with me."

"You are too old to carry it by yourself," she said, reaching again for my bag.

"You forget. You are too old, too. One year older already." And finally she let me and my bag go.

All night long I cleaned my house to forget. I shook my curtains, beat my sofa, dusted my tables and the rail going up my stairs. I wiped down the TV set, wiped the picture frame on top, the glass, looked at the picture underneath: Jimmy, always so young.

I went into my bedroom, changed the sheets on my bed, the same bed I shared with Jimmy, the curve of his body still sunken in.

I went into Samuel's room. I dusted the plastic airplanes he made, Japanese and American bombers, the little soldiers running away on his desk. I opened a dresser and saw a *Playboy* magazine. Ai! It was like an old slap to my face. I once told Samuel to throw that magazine away: 1964, it said, the same year Jimmy died, when everyone stopped listening to me.

I went into Pearl's room. So many hurts and fights in this room. The Barbie doll I let her have, but no Ken. The perfume I wouldn't let her wear because it made her smell like cheap stuff. The curved dressing table with the round mirror and silver handles, the one I loved so much, but gave to my daughter instead. And when she saw it, she said she hated it! "You picked this one out just to torture me," she shouted.

I was remembering this, dusting her table. That's when I saw tiny words carved into the top of the dressing table: "I love RD."

Who is RD? Who does my daughter love enough to ruin this furniture she hates so much? Is he American or Chinese? And then I became angry: Look what she did to my good furniture!

Of course, after I calmed down, I realized Pearl didn't do this recently. That was maybe twenty-five years ago. Because now Pearl is over forty years old. And she is no longer in love with RD. She is married to Phil Brandt, not Chinese, but still a nice man, a doctor, although not the best kind.

When Pearl first introduced him to me, I tried to be nice. I said, "Oh, a doctor. I'll send all my friends to be your patients." And then he told me what kind of doctor he was. A pathologist!—

someone who looks at people only when it's too late, after they've died. How could I send my friends to that kind of doctor?

But Pearl has a good job, a speech therapist for retarded children, although she told me never to say that. A few years ago, she said, "We don't call them retarded or handicapped children anymore. We say 'children with disabilities.' We put the children first, the disabilities second. And I don't do just speech therapy. I'm really what's called a speech and language clinician. And I work only with children who have moderate to severe communicative disorders. You should never call them retarded."

I asked her to tell me what she did again and she wrote it down: "A speech and language clinician for children with moderate to severe communicative disorders." I practiced saying this many, many times. I still have those words in my purse. I still can't say them. So now maybe Pearl thinks I'm retarded, too.

Of course, Pearl's two daughters have no problems speaking English. When the older one was only two years old, she ran up to me at the door, shouting, "Ha-bu! Ha-bu! Ha-bu is here!" How clever, I was thinking. She knows how to call her Grandmother in Shanghainese. And then my granddaughter said in English: "What presents did you bring me? What kind? How many? Where are they?"

"Isn't it amazing?" Pearl said. "She already speaks in complete sentences. Most kids her age use only two-word phrases. She's really smart."

And I said, "What good is it to have her be this kind of smart? You should teach her manners, not to ask too much, same way I taught you."

My daughter gave me a smiling-frowning look. She said, "Oh, Ma." That's all she said. "Oh, Ma." No more argument.

I was thinking about this, while cleaning her room. That is how she is. That is how I am. Always careful to be polite, always trying not to bump into each other, just like strangers.

And then my hand knocked into something underneath her bed. Those granddaughters—so messy when they play. I pulled it out. In my hands I held a pink plastic box. It was locked, no way to open it without a key. "My Secret Treasures," it said on top.

Oh, I remembered. I gave Pearl that box when she was ten, for her birthday. Back then she had opened the box, looked inside.

"It's empty," she said. She looked up at me, as if I should change this.

"Of course. Now it is empty. Later you can put things inside," I told her. Maybe she thought the box was too old-fashioned, just like the dresser. But to me it was modern, something I thought she would like very much.

"What kind of things?" she asked.

"Secrets, privacy, American junk."

She said nothing, only stared at the lid. It showed a girl with a yellow ponytail, lying in bed, her feet on the wall, talking on the phone. We had lots of fights about that too, talking too much on the phone.

But now I could see: Where the ponytail had once been yellow, now it was black. And the box, once empty and holding only her disappointment, now was so heavy, lots of things inside.

Oh, I was excited! To open the treasures of my young daughter's heart, all those things kept hidden from me for so many years.

I looked in other drawers, searching for the key to the lock. No key. I looked underneath her bed. I found an old pair of Chinese slippers with a hole at each big toe.

I decided to go downstairs, get a knife and cut the latch open. But before I could take even one step forward, my mind walked ahead of me. What was inside? What hurts and disappointments? And if I opened the box and saw a stranger, what then? What if this daughter inside the box was nothing like the one I had imagined I had raised?

I was trying to decide what to do. Cut the lock or not? Put the box back or open it later? And as I asked myself these questions, I smoothed my hair. My hand brushed against a bobby pin, and it was like an instant answer. I took that bobby pin and put it in the lock.

Inside the box I found two tiny lipsticks, one pink, one white. I saw some jewelry, a silver necklace with a cross, a ring with a fake ruby on one side and bubble gum on the other. Underneath that, more junk, even terrible things—tampons, which I warned her not to use, blue eye makeup, which I also warned her not to use. And underneath that were silly things, an announcement for something called "Sadie Hawkins Day Dance," and letters from her friend Jeanette. I remember that girl, the one whose mother always let her go boy-crazy.

Pearl fought me. "Why can't I ask a boy to Sadie Hawkins? Jeanette's going. Jeanette's mother is letting her go."

"You want to follow a girl who has no sense? You want to listen to her mother? That mother doesn't even have concern for her own daughter!"

I was seeing all this again in front of me. I opened one of Jeanette's letters. What was this? "Hey, ding-dong. He's bonkers for you. Fake him out. Make out."

I was right! That girl made no sense.

And then I saw something else. My breathing stopped. It was a small card with a picture of Jesus on one side. On the other side, it said: "In loving memory, James Y. Louie." More words, the date he was born, April 14, 1914. But then look: The date he died. It was covered with black marks, so many angry marks.

I was happy and sad all at once, the way you feel when you listen to old songs you had almost forgotten. And you can only weep that each note is already gone the moment you hear it, before you can say, "How true! How true this was!"

Because right then I realized I was wrong. Right away I wanted to call Pearl and tell her, "Now I know. You were sad. You were crying, if not outside, then inside. You loved your daddy."

And then I thought about Helen, what she said last night, how she would tell Pearl all my secrets, my lies. And after that, why should my daughter believe me anymore?

I took out my vacuum cleaner to catch all the dust I had thrown into the air by bringing out this worry. I went into my hallway and vacuumed the top of my carpet, the plastic runner, the sides where the carpet showed. I lifted the runner to clean the carpet underneath. I saw how the carpet was still bright underneath, like gold-colored brocade. But on the sides, where the carpet showed, it was worn and dirty-looking. And no matter how much I cleaned, it didn't matter. It would always look this way. Just like this stain from my life. I could never get it out.

I went downstairs and sat on my sofa. And when morning came, I was still sitting, still awake, holding that letter from Beautiful Betty. I was thinking about all those times Wen Fu could have died, should have died: During the war, when so many pilots died all at once. When he crashed that jeep and killed someone else. When the Communists took over and killed the Kuomintang. During the Cultural Revolution. All those other times when so many other people died, when he should have died but did not die.

And now this letter from Beautiful Betty, telling Helen how he had died in bed, his whole family watching: his other wife and his children by that other wife, his brother and his brother's wife, his old pilot friends.

In my mind, I could see them all: dropping tears on Wen Fu's face, smoothing his hair, wrapping warm bricks to put at his feet, calming him, soothing him, calling to him, "Don't go! Don't go!"

He died peacefully, the letter had said, died of a bad heart at age seventy-eight.

I slapped that letter in two. It was his bad heart that kept him alive! And now I was the one left with a bad heart. I sat on my sofa, crying and shouting, wishing I had been at his deathbed, wishing he were still alive. Because if he were, I would lean over his bed and call his name. I would pry open his eyes and tell him, Wen Fu, now I have come back. And when he saw my heart through my eyes, I would round my lips and spit hard in his face.

Look what he started by dying! Dead and he still comes back. And all the time, Helen is saying, "What does it matter?" What would she tell her children? How much would she tell them?

Sure, I could tell my children first: I had another marriage, to someone else. It was a very bad marriage. I made a mistake. But now that man is dead.

I could tell them: I had other children from that first marriage, but I lost them, so sad, but that was wartime, long time ago.

I could tell them: I pretended I was already married to your father so I could come to this country. I had to, the Communists were taking over. And Helen lied for me, so later I had to lie for her too.

And then I would see Pearl's face, always suspicious. No, no, I would say, it is not as bad as you think. I really did marry your father, right after I arrived. And then I had both of you, you first in 1950, Samuel second in 1952. And we really would have lived happily ever after, just like in those stories, if only your father had not died.

But even if I told it to them that way, Pearl would know. That's not all that happened. She would see it in my dark eyes, my still hands, my shaky voice. She would not say anything, but she would know everything, not the lies, but the truth.

And then Pearl would know the worst truth of all—what Helen does not know, what Jimmy didn't know, what I have tried to forget for forty years. Wen Fu, that bad man, he was Pearl's father.

I have tried to think how I would tell my daughter. But every time I begin, I can hear her voice, so much hurt, "I knew it. You always loved Samuel more." So she would never believe me.

But maybe if I told her, This is not true. I loved you the most, more than Samuel, more than all the children I had before you. I would tell her, I loved you in ways you never saw. And maybe you do not believe this. But I know this is true, feel my heart. Because you broke my heart the hardest, and maybe I broke yours the same way.

I will call her, long, long distance. Cost doesn't matter, I will say. I have to tell you something, can't wait any longer. And then I will start to tell her, not what happened, but why it happened, how it could not be any other way.

# 5

# TEN THOUSAND THINGS

First I told my daughter I no longer had a pain in my heart, the reason why I said she had to come right away.

She still had a big worried look on her face. "Maybe we should take you to the doctor anyway. Just to make sure."

"I am already sure," I said. "Now I feel better. Now I don't have to pay a big doctor bill. Take your coat off."

"I still think we should go see a doctor."

"Eat some noodle soup first. See what I made? Same kind when you were a little girl, lots of pickled turnip, a little pork just for taste. On cold days, you were so happy to eat it!" I was hoping she would remember how soothing my soup made her feel. She took off her coat. She sat down to eat.

"But what did it feel like, the pain?" she said, one spoonful already going into her mouth.

"Too hot?" I said.

"Not too hot," she said.

"Not hot enough?"

"It's good, really."

I gave her more. I watched her drink my soup. And then I told her.

It is the same pain I have had for many years. It comes from keeping everything inside, waiting until it is too late.

I think my mother gave me this fault, the same kind of pain. She left me before she could tell me why she was leaving. I think she wanted to explain, but at the last moment, she could not. And so, even to this day, I still feel I am waiting for her to come back and tell me why it was this way.

I never told you about my mother? That she left me? Oh. That's because I never wanted to believe it myself. So maybe that's why I did not tell you about her.

Of course, that does not mean I did not think about her. I loved her very much. In fact, when I was young, and for many years, I kept her hair, three feet long, curled up in a small tin box. I saved it for her all those years, thinking she would someday return, and I could give it back to her, like a gift. Later, when I believed she was dead, I still kept her hair. I thought I could someday find her body, and she and her hair could be reunited. That way, in the other world, she could loosen her hair. And once again she could let all her thoughts run wild.

That is how I remember her, in her room, untying her hair, letting it down. She let me touch her hair.

What else? Of course, I do not remember everything about her. I was only six years old when she disappeared. But some things I can remember very clearly: the heaviness of her hair, the firmness of her hand when she held mine, the way she could peel an apple all in one long curly piece so that it lay in my hand like a flat yellow snake. You remember? That's how I learned to do that for you.

Other things from my memory are confusing. I saw a painting of her once. This was after she was gone. And I did not remember the mouth in that painting, so stiff, so firm. I did not remember those eyes, so sad, so lost. I did not recognize the woman in the painting as my mother. And yet I wanted to believe this painting was my mother, because that was all I had left of her.

I used to hold that painting in my lap, peer at her face from one side to the other. But her face always looked in another direction, never at me. She showed no thoughts. I could not tell what she was thinking before or after her painting was made. I could not ask her all the questions I had before she left: Why she talked so angrily to my father, yet kept a big smile on her face. Why she talked to her mirror at night, as if her own face looking back belonged to someone else. Why she told me that she could no longer carry me, that I would have to learn to walk everywhere by myself.

One day, when I was perhaps ten—this was after she had already been gone for several years—I was again looking at her painting. I saw a little spot of mold growing on her pale painted cheek. I took a soft cloth and dipped it in water, washed her face. But her cheek grew darker. I washed harder and harder. And soon I saw what I had done: rubbed half her face off completely! I cried, as if I had killed her. And after that, I could not look at that picture without feeling a terrible grief. So you see, I did not even have a painting anymore to call my mother.

Over the years, I tried to remember her face, the words she said, the things we did together. I remember her ten thousand different ways. That is what Chinese people always say—*yi wan*—ten thousand this and that, always a big number, always an exaggeration. But I have been thinking about my mother for almost seventy years, so it must be ten thousand different times. And it must be that she has changed ten thousand different ways, each time I recalled her. So maybe my memory of her is not right anymore.

So sad! That is the saddest part when you lose someone you love—that person keeps changing. And later you wonder, Is this the same person I lost? Maybe you lost more, maybe less, ten thousand different things that come from your memory or imagination—and you do not know which is which, which was true, which is false.

But some things I know for certain, like my legs, how they got to be this way. Look how my legs are still thin, no muscles on the calves! My mother used to carry me everywhere, even when I was six years old, so spoiled. I refused to walk even ten steps by myself. And this was not because I was sick or weak. I always wanted to see the world at her same height, her same way.

So that's why I do not remember too much of those early days when we lived in the fancy Shanghai house. I did not come to know that house and the people who lived in it the way you would if you were a child walking around by yourself, discovering how one corner turns into another. Whenever I think about those early days,

I remember only my mother's room, the one I shared with her, and the long staircase that took us down to an entryway with watery patterns on the floor.

In my mind, I can still see that steep tunnel of stairs that wound down one floor after another, and my mother holding me as she leaned over to look down to another level, where other relatives lived. I think my father's other wives lived on the floor below, although this is only my guess now. My mother was telling me to be very quiet, not to laugh or ask questions. I was holding my breath, trying to obey, although I wanted to cry out, to tell her I was scared looking at the staircase falling beneath us. And then we heard servants' voices, and she leaned back. We both breathed deeply at the same time and I held onto her tight, so glad we both did not fall down.

Whenever I think about that staircase, I remember the room, and then I remember something else, more and more, until it becomes the time just before she left. Or maybe it is all my memories and imagination of her, now gathered into one day.

After looking down the staircase, we returned to our room. It was early in the morning, and other family members were still sleeping. I do not remember why we were already awake, cannot even guess. To judge from the color of the sky, it would be perhaps another hour before the servant girl would come with our morning meal.

My mother was playing a game with little red and black tablets spread out on a board. She said this was a foreigners' game called *chiu ke*, "prison and handcuffs."

It is only now that I think of this game—*chiu ke*—that I realize she must have been talking about checkers. She was sliding the tablets across the board, explaining that the different colors were people fighting under different warlords, trying to capture each other. But when she started to explain more, my young mind became confused. Of course, I did not know how to say I was confused, so instead, I complained that I was hungry.

I could do this with my mother, complain and demand things. She was not strict with me, not the way some mothers can be. She was perhaps even more lenient than I was with you. Yes, can you imagine? If I wanted something, I could always expect to receive it, never thinking I would have to give something back in return. So you see, although I knew my mother only a short time, I learned this from her, a pure kind of trust.

That day, when I said I was hungry, I already knew my mother had a box of English biscuits hidden on top of her tall dresser. She brought the tin box down. These biscuits were her favorites, my favorites too—not too sweet, not too soft. My mother had many favorites from different countries. She liked English biscuits, of course, and also their soft furniture, Italian automobiles and French gloves and shoes, White Russian soup and sad love songs, American ragtime music and Hamilton watches. Fruit could be from any kind of country. And everything else had to be Chinese, or "it made no sense."

My father owned several cloth factories, and once a foreign customer gave my mother a bottle of French perfume. She had smiled and told the man she was honored to receive such a fine gift from a big, important customer. If you knew my mother, you would have known she did not like this man, the way she called him a "big, important customer."

Later, she let me smell the insides of the bottle. She said it smelled like urine, and that's what I smelled too. "Why do foreigners always pay big money to put such a stink on themselves?" my mother said. "Why not just wash more often? It makes no sense." She emptied out the perfume into her chamber pot and gave me the round crystal bottle. It was a deep blue color. And when I held it up to the window and shook it, it threw dancing colors all around the room.

That morning I was eating my English biscuit, playing with my French bottle. I could hear the sounds of the morning. My mother was the one who taught me how to listen. She was always lifting her ears up to catch a sound, showing me how to judge its importance. If the sound was important, her ears stayed up; not important, she went back to what she was doing. I copied what she did.

Together we heard servants walking up and down the hallway, removing chamber pots, lifting them with a small grunt. We heard someone dragging a box down the stairs and someone else whispering loudly, "What's the matter, wind in your brains?" Outside, a big bucket of water was thrown out of a high window so that it splashed all at once onto the back courtyard—pwah!—sounding just like hot frying oil. And after a very long time, we finally heard the little *ting-ting-ting* of chopsticks hitting against the sides of porcelain bowls, an announcement that servants were entering rooms to bring in the morning meal.

They were all the usual sounds, what we heard every morning. But that morning my mother seemed to be paying attention to all of it. Her ears stayed up, mine too. And it is still a question in my mind—if she heard what she was listening for, if she was disappointed or relieved.

Before I finished my breakfast, my mother left the room quickly. She was gone for such a long time, although maybe it was only a few minutes. You know how children are, one hour or one minute, it doesn't matter, they become impatient. You were the same way.

When I could wait no longer, I opened the door and peeked outside, then toward the end of the hall. I saw my mother and father standing there, talking in harsh voices.

"This does not concern you," my father said firmly. "Do not mention it again."

"My mouth is already open," my mother said quickly. "The words have already fallen out."

This was not the first time I had seen them argue. My mother was not like my father's other wives, the ones who used the same kind of fake manner, acting more pleasant than someone else, as if they were in a contest to win something big.

My mother's manners were genuine. She could be gentle, of course, but she also could not stop herself from being honest and open. Everyone said this was a fault of hers. If she was mad, she let everything come out, and then trouble would follow.

So that morning when I heard my mother and father talking that way, I was scared. They were not shouting, but both were angry, I could tell. My father's voice made me want to close the door and hide. While my mother's voice—it is so hard to describe a sound according to how a little girl felt it—I can only say it sounded ragged, like good cloth already torn, never able to be mended.

My father turned to walk away. And then I heard my mother say, "Double Second," as if the words were a curse. My father did not turn around. "You can never change this," was all he said.

"You think I cannot change this?" said my mother, as my father walked away.

Back then I did not know what these words meant, "Double Second." I only knew those words were very bad, the worst name someone could call my mother, a name that always made her spend many hours in front of her mirror, accusing the double second that stared back at her.

Finally my mother turned around. She was wearing a strange smile, one I had never seen before. At that moment she saw me. "Still hungry," I complained right away in a small voice.

"Coming, coming," she said softly. And then her smile changed back to the kind one that I recognized, although I was still thinking, Why is she smiling when she is so angry?

Back in our room, she told me to get dressed. "Good clothes," she said. "We're going outside."

"Who else is going?"

"Just we two," she said. This was very unusual. But I did not question her. I was glad for this rare opportunity. And then she took a long time to prepare herself. I watched. I always liked to watch my mother getting dressed. She put on a Western dress, looked at herself in the mirror, then took that off. She put on a Chinese dress, took that off, put on another Chinese dress, frowned. Finally, after many more dresses, she put the first dress back on, and that's what she wore, a jade-green dress with short sleeves and a long straight skirt of smooth pleats running down to her ankles.

I waited for her to pick me up, so we could finally leave.

But instead she patted my head. *"Syin ke,"* she said, "you're already so big." She always called me *syin ke,* a nickname, two words that mean "heart liver," the part of the body that looks like a tiny heart. In English, you call it gizzard, not very good-sounding. But in Chinese, *syin ke* sounds beautiful, and it is what mothers call their babies if they love them very, very much. I used to call you that. You didn't know?

*"Syin ke,"* my mother said, "today I will teach you important secrets. But first you must learn to walk by yourself." And before I could cry or complain, she was walking ahead of me, saying, "Let's go, let's go," as if all kinds of fun lay ahead. I followed, and then we were out the front gate and into one of the new-style

93

pedicabs that darted in and around the city faster than the old rickshaws.

It was the beginning of summer, so it was still cool in the morning, although by afternoon it would be steaming hot. As we drove farther away from our house, I started to hear different kinds of sounds: the shouts of vendors, trolley cars grinding by, motorcars honking, and so much hammering—old buildings were being pulled down everywhere, new ones being pushed up. Hearing all those sounds, I was so happy! My mother seemed happy too. She became a different person, laughing, teasing, pointing, and shouting in a glad voice, just like a common person.

"*Syin ke,* look!" And it was a shop-window display, filled with calfskin gloves for ladies. We stepped out of the pedicab to look in the window. "So many thin hands reaching into the air for customers," my mother said. I made my hands move like a snake, and we both laughed. We got back in the pedicab.

"Look!" I cried a little while later. I pointed to a man spitting a long stream of bean-curd paste into a pot of boiling water. I was proud I had found something interesting to show my mother. "He looks like a fish," I said, "a fish in a fountain!" I stood up in the pedicab. The spit had curled into doughy threads.

"He is using his mouth just like a cooking tool," my mother explained.

We passed so many interesting things that day. It was as if my mother wanted me to open my eyes and ears and remember everything. Although maybe it is just my imagination now that makes me think this. Perhaps she had no such intention. Maybe we saw none of these things as I have described. Maybe we did not go to all the places that I now remember. For how could we have done all this in one day? But that is what I remember, and even more.

That day we also went to all the places where the best things in the world could be found. To Zhejiang Road, where she said they made the best French-style leather shoes; she did not buy any. To Chenghuang Miao, where she said they sold a beauty tonic of crushed pearls. She let me put some on my cheeks, but she did not buy this either. To Bubbling Well Road, where she bought me the best American ice cream sundae; she did not eat any, told me it was "too messy, too sweet." To Foochow Road, where she said you could buy any kind of book, any kind of newspaper, Chinese and foreign too. And there she did buy something, a newspaper, although I do not know what it was exactly, since I could not read.

And then we went to Little East Gate, where all the best seafood vendors put up their stands. She said she was looking for a delicacy she had not tasted for many years. It was a rare little fish, called *wah-wah yu,* because it cried just like a baby—wah-wah!—and it could wave its arms and legs. And when we found that fish, I heard it cry out loud, I saw it move just as my mother promised it would.

"Long ago I loved to eat this fish," she said. "So tender, so delicious. Even the scales are as soft and sweet as baby leaves. But now I think it is sad to eat such a creature. I have no appetite for it anymore."

I was paying attention to all these places and things my mother found. And I remember thinking, This is important. Listen carefully. So many desires to remember, so many places to find them. I thought my mother was teaching me a secret—that my happiness depended on finding an immediate answer to every wish.

That afternoon we also went to the theater. It was already very hot outside, the full sun was out, and I felt sticky. So I was glad to think we would go into the dark theater. Of course, I was mistaken in thinking the theater would be cool. The last time I had been there must have been during the winter or spring. But that day, it was steaming hot inside, like an oven—and dark. The moving picture was already playing when we arrived, a story about a little blond-haired girl. Someone was playing a piano, loud crashing sounds.

"I can't see, I can't see," I cried to my mother, afraid to take even one step forward.

"Wait a little," my mother said. And when my eyes took in all this darkness, I could see rows of people, everyone waving a paper fan. My mother counted off the rows, ". . . six, seven, eight." I did not wonder why she was doing this, looking for the number-eight row from the back. I was interested only in her counting, because that was what I was learning to do. And then we were standing at that number-eight row, pushing our way toward the middle, until my mother came to an empty seat. She whispered to someone sitting on the other side. At the time I thought she was saying, "Excuse us." It was not until later that I came to think she was saying something else.

I had seen many moving pictures before with my mother, all silent: Charlie Chaplin, the fatty man, policemen and fire engines, the cowboys running their racehorses in a circle. That afternoon the picture show was about an orphan girl who had to sell matches in the snow. She was shivering. A woman in front of me was crying, blowing her nose, but I was thinking that little girl was lucky, to be so cool on a hot day. That's what I was thinking before I fell asleep in the dark theater.

When I awoke, the lights had come on and my mother was leaning toward the man sitting next to her, whispering to him in a solemn voice. I was alarmed. This seemed a dangerous thing she was doing, talking to a stranger. So I whined a little and pulled my mother toward me. The man leaned over and smiled at me. He was not too old. He looked refined. His skin was smooth and light-colored, not like the face of someone who worked outdoors all day long. Yet he was wearing a common villager jacket, plain blue, although very clean. My mother thanked him, and then we stood up and left.

On our ride home, I fell asleep again, all my excitement used up. I woke up only once—bumped out of sleep by the pedicab driver cursing a slow cart on the road. My face was leaning against my mother's hair. I found myself looking at the color of her hair. How different it looked from mine, from that of other women in our family, from anyone else's I had ever seen. Not a brown-black or black-brown. Not any kind of black with a name.

My mother's hair was a color you could feel more than see— very, very black, as black and shiny as water at the very bottom of a deep well. And winding through her bun were two white hairs, like little ripples when tiny stones are thrown in the water. And still, these words are not enough to describe it.

I remember only a few more things, what happened that evening. I was already very tired from the day. We ate a simple meal in our room. Afterward, my mother showed me how to do an embroidery stitch, one she said she invented herself. I copied her very badly, but she did not criticize me, not once. She praised what I had done. And then, as she helped me undress for bed, she gave me another lesson, how to count my fingers and toes. "Otherwise, how will you know if you wake up each morning with the same number?" she said. ". . . six, seven, eight, nine, ten."

You see how educated and clever my mother was? She always found a reason why I should learn. She told me once she had wanted to be a schoolteacher, just like the missionaries who had taught her.

And then she sat at her stool in front of her dresser, and I watched her take off her clothes, her jewelry. She pulled off her gold bracelet, her jade earrings. She saw me looking at her in the dresser mirror. She turned around and held up the earrings.

"Someday these will be yours," she said in a somber voice. I nodded.

"And all this." She patted her jewelry box. I nodded again.

"When you put them on, people will think your words are worth more." I nodded once more.

"But you should never think this way, never," she said. I shook my head right away.

She climbed into the bed we shared and smoothed my hair away. As I looked up at her face, she sang me a little song—about a naughty mouse who stole lamp oil. Do you remember? I used to sing you that song. That night, before I could hear the ending, I fell asleep.

I dreamt about all the things I had seen that day. A fish that cried and sang a song about a little mouse. The blond-haired girl trying on fancy French shoes. My mother's hair, the way my fingers wove through it only to discover it was not hair at all, but embroidery and jewels. My mother, sitting at her dressing table, combing her hair, crying to her face in the mirror, "Double Second! Double Second!" Although maybe this last part was not a dream.

The next morning, when I awoke, she was not there. I thought she had slipped quietly out of bed and walked to the staircase, the same as we had done the day before. I opened the door and looked out. I saw only the servants, carrying away chamber pots. I went back in the room and sat down to wait for her return. And then—*ting-ting-ting*—the servant came in with two steaming bowls of *syen do jang*. You know the one, the salty-tasting soy-milk soup we can get at Fountain Court on the weekend. Last time, Cleo ate a big bowl by herself, no spills.

Anyway, that morning I had no taste for *do jang*. "My mother—where is she?" I demanded.

The servant did not answer me, only looked around the room, puzzled. She put both bowls down on our table.

"Now eat fast. Don't let it get cold," she scolded, and left the room in a hurry. I let my bowl become cold. I waited, and when I became impatient, I began to cry, just a little. A lump grew in my throat, and I waited for my mother to return so I could release it, cry and tell her how long I had waited. I decided that when she did return I would point to my cold bowl. I would demand some English biscuits, at least three to make me happy again. I waited some more. I tipped over my bowl and made a big mess. I stood on a chair and brought down the biscuit tin myself. And still she did not come.

The servant came back to take our bowls away. She looked at the mess I had made. She looked around the room. "Look what you've done!" she scolded, then left quickly. As soon as she closed the door, I opened it. I saw the servant talking to the head servant. They both rushed down the stairs, and I ran over to the staircase to watch them going down. And then I heard loud voices downstairs, more people walking, doors opening and closing. I could see Nai-nai, my grandmother, walking slowly up the stairs with the servant talking fast next to her. Nai-nai was not the kind of grandmother who patted my head and told me I was pretty. She was the big boss of all the ladies of the house, and I was the smallest girl, the one she noticed only when she wanted to criticize. I raced back into the room and sat on my bed, scared. Trouble was coming, I knew this.

I cried as soon as they walked in the door. "Where is your mother?" Nai-nai asked again and again. "When did she leave? Did she take anything with her? Did someone come get her?"

What could a little girl say, a girl who knew nothing? I shook my head, cried and cried, "She's not gone! She is still here, right here."

Suddenly another person burst into the room. I don't remember who, because I had eyes only for what she was holding in her hand. It was my mother's hair, chopped off, now hanging down like a horse's tail! I screamed. Of course I screamed. It was the same feeling as seeing her head cut off. How bad!

And now my memories of that time are very cloudy. I only remember that everyone was nervous, whispering secrets. And my father was angry. He came into my mother's room. He opened her drawers, the armoire, her jewelry box, all full. He sat down, quiet. He looked at me sternly as if something were my fault.

"Where did she go?" he asked. And I was trying to be obedient. I tried to guess for him. I said Zhejiang Road. I said maybe Cheng-huang Miao. I mentioned the fish stand at Little East Gate. I said she was at the picture theater.

I did not leave the room for three days. I sat there, waiting for my mother. Nobody told me I had to stay there. But nobody came to get me either. The servant who brought me my food said nothing, and I did not ask her any questions.

On the fourth day I went downstairs by myself. As I already told you, my mother used to carry me everywhere. So my legs were never too strong. That day they were very, very weak. But perhaps this was also because I was afraid of what I might see.

Let me tell you, it was worse than what I had imagined. I saw funeral banners hanging on the door. I knew what this meant, without asking. Yet I did not want to believe it. So I walked up to the girl who washed our laundry and asked who had died. The girl said, "How can you ask such a question!" I walked up to Old Aunt, who had arrived that day, and she said, "Don't talk about this anymore."

Maybe one week later, maybe sooner than that, I was sent to live on Tsungming Island with my father's younger brother and his two wives, Old Aunt and New Aunt. The island was two hours from Shanghai by motorboat, up the Huangpu River until you reach its mouth. That's where my father's family came from originally, the island countryside. On a map, maybe it is only a little dot stuck in the water, close to nothing, cut off from everyone.

Anyway, by the time I arrived I was sick to my stomach, because of that motorboat ride, because of my grief. I was crying loud, so heartbroken I didn't care that Old Aunt was threatening to slap my face in two. I shouted, "I want my mother! I want to be with my mother! Tell her where I am, she'll come get me."

And that's when Old Aunt told me, "Shuh! This is where your mother is buried, on this island."

If you ask me today what really happened to my mother, I could not tell you exactly, only what everyone told me. And that would not be the truth, only gossip.

I knew this, though: What my mother did was a big disgrace. That's why they said she died, to bury her scandal. That's why no one would ever talk about her to my father. That's why they sent me away, so I would not remind him of her.

And yet, many times they gossiped about her. They all did— Old Aunt, New Aunt, Uncle, and their friends—over tea, during meals, after the noontime nap. For many years, my mother was the source of funny and bad stories, terrible secrets and romantic tales. It was like digging up her grave, then pushing her down farther, always throwing more dirt on top. Can you imagine how a little girl would feel, hearing this about her own mother?

I heard what they said. I felt so bad to hear them. And yet I could not stop myself from listening. I wanted to know how it could be that my mother left me, never telling me why.

So that's how my mother became a riddle, each piece of gossip making another question in my head. If she was dead, why did they hold no funeral? If she was alive, why didn't she come back to get me? If she ran away, where did she go?

Sometimes I would try to put together all the pieces of gossip I heard, I would try to make one whole story. But then each part would contradict the next, until no part made sense.

So then I looked at what I knew about my mother, both good things and bad. I tried to think of all the reasons why her life went one way or the other. And this is what I think happened, how my mother came to be the second wife to my father and, later, why she left.

My mother was not like the Chinese girls Americans always imagine, the kind who walk around with tiny bound feet, choosing their words as delicately as they choose their steps. My mother was a modern girl. Many girls in Shanghai were. They were not peasants, nothing of the kind. When my mother was eight years old, her feet were already unbound, and some people say that's why she ran wild.

She had been born into a wealthy, educated family in Shanghai, the only child of a Ningpo father and a Soochow mother. Soochow is that city of ladies with beautiful soft voices; even a Shanghainese would tell you a Soochow accent is the best. And Ningpo people are such good businesspeople they continue to argue even after they have already made a bargain. So you see, my mother was born with a double character already fighting inside of her.

I think my mother must have been a classic beauty, the kind other girls would read about in a story and cry over, wishing they were reading about themselves. My mother once read me a story like that, about a beautiful but lonely girl. One day, she looked in a pond and thought she had finally found a friend, someone who did not envy her. She did not know that the shimmering face smiling back at her was her own reflection. At the end of the story, my mother exclaimed, "Nonsense! What girl would not know her own self looking back at her!"

In any case, my mother did not look in a pond, she looked in a mirror. Every night she did this. So if I am honest, I would have to say my mother was proud of her looks, maybe even vain, just a little.

Of course, she had reason to be proud. Her skin was the color of white jade. Or maybe it was the color of a summer peach. Or maybe I am only remembering my mother as another classical tale, all those phrases about ladies with voices as pretty-sounding as lutes, skin as white as jade, their gracefulness flowing like calm rivers. Why did stories always describe women that way, making us believe we had to be that way too?

Maybe my mother was not pretty at all, and I only want to believe that she was. But then I think, Why else did my father marry her? He was an important man. He could have had all kinds of wives—which he did. Back then there was no other reason to marry a second, third, or fourth wife, except to use a woman's prettiness to add to a man's prestige. So I think my mother must have been pretty. It is not just bad classical stories that make me think this way. There was a reason why she had to be.

She was also smart and clever, quick-thinking too. I have already mentioned that she was educated. She went to a missionary school in Shanghai, the first Chinese school girls could go to. That's because her father, my *gung-gung,* was very educated himself, a scholar-official, like a bureau chief in charge of reforms for foreign affairs, something important like that. In any case, many of the officials at that time were sending their daughters off to get an education. That was the modern thought—educate sons, educate daughters a little to prove you were not too feudal-thinking. But Gung-gung did not want to send her to France, or England, or America, the way some families did just to prove how rich they were. All those girls came home with short hair and dark faces from playing tennis outside in the sun. Why should he educate a daughter only to turn her into a girl he did not like? So in 1897, when the missionary school first opened in Shanghai, Gung-gung sent my mother there.

I heard my mother even learned English at that school, although I never heard her say any English words, except "biscuit." New Aunt, who went to the same missionary school, said my mother was not a good student, not very good at all, maybe that's why I was the same way. She said my mother had a fighting temper, maybe that's why I was the same way. She was naughty, maybe that's why I was the same way.

New Aunt said that once, during prayers at that school, an old nun let out a loud fart—by accident, of course—and my mother burst out laughing and said, "God heard that!"

"I don't know why the nuns liked her so much," New Aunt said to me. "They told her, 'We're praying hard for you, little one. If you become a Christian, you can go to heaven when you die.' And your mother, so willful, she said, 'When I die, I don't want to live in a heavenly foreign concession.' Do you know what those nuns did? Laughed—only that!"

New Aunt was so jealous. She used to say, "I was never bad like your mother. So why didn't the nuns pray hard for me?"

Old Aunt, on the other hand, did not go to that school, no school whatsoever. She was raised in a feudal family, the traditional way: The girl's eyes should never be used for reading, only for sewing. The girl's ears should never be used for listening to ideas, only to orders. The girl's lips should be small, rarely used, except to express appreciation or ask for approval. Of course, all this feudal thinking only made Old Aunt more opinionated on all kinds of matters.

"Her education was the cause," Old Aunt would always say.

"They put Western thoughts into a Chinese mind, causing everything to ferment. It is the same way eating foreign food—upset stomach, upset mind. The foreign teachers want to overturn all order in the world. Confucius is bad, Jesus is good! Girls can be teachers, girls do not have to marry. For what purpose do they teach this? Upside-down thinking!—that's what got her into trouble." And then Old Aunt would warn me, "Weiwei-ah, do not follow your teachers too closely. Look what happened to your mother."

If you were to ask me, what happened to my mother was not a bad education but bad fate. Her education only made her unhappy thinking about it—that no matter how much she changed her life, she could not change the world that surrounded her.

Uncle used to say that none of this would have happened if my mother had not been the only child. All the will and stubbornness that should have been given to a boy went into her. Worse, her parents let her stay at home and grow stronger and stronger. They were thinking they could wait and pick a husband for their only daughter when she was maybe twenty-two.

Before that could happen, the revolutionaries came and threw the Manchus out. That was in 1911, when my mother was just twenty-one years old. No more Ching Dynasty, no more scholar-official job for Gung-gung.

A servant told Gung-gung this bad news while he was eating his noontime meal. He was chewing a piece of steamed tendon. Suddenly Gung-gung yelled like a wild animal, then bit his tongue right in half. Or perhaps he bit his tongue first, then yelled. In any case, he fell over backward, chair and dead body together. And in one fall, my mother's family plummeted ten thousand feet. Because everyone said Gung-gung committed suicide, so sorry to see the Ching Dynasty end.

Now my mother's mother, my *ha-bu*, was a widow, not so rich anymore. She was in no big hurry to marry off her daughter. Her daughter could take care of her into her old age. That's what Confucius would have said. I don't know why everyone always thought Confucius was so good, so wise. He made everyone look down on someone else, women were the lowest!

In any case, my mother was already twenty-one years old, and she had been educated against Confucius thinking. Maybe she wanted to marry, maybe she did not. Who knows? In any case, she would choose for herself. Uncle used to say, "That's what got her into trouble, thinking for herself."

New Aunt did not agree. The real trouble, New Aunt said, was romance, a foolish desire on my mother's part to marry for love. She had met a student from Fudan University, a journalist. He was older, maybe twenty-nine, so he was very late in starting his education. My mother was already twenty-six years old at the time.

This student was a man named Lu, a Marxist, just the kind of person Gung-gung would have hated. New Aunt said she knew all about him, because after my mother left, New Aunt searched through her belongings and found a newspaper story about a student revolutionary named Lu. It must have been the same student she loved, New Aunt said. Why else would my mother have saved the article?

The newspaper story, New Aunt said, was very badly written. A tale of inspiration and heroes, so maybe only part of it was facts, the rest just more and more water added to old rice. In any case, this is how the story went, like an old revolutionary tale, something like this, very romantic.

Lu had been born in Shandong, that place up north of Shanghai where all the good seafood swim. He was a fisherman's son, so all he could look forward to in life was inheriting the holes in his father's nets, the ones he repaired every day. He had no education, no money, no way to change his life. And really, this was the kind of life everybody had, except for, of course, the scholars, the foreigners, and the most corrupt. But one day, a good Marxist came up to him and showed him a piece of paper.

"Comrade, can you read this for me?" said the man with the paper. And Lu said, "Sorry, I was born a fool."

Then the man said, "Comrade, what would you say if I told you I can teach you to read this and anything you want in ten days? Come to a meeting and find out." This good man told Lu about a new method for teaching laborers and peasants how to free themselves from slavery. It was called One Thousand Characters in Ten Days.

At this meeting, the Marxists said that if a person was hardworking enough, he could learn to read and write one hundred characters a day, one thousand characters in ten days. He could be instantly educated, able to read common newspaper stories, write letters, conduct business, free himself from the bad life given to him!

When they asked Lu to join, he answered, "The only plentiful thing I have is hard work and bad luck."

So Lu worked hard and changed his luck. But he did not stop at one thousand characters. He kept learning more and more, his diligence was that strong. He learned two thousand, four thousand, then ten thousand. He learned enough until he was able to pass examinations and get into Fudan University. And because he was so grateful for being able to change his life, he vowed he would someday write about the hardships of peasants and laborers, to be their mouth, to tell their story, to tell them they could change their fate—by revolutionary ideas!

So now you see why New Aunt said my mother ruined her life for romance. How could my mother not fall in love with such a man?

I think this Lu person also must have been handsome. Maybe he had the same features my mother admired in herself: big eyes, light skin, a face that was neither too broad nor too thin, small lips, and very black hair. And he must have been modern-thinking in other ways, because he asked my mother to marry him, no waiting to ask permission or use a go-between. That must have been very exciting to my mother—a revolutionary marriage! She said yes immediately, and then went home to tell her mother what she had done.

Ha-bu shouted at my mother, "How can you even think such a thing! How could you even talk to such a man! This is what happens when there are no emperors to rule the country."

That's when my mother threatened to swallow gold if she was not allowed to marry Lu. In fact, that afternoon she melted down half a gold bracelet. She showed her mother how serious her threat really was. "Half a bracelet!" New Aunt used to say when she told this part. "That's how fierce her will was."

Of course, my mother did not swallow her bracelet. Otherwise, she would have died. She only pretended to swallow it. She painted a gold drop on her lip, then lay down on her bed, very still. Meanwhile, Ha-bu kneeled in front of the family altar and prayed in front of her dead husband's shrine. She begged for forgiveness, for guiding her daughter to such a bad conclusion. While praying like that, Ha-bu thought she heard her dead husband say, "Go see my old friend Jiang Sao-yen."

So Ha-bu went. She told Jiang about my mother, how bad she had become, how she threatened to kill herself—over love for a revolutionary! She asked Gung-gung's longtime friend what she should do.

That afternoon, Ha-bu and Jiang Sao-yen made a contract. Jiang agreed to take the bad daughter of his old dead friend and make her his second wife.

Whenever I remember this part of the story, I always think to myself, Why didn't Ha-bu protest? Why didn't she say to Jiang, "Second wife? Why not make her the first?" After all, the first was already dead.

But maybe Ha-bu was happy only to have her big problem solved. In any case, she agreed to everything. And that's how Jiang got a beautiful woman for his second wife—not a slave girl or some girl from a low-class family, but an educated girl from a once respectable family.

The next day, my mother saw the contract. She ran to Lu and asked him what she should do. Perhaps they kissed. Perhaps they squeezed tears from their eyes. I'm still thinking my mother was very romantic.

And Lu said, "You must resist. That is the only way to put an end to the old marriage customs." And then he told her a story about a revolutionary who did exactly that.

She was a young village girl, very beautiful, and she too had been told she had to marry an old man she did not even know. She said to her family, "I want to choose my own husband, or I refuse to marry." Her father was so angry he locked her up in a pig shed. Every day she shouted she would not marry the old man. She shouted until the day of her wedding. When she came out of the pig shed she was very quiet, also very dirty, as you can imagine.

Her mother and aunts cleaned her up, dressed her up, then put her into a locked-up wedding sedan. Six hired men carried her the long distance from her village to the old man's house one village over. When they arrived, many people were already celebrating—playing loud music, ladling out good food. They laughed and shouted good wishes, then opened the sedan door to welcome the bride. Welcome! Welcome!

Ai!—she was dead. She hanged herself with the rope of her own hair, tied to the sedan slats on top.

"So you see," Lu said to my mother, "you must resist too—not just for love, but for your country."

My poor mother, all she could think about was that girl hanging by her own hair. She thought this was what Lu meant when he said, "You must resist." She went home, wondering if she was strong enough to fight fate, brave enough to die for love. In two days, she left to go to Jiang's house as his second wife.

Yes, that's what I'm saying. She married that man Jiang, my father, your grandfather, an old man before I was even born.

Worse than that, when my mother arrived, she found there was already a third, fourth, even fifth wife. The servants told her the first had died of tuberculosis. And the second had killed herself when Jiang did not promote her to take the first wife's place. And now everyone said my mother had come to take over this bad-luck position—a replacement for the dead second wife.

So that's how my mother became the Double Second. And even though the other wives did not want my mother's bad-luck spot, they still envied her, made her miserable for having a higher position. They often told her, "Hnh! Second Wife. Really, you are only the Double Second, half her strength."

Sometimes I think my mother was finally chased away by those other wives. They made her life miserable, complaining if she ordered a special kind of noodle for herself, making fun of the foreign French shoes she liked so much, teasing her for reading newspapers, since they were not educated. And they envied her hair, her black-black hair—saying that was the reason my father had married her, for her hair.

So maybe that's why she cut off her hair. She left it for those wives to fight over.

But then I think: My mother was strong enough to stand up to those other wives. Anyway, all wives in a family did that, complained all the time, fought over little things. And I knew those wives, San Ma, Sz Ma, and Wu Ma—that's what I called them, Third Mother, Fourth Mother, Fifth Mother. They were not so bad, not really. San Ma, for example, she had a typical Shanghai

manner—teasing people if they acted too proud, criticizing everything equally so you didn't know what she really liked or didn't
like.

So maybe the real story is this: My mother ran away to go back
to Lu. Of course she did. She loved him from the beginning. And
that man in the movie theater the day before she disappeared?—
that was probably Lu. They were arranging how to meet, how she
should run away, that's probably what she was doing.

Perhaps she was becoming revolutionary in her thinking as well.
That's why she took me into the city that day, to show me all the
imperialist evils in Shanghai, to teach me what Lu had already
taught her—what things were too messy, too sweet, too rare, too
sad. And that's why she cut off her hair, too, to show she was just
like that girl who hung herself in her sedan chair, free at last.

But then I think, If she did run away with Lu, then she would
have been alive and she would have come for me. I was her *syin
ke*! She would have tried to visit me at my school, the same school
she had gone to. She would have made a secret boat ride to the
island, hidden behind some bushes. She would have popped out to
say, "I've come to take you back. Meet my new husband."

So then I think she must have run away because she was sad,
too sad to stay in this world. Maybe she found out Lu had died.
She was reading the newspaper, the one she bought at Foochow
Road. Perhaps she had bought it earlier in the day than I remembered. And she read that he had been shot, killed while teaching
more peasants how to read. Many revolutionaries were killed that
way. And her sudden grief reminded her of their long-time-ago
love. While I slept in the dark theater, she thought about this,
crying to think of her loss. While we were shopping for *wah-wah
yu*, she was overcome with guilt, remembering how she did not
resist eating this fish or resist her loveless marriage. As I slept in
the pedicab on the way home, she felt shame that she had grown
comfortable with her imperialist life-style—all the things Lu hated
and fought against. And when she stared at herself in the mirror
that night, she hated herself, decided to purify herself all at once.

So she cut off her hair, a sure sign she could not turn back. She
became a revolutionary in hiding, and her leaders ordered her not
to see anyone from her past. And she obeyed without question—
that's why she did not come back and get me.

But then I think: My mother was not the kind of person to obey anyone. She followed her own mind. And maybe she followed her mind until she became lost. Maybe that's what happened: She ran out the door, crazy, not knowing where she was going.

And sometimes I think my mother cut off her hair and became a nun. It was those nuns at her school, they prayed my mother would follow God's will. And that's what happened, after that no will of her own.

And sometimes I think it was the dead second wife—so jealous of my mother. Her ghost came back and took my mother away.

And sometimes I think it is what everyone said. She suddenly took sick, then died that same night, and now she is buried on Tsungming Island.

Now I no longer know which story is the truth, what was the real reason why she left. They are all the same, all true, all false. So much pain in every one. I tried to tell myself, The past is gone, nothing to be done, just forget it. That's what I tried to believe.

But I cannot think this way. How can I forget the color of my mother's hair? Why should I stop hoping I will see it again?

Of course, in my mind, I know she will never come back. But I still remember. Many times in my life I remember. And it is always like this.

In my heart, there is a little room. And in that room is a little girl, still six years old. She is always waiting, an achy hoping, hoping beyond reason. She is sure the door will fly open, any minute now. And sure enough, it does, and her mother runs in. And the pain in the little girl's heart is instantly gone, forgotten. Because now her mother is lifting her up, high up in the air, laughing and crying, crying and laughing, "*Syin ke, syin ke!* There you are!"

# 6

# · PEANUT'S FORTUNE

So you see, I did not have a mother to tell me who to marry, who not to marry. Not like you. Although sometimes, even a mother cannot help her daughter, no matter what.

Remember that boy you thought you could not live without? What was his name? Randy. You don't remember? He was the first boy to pay you any attention. You brought him home one time for dinner.

I watched how you smiled every time he spoke, how he paid no attention when you spoke. You said, Have something to eat. And he did not say, No, no, you first, you have something to eat yourself. He said, Do you have any beer in the house? And you were so embarrassed, you said, Sorry. I'm real sorry.

Later I told you, Be careful, be careful. And you said, What are you talking about? I said, That man considers himself first, you second, and maybe later you will be third or fourth, then never. But you would not believe me. So I said, If you always tell him you are sorry now, you will always be sorry later.

You know what you said to me? "Ma, why are you so negative-thinking?" This was not negative thinking! This was thinking for my daughter because she could not think for herself.

And later, you did not mention his name anymore. But I saw your broken heart, your good heart, trying to keep all the pieces together, trying not to let me know. So I said nothing. You said nothing.

I wasn't going to tell you "I told you so." Nothing of the kind. My heart was breaking for you too. Because I know how it is to have a good heart, an innocent heart. When I was young, I had a good heart too. I did not know how to look at a person like Wen Fu and think to myself, This man can cause me lots of trouble. This man can take my innocence away. This man will be the reason why I will always have to tell my daughter, Be careful, be careful.

When I met Wen Fu, he was already in love with my cousin, Huazheng. She was New Aunt's daughter, the one we called Huasheng, "Peanut," because she was small and plump like the two rounds of a peanut shell. So you see, she was the one who was supposed to marry him. And now I am wondering why it happened the other way.

At the time, I was living in the house on Tsungming Island, my home for almost twelve years. In all those years, I had not seen my father, not even when I was sent to boarding school in Shanghai. And every time I returned to my uncle's house, I had to act like a guest, never asking for things, waiting instead for someone to remember what I needed.

If I needed a new pair of shoes, for example, I would wait until guests came to visit. We would all be sitting downstairs having tea, and Old Aunt and New Aunt would make the kind of easy conversation that meant they had no problems or worries in this world. That's when I would let my old shoes peek out under everyone's nose. I would tap my foot a little, something Old Aunt always scolded me for. And then I would wait for her face to turn red when she and all the family and guests saw my big toe sticking out of a hole.

So you see, I never felt I belonged to that family. Yet they were the only family I knew. They were not mean to me, not really. But I knew they did not love me the way they did Peanut and my boy cousins. It was like this: During the evening meal, Old Aunt or New Aunt might say to Peanut, "Look, your favorite dish." They might say to the little boys, "Eat more, eat more, before you blow away with the wind." They never said these things to me. They noticed me only when they wanted to criticize, how I ate too quickly, how I ate too slowly. And there were other differences. When Peanut and I returned home from boarding school, Uncle would always give Peanut a secret gift—candied plums, money, a peacock feather. To me, he would give a pat on the head and say, "Weiwei, you're back." That was all. My own father's brother, he could not think of anything more to say.

Of course, I hurt. Remembering this now, I hurt. But how could I complain? I was supposed to be grateful. They took me in, left-overs from my mother's disgrace. By their standards, they were good to me. They had no intention to be mean, no intention at all. And maybe that was why I hurt—they had no intentions for me. They forgot I did not have my own mother, someone who could tell me what I was really feeling, what I really wanted, someone who could guide me to my expectations. From that family, I learned to expect nothing, to want so much.

And then one year, all that changed. This was when I was eight-een years old, during the Small New Year, right before the Big New Year celebration began, when everyone turned one year older. So maybe it was 1937 by the Western calendar, in any case, before the start of the war.

The New Year was a time when you could change your luck. Oh, we didn't have a kitchen god, not like Auntie Du. We were country people, but not that old-fashioned. Of course, maybe the servants had a god like that and I don't remember it. In any case, we still had ways to think about luck, some just for fun, some more serious. And that day, I too was dreaming of a better life. Better than what, I don't know. I wasn't dreaming of winning a million dollars, not like you do with the lottery. I had only a little hope in my heart that something would change. Maybe I wanted to be less lonely. So you see, maybe that's why it happened, why I met Wen Fu.

Our New Year celebration was not like what you have in the United States today—parades and firecrackers, lucky money for children, only fun, fun, fun. It was a day of thinking. According to our custom, when the new year began, not one single speck of dust from last year could remain. Not a single copper's worth of debt could be left unpaid. And not a single bad word could fall from anyone's mouth for three days. I loved the New Year for that reason, no scolding from Old Aunt no matter what. But three days before—that was different—you should have heard the shouts.

As the sun rose on that last cold morning before the new year, Peanut and I could already hear her mother ordering the servants around: Clean this, clean that, not that way, this way!

Peanut and I shared the same bed, although, of course, we each had our own quilt. We did not have blankets and sheets the way you do in this country, everything lying flat on top of you. Our quilts were rolled around us, like two thick cocoons, very warm.

That morning, Peanut was pulling her quilt over her head to find where her sleep had gone. But then we heard New Aunt calling, "Peanut, you lazy girl, where are you?"

You see how she called for only Peanut, not me? Her mother was not being nice to me, letting me sleep. She wanted her daughter to get up and learn how to put a house in order, so that one day Peanut would know how to be a proper wife. New Aunt did not consider these were skills I should learn too. But I watched. I learned without anyone telling me what to do.

I saw how the cotton batting of quilts had to be pulled out and beaten just so, the covers washed fresh, no dirty spots left. Table legs had to be wiped down with oil until the wood shined back lustrous bright, not greasy-looking. And everything had to be pulled back from the walls—cabinets and armoires—so you could see where all the dust, spiders' nests, and mouse droppings were hiding. And I too heard the right way to scold a servant, the way New Aunt said: "Why is this dirty when you say it is clean?"

And later I watched Old Aunt in the kitchen. She was ordering the cooks to chop more meat and vegetables. And then she checked all her supplies. She lifted the lids on jars of peanut oil, soy sauce, and vinegar, smelled each one. She counted the number of fish swimming in a wooden bucket, the number of ducks and chickens pecking in the courtyard. She poked the sticky rice cakes filled with date paste to see if they had steamed long enough. She scolded a cook's helper for letting too many clouds of fat float in the chicken broth, scolded another one for cutting strips of squid the wrong way: "Stupid girl! They must curl up into a lucky ball when cooked. The way you've done it, they'll look like leftover strips of cloth. Bad luck."

I learned all those lessons for my future. Oh, I tried to teach you these same things when you were growing up. But you never listened. You said, "It's boring. Too much trouble. I'd rather eat McDonald hamburgers instead." Yes you did. you said those things! You see how eager I was to learn? When I was young, I already knew everything must look good, taste good, mean good things. That way it lasts longer, satisfies your appetite, also satisfies your memory for a long, long time.

What else happened that day? Oh, I remember, everyone had a task to do, not just the servants. As for me, I had to finish sorting through the family's clothes. For one week I had been doing this, mending anything that showed unlucky signs of prosperity coming apart—a loose thread, a little hole, a torn spot, a missing clasp or button. That morning I was in a big hurry to finish, so Peanut and I could later go shopping in the marketplace.

The night before, New Aunt had given us enough money to buy New Year's gifts at the special stalls set up at the marketplace. I was one year older than Peanut, but New Aunt did not hand me the money. She counted it into her daughter's hand. Of course, Peanut was supposed to share. Without New Aunt's saying so, Peanut was supposed to do that. But I knew what would happen. Peanut would spend that money fast on her own desires, or hold it tight in her hand until I had to embarrass myself and throw big hints her way.

"Both of you, finish your tasks early. then you can go," New Aunt had said. "But don't forget, even with luxuries, be frugal." That meant we were supposed to bargain down the shopkeepers. "And do not let your brothers eat too many sweets." That meant we were supposed to take Little Gong and Little Gao, who were ten and eleven.

I took my mending outside, thinking I could sit on a quiet bench at the front of the house and dream about my secret desires. But Lao Gu, the servant who was head of the household, was already out on the lawn, showing hired workmen what needed repair. He pointed to the dark wicker-woven fence that surrounded our house like a large fish steamer. One workman was shaking his head. He stuck his hand through a big hole that Little Gong had made two weeks before while riding his new bicycle.

And then Lao Gu pointed to different parts of the house, saying,

"For Old East, fix this. For New West, fix that." He was talking about the styles of the two halves of the house.

Old East was the part where everyone lived, slept, and cooked, where babies were born, where old people died. It was a big Chinese house, only one story, with a square courtyard bordered by walkways and living quarters, all the doors and windows facing in. The most important rooms faced east: the kitchen at one end, Uncle's room and the sitting rooms at the other.

New West had been added later, maybe fifty years before, when our family first became rich on foreign money, selling silk thread for velvet, curtains, and carpets. True to its name, New West faced the west and stood two stories high, with three chimneys sticking out of the roof. It was fashioned after a fine English manor, that's what Old Aunt once said. But over the years, everyone kept building something else onto the front of the house, and after a while all the good parts were covered up. So now it looked just like the back of an old farmhouse.

That's where I went, up the front wooden steps of old New West and into the porch area, thinking I would do my mending there. Uncle had added this porch maybe ten years before. The summer after that, Old Aunt enclosed it top to bottom with wire-mesh screens to keep insects out. But a few always managed to sneak in, and Old Aunt promptly squashed them with the bottom of her slipper. So here and there I still could see the broken remains of mosquitoes and dragonflies stuck to the mesh, their wings flying in the breeze like torn rice paper. Everything was rusted, the porch door sang with the wind—*yee-yee! yee-yee!* I felt I was stuck inside a cricket cage. This was not a good place to dream about my future.

So I left the porch, and that's why I finally ended up in the greenhouse, the secret hiding place of my childhood. I looked in to see if it was empty. I wiped a windowpane as carefully as if it were the eye of a waking child. Empty, so many years empty.

When he first came to the island, Uncle had added the greenhouse to the south side of New West, the side facing the sun. It looked like a drawer pulled out, left out. He used to boast that this was what English gentlemen did for a "hobby"—grow roses, grow orchids, grow luxuries that had no lasting value. He always called it "hobby," just like the English, no Chinese word for doing something only to waste time, waste money. I don't know why he thought this was good, to imitate what foreigners did, as if everything Western were good, everything Chinese not so good. Every year, Uncle found a new hobby. And Old Aunt would shout at him, calling his new hobby *ha pi*, "breathing out farts," which meant his ideas were worthless.

After Uncle tired of the greenhouse, he became interested in English dog-racing, greyhounds, animals he could starve on purpose to make them run faster. And when the dogs died, he bought rifles and shot pigeons, real pigeons because the clay ones were too expensive. And after that, it was smoking pipes that made him sick, then English books wrapped in leather that he never read, then insects stuck on pins. He could have sat in the porch for that one.

But the greenhouse was the first hobby. And after he abandoned it, the greenhouse was used only as a strange storage place. When New Aunt sat down one day and broke a chair—into the greenhouse. When Uncle tired of his hobby of shooting rifles or sticking insects—into the greenhouse. When Old Aunt complained that Uncle kept too many paintings of unknown ancestors, too many memorial scrolls—into the greenhouse. That place was where things went when someone decided they belonged nowhere else. When I was little I used to sit on the broken chairs. I would touch the rifles, imagining their noise. I would have pretend-tea with my unknown ancestors. Every year more things were thrown in there that nobody wanted, and I saw them all.

One day, when I was nine or ten, I found a painting of a pretty woman, wearing a plain blue dress, her hair pulled back, looking straight ahead, so somber I almost did not recognize her. "Mama?" I called, and I truly thought she would look at me. I imagined her climbing out of her picture frame, looking as flat as her painting, asking me, "Weiwei treasure, what is this place with so many tiny windows?" And I realized that was the kind of place my mother and I belonged to, only that kind of place, where things are thrown away. Even when I was older, I still felt that. Anyway, that's where I did my New Year's mending.

I was working on my cousins' clothes—the boys who always fell down on purpose. Big holes at the knees and elbows! So many stains! I decided most of those clothes were too bad to fix. Maybe I could give them to the servants, not to fix, but for their children to wear. If Old Aunt scolded me later, I would tell her I was thinking only of my cousins, how they would be destined to roam the streets as beggars if they wore clothes as poor as these. And then I smiled, remembering how I had secretly left a little hole in one of Old Aunt's jacket pockets. Maybe some of her powers would drain away.

Why are you laughing? You thought your mother was always well behaved? You thought I did not know how to be naughty in a secret way? How else did I know you were being naughty? Like that time you hid that dirty book, *Catch Her in the Ride*. I knew you were not reading the Bible.

I did the same thing at that age, hid a book in my mending basket. It was a romance story called *Chin Ping Mei,* a forbidden book. Sister Momo at our boarding school told us many times that we were not allowed to read it. So I borrowed it from a girl named Little Yu, a naughty student who always did what she was told not to do. She said it was a book about sex things: what a husband likes, what a wife likes, what a husband likes more than a wife, how often a husband needed to perform his duties, how often for a wife. She told me it had many secret words too—"jade pavilion," "playing the flute," "clouds and rain"—but she would not tell me the meanings. Read it yourself, she said.

So that morning, I was reading that book myself, searching for those secret meanings. But after ten pages, I had read nothing wrong, only the usual things I had been taught to obey—how many gifts to give people depending on their importance, how to keep all your relations happy, why you should never think only of yourself and matters of this brief world. And then I thought, Maybe this book is like a riddle and I am too innocent to see what it means. Perhaps this description of beautiful pine trees was really one of those secret words, hidden inside some other kind of knowledge. What about this man receiving two tea cakes from someone else's wife? This certainly did not sound proper. And why two tea cakes? Why not just one? What if she had given him two oranges?

Before I could think about this more, I heard Peanut calling my name in her complaining voice: "Weiwei-ah! Where are you, silly girl?" And I almost did not answer her, same as when I was little. But then, of course, I remembered about the marketplace. I hid my book behind two stacks of pots and hurried out with my basket of clothes.

As we went to our room to get ready, Peanut was again rehearsing which stalls we should visit first, what kinds of things we should buy. Perhaps paper puppets or lanterns in the shape of animals for her brothers. Good tea for the grownups. And little money purses for our other cousins, Old Aunt's daughters, who would come visit with their families sometime during the New Year period. And then we both agreed to flower-shaped hair ornaments for ourselves. And of course, a reading by the fortune-teller to determine what good things lay ahead for the next year.

"We shouldn't go to that woman with the crooked teeth," Peanut said. "Last year she gave me the worst fortune, all warnings, how the bad parts of my character mixed with the bad parts of the new year."

And I remembered what that fortune-teller told her last year. How she was a sheep, always trying to hide behind her thick skin. During the Rat year, the fortune-teller had said to Peanut, someone could chew through her wool coat and expose her faults if she was not careful. Peanut had asked for her money back, she was so mad. The woman refused. Then Peanut raised her voice, letting everyone around her hear: "This woman cheated me, gave me bad advice. No luck to be found here. Better stay away!" I was embarrassed, but I was also thinking, How does this fortune-teller know so much about my cousin?

"This year," said Peanut, "I want to know only about my future husband and his family."

And then Peanut began to think about her appearance, how she should look when walking around the marketplace. She twisted her curled hair off to the side. "I saw this in a foreign beauty magazine," she explained. And I pinched up my mouth to let her know this was not a good style for her, but as usual she did not pay attention to me. And then she spent a lot of her worries on which dress to wear, which coat to put on top.

As the family favorite, she owned many fine clothes, most of them French- or English-made, bought in expensive shops in Shanghai. One coat was a black curly lamb with a stiff rolled collar and shawl of padded brocade. When fastened with tiny clasps down the middle, the coat tapered down to her ankles, making it impossible to walk, except in tiny steps. Ridiculous! That was the coat Peanut decided to wear, along with a pair of new high heels. They were sure to be eyesore luxuries to the local villagers—those people considered themselves lucky if they had one piece of cloth for making a new pair of pants! But this was the New Year, a time to show off wealth.

We were the richest family in our village. Of course, richest only by the standards of that small part of the island, the little village called the Mouth of the River, only a half-mile long and a quarter-mile wide, not counting the road from the port and the small stores scattered in between. A village that small could produce only one top-class house, maybe a few middle-class people. Almost everyone else who lived there was poor.

I am not saying this was right, to have only one rich family, to have so many poor. That was the kind of life everyone had back then, no questions asked, the fate people were born with. That was China.

Many of those poor people worked for my family's textile factory, so they didn't starve. They lived in small houses made out of clay, rented from our family. They owned no land, only the dirt that gathered on their floors. But once a year they could look forward to the big party our family gave, the New Year's celebration at the Jiang family house by the Mouth of the River. At least that, a big feast three days after the New Year.

Of course, I did not think about these matters when I was getting ready to go to the marketplace. I was like Peanut, putting on pretty clothes: a festive long skirt with bright red bands, my best padded jacket on top. I wound my braid into a grown-up knot at the back of my head. And then I saw Peanut tiptoeing out into the covered walkway. She listened for sounds coming through the courtyard, heard her mother's voice across the way, still shouting instructions. She came back, opened a drawer, then took out a package wrapped in thin white paper and tied with a red ribbon. From this she removed three round boxes of different sizes. She sat down in front of her mirror. Face powder! In a few minutes, she had covered her plump cheeks and small nose with a fine rice-white coating.

"You look like a foreign ghost," I said quietly, and bit my lips. I was scared for her, for myself. I was one year older, and New Aunt might blame me for not guiding Peanut properly. But if I scolded Peanut, Old Aunt would say, "Who are you to criticize? Criticize yourself first."

So I said nothing. I watched as Peanut took out another box, this one smaller, with a pearl-colored top. She painted her lips cinnabar red.

"Wah, your mouth looks like a monkey's bottom," I teased, thinking this might discourage her.

She twisted open the last box, the smallest, then opened up her foreign beauty magazine. And with a smiling movie star as her guide, she quickly dabbed two dark smudges above and below each eye, then drew a thick line on her eyebrows so that they resembled two dark cricket legs about to leap. Really she looked quite frightening, not pretty at all. When she looked down, the dark smudges looked just like a pair of evil eyes staring back at me.

Lucky for Peanut, she was able to hide behind the stiff collar of her coat and flee down the dark walkway and out the back door before anyone noticed her new face. I fetched Little Gong and Little Gao and brought them to the road. And when they saw their older sister, they laughed in whispers, then out loud, until Peanut walked over and slapped both their heads. They shrieked and ran off, carrying their laughter farther up the road, then turned around to dance and point once again.

The walk to the marketplace usually took us ten minutes. But that day it required nearly forty. Peanut walked with three high-heeled steps to each one of mine. And as villagers on the road walked past her, they stopped to stare and bow, then laughed as they went on their way. Oyo! You should have seen Peanut! She huffed like this—hnh! hnh! hnh!—looking as mad as a queen whose servants had run off with her sedan. If she was blushing under her white powder, I could not tell.

Look at my skin, how smooth it still is. When I was young, I wore no makeup. I had no need—no dark spots, no little dots, no scars or marks. Many people told me I had a lucky face, so why would I have to cover this up?

Now let's go in the kitchen and make some tea. And then I will tell you how Peanut changed my luck for the new year.

The marketplace was already crowded at eleven o'clock that morning, and everyone was doing a good business. And all this busyness raised my excitement even more. That day even the woman who sold soup from the front of her house did not have to cry out, "Wonton! Try some, best wonton!" Both tables were full of people with cold red cheeks poised over steaming bowls, and a dozen more were squatting on the ground, bowls balanced between their legs.

We passed the usual stalls that sold fruit and vegetables, eggs and live chickens. But that day, the fruit looked bigger, the chickens more lively. Red banners hung everywhere. Firecrackers exploded at every step, and babies were screaming as their mothers reached for pears and oranges, pomelos and persimmons. Little Gong and Little Gao were watching a monkey dancing. At the end of the show, they threw two coppers on the ground. The monkey picked them up, bit them to see if they were true, tipped his hat to the boys, then handed the money to his owner, who gave him two dried lizards that he crunched on right away. We all clapped.

And then Peanut found a fortune-teller she liked, a fat woman with a big smile who promised she knew everything—love, marriage, wealth. A sign in front of her stall bragged that she had the luckiest fortune sticks, knew all the lucky numbers, the right lucky marriage combinations, the best days for making lucky business decisions, remedies for changing bad luck into fantastic luck. Everything guaranteed.

"Little sisters, ah," she said to us, then patted her stomach. "See how rich and fat I've become following my own advice. I don't need to do this to make my living, not at all. I do this only because the Goddess of Mercy asks me to, to advance myself in the next world. So you see, my good fortune for you does us both a favor. Come see, best fortune, hanh, I can prove it to you."

And then the fortune-teller did a remarkable thing. She said to Peanut, "Your lucky number is eight, isn't this true?"

And Peanut remembered that she was born in the eighth month, that her eighth year had been especially happy, and she would be eighteen as soon as the new year came. And so, with half her mouth dropped open and half the money New Aunt had given her, Peanut bought a fortune that promised that within the year she would marry a man who would make both her parents happy. Her mother-in-law would be too good to be true. Her future household would have enough riches that she would never desire anything else. And of course, she would have many children, one right after another.

"What will my husband look like? Not too old, I hope," Peanut said in her complaining voice. "And where does his family live? Will I have to stay here forever at the Mouth of the River?"

The woman picked up another stick, then frowned, looked puzzled. Another stick, more frowns, and then another. "Mm," she said. "Your husband is young enough, it seems, only a few years older than you. But your destined family lives close by here, that's what I see. This is not too bad, but perhaps I can make it better for you."

After more money was exchanged, the woman wrote Peanut's name on a piece of red paper, along with her birthdate and the date of the fortune, then added a piece of paper with some sort of rhyming poem. It went something like this: "Happiness comes from nearby, as far-reaching as the East Sea."

"What does this mean?" Peanut asked after reading the rhyme.

"Ah," said the woman, and she held the poem close to her eyes. Finally she pointed to the words "nearby" and "happiness," and said, "See this? This is the local man you were supposed to marry, but now I've chased him away, sent him to someone else." And then she pointed to the words for "East Sea." "And this means your new husband is someone who lives farther away—not as far as another country, of course, but not from this island. Maybe as far north as Yangchow."

Peanut had an ugly scowl on her face.

"Maybe as close as Shanghai," the woman said. And when she saw Peanut smile, she added, "That's what I see. And riches beyond imagination. Five sons, all of them dutiful. And no other wives, you are the only one."

The woman put all the slips of paper and the poem on top of a golden tray, along with Peanut's money, and laid this in front of a statue of the Goddess of Mercy.

"Now there are no more worries in your life," the woman told Peanut. And then the fortune-teller smiled at me. "But how about you, little sister? I feel there's a husband in your future too."

And then she peered at my face, looked at me closely, and her mouth dropped open. "Ai-ya! But look, there is a problem, I can see this now, sitting right above your eye! This little speck here, it can make everything you see turn black."

And she pointed to the mole just above my eye, below my eyebrow. "I can fix this," she said quickly. "It is not easy, of course, to find a charm to fix bad fate. But I can do this for you, remedy this before the new year. Your decision." She wrote down a number, the amount I should pay her.

But Peanut was already pulling my elbow in another direction, telling me she had heard about a stall that sold foreign-made chocolates shaped like all twelve animals of the horoscope. Of course, I wanted to hear my fortune, get my charm, change my bad-luck future. But how could I say this in a crowd!—"Eh, Peanut, give me money so I can find a better husband too."

Maybe that fortune-teller could not have told me anything to change my fate. Maybe she used only the most ordinary tricks and nothing she said was genuine. But what she said was certainly true about me: Unhappiness was coming my way, and I did nothing to keep that speck from blowing in my eye. And this came true as well: Peanut did not marry the local boy she was supposed to get with the first fortune. She married someone from Shanghai. And the local boy she chased away with a rhyming poem? Those leftovers went straight to me.

No, I'm not being superstitious. I am only saying that's how it happened. And how can you say luck and chance are the same thing? Chance is the first step you take, luck is what comes afterward. Your kind of chance makes no sense, it is only an excuse not to blame yourself. If you don't take a chance, someone else will give you his luck. And if you get bad luck, then you need to take another chance to turn things from bad to good. Of course everything is connected.

How do I know? Well, you can see for yourself—one thing was said, then the same thing happened. We lost Little Gong and Little Gao, then we found Wen Fu. I did nothing about it, then—well, here's what happened.

We were looking for Little Gong and Little Gao, walking through the marketplace. Peanut scolded them as if they were there: "Bad boys, always getting in trouble. Why don't you listen to your big sister?" We walked from one stall to another, pushed our way through the thick crowds, always looking for them, unable to rest our eyes for even one moment on interesting trinkets.

At last we found them. They were standing at the front of an audience, everyone waiting for a play to begin. The audience was enclosed in what looked like an arena partitioned off by ropes. A big sign over the stage said: "A New Year's Play in Honor of the God of the Village. Debtors Welcome."

"You remember this," I said to Peanut. "Same as last year." And we decided to stay with the boys and watch. This was the mock play the village people put on every year on the last day, the same old tradition. In the old days, if someone owed you money, you could chase him down and make him pay. But only until the last hour of the last day before the new year. After that, too bad. So landlords and merchants were always running after poor people, chasing them until dark. And the only safe place a poor person could go was to this play, a play dedicated to the god of the village. As long as you stood inside the roped-off area, nobody could demand payment from you.

Of course, it was still true that you were supposed to pay your debts before the end of the year. That was the honorable thing to do. But now the village play was only for fun. And the people inside the ropes were not really debtors; they had been pushed inside to become part of the play itself.

I can still see and hear it. Cymbals and drums sounded loudly, and actors in cheap-looking costumes appeared on the stage. An old woman walked on, sweeping a straw broom, crying over her lost son, the bandit. Off in the distance a dragon was rising out of the sea, his tail rippling like waves. The dragon was bellowing about his hunger for the ships of greedy men. These were two operas all mixed together, awful.

Suddenly the actors stopped what they were doing. A beggar man in a tattered jacket jumped up from the audience and went running up and onto the stage. He raced around the old woman and the dragon, grabbing a broom, grabbing a tail, crying to someone behind him, "I don't have your money! I swear it!"

Another man jumped out of the audience, this one holding a lantern high in one hand. "Ah!" whispered the crowd. "The evil landlord!" He too rushed across the stage, and three times almost caught the beggar—by his hair, an ear, the tail of his tattered jacket—but the beggar managed to spin away each time. The audience roared with relief and laughter.

The actress playing the old woman pretended to be annoyed.

"Stop! Quiet! We are performing an important play," she cried, and as the two men whirled around her again, she threw her broom at them, but missed—ponk!—striking the dragon's tail instead. More laughter! And then the man holding up the tail of the dragon peered out, rubbed his aching head, and asked, "Where am I?" The audience laughed even louder.

Then more shouts: "Make way! Stand clear!" And two men in the audience were pushing everybody back. One moment later, the beggar ran off the stage, sprang onto his hands, then bounced forward three times, head over heels, before landing within the safety of the ropes. The crowd clapped. The landlord with the lantern was now on the other side of the ropes, stomping his feet, while everyone jeered at him.

Little Gong and Little Gao did not tire of this until the whole scene had been repeated two more times, with different acrobats playing the beggar and the same actor playing the landlord. At the very end, the landlord was so mad he broke his lantern in two, then announced he was going home. "Forget the debt," he shouted. Everyone cheered in victory, as if they too had won. But as the landlord started to walk away, he suddenly turned around and called to the audience, "I'm going home, it's true, but all of you now owe our fine actors a token of your New Year's generosity!"

And then all the actors jumped into the audience with begging bowls in hand. The tail of the dragon was nudging Peanut, and he turned out to be Wen Fu. He must have thought Peanut would give him a big donation, to judge by the way he eyed her fine clothes and called her "generous lady."

Let me tell you, he was not the kind of man that would make you say, Oh, this man is very handsome. I should marry him. Not like your father. But Wen Fu had a way that made your eyes follow him right from the start, a manner that was unusually confident, very bold. When he said "generous lady," his tone sounded so sincere, yet his face was teasing: turtle eyes that blinked slowly but did not look away, a wide grinning mouth. He was—how do you say it here?—charming.

And there were other things I saw about him—which Peanut later told me she noticed too—signs that he was raised in a good family, that he was elegant, a person you did not have to look down on. His clothes fit him well, everything falling to the exact length of his arms and legs. And he wore Western-style clothes: a wide-collared shirt, open at the neck, tailored pants with a thin belt at the waist and sharp cuffs at the bottom. His hair was full and shiny, cut neatly all around, not stringy or chopped off at the bottom like a farmer's. His eyebrows—we both liked his eyebrows. They were thick and nicely tapered, like two ends of an inkbrush. And he had strong-looking teeth, all straight, not one tooth missing in front.

He held out a small money bowl. "Not for me," he explained again in that soothing, sincere voice. "For the hospital we are building at the south end of the island." His eyebrows rose up in the middle, a look of concern. He looked at Peanut, then at me. Of course, I was embarrassed that I had no money to give. So I gave him a stern look instead, as if he should not be bothering us.

Peanut smiled at him. "Such hard work to be a dragon," she said. And then she gave him a few coins, and we both turned to walk away. But now Wen Fu was calling to Little Gong and Little Gao: "Hey, little brothers, I have some lucky money for you in return." He pulled out two red money envelopes from his pockets and tossed a packet to each of them. In a moment, they discovered the envelopes contained some sort of candy in the shape of coins, wrapped in gold foil. "Are they real?" Little Gao cried, holding one up to the sun, watching it shine. They put their coins back in the envelope with much respect.

"Thank you, Uncle," they said.

"Did you see how well I worked the dragon tail?" Wen Fu asked them. They nodded shyly, smiled. "Maybe you would like to see the whole dragon?" And then they threw all shyness away, jumped up and down, and ran to the stage. Wen Fu looked at Peanut, then me, and shrugged as if he had no other choice.

For the rest of the afternoon, Wen Fu followed us. Or rather, he led the boys to see different sights—a cockfight, a game with wooden boats being sunk by sand bombs, a stall that claimed to sell tiger teeth—and we were the ones who followed. Of course, we protested at first, saying, "No more, you've already gone to too much trouble." But I think both of us secretly thought he was exciting. We sighed as if we had no other choice, then giggled because we did not know how to express our excitement any other way.

He carried our packages, spent his own money on little treats for the boys. And then he tried to buy things for Peanut and me, luxuries he saw us admire—a paper dragon on a string, a chocolate candy in the shape of a sheep that Peanut had been eyeing. "You should not do this!" we protested each time. Or maybe only I protested. Peanut only smiled.

So you see, I never took those gifts from Wen Fu. Peanut did. She said she would tell her mother she bought them herself, so many good bargains. But I knew this was wrong, not just the lying but taking something from a man. There were many sayings about that: Take even one sweet, and lose your whole life to bitterness. Eat forbidden candy and your stomach pops out.

And I could see how those sayings were right. Something was already happening. Wen Fu was winking at Peanut, his inkbrush eyebrows dancing. All afternoon it went like that.

You have an American expression for what Wen Fu did to Peanut: He swept her off her feet. That's what he did, exactly that. At the end of the day, when Peanut complained that her feet ached like two burning coals, he found a farmer willing to rent his wheelbarrow for a few coins. And then he lined the dusty insides of the wheelbarrow with his own jacket, and invited my giggling cousin to ride home in her new sedan. As he pushed her home, he sang to her, happy songs, sad songs, songs about secret gardens and dark pavilions. I kept thinking to myself, Are these like those words from *Chin Ping Mei*?

By this time, most of Peanut's white powdery face had rubbed off onto her coat. And I could see her cheeks were as flushed as mine. She was happy. And I can admit this: I was sick in my heart, such a bad feeling.

You see how he was? Always flamboyant, showing off in a big way, just like the actor he was that day. Charming!

A man with good manners would have found a pedicab. He would have secretly paid the driver before we knew it, then sent us home. Or maybe he could have shown his concern by inviting the girl and her cousin to rest a little, to take some simple refreshment at a teahouse. He would not have remarked about her feet, how small and delicate they looked, no wonder they were tired. And a good man would not play favorites, filling one girl's heart with pride, the other's with envy. And whatever interest he showed, he would never ask the girl for anything in return.

But Wen Fu asked. He pushed Peanut down the road. He saw our big house. He saw the banners for our celebration. He asked to come in four days, the third day of the first month of the lunar new year, to pay his respects to Peanut, her family, and of course, me.

The next day was the new year. Everyone pretended to be happy and kind, shouting, "Ten thousand generations!" "Long life!" "Highest position!" "Biggest prosperity!" That sort of thing, all meaningless, but good-sounding.

The servants were especially happy, because they did not have to work that day. All the cooking was done, and now no knives could be touched, no sharp words could be thrown. We ate sweet things and cold dishes.

Peanut and I talked about Wen Fu, wondering if he would come in three days. We wondered what kind of house he lived in on the other side of the island. We wondered if his mother was too good to be true. I did not say anything to Peanut about the rhyme she had used to chase this local marriage away.

The next day Peanut woke up crying. She said she must refuse to see Wen Fu! How could she see him? He had seen her when she was a vision of beauty, with her face powder and lipstick on, wearing her most sophisticated clothes. She could not put powder on her face, wear that in front of her mother and father. She could not show Wen Fu what she looked like underneath. I tried to tell Peanut that Wen Fu would find her even more attractive when she looked natural. I did not say this only to be kind. It was true. If he liked her when she looked ridiculous, why should he not like her the other way?

But I could not convince Peanut in time. When Wen Fu came, she hid herself. She was there, of course, watching him from different hiding spots: at the top of the stairs, behind the door of a dark room, through the windows of the greenhouse.

And then Old Aunt and New Aunt met Wen Fu. He called to them in such a sincere voice, "Auntie, Auntie," as if this were a happy reunion. At first they were puzzled. They could not recall who he was. Then he presented them with a basket of expensive fruit. He sent respects from his mother and father, especially from his mother, who seemed to be a longtime friend of Old Aunt's. Eventually, Old Aunt thought so too. She struggled with her memories until she found one that matched. "Ah, you are Mrs. Wen's son. Only a little baby the last time I saw you, I think."

I heard this and laughed. I admired Wen Fu. If I had any good feelings for him in my entire life, it was at that moment, maybe a few others like that. He was so bold, so clever, funny, and daring. So you see, even now I can still remember a few good things about him.

Lucky for Wen Fu, the house was soon filled with hundreds of people, all the villagers who had come to eat *nian gao,* the sticky rice cakes with a name that sounds like you are saying "Happy New Year." So if Old Aunt and New Aunt were confused by Wen Fu's visit, it seemed only a natural part of the day. Too many people to keep track of anything.

I was ladling out bowls of boiled dumplings when Wen Fu approached me. "Where is she?"

"She's shy," I said.

"She does not like me?" he asked. His eyebrows were pushed into a frown, but he was smiling.

"Only shy," I said again. It did not seem proper to confess that Peanut liked him.

"Why suddenly shy?" he said with a laugh. "Does shy mean she likes me?" And then he turned to me. "You aren't shy. Does this mean you don't like me? Ha! Is this the case?" He had that same teasing look.

I almost could not answer him. "I'm not that way—that is, not shy."

"So perhaps you also like me," he said right away.

"Being shy does not mean you like or do not like," I said.

On and on we talked that way, until my head hurt from trying to be polite, from trying to hide from his tricky questions. Finally he pulled an envelope from his pocket.

"Little sister, please give this to her," he said. "Please tell her to answer me tomorrow." And then he left.

Peanut had been watching all along. So when Wen Fu left, she dashed out from behind the kitchen door and demanded the letter from me.

"What does he say?" I asked her. I felt I had as much claim on reading the letter as she. I had worked so hard for her. Peanut hunched her shoulders over the letter, protecting it from me the same way a mother duck places her wing over her babies. She was giggling, biting her fingers, squeezing her fist, pulling a strand of her hair.

"What does he say?" I asked again.

Peanut looked at me. "He needs an answer tomorrow," she said. "Tell him I have no answer yet. Tell him to wait." And then she walked away.

So I helped Peanut and Wen Fu: carried their love letters back and forth, brought them to the marketplace, to the middle of our road. I was helping them to each other. I did not have it in my mind to steal Wen Fu away from Peanut. I swear this. I am not remembering this differently so as not to blame myself.

Each time I delivered a letter to Wen Fu, I used my words to carry a picture of Peanut to him. I told him what color dress she was wearing that day, rose-colored, the same as her cheeks. I reported how she had put a little decoration in her hair, a dragon pin, thinking about him. I hinted that she was unable to eat and was becoming thin.

Of course, none of this was true. I was only using my imagination to talk about all those silly, lovesick things girls did for romance back then.

So how did I come to marry him? Sometimes I think about asking Peanut. If she is still alive in China today, she would agree, I'm sure of it. I did nothing to make Wen Fu turn his eyes and look at me, nothing at all. Wen Fu changed his own mind.

I had a good heart, just like you. I was innocent, just like you. So maybe you can understand how your mother once was: a lonely girl, a girl with no expectations, wanting so much. And suddenly someone came knocking at my door—and he was charming, a reason to dream about a better life.

What else could I do? I let him in.

# 7

# DOWRY COUNTING

You remember how Helen always tells people she was my brides-maid. She tells people I had a big, big Chinese wedding.

And this was true, just the way Helen always tells people. Only, Helen was not there. Peanut was, with her whiteface makeup, and red monkey-bottom lips, smiling big, as if she truly were happy for me.

But the month before my wedding, you should have seen Peanut, so mad she would not look at me. She said it was my fault that I was marrying Wen Fu and she was not. She pretended she had no ears when I reminded her how I had helped her and Wen Fu.

This was true. I continued to carry their letters back and forth, the ones she didn't let me read. And later I found a secret place in the greenhouse where Peanut could put on her makeup. I told Wen Fu when to come, where to hide his bicycle. I took him to Peanut so they could talk while everyone slept for two hours after the noontime meal. And I stood by the door, watching out for Old Aunt and New Aunt, while Wen Fu and Peanut kissed.

Of course, I didn't see this, the kissing part. But I knew that they had done this—kissed like crazy lovesick people!—because later, when they came out from behind the broken pots, Peanut's face and neck were covered with red smudges, all those places where Wen Fu's mouth had been. And Wen Fu's own mouth was stained red from Peanut's lipstick, his cheeks were dusted with her white face powder. He looked like an opera singer. I watched him as he pushed off on his bicycle, a big, satisfied grin on his face.

And then I had to hurry to help Peanut wipe off those kiss marks, clean off her makeup. I scolded her: "Why did you let him kiss? Why not just talk, hold hands?"

This was a terrible thing to do, giving your mouth to a boy your family did not know. Of course, it was not as bad as giving away your other body parts.

"I liked it," Peanut said, so naughty the way she smiled.

"What! You like it, so you throw your family's name in the gutter just to satisfy your own desires? Just like two mindless dogs, running up to sniff each other's dirty tails!"

But as I scrubbed Peanut's face, she was still dreaming about Wen Fu, telling me the praises he had for her soft cheeks, her delicate hands. "Ai!" she squawked. "You're rubbing my skin off completely!"

"Your fault," I said. "This one won't come off. He bit your neck like a spider. And now everyone will be waking up soon. Ai, trouble now."

Peanut only giggled, reached for the mirror, and said, "Let me see. Ayo! Look what he did!" She pulled her collar up and giggled some more.

She wasn't considering what a big risk I took to help her. She knew that if her mother found out about this, I would be in more trouble than she. Peanut was younger than I was, so I was responsible for her behavior. And I was scared of what Old Aunt and New Aunt would do.

Of course, you probably don't understand this kind of thinking, how I could be in trouble for Peanut, why I was scared. In China back then, you were always responsible to somebody else. It's not like here in the United States—freedom, independence, individual thinking, do what you want, disobey your mother. No such thing. Nobody ever said to me, "Be good, little girl, and I will give you a piece of candy." You did not get a reward for being good, that was expected. But if you were bad—your family could do anything to you, no reason needed.

I remember the threats. "Do you want to be sent away forever and become a beggar, just like your mother?" Old Aunt would say. "Do you want to get a terrible disease that eats away your face, same as your mother?" From the time I came to live on Tsungming Island, Old Aunt told me things like that—didn't matter if they made no sense. I did not know what had happened to my mother—whether she had escaped from her marriage, the way Peanut said she had; whether she had died of a strange sickness, the way my father said she had; whether she had been sent away because she made my father angry for some unknown reason, the way some people whispered when they thought I was not listening. When I first came to the island, Old Aunt had only to say my mother's name—and I would burst into tears.

Later, I no longer cried. I tried not to remember my mother so much, or the feelings of hope I once had that she would someday come back for me. So Old Aunt thought of new threats to make me afraid. Once, she took me and Peanut to visit a family in Shanghai. She pointed to a servant girl, sweeping the courtyard.

"Look at that poor girl," Old Aunt said with a pitying voice. The girl was wearing ragged pants too short for her thin legs. Her eyes had no feeling left behind them. And then Old Aunt said the girl was a slave, sold by her father because she would not behave after her mother died.

And there were more threats. When Old Aunt thought I was not acting fearful enough—when I didn't bow down fast enough and beg for forgiveness—she would slap the side of my head. "So willful, that rebellious! What kind of family would want you for their son's wife? Maybe I should marry you off to Old Shoe Stink!"

She was referring to the old beggar shoe-mender who walked from door to door, whose breath and body smelled as bad as the old shoes he fixed and tried to sell. I think all the mothers in our village threatened to marry their daughters to Old Shoe Stink. And those daughters must have obeyed. Otherwise, Old Shoe Stink would have had twenty wives!

I do not think Old Aunt said these things to be mean to me or to lie for no reason. I am not being generous in saying this. Giving threats to children was the custom in old families like ours. Old Aunt's mother probably did this to her when she was a child, handing out warnings about another kind of life, too terrible to imagine—also giving examples of obedient children too good to be true. This was how you made children behave. This was how you drove selfish thoughts out of their foolish heads. This was how you showed you were concerned for their future, teaching them how they too could keep order in the family.

But this was also the reason why I was afraid for myself that day in the greenhouse. How bad Peanut was to let Wen Fu kiss her! She could have cost me my own future. So of course, the next time Peanut asked me to carry a letter to Wen Fu, I refused.

"Carry it yourself," I said. "I am no longer your go-between." Peanut had cried and begged, then shouted names at me. She did not speak to me for the rest of the day. And I thought I had put an end to my troubles. How could I know I was only making them worse?

I found out later: Wen Fu became angry too. He waited many hours for me to come down the road with Peanut's letter. And when I did not come the next day or the day after that, he didn't wait any longer. He found a real go-between, a woman who could deliver not only letters but a marriage proposal.

You see, Wen Fu decided he really did want to marry Peanut, not because he loved her sincerely—he wanted to marry into her family. And really, he was no different from most men back then. Getting married in those days was like buying real estate. Here, you see a house you want to live in, you find a real estate agent. Back in China, you saw a rich family with a daughter, you found a go-between who knew how to make a good business deal.

The matchmaker he found was an old lady we called Auntie Miao. She was famous for matching the right girl to the right boy so that they would both produce the highest number of sons. She had helped arrange marriages for Old Aunt's two daughters several years before. Now that I think about this, Auntie Miao was also the one who helped Old Aunt chase away another boy, a son from a family named Lin. I never met him, but he was the one I should have married. But before I could even get my hopes up, that chance was gone.

"No money in that match," Auntie Miao had told Old Aunt. "The Lin father is educated, this is true. But to what purpose? He never received even the lowest-ranking official position. And look at his wife—almost forty years old when she had her last baby. No morals, no shame."

But that was not the real reason Auntie Miao did not like the Lin family. The real reason was a feud that had happened many,

many years before. Peanut overheard Uncle talking about it, how the Lin family had made another marriage contract with a local girl. "A few months before the wedding," Peanut said, "the Lin son ran off and married a girl from Shanghai instead—married for love, just like that! Of course, the family could have forced the Shanghai girl to become the concubine, while the local girl still became the wife. But how would that look? A man who dislikes his future wife so much he takes on a concubine first to spite her."

And then Peanut laughed. "That local girl from a long time ago was Auntie Miao. So embarrassed, so mad—she had to wait another three years before anybody would consider her for a daughter-in-law."

This was the same Auntie Miao who now often dropped by our house for tea, to chat with Old Aunt and New Aunt, to mention who was sick, who got a letter from overseas relatives, whose bad son had run off and joined the Communists.

To her face, Peanut and I called her Auntie Miao. But behind her back, we called her Miao-miao, because she was just like a cat. Her ears turned in every direction, ready to pounce on a secret.

I'm sure Auntie Miao must have told Wen Fu all kinds of secrets about our family: How Uncle owned a good business, but lost a lot of contracts. How New Aunt was his second wife, the one who pleased him. How Old Aunt was his first wife, the one everyone had to please. How Peanut was the youngest daughter, the favorite of the family. How I was Peanut's cousin, sent to the island right after my mother disappeared—killed or captured by bandits, drowned in the sea or swallowed up by the earth, nobody knew. How I was also the daughter of a man so rich he could afford to give his younger brother an entire factory and the richest house in the Mouth of the River, because he had more, much more, in Shanghai. I know Wen Fu must have asked these questions, because this is what happened next:

Soon after I refused to carry any more letters, Auntie Miao came knocking on our door, and she brought Wen Fu's mother and father. The afternoon they came, Peanut was so excited she almost dropped the tea she was serving them. She was giggling so much New Aunt had to scold her twice for not giving Uncle more tea as well. But I saw that Wen Fu's mother was not noticing Peanut and all her silly ways. She was staring at me with a critical eye.

She asked me if I had made the dress I was wearing. She examined the stitches at the ends of my sleeves, then said my workmanship was not too bad, but could be improved. She asked about the paleness of my skin—Was this my natural color, or had I been ill recently? Why was I so quiet? Did I have a cough? Was I easily tired?

The next day, Old Aunt and New Aunt went to pay a visit at the Wen family house on the other side of the island. Peanut was so excited she was already deciding what kind of Western wedding dress she would wear. And the day after that, Old Aunt announced a marriage proposal from the Wen family—not for Peanut, but for me.

I did not say yes. I did not say no. Nobody asked for my answer because it was not my choice to make.

Of course, I did not clasp my hands and thank my aunties for planning such a good future for me. But I also did not run into my room and refuse to eat, turn white and threaten to die, which is what some girls did when their families chose bad husbands for them.

If you asked me how I felt when they told me I would marry Wen Fu, I can say only this: It was like being told I had won a big prize. And it was also like being told my head was going to be chopped off. Something between those two feelings.

After the announcement, I continued to sit at the table, blank-faced, too confused to say anything. Peanut was pouting. "Why does Weiwei have to marry?" she asked.

New Aunt mistook her daughter's complaints for a better meaning. "Don't be selfish! She can still come visit you often. But now she must marry and leave us. She's the oldest. She's the right age, five years younger than her husband. Later, you can go visit her at her new family's house."

I sat quietly, trying to imagine Wen Fu as my husband. I saw myself running to meet him on the road, the way Peanut did. Only now he was kissing me, not Peanut. He was laughing and grinning. He was telling me I had pretty cheeks, rose-colored like the dress I was wearing. He was giving me a love letter. And I could already feel my heart jumping, ready to read his letter.

I looked at Peanut, still pouting, unable to speak, her anger blowing out of her nose. Hnh! Hnh! Just like a dragon whose tail had been stepped on. She did not know how to hide her feelings the way I did. And so it was only then that I realized I had hidden my true feelings for so long and so well that I did not recognize them myself—until now. All those times I was angry at Peanut for letting Wen Fu kiss her—now I knew. I had wanted him for myself.

No, this was not love! That's not what I am saying, no such thing. This was a foolish kind of hope. This was learning to hope for myself.

You don't believe me? Did Auntie Helen tell you this story herself? Well, she wanted to. I stopped her. I knew if she told you she would get it all wrong. She would tell you, "Your mother fell in love. So romantic."

But you know how she is. If something is false, she thinks it is true. If something is true, she thinks it is false. Like her brain tumor—she has no brain tumor. I told her so, but she didn't believe me. She thought I was saying that just to be nice. "Why should I be nice?" I asked her. "Because I am dying," she said. How can you argue with someone like her?

That's why I'm telling you this story, not Auntie Helen. And you must believe me, because I am your mother. I did not love Wen Fu, even at the beginning. I was happy, of course, but only because I saw my marriage as a new chance. Although maybe I too confused my happiness for love, just a little.

A few days after the announcement, I listened to my aunties carefully, keeping my head bowed in a respectful manner. I heard them tell me what a good family the Wens were, how lucky I was. Old Aunt said my in-laws accepted me, in spite of my mother's bad background. They told me that the Wens ran a successful overseas business, that Wen Fu could help my father and Uncle sell our family's silks and cottons in foreign countries. He had already promised this. They said that Wen Fu's mother was very talented, a seamstress and a landscape painter, a good cook and an efficient manager of the house. She could teach me lots of things. And the house itself—of course, it was not as good as ours, but it was a very fine house, with plenty of servants. They even had an automobile!

The more I heard, the more I wanted to believe them. I imagined Wen Fu driving up in the automobile to take me away, and I would be so glad to leave my old life. I dreamt of living in a happy household where nobody ever complained. I was thinking of a mother-in-law who was too good to be true, who praised me, never scolded me. I could already see servants filling my teacup before I even knew I had a thirst. And running through my mind were many children, all the same size, chasing my skirt, one after the other, making me laugh. When my aunties told me I was marrying Wen Fu, that's what I imagined, what the fortune-teller had told Peanut.

Of course, with all these good things about to be mine, I felt sorry for Peanut. But then she began to accuse me, told me I had betrayed her. During the time before the wedding, we still had to share the same bed. When I walked into our room, she spit on the floor. At night, she kicked my legs, pushed me and my quilt off to the side, whispered that I was worse than worms that ate a dead animal.

"You heard your mother," I protested. "I am the oldest. I have to marry first. I have to obey. If you want to change this, you argue with your mother."

If I had thought about this more carefully, I would have realized: My aunties did not care if I was the oldest, Peanut the youngest. Peanut was the favorite. Everything they gave to Peanut was always better: better clothes, better praise, more spending money, better charms for attracting good luck, more remedies when she became sick. As I have already said, they did not mistreat me. They just treated Peanut better. So why was I so stupid? I should have known—if they were giving me to Wen Fu's family, then maybe it was not such a good deal.

And then something happened that made me think all these good things would go away. My aunties said they were taking me to Shanghai to see my father, to ask his permission for my marriage. They showed me his letter, telling us when we should come, only that, no words of congratulations. Back then, we had no telephone lines connecting Shanghai to the island, and this letter had come by messenger, not the regular mail service. So the letter I held in my hand seemed very serious.

Imagine with your heart how I felt. I had not seen my father for almost twelve years, ever since he sent me to the island. My aunties had never taken me to see him all those times we visited Shanghai.

He had never written to me, had never come to see me on the island or at my boarding school. So I did not know whether he would be mad or happy to see me. I did not know whether I should be fearful or happy to see him.

That morning Old Aunt, New Aunt, and I took our baths early. We put on our best clothes, bright silk dresses and jackets. We bought first-class tickets for the two-hour motorboat ride down the river to the Shanghai harbor. When we got off the boat, a long black automobile with a driver was already outside the gate, waiting to take us to my father's house on Julu Road. Everything was like a happy fairy tale.

But as we walked up the pathway to the house, I knew we had made a terrible mistake. Our clothes were too bright, too showy, letting everyone know how unimportant we were. And then the door opened, and I was standing in the big hallway of a house I once lived in but could not remember.

The house was ten times bigger and better than our place at the Mouth of the River. Or maybe you could not even compare it that way. It was the kind of place where everything you saw you wanted to touch, yet you were afraid to move one step in case you knocked something down. Next to me were two tall ornate stands that held small white statues, one of a hunter chasing a deer, another with two girls walking in English dresses. One sneeze, one cough, one word said too loud, and surely you would break those statues.

I was looking at my feet, wishing I could stoop down and wipe the dust off my new shoes. That's how I came to stare at the white marble floor.

I suddenly remembered the pattern running through it—my mother once told me they were jewels left by a river flowing over the marble rock. And in front of me, on the surface of the floor, different-colored lights were dancing. The shadows of colorful fish from the same river, my mother had said.

And then I looked up to see where the colored lights came from— the big stained-glass window at the top of the first stair landing, the flowers, trees, and sky in the glass. And as I struggled to re-member that as well, I saw the wide spiral staircase, tried to recall the smooth dark wood along the banister, the feel of running my hand along it.

And that's when I saw my father walking down the stairs, one slow step at a time, looking like a god descending from heaven.

I remembered that manner of his, as if he was never in a hurry. I remembered that feeling of always waiting, of always feeling scared, not knowing what would happen next.

But now he was standing on the bottom step, staring at me, no color in his face. And I'm sure I looked the same way. It was like one ghost staring at another. Oh! Perhaps he was seeing my mother in my face and hated me. I bowed my head.

"Daughter," he suddenly said, "you should invite our guests to sit down."

I turned to the side to see if he was speaking to someone else in the room. But Old Aunt nudged me, and I found myself pointing to a sitting room to my right, saying, "Please sit down, come in and sit. Don't be polite, sit," as if I had always welcomed my aunties to a house I did not live in.

We were all sitting very quietly on sofas with feather cushions that sank down low and made me feel stuck. Old Aunt was nodding nervously toward my father: "How are you, Big Brother? Good health, I hope." New Aunt repeated the same thing: "How are you? How are you?"

My father smiled, slowly crossed his legs, then said, "Not bad, although not the best. You know how it is when your bones grow a little older."

"Ai, this is true!" Old Aunt burst in right away. "It's the same way with me. I have stomach pains, all the time, right after dinner, and here in my bowels—"

One of my father's eyebrows shot up, and everyone fell silent again. The gong of a clock sounded in another room, and my aunts pretended to listen with great delight, then agreed that this was the most beautiful noise they had ever heard.

I was quiet. Sitting there, I saw that my father looked like an older, thinner image of Uncle. His face was more stern, also more intelligent-looking. He wore glasses with round gold rims, a dark Western suit with a Chinese vest underneath. He was not very tall, although he had the air of a large man, the way he slowly turned his head halfway back toward a servant, then slowly waved the servant forward with his hand. But instead of telling the servant something, he turned to me.

"Daughter, you decide. Should we have Chinese snacks or English biscuits with our tea?" My mind felt like two horses running off in opposite directions. Which one? Which answer was correct?

"Something simple," I finally whispered.

And he smiled. "Of course, that's what you always prefer." He waved his hand once again to the servant, told him to bring English biscuits, Chinese pears, and Belgian chocolates.

I thought about what he did. His manners were so elegant, very strange to me. Yet he seemed to know me. If I had truly spoken my desires, that's what I would have said, all those things.

Over tea, which did not last too long, Old Aunt told my father all about the Wen family—how they were the best match for his daughter, a good ally for his family business. I stared at my hands folded in my lap, glancing up every now and then to see my father's reaction. And we all listened as Old Aunt took a little piece of truth and stretched it in all directions.

The Wen family's export business became an international shipping company. Wen Fu's knowledge of overseas business became handshake friendships with the presidents of the most important companies in England and America. And the Wen family mother now had talents so great—well, hearing Old Aunt, you would think she could charm a winter tree into growing back its leaves overnight!

My father was not a stupid man. He listened quietly, sipped his tea. And every time Old Aunt exaggerated too much, he stared at her without saying anything, no expression on his face, until she became flustered and moved her estimate of the Wen family down just slightly.

"Oh, naturally, their business is not successful by your same standards, not nearly as high as your position. But they are very comfortable and very, very respected. That's the most important thing for your daughter, I was thinking, a respected family."

And now Old Aunt had exhausted herself with good things to boast about the Wen family. Still, my father did not say anything.

"A good boy, a respected family," New Aunt said to fill in the quiet.

My father was looking at me. I was confused, and tried not to show this. Perhaps he was against the marriage. Maybe he was still angry with my mother, angry with me.

"I know this family," he said at last. "I have already had some people look into their business, to find out about their background."

He waved his hand back, as if chasing away a mosquito. "But it is good to hear what my own family has to say as well."

This news startled Old Aunt and New Aunt. They looked like two thieves caught stealing beans. They hung their heads down, guilty, waiting to hear what my father would say next, what he already knew.

"Daughter, what do you think?" His voice was low, almost hoarse. "Is this what you want?"

I bit my lips. I pinched my fingers. I plucked at my dress, trying to think how I should answer.

My father waved his hand again. "This is what she wants," he said to my aunties, then sighed. "How can we stop her?"

My aunties both laughed a little, as if this were a joke. But I heard something different. That tone in his voice, he sounded sad. Before I could think about this anymore, my father started asking questions about business matters, so perhaps I was mistaken.

"How big a gift is the Wen family offering?"

Old Aunt handed over the envelope. My father quickly counted out four thousand yuan, then nodded. I was relieved. This was a large sum, a respectable amount, the same as two thousand dollars in U.S. money, maybe worth forty or fifty thousand today. A middle-class Chinese person would have to work more than ten years to earn that sum of money. But it did not mean the Wen family was really giving my father that money. He was supposed to hand back the money on my wedding day, give it to the Wen family, saying, "You are sharing a lifetime of your family's wealth with my daughter. That is already enough."

And my father was then expected to give me a money dowry that was the same size as their gift, telling me, "This is some extra money so you are not too much of a burden on your new family." And that money would be mine, put into a bank account under my name. I didn't have to share it. No one could take it away from me. But it would be the only money I would have for my entire lifetime.

"How big a dowry does the Wen family expect?" my father asked next. And here he was referring to things beyond the money dowry.

Old Aunt had to be very careful how she answered. If she said the Wens did not want very much, it would appear that they were not a family worthy of joining. If she said they wanted a lot, it would sound as if I were not worthy of them. But Old Aunt had already had experience marrying off her two daughters, so she simply said, "The furnishings for her and her new husband's room," meaning the room we would have in the Wen family house. That kind of answer did not make the Wens sound greedy. That kind of answer was like a turn in a poker game. It was now up to my father to show how extra generous he could be.

"Of course," added Old Aunt, "the husband's family will buy the bed." And here she was referring to old custom, because all generations of sons always had to come from the husband's bed.

"More tea?" my father asked. And because he had asked, rather than ordered the servant to pour the tea right away, that was our sign the visit was over. My aunties and I jumped up quickly.

"No, no, we must go," Old Aunt said.

"So soon?" my father said.

"We are already late," said New Aunt, which was not true. We had nowhere else to go at that hour of the afternoon; our boat would not leave until the evening. We started to walk out of the room.

But then I heard my father call me. He did not say "daughter." He called me by my name. "Weiwei-ah," he said. "Say good-bye to your aunties. Then come to my study so we can talk about your dowry."

What small hopes I carried to my father's house that afternoon! And now what great wishes wanted to leap from my throat with a shout! He was treating me as if I was truly a daughter, all those years in between completely forgotten.

Of course, he did not hug me and kiss me, not the way you Americans do when you have been reunited after five minutes' separation. We did not even talk very long after my aunties left. But what little he did tell me has made me wonder, even to this day: Did he truly think he was sending me to a good marriage? Or was he finding an easy way to be rid of me forever, this reminder of his own unhappy marriage?

And so I have remembered clearly his few words spoken to me that afternoon. I do not think I changed them in my mind to make the meaning of his words go the way I wanted.

His face was solemn, his expression frank. He spoke of no apologies for what had passed as twelve years' separation. "Now that you are getting married," he said, "you will learn your true position in life." And then he pointed to an old-style painting that stretched from one end of the wall to the other. It showed one hundred different people: men, women, and children. And they were doing one hundred different things: working, eating, sleeping, all brief moments in life captured forever.

"When you were a small child," my father said, "you would come into this room and look at this painting over and over again. Do you remember it?"

I stared at the painting for a very long time, hoping to recognize it. And at last, I remembered a small figure in the corner. It was a lady looking over a balcony. I nodded.

"When I asked you if you liked the painting, you told me it was a very bad painting. Do you remember?"

I could not imagine myself saying such a thing to my father, even as a young child. "I am sorry, I do not remember this," I said. "I am even more sorry that what you remember is a disobedient child."

"You said the painting was very confusing. You could not tell if the lady playing the lute was singing a happy or a sad song. You could not tell if the woman carrying a heavy load was beginning her journey or ending it. And this woman on the balcony, you said one moment she looked as though she was waiting with hope, the next moment watching with fear."

I covered my mouth and laughed. "What a strange child I was," I said.

My father continued talking as if he had not heard me. "I liked this in you, so unafraid to say what you thought." And now he looked at me and his face looked empty of any thoughts or feelings.

"So tell me, what do you think of this painting now?" he said.

My mind ran fast, trying to think of the answer, one that would please him, that would show him I had not changed in my honesty.

"This part I like very much," I said, nervously pointing to a man pleading before a magistrate. "The proportions are good, the details are very fine. And this part of the painting I don't like at all. You see, it's too dark, heavy at the bottom, and the features are too flat—"

My father had walked away. He was nodding, although I did not think he was agreeing with me.

He turned around to face me. "From now on," he said at last with a stern look, "you must consider what your husband's opinions are. Yours do not matter so much anymore. Do you understand?"

I nodded eagerly, grateful that my father had taught me this useful lesson in such a subtle way. And then he said I would stay in his house for the next week so I could shop for my dowry.

"Do you know what you need?" he asked.

I looked down, still shy. "Something simple."

"Of course," he said. "Always something simple." He smiled, and I was so happy I had said just the right thought.

But then his smile was gone. "Just like your mother," he said, "always wanting something simple." And then his eyes grew small, as if he were still seeing her in some distant place. "Always wanting something else," he said, then looked at me sharply. "Are you the same way?"

His meaning—it was like that painting, changing at each moment. And I was like the lady on the balcony, waiting with hope, waiting with fear, my heart swelling and shrinking with every word. So that in the end, I did not know how to answer him. I said only what flew out of my mouth, honest and true. "The same," I said.

That afternoon, a servant showed me to the room I once shared with my mother, then left me so I could rest up before the evening meal. As soon as the door closed, I inspected and touched everything.

The quilts were different. The paintings and curtains she had chosen were no longer there. Her clothes, her brush and comb, the lavender soap, all her smells—nowhere to be found. But the furniture was the same: the bed, the tall dresser, the stool and vanity table, the mirror that once held her face. I cried, so happy to return at last. And then I cried a different way, just like a little child again, wondering when my mother would come back.

I found out later: No one wanted that room that had once belonged to my mother. It was considered a bad-luck room. And so no one had used that room in all those years, even though the house was filled with many people. San Ma and Wu Ma still lived there. You remember them—my father's other wives. Sz Ma had already died a few years back. And my father's sons, now with wives and children of their own, they lived there as well. So did the servants and their children. All together, the house contained maybe twenty-five or thirty people.

But even with that many people, the house seemed very quiet. When I went downstairs for the evening meal, people were talking in quiet voices. They greeted me politely enough, and of course, no one mentioned the reason for my absence for so many years. I think they didn't know how to treat me.

And then the food began to arrive on the table. I started to sit next to a half brother's wife, but my father motioned that I should sit next to him. Everyone turned to watch me. My father stood up and announced, "My daughter Jiang Weili is to be married in one month." And then we waited—and waited and waited—as the servant slowly poured a special drink into small jade cups the size of thimbles.

Finally my father spoke again, a simple toast in my honor: "In your marriage, may you find all that you wish. *Ganbei!*" Bottoms up! He tipped his head back and emptied his cup in one quick swallow. We all followed. And soon I found everyone congratulating me, talking loudly in the manner of a happy family. My tongue burned from the liquor, my eyes burned with tears of joy.

As it turned out, my father asked San Ma to help me shop for my dowry. She was the senior wife, the one who approved the spending of household money. And of course, she was also familiar with all the things a girl needs when she marries. She had already done this for Sz Ma's three daughters, who married after Sz Ma died. That's what she told me as the automobile took us to Yung An Gungsi, the first-class shopping store on Nanking Road.

"Sz Ma's daughters," she was saying, "they each inherited the worst flaws of their mother. Tst! Tst! Number one lacked generosity, the kind of person who would never put one copper into a beggar's bowl. Number two lacked compassion, the kind of person who would throw dirt into the bowl. Number three, so greedy—you know what she would do?—steal the dirt and the bowl! So I did not buy them too many things for their dowry. Why should I, girls as bad as those?"

I was very careful how I acted toward San Ma. I remembered she was the wife most jealous of my mother, envious of her hair, her position, her education. I did not want to give her any reason to tell my father that I was greedy.

So when she asked me to choose a chair, I pointed to one with a very simple design, no fancy carvings. And when she asked me to choose a tea table, I pointed to the one with the plainest legs. She nodded and walked over to the salesman waiting to help us. But she did not order the pieces I had picked; she ordered others that were three grades better!

I thanked her many times. And then I thought we had finished our shopping and would return home. That's all I thought we would be buying, a chair and a tea table. But San Ma was already encouraging me in a gentle way to remember what a proper wife needed. "What style dressers?" she said.

Can you imagine how I felt? Do you remember how I had been hoping and praying for a better life? And now everyone was being so good to me. I was no longer lonely. I had all that I wished. I would have no need to wish for anything else, just as the fortune-teller had predicted.

All day long San Ma and I shopped. It was just like that game show—the one where the woman has one minute to grab onto anything she wants from the store shelf. And she has no time to decide—if she sees something, she should just take it. I was doing the same thing, only I had one whole week. So you can imagine how many things we bought, how the dreams of my future life began to grow and grow and grow.

That day we also found a triple dresser and a triple armoire, very handsome. And this was my favorite piece: a vanity table in a modern style I had picked out myself. It had a big round mirror framed in silver. Both sides had two drawers, one short, one long. And the front of each drawer was inlaid with mahogany, oak, and mother-of-pearl in a pattern that burst open like a fan. The drawers were lined with cedar, so that the moment you opened them, a good scent flew out. The center part dipped lower than the rest. It was a square table that was also inlaid on top. And beneath the table was a little curved bench covered with green brocade. I imagined myself sitting at that vanity, looking just like my mother.

Now you know what I am talking about, the same style of furniture I bought for you. I looked so long to find it. So you see, I didn't buy that table to torture you. That was my favorite.

On the second day, San Ma helped me buy fun things: a radio, a sewing machine, an RCA phonograph that changed records by itself, a porcelain fishbowl big enough for me to fit in! Wen Fu and I would have plenty of ways to have a happy life.

On the third or fourth day, San Ma and I went shopping for my private married-lady things. Oh, I was embarrassed! I could only laugh whenever she mentioned what I needed and why. First we found a washbasin, which was really a very nice piece of furniture—a green marble top and a carved wooden cabinet. San Ma showed me the little cupboard down below for hiding female things. We used cloth napkins back then, just like diapers.

And after that came two kinds of tubs, a tall wooden one for washing my whole body in the morning, and then a smaller porcelain one, which was for washing only my bottom and my feet. That's what most people in China always used, because they didn't have time to wash all over every day, only partially. San Ma said, "You should wash your bottom every night before joining your husband in bed. That way he will always welcome you." This made sense. I remembered times when I wanted to push Peanut out of our bed.

But then San Ma said to me, "Later at night you should do a small wash again." And she did not explain why I had to do this. Although I began to think men were more fussy than women, and women were naturally more dirty.

And then San Ma made me buy three chamber pots. My face burned just to look at them, to imagine that Wen Fu and I would share this as well. The pots had wooden lids and the insides were painted red, then sealed off with a very strong-smelling oil.

On the fifth day, San Ma helped me buy travel and storage things: big suitcases, all leather, and two cedar chests. We filled the chests with pillows and quilts. And then it was as if San Ma went crazy! She insisted I buy more quilts—twenty!

"Of course you need this many," she said. "How else can you keep all your future children warm?" So I chose good, thick quilts—all Chinese made, with lots of fine-weave banding around the sides. Inside, they were filled with the finest cotton batting, the most expensive, beaten many times until it rose up high. And for these blankets, I chose beautiful covers, all silk, not one of them cotton. And each one was embroidered with different flower patterns, never the same pattern twice.

On the sixth day, we bought all my things for entertaining guests and honoring ancestors: sofas and chairs, an altar table, four stools, and a short round table. This last piece was made out of very thick dark gleaming wood, and it was carved in the Chinese style with claw feet and long-life characters running around the border. Underneath the table were four smaller tables that could be pulled out, in case more guests arrived.

On the seventh day, the last, we bought all my dishes and silver. By this time, I had been living at my father's house long enough to know what I needed: two sets of everything!

I got one set for banquets, one set for everyday use, ten of everything for each set. And it was not just plates and knives and forks like Americans have, one plain, one fancy. Everything was fancy! Ivory or silver. Can you imagine? This was Chinese silver, pure, soft silver, just like money you can exchange.

At the store they had a big long table, and we set the table with all the things I was choosing. I danced around the store, picking this, picking that, as if I had done this every day of my life, no cares about how much money everything cost. I had silver cups for holding soy sauce, silver cups for drinking tea, silver cups for drinking wine, a silver dish only for holding a little soup spoon. And I had many sizes of spoons, one for drinking a meat soup, one for sipping dessert, like the lily-flower seed soup I loved so much, then two more sizes, one small, one big, although I cannot remember what their purposes were. And to match those I had four sizes of soup bowls, not in silver, but only because then they would be too hot to hold. But they were made out of very good porcelain, painted around the edge in gold. Then I had two sizes of plates, one small, another smaller than that, because as San Ma pointed out, "If you choose a plate that is too big, it is as if you are saying you will never get another chance to eat again."

My chopsticks were the best, silver too, each pair connected by a little chain, so they could never be separated, never lost. And just when I thought I was done with my shopping, the salesman showed me a small silver piece, shaped like a fish leaping up. And I knew right away I needed to have that too, because this little ornament was a place for resting your chopsticks, a way to stop eating for a few moments, to admire your table, to look at your guests, to congratulate yourself, and say, How lucky am I.

On the seventh day of my dowry shopping, only a few weeks before my wedding, that was precisely what I was thinking: How lucky am I. I had nothing but good thoughts in my head. I was sure that my life had changed, was getting better every moment, that my happiness would never stop. And now I would have to pray to the gods every day, but only to offer my never-ending thanks for so many never-ending blessings.

Imagine me in that store, smiling, sitting at the long, long table with all my things. I tried out my happiness with San Ma and the salesman watching. I picked up my silver chopsticks. I pretended to pluck a delicate morsel off a silver plate. I turned to one side, and I was imagining myself saying, "Husband, you eat this, the best part of the best fish. No, not for me, for you, you take it."

That was how I was, dreaming of all the ways I would respect my husband. And I can admit this: I was also thinking of ways to show off—all the banquets I would hold. One for my father, whom I now respected so much. One for San Ma, to respect her as my honorary mother. One for my future mother-in-law and father-in-law, whom I was sure I would learn to respect. One to welcome my first son, when he chose to be born. One in honor of Old Aunt and New Aunt, for letting me go. And one for Peanut, maybe even her, when I chose to forgive her.

I found out later: San Ma had bought a dowry five times bigger and better for Sz Ma's daughters. I found out: My father knew all along the Wen family character was not so good. So by allowing me to marry into the family, he was saying I was not so good either.

But I'm sure even he could not imagine just how bad the Wen family really was. All that dowry furniture I had chosen over those seven days?—Wen Fu's family took it all, shipped everything to America and England as part of their overseas export business.

The quilts and their silk covers?—Wen Fu's sisters and his brothers' wives took them all. And the wedding gifts from other family and friends, the fancy silver picture frames, the heavy silver hairbrush and mirror, the pretty English basins and painted pitchers?—Wen Fu's mother put those on top of tables in her own room.

There was only one thing from my dowry they did not steal—because someone else stole it first. It happened the day a servant left to care for her sick mother in the south. And Wen Fu's mother, who never liked this servant in the first place, soon came to an angry conclusion. While she was cursing this runaway thief for stealing her ten pairs of silver chopsticks, I was hiding those same things under the lining of my suitcase.

For many years after that, when times were bad, I would take out a pair of those chopsticks and hold them in my hand. I would feel the weight of the silver resting in my palm, solid and unbreakable, just like my hopes. I would dangle the chain that meant a pair could never be separated, never lost. I would pluck at the air, at nothing.

Can you imagine how innocent I was, how strong my innocence? I was still waiting for the day I could finally bring those silver chopsticks out in the open, no longer a secret. I was still dreaming of celebrations I would hold, of happiness yet to come.

# 8

# TOO MUCH YIN

Now you see how I once was. I was not always negative-thinking, the way you and Helen say. When I was young, I wanted to believe in something good. And when that good thing started to go away, I still wanted to grab it, make it stay.

Now I am a little more careful. I don't know why Helen criticizes me about this. She should criticize herself! You see how she is. She sees something good—her children acting nice—she thinks something bad. I'm asking you, isn't that negative thinking, to think you are going to die because everyone is nice? We have the same expression in Chinese, *daomei* thinking, only maybe it is even worse. If you think *daomei, daomei* will happen. If Helen thinks she is going to die—well, we shouldn't even say these words.

All I am saying is this: I know how it is to hear bad stories and believe they are true. You're lucky this has never happened to you. But that's what happened to my marriage—right from the start.

Of course, maybe my marriage never really had a chance. If you marry a no-good husband, you have a no-good marriage, no avoiding this. But without the worries Peanut put in my head, maybe I would have found a few moments of happiness before all the truth came out.

So this is what happened: Three days before my wedding, Peanut did a very bad thing. She fed me news about the Wen family that soured in my stomach. And the next day, she told me a secret story, about the dangers of loving Wen Fu too much. And the day after that, I left for Shanghai to get ready for my wedding, already worried that my marriage was doomed.

At the time, I did not think Peanut was telling me these things to get revenge for my marrying Wen Fu. After I returned from my father's house, she began to act friendly again toward me. She showed me an American magazine with pictures of brides, told me what style wedding dress would be best for me, a white satin one with a train ten feet long. She pointed to the dress she thought she should wear, even though I had not asked her to be my bridesmaid.

I told her Old Aunt had already picked out my wedding dress: a long red *chipao* with an embroidered jacket. Peanut wrinkled her nose. "Villager wedding clothes," she said, and sniffed. "You must have a Western wedding dress. No respectable Shanghai girl gets married in only Chinese clothes anymore. How old-fashioned! Look at this magazine." Peanut was always that way, rebellious toward the old customs, but with no new ideas of her own.

"Old-fashioned or not," I said, "Old Aunt will never agree to a white wedding dress."

"Only uneducated people think white is for mourning," Peanut argued. "If you let her decide everything, she'll have you going to your wedding in a red sedan chair—with the village band clanging up a parade of beggars along the way! And all those important friends of your father's will get out of their automobiles and laugh." Peanut laughed out loud like a horse to let me know what I would hear on my wedding day.

I had never thought of this.

"Eh! Don't look so serious," she said. "I'm going to talk to my mother about this right away. Also why we must both wear makeup for the wedding. Girls from the best families wear makeup, not just singers and actresses and low-class girls. Look at the Soong sisters."

Now that Peanut had told me she was going to help me, I let my excitement about the wedding come out a little bit at a time. I told her about the two banquets that would be given, one at a good restaurant owned by friends of the Wen family, the other at the YMCA, which was a modern, very stylish building in Shanghai, at least this was the case in 1937. Now the name does not sound so good. but I am telling you, back then it was a very good place to hold a banquet.

I also told Peanut about some of the furniture my father had bought me for my dowry, about the vanity table with the inlaid fan design—the same things I told you. I told her that Wen Fu's family had given four thousand yuan as a money gift. "See how generous they are. See how much they value me," I said. And here, I knew I was bragging just a little.

"I expect my future family to pay at least forty thousand," Peanut said. a smug look on her face.

Her remark was like a slap. I stared at her.

"You remember what the fortune-teller said," Peanut added. "My marriage will be to a wealthy family in Shanghai, much richer than the local marriage I gave up."

And then I realized: She was telling me that it was her choice, long before my marriage proposal, to give up Wen Fu for someone better. So in this way she was saving both our faces, hers for losing Wen Fu, mine for taking him away from her.

I thought this was very generous of her, to find an excuse to let both of us accept what had happened. And that's how we came to be as close as sisters once again for the rest of the time I had left with my family. In fact. from that day forward, until I was married, we called each other *tang jie,* "sugar sister," the friendly way to refer to a girl cousin.

But all that talk about money was not the bad thing Peanut told me. That only made me think she was sincere.

Three days before the wedding, our house was crowded with relatives who had come from far away—Old Aunt's people, New Aunt's people. cousins connected to us by complicated marriages. With so many people, it was too noisy to sleep after the noontime meal. So Peanut went outside for a walk, and I began to pack my clothes and wrap my jewelry in soft cloths.

A few days before, many things had been presented to me at a big family dinner: an oval jade ring from my father's mother, a gold necklace from my father, two gold bracelets, one each from Old Aunt and New Aunt. And there was something else; Old Aunt gave this to me when nobody was looking: the imperial jade earrings that had once belonged to my mother, the ones she said would someday be mine.

I was trying them on, remembering what my mother had said—about the worth of the earrings, the worth of my words—when Peanut ran back to our room. She whispered she had to tell me something, that we should go to the greenhouse to talk. Right away I stopped what I was doing and we walked outside. Secrets told in the greenhouse were always the best, dangerous to know, dangerous to others. We wound our way past the broken pots, then found our childhood tea furniture, two wooden lawn chairs with the backs broken off.

Peanut said she had been sitting on the front steps of the New West part of the house. And behind her, in the screened porch, she could hear the men relatives talking. Old Aunt had kicked them out of the sitting room, because they had been smoking cigars, and she discovered a few of them liked to spit on the rug as well. So there they were, in the porch, smoking and spitting.

Peanut said she had heard them talking about the same boring things: the new Japanese premier, factory explosions, strikes, and then a new subject—*la-sa,* or garbage, businesses.

"One uncle was saying how people in Shanghai were crazy to find any kind of way to get rich off foreign *la-sa.* The Americans, the British, the French—they're always throwing away leftovers from their businesses, throwing away food, just because they made too much. They pack things in wooden boxes, and when they unpack they throw the boxes away. They abandon furniture when they go back to their foreign countries.

"Uncle said it's easy to get rich off foreigners. You don't have to be so smart. You tell them, 'For a small fee, I can take your garbage away—your old clothes, your wood scraps, leftover furniture.' And after they pay you, you turn around and sell these same throwaway things to someone else. That's how you can make three generations' worth of fortune almost overnight."

"Why are you telling me this?" I asked Peanut. I did not think this kind of business talk was worthy of a greenhouse secret.

"I'm not finished," said Peanut. "I only told you the first part, because then another uncle mentioned that at least that kind of garbage business was not as bad as another kind, at least not dishonorable."

"What kind of dishonorable business?" I said, and I was imagining Peanut was going to tell me about "missionary wives." That's what desperate beggar girls said to foreigners: "Be your missionary wife tonight. You save me. Please save me."

But Peanut said instead, "He was talking about the Wen family business. He said they sell *Chinese* garbage to the foreigners, especially people from America and England."

I immediately felt weak. "What kind of garbage?"

"They sell anything that is broken, or strange, or forbidden," said Peanut. "The broken things they call Ming Dynasty. The strange things they say are Ching Dynasty. And the forbidden things—they say they are forbidden, no need to hide that."

"What kind of forbidden things?"

"Uncle said the Wen father travels to small villages, countrysides plagued by drought or flood or locusts. And he quickly finds out which families cannot pay their rent, which ones need to sell off their last piece of land to keep from starving. And for a few coppers, he buys paintings of dead ancestors. It's the truth! I am not lying. Those people are so desperate they would part with their own relatives' shrines. Can you imagine? All those ancestors immigrating to America against their will. Then one day they wake up, and—ai-ya!—they are hanging on Western walls, listening to people arguing in a language they can't understand!" Peanut was laughing hard.

This was a terrible thought. I was thinking about the painting of my poor mother. Where was it?

"This can't be true," I said. "The Wen family ships only good-quality merchandise, the best. Auntie Miao said so."

"Miao-miao's husband was there too," said Peanut. "And even he thought the Wens ran a bad business. True, they make a lot of money, he said. Foreigners love those paintings. But it is riches made from someone else's tragedy. The reason why they had to sell, that's one kind of tragedy. But the worst tragedy is still to come. Auntie Miao's husband said that when the Wens die and try to go to the next world, you can be sure all those people's ancestors will be standing at the front gate, ready to kick them out."

I jumped up and brushed the dust off the bottom of my dress. "I don't believe it. Those other people are only envious. You know how Miao-miao's husband is, the others. Always lying."

"I am only telling you what I heard. Why are you mad at me? Maybe it isn't true. What does it matter? It's still a good business. They aren't doing anything illegal. That's how they do a modern business with foreigners."

"People shouldn't say this about my husband's family," I said. "You must never repeat this lie to anyone else." I shook my finger at her.

I thought about what Peanut said all day, all night. I kept telling myself, This is not true. But my stomach fought me, and made me feel the truth another way. I got sick.

Of course, I had other reasons to be nervous, just thinking about my wedding, all the people who would be there, my father, his important friends, my half sisters, their husbands and children. When I told Old Aunt I felt ill, she said, "Of course, you should feel ill. You are about to leave your family, start a new life." She put me to bed and fed me a hot, bitter soup, and I felt I had never known her to be so kind.

Peanut came to see me the next afternoon while I was lying in bed. She said she had been to the porch again, and she had overheard another story.

"I don't want to hear any more stories," I said.

"This isn't about the Wen family," she insisted. "Nothing about business. It's a good story." And then she leaned forward and whispered in my ear, "A sex story."

When I heard Peanut say those words, "sex story," I opened my ears. We both giggled and I sat up to listen.

I was very naive back then, more so than most Chinese girls. I was not like you, watching movies in school about your body, dating at sixteen, falling in love with someone your first year of college, that Randy boy. You were naughty with him, weren't you? See, even today you can't admit this. I saw your face when you were with him. I see your face now, embarrassed. Your mother is not so naive. Of course, just before I was married, that was different.

I thought of sex as something mysterious, like going to a remote place in China. Sometimes it was a cold, dark forest. Sometimes it was a temple in the sky. That was my feeling about sex.

And I also knew some facts—through gossip Peanut told me, or stories we heard or imagined together. I knew that sex was another kind of forbidden thing, not the same as selling ancestor paintings, of course. I knew that a man touched a woman in secret places, her feet for instance. I knew that a woman sometimes had to take off all her clothes. And that a man had a male-thing—nobody had ever taught me the proper word, only the little-boy word, because I had seen the *ji-ji*s of my little boy cousins. So I knew what a male-thing looked like: a little lump of pink, soft flesh, as small and round as one of my toes. And if a man did not want to get up and use the chamber pot in the middle of the night, he could just ask his wife if he could put his *ji-ji* between her legs.

This was all I knew about sex from stories I had heard. I remember Peanut and I used to laugh until tears fell from our eyes. Oh, this was terrible. A man goes *shu-shu* in a woman, flooding her like a chamber pot! You see how innocent I was?

We thought it was so funny back then—that this was what happened to Old Aunt and New Aunt. But right before my marriage, I started thinking about it a different way. And I was worried that now this would happen to me. I would become my husband's chamber pot! That's why I had bought three for my dowry, one extra to put close to our bed.

So you can understand how eager I must have been to hear Peanut's sex story, especially since I would be married in another two days.

"This afternoon," Peanut said, giggling already, "one of our uncles told a sex story about newlyweds."

"Which uncle was this?"

"Old Aunt's cousin from Ningpo. You know who I am talking about."

"Turtle Uncle!" I exclaimed. We always called him that, after Little Gong put a live turtle in his soup, and he complained to Old Aunt that the soup had not been cooked long enough. This was a very bad name to call a man, "turtle." That's what you said if a man was too stupid to know his wife was fooling around right in front of his face.

In any case, that's what we called him. And Peanut was telling me what Turtle Uncle had said in the porch.

"He was telling everyone how he ran into an old schoolmate friend recently," Peanut said. "And the schoolmate said, 'You remember Yau, my cousin on my mother's side?' And Turtle Uncle answered. 'Of course, the thin young man who was at the horse races with us maybe three years ago. He bet on that nag who couldn't even cross the finish line. How is he? Not betting on horses anymore, I hope.'

"Then the schoolmate became very serious and reported that last year Yau had married a girl his family did not like. Her family was not very respected, some kind of middle-class merchant doing a small trade in Japanese soy sauce, in any case, much lower than Yau's family position. And she was not a great beauty. So she must have seduced Yau, body and mind, convinced him he should stand up to his family and say, Sorry, Mother and Father, but I must marry this girl, no matter what."

At this point, Peanut leaned toward me. "Then Turtle Uncle whispered to everyone on the porch what he thought the girl had done to seduce Yau." She sat back again. "But everyone was roaring with laughter, so I could not hear exactly, except for the words 'chicken love,' and 'cow-milking hands,' and 'night garden tricks.' "

"What do those words mean?" I asked.

Peanut frowned, thinking about this. "It's some kind of magical tricks a girl can do with her body. I think it means she learned this from a foreigner. In any case, Yau's mother and father resisted his marriage choice, threatened him. They said the girl had very bad manners and was too fierce, too strong. If he married the girl, the family said, they would cut him off.

"But by then, Yau was so drawn to the girl he didn't know how to stop himself. Finally the family gave in, because he was their only son—what could they do? So Yau married her and they lived in his parents' house. For a while it seemed as if all would work out. The girl and her in-laws were having fewer and fewer fights. And Yau grew more and more dazed with love for this girl, even though she was already his wife."

Peanut took a deep breath, sat up, and breathed out in a big smile, as if that were all to her story, this happy ending. But suddenly, she took a big breath and said, "Then guess what happened?"

I shook my head, leaned forward.

"When Yau and his bride had been married only three months—disaster! Late at night, the mother woke up and heard her son and daughter-in-law fighting. Yau was cursing and the girl was crying and begging. And the mother thought, Good, now he is teaching her to be more obedient. But then—funny!—her son's cursing stopped, but the girl was still begging. And after a few minutes, the girl began to scream, just like an animal. She screamed and screamed and wouldn't stop.

"The mother and the rest of the family ran into the son's room. Ai, guess what they saw? The naked couple, Yau lying on top, his bride screaming below, trying to push her husband off. But Yau did not roll off. He was not moving. He seemed as wooden as a carved statue. And the girl was screaming, 'We're stuck together. Help me! Help me!' It's true, they were stuck, just like dogs."

"This can't be!" I exclaimed.

"It's true, it's true! The mother tried to pull them apart, slapped her son's back and told him to wake up. She pushed and pushed, until her son and the girl rolled to the side. That's when she saw her son's gray face, his eyes pressed together in pain, his mouth wide open. And the mother started crying and slapping her daughter-in-law. 'Let him go! Let him go, you fox-devil!' she screamed.

"Now it was the father's turn to save his son. He pushed the mother out of the room. He called to a servant to hurry and bring in buckets of cold water. And the father splashed the water on top of the couple, because he had seen this work with dogs. One bucket, two buckets, another and another—he nearly drowned the poor girl. Then he too gave up and called the herb doctor.

"The doctor arrived, went to the son first and found he was already cold and stiff. But rather than alarm the family, who were already talking about killing the girl to make her release their son, he quietly instructed the servants to bring a pallet. Then he quickly mixed together a concoction of moxa leaves, dried alum, and warm vinegar. He tried rubbing this down where Yau and the girl were stuck. And when they still did not become unglued, he made the girl drink a lot of *maotai,* until she was a senseless drunk. And as she lay on the pallet, laughing and crying, the servants carried her out of the house with her dead husband still on top of her.

"Turtle Uncle said that at the hospital they finally got the husband and wife apart. And all the other uncles began to murmur among themselves, guessing what had finally worked: 'They put her on a bed of ice until she sneezed him out.' 'They applied hot oil to make them slide apart.' Then I heard Turtle Uncle tell them he truly didn't want to explain—but wasn't it terrible that his old friend

Yau had to go to the next world as a eunuch? Wah! And then everyone laughed and spit on the porch floor.

"Can you imagine? They laughed, no compassion at all for that poor man and his bride. And then Turtle Uncle was telling them to be quiet. He said it was a true story. His schoolmate had gone to the funeral, that's how he found out what had happened. And even though the family tried to keep the scandal a secret, by the time they put Yau in the ground, it was common knowledge that the parents had been right all along. That girl had been too strong. She had too much *yin*, the woman essence. She had grown to love her husband with so much will that when he connected his body to hers, she locked him in there, wouldn't let go. She began to drain him of all his semen. And all his semen kept pouring out, wouldn't stop, until there was nothing left and he died."

"What is this word 'semen'?" I asked.

"Anh! You don't even know this!" Peanut exclaimed. "It is a male essence, his *yang*. A man stores it like a potion inside his body—in here." Peanut used her finger to draw a line from the top of her head to the spot between her legs. "It's a man's ten thousand generations passed on from his male ancestors, father to son. That's why a man is a man, because of this *yang* potion."

"Then why would a woman want his *yang*?"

"This is because—" and then Peanut frowned.

"Be frank," I said.

"It's this way. If a woman can get enough *yang* inside her, she can make sons. Not enough, then she only has daughters. So you can see, if a woman has too much *yin*, she draws a lot more *yang* from her husband. That girl took all her husband's potion, his current life and all his future generations."

"What happened to that girl?"

"Of course, the parents now hate her so much. But they didn't kick her out. And she didn't leave. Where could she go? She could never remarry—who would want such a wife? So today she is still living in her dead husband's house. The mother-in-law treats her as bad as she can. They tell her they are only keeping her there so that when she finally dies, which they hope is very soon, they can bury her with their son. That way, he can once again be rejoined with all the *yang* she took away from him, now swimming in her body."

Peanut slapped my leg. "Don't look at me that way. It's a true story. Turtle Uncle knows that family. Maybe he even knows where that girl lives, somewhere in Shanghai. Maybe we can find out. Maybe we can go by someday and see her in a window. I wonder what she looks like, a girl who loved her husband so much she squeezed all the life out of him. Why are you looking at me that way?"

"This is a true story?" I whispered.

"This is a true story," Peanut said.

Two nights later, on my wedding night, I was scared. When my husband took off his clothes, I screamed. Wouldn't you scream if you saw that your husband's *ji-ji* looked nothing like that of your little boy cousins? Wouldn't you think all his *yang* was bursting to pour out?

I have confessed this. I was afraid to love my husband right from the beginning. Of course, I was a foolish young girl then. I believed Peanut, a girl who had a lot of silly pride. But if I was foolish, then Peanut was foolish too. Because she believed Turtle Uncle, a man who was as slow-minded as the creature he found swimming in his soup. And Turtle Uncle was foolish because he believed his schoolmate, who later turned him in during the Cultural Revolution. And who knows who that schoolmate believed?

Why do people say these things? How does anyone know who you are supposed to believe? And why do we always believe the bad things first?

Lately I have been dreaming of that girl, imagining what happened to her. I am dreaming of writing Peanut a letter.

Peanut, I will say, do you remember that girl from more than fifty years ago, the one you said drained her husband? Yesterday I saw her. Yes, that's right, in America I saw her. Her in-laws died during the war, typhoid fever. And then she came to this country and married someone new, Chinese of course.

She is now much older, but you can still tell, when she was young she was pretty, much prettier than the way Turtle Uncle described her. And she and her second husband are still very happy together—that's right, after forty years of marriage.

They live in a big house in San Francisco, California, two stories high, low mortgage payment, three bedrooms, two baths, big enough for all her grandchildren when they come to visit. And the grandchildren visit all the time—four of them—two granddaughters made by her daughter, two grandsons made by her son. Yes, can you imagine—both daughters and sons from a woman with too much *yin*!

Of course it's a true story. I saw her myself. I found out where she lives. I walked by her house. And she waved to me from her window.

# 9

# BEST TIME OF YEAR

After I married, that's when I met Helen. And I can tell you, we are not the same people we were in 1937. She was foolish and I was innocent. And after that year, she still had her foolishness, and became more stubborn about it. And I lost my innocence, and always regretted what I lost. And because I lost so much, I remember so much. As for Helen—she only thinks she remembers.

Whenever Helen talks about the past, she says, "We were both so young and pretty, remember? Now look how thick my body has become!" She laughs and sighs, as if she is letting go of her prettiness just now, for the first time. And then she goes back to her knitting, shaking her head and smiling, thinking to herself, How good it is to remember!

But that's not the way it was. Because I remember what Helen looked like when I first met her.

This was in the spring of 1937 in Hangchow, where Helen and I both lived for maybe five months, while our husbands finished their training at an American-style air force school just outside the old city. I was only nineteen back then, still thinking I could find an answer to every wish. And because I had been married to Wen Fu for only one month, I was still thinking I was lucky too, proud to be married to a future hero. Back then, before the war, everyone thought we were the lucky ones, married to air force pilots, only three or four hundred in all of China.

At the time of my wedding, I did not know I was marrying someone who had just joined the military. I was not a stupid person. Nobody thought to tell me this. Anyway, two or three weeks afterward, I knew. Wen Fu told me he was going to be a pilot. The pilots, he said, had been chosen from the best families, from the best schools. And now the announcement had come: They would be sent to Hangchow for special training, with congratulations from Madame Chiang on behalf of her husband, the General. Wen Fu said he had to leave in only a few days. What could I say? I went too.

When we arrived in Hangchow, all the pilots were honored at a big banquet given by that famous American general with a lady's name, Claire Chennault. Of course, he was not famous then, not in the beginning. He was not even a general. But I remember the pilots gave him a good-sounding Chinese name, Shan Nao, which sounded like "Chennault": *shan* as in "lightning," *nao* as in "noisy." Noisy lightning was like the sound of airplanes racing across the sky—zah! And that was why Shan Nao came, to teach the pilots how to fly.

I was there at that dinner, when old Noisy Lightning told the pilots something that made all the American instructors scream and shout like cowboys, and throw their caps in the air. But all the Chinese pilots remained seated, only smiled and clapped, waiting until it was quiet enough for the translator to tell them: "Shan Nao says we should give the Japanese a new kingdom."

Then all the pilots were talking among themselves, disagreeing, saying Shan Nao could not have meant to give the Japanese new territory. Whose kingdom did he mean? And finally, after much discussion, more arguments, many translations, we learned what Shan Nao had really said: "With your help, we won't be sending the Japanese back to Japan, but to kingdom come." And everybody was laughing and saying, "It means we will kill them all! Kingdom Come is hell!"

I remember many arguments like that: the Americans said one thing, we understood another, everybody fighting someone else. It was like this at the very beginning, when we arrived at the training camp just outside Hangchow, when we learned we had no place to live. The first class of pilots and their families were still living in the bungalows, walking around in circles, talking angrily among themselves. And later we heard why: The Americans were telling their leaders that the Chinese pilots were still not qualified to fly, that they had failed the test.

And this made the first class of pilots feel they had failed not just a test but all of China! Lost face, big faces. Many of them came from very important Chinese families and they complained to their leaders: It was only because the Americans concentrated on all the wrong things—shiny shoes and ties and hats put on straight the same way. And the foreign-built airplanes were bad, broken down—of course no one could fly them properly. And then my husband's class, the second class, was shouting, "No more wasting time. We need to be trained too—to save China." Until finally the Americans agreed to give the first class more training. And the second class would also begin training. But the complaining didn't stop right away, because we still had no place to live.

That's how everything was in China then. Too busy fighting each other to fight together. And not just the Americans and the Chinese. The old revolutionaries, the new revolutionaries, the Kuomintang and the Communists, the warlords, the bandits, and the students—gwah! gwah! gwah!—everybody squabbling, like old roosters claiming the same sunrise. And the rest of us—women and children, old people and poor people—we were like scared hens, letting everyone chase us from one corner to another. So of course the Japanese saw an opportunity to sneak in like a fox and steal everything.

The second class of pilots and their wives ended up living in a place in Hangchow that had once been a monastery, halfway up in the mountain where the monks grew dragon-well tea, the best tea in all of China. The monks had donated this place temporarily to the air force, because they believed the air force was going to save China. Every Chinese person believed the same: that we were about to push the Japanese out of China forever.

Most of the pilots slept in a big common room. But if you had a wife or were an American, you had your own room with a narrow bed. Everyone shared the kitchen located at the end of the building, as well as an unheated bathhouse, which had five small wooden tubs. That bathhouse was also used by some Americans, but fortunately, they took baths only once a week, on Saturday nights.

So our housing was not comfortable. Yet we did not complain too much, perhaps because of the clever way the monks had greeted us. We had arrived in the late springtime. The hills were already fragrant with tea. And we were also told that we had come at just the right time. This exact week in spring was the best time of the best season, they said—when the sweetest leaves of the most fragrant tea in the world could be harvested. When the most beautiful lake under all the heavens was at its loveliest. When the weather seemed like a daily blessing. And this news that welcomed the pilots at their new home made them feel immediately pleased with themselves, victors already.

Oftentimes at dusk, a group of us would walk along the lake and someone would say, "This is when the lake is clearest, this time of the year." And someone else would add, "Look, the sun, over the lake, and in the water—two, no, three suns setting at once." And another person would sigh and murmur, "A sunset like this, I can watch it all day."

You can see how none of us was thinking that this small bit of luck—of arriving at just the right time—would soon pass, and perhaps something less kind would take its place.

All that beauty was almost enough even for me. I would often walk around the lake by myself, and I would not be thinking about my past unhappiness, or my future life with my husband. I was only watching the birds who floated above the lake, then landed so lightly on the water that no ripples appeared. Just that moment. Or I would be admiring the web a spider had woven on a bush, perfectly formed and sparkling with pearls of dew. And I was wondering if I could later knit a sweater in the same design, using only this memory as a pattern.

But then the birds would suddenly call to one another, and they sounded just like a woman crying. Or the spider would feel my breath and clench its body small and tight before scurrying away. And I would be thinking about my fears, the questions I already had in my marriage.

I had known Wen Fu only a short time before we were married. And after the wedding, we lived one month with his parents, in their family house on the island. So in truth, I knew Wen Fu's mother's nature better than I knew his. She was the one who taught me how to be a good wife to her youngest son. This mother who spoiled him—she was the one who taught me how to be dutiful to a terrible person. And I listened, because I had no mother of my own, only Old Aunt and New Aunt, who each raised me to be afraid in different ways.

So this is what my mother-in-law taught me: To protect my husband so he would protect me. To fear him and think this was respect. To make him a proper hot soup, which was ready to serve only when I had scalded my little finger testing it.

"Doesn't hurt!" my mother-in-law would exclaim if I shouted in pain. "That kind of sacrifice for a husband never hurts."

And I believed she was also saying that this kind of pain for a husband was true love, the kind that grew between husband and wife. I had also learned this in the movies, both Chinese and American. A woman always had to feel pain, suffer and cry, before she could feel love. And now that I was living with Wen Fu in a little monastery room in Hangchow, I suffered a lot. I thought my love was growing bigger and bigger. I thought I was becoming a better wife.

And now I have come to the part where I must be frank. I was thinking I should not talk about these things with you, sex things. But if I didn't tell you, then you would not understand why I changed, how he changed. So I will tell you what happened, although maybe not everything. Maybe I'll come to a part where I cannot say any more. And when that happens, you just have to imagine what happened. And then you should imagine it again—and make it ten times worse.

Every night Wen Fu wanted me. But it was not the same way as when we were at his parents' house. I had been shy then, and he had been gentle, always coaxing me, soothing me, stopping when I became too afraid, before I screamed too much. But in Hangchow, he said it was time I learned how to be a proper wife.

I thought I was going to learn something that would make me less afraid. I was still nervous, of course. But I was ready to learn. The first night in the little monastery room, we were lying on that narrow bed. I wore my nightgown, Wen Fu had only his pants on. He was kissing my nose, my cheeks and shoulders, telling me how beautiful I was, how happy I made him. And then he whispered to me to say dirty words, words for a woman's body parts—not any woman's parts, a saltwater whore's, the kind who would give her body to foreign sailors. My ears hurt just to hear them. I pulled away.

"I cannot say those words," I finally told him.

"Why is this?" he asked me, and he looked gentle, very concerned.

"A woman cannot say these things," I said, searching for a reason. And then I laughed, just a little, to show him I was embarrassed even thinking about it.

Suddenly his smile went away, and he was a different person. He sat up quickly. His face was ugly, mad, and I became scared. I sat up too and stroked his shoulder, eager to win him back.

"Say them!" he shouted suddenly. He repeated the words, three or four dirty words. "Say them!" he shouted again.

I shook my head and began to cry. And then he became tender again, wiping my eyes and saying how much he cared for me, rubbing my back and my neck, until I thought I would faint with relief and joy. He was only teasing, I thought happily. How stupid of me! And then he was helping me to stand up. He lifted my nightgown off, and when I was naked, he took my two hands and looked at me sincerely.

"Say them," he said in a quiet voice. And hearing this once again, I started to collapse to the floor. But before I could do so, he pulled me back up, dragged me toward the door like a bag of rice. He opened the door, then pushed me outside into the corridor of the monastery, where anyone passing by could have seen me, naked like that.

What could I do? I could not shout. Someone would awaken, look out, and see me. So I was whispering to him through the door, pleading, "Open the door! Open!" And he said nothing, did nothing, until several minutes had passed and I finally said, "I will say them."

After that, it was the same way every night. Here is where you should imagine more, here is where you should make it worse.

Sometimes he made me take off my clothes, get on my hands

and knees, then act as if I were begging him for a good "stuck-together" time, so desperate I would do anything for this favor. And he would pretend to refuse, saying that he was tired, or that I was not pretty enough, or that I had been a bad wife that day. I had to beg and beg, my teeth chattering, until I truly was begging so I could get off the cold floor. Other nights he made me stand in the room naked, shivering in the night chill, and when he named a body part, I was supposed to say the same coarse word, then put my fingers there, touch myself—here, there, everywhere—while he watched and laughed.

And often in the morning he would complain, telling me I was not a good wife, that I had no passion, not like other women he knew. And my head and body would hurt as he told me about this woman and that woman, how good she was, how willing, how beautiful. I was not angry. I did not know I was supposed to be angry. This was China. A woman had no right to be angry. But I was unhappy, knowing my husband was still dissatisfied with me, and that I would have to go through more suffering to show him I was a good wife.

I discovered another thing about my husband during that first month. All the other pilots always called him Wen Chen. And this was strange to me, because I knew my husband's name was Wen Fu. Oh, he did have two older brothers, and one of them had been named Wen Chen. But that brother had died two years before, in 1935—of tuberculosis, I think. The family used to talk about him: a smart son, devoted, but always sick, always coughing blood. I thought the pilots were only confused, that maybe Wen Fu had mentioned this dead brother and now they thought it was Wen Fu's name. My husband was just being polite in not correcting them.

But then one day I heard him introduce himself, and—strange!—he said his name was Wen Chen. Why was this, I asked him later. And he told me I was hearing things wrong. Why should he say his name was something else? And then later I heard him say it again, that his name was Wen Chen. And that time he told me that the air force had written his name down wrong. How could he correct the whole air force? He said he would have to tell them Wen Fu was his little-boy name, just a nickname.

I accepted what he said. This made sense. But later, when I was sorting through boxes, putting away some things, I found a diploma and an application for the air force. They were papers for Wen Chen, my husband's dead brother, who had graduated with top honors from a merchant seaman school. And then I knew: My husband was not smart enough to get into the air force, but was clever enough to use his dead brother's name.

I now felt as if my husband were two people. One dead, one alive. One true, one false. I began to see him in a different way, watching the way he lied. So smooth, so calm. He was just like those birds who land on top of the water without making a ripple.

So you see, I tried to be a proper wife. I tried to love the half of him that was not so bad.

I met Helen maybe two weeks after we arrived in Hangchow. She was also very young, maybe eighteen, and I heard she was also newly married—no, not to my brother. But I will get to that later.

I had noticed her many times before—in the dining hall, or around the monastery grounds, where we both walked, or in the city below, shopping for meat and vegetables at the open stands. All the women in the monastery noticed one another, because there were only six of us. Most of the pilots were very young, really just boys, so only a few had wives. And the American advisors did not have their wives or girlfriends with them, although sometimes they brought a bad local girl to their rooms. It was always the same girl, I heard later, because five of the Americans caught her same disease, a type of invisible body lice that everybody said now lived in the bathhouse.

In fact, it was because of that girl and her lice that I met Helen. None of the wives wanted to use the bathhouse anymore, even after the monks claimed it had been disinfected. We had heard that it was impossible to kill this lice. And if a woman caught it, no one could tell the difference between her and a prostitute. Because then she would be constantly scratching between her legs, and the only relief she could get was if a man scratched her further between her legs.

I was thinking how I would then have to truly beg my husband. And of course, I was also remembering that time on Tsungming Island when I was bitten by fleas, how I had scratched myself, shouting "*Yangsele!*" How this kind of behavior was just like that of an unfaithful wife, one who itched for sex so much she would allow herself to become just like a prostitute—to Chinese, Americans, lepers, it didn't matter. This was common knowledge among young women about to be married. Of course, we believed these things. Who else could tell us otherwise? You think I was the only stupid one?

So all of us—the five women and myself—decided not to use the bathhouse anymore. Instead, one of the wives—a stuck-up girl who complained about every little thing—found an extra room that had once been used to store the dragon-well tea leaves brought down from the mountainside. The floor was still covered with old leaves from many harvests ago. And there was a woodstove in one corner that had been used to dry the leaves. We decided immediately to use this stove to heat the room and make it better than the bathhouse. Using the drying lines already stretched across the room, we draped sheets to make a partition.

And then we took turns, one of us boiling water, two of us running back and forth between the tea-drying room and the kitchen at the other end of the building, carrying buckets of hot water and boiled cloths. The other three would sit on stools behind the sheets, dipping the cloths into the washbasins, wiping their bodies down. The water would trickle down to the floor and onto the leaves. The steam would rise from the buckets on the floor. And soon the air was the scent of dragon-well tea. We would all breathe and sigh, breathe and sigh, letting this fragrant dew fall on our faces.

So we did not mind about the bathhouse. Even the stuck-up girl laughed and said she was glad the Americans had caught this disease. And every evening I now felt I had an important job, as I carried those buckets of hot water to and from the kitchen with a girl named Hulan.

That's what Helen used to be called: Hulan.

So you see, Helen is not my sister-in-law. She is not your real auntie. How could I tell you this, that I met her during the war in China? When you were little, you didn't even know there was a war in China! You thought World War Two started at a place in Hawaii with your same name, Pearl Harbor. I tried to tell you, but you were always correcting me. You said, "Oh, Mommy, that's Chinese history. This is *American* history." It's true, it's true. You told me that once. If I told you Auntie Helen was not your auntie, maybe you would have corrected me about that too! See, you're still trying to correct me.

Anyway, this is the truth. I met Helen in that bathhouse. And she was called Hulan. And the first few evenings I did not say very much to her, perhaps only to ask her every now and then, "Is the water already hot enough?"

She was the wife of a vice-captain, Wen Fu's boss. So I thought I should be careful what I said to her, not complain about our living conditions or say that I wished I could stay in Hangchow forever. She might think I didn't want our pilots to pass their training.

But from the beginning she was very friendly, even announced out loud to me that the monks were not very clean, that they were actually very dirty, because she had found toenails and bits of hair behind her bed. I did not agree or disagree, although I too had found dirty things behind my bed, also on the walls.

And then she told me that her husband, whose name was Long Jiaguo, had complained that the training was still not going well. She said the Americans had many disagreements with the Chinese leaders. And now there was talk of sending everyone to an Italian training camp in Loyang. She said that would be terrible, because Loyang was a sad place to live, a city of only two seasons: floods and dust storms. And while it had once been famous for its hundred thousand Buddha statues, in recent years most of the Buddhas had had their heads cut off. So going to a place filled with wounded Buddhas could only bring the air force the worst kind of luck.

I wondered how she knew this about Loyang, whether she had come from a village near there. She spoke in a slow but loud manner, with a countryside accent I could not identify. And all her movements were large and clumsy, not refined at all. If she dropped a hairpin, she would simply bend over with her bottom sticking out, pick up the pin, and poke it back anyplace in her hair. When she walked, she took big, wide steps, swinging her arms, just like someone who had always carried two buckets of water back and forth for someone else.

Really, she had the manners of a village servant. And this made me wonder how she had come to marry a vice-captain, someone who was educated and handsome, certainly from a refined family. I had known other girls who had been born poor, who had later married well. But their beauty had been exceptional, and their mothers-in-law had quickly trained them how to behave properly.

Hulan could not be called pretty, even if you judged her with an old-fashioned eye. She was plump, but not in that classical way of a peach whose pink skin is nearly bursting with sweetness. Her plumpness was round and overflowing in uneven spots, more like a steamed dumpling with too much filling leaking out of the sides. She had thick ankles and large hands, and feet as broad as boat paddles. While she had cut her hair in a popular Western style— parted deep on one side like this, combed back smooth, and curled halfway down—she had applied the curling sticks to her hair unevenly. So here it was lumpy, there it was flat. And she had no sense of fashion, none at all. One day I saw her wearing a Western-style flowery dress on top of a yellow Chinese dress that hung down like a too long slip. On top of this she wore a sweater she had knit, with the sleeves too short. She looked just like laundry hung out to dry.

I am not being critical in remembering her features just because I am angry with her now. Why am I angry? Because she wanted to tell you my story, throw everything into the open before she died. Of course I would have told you eventually myself. I was waiting for the right moment. And you see, now you are here and I am telling you everything.

Anyway, even though I am angry I can remember many good things about Hulan as well. Yes, her eyes were kind-looking, big and open. And her cheeks were nicely rounded, pushing in her mouth to make it seem small and sweet. And she had a nice-shaped chin, not too big, not weak-looking either. And she was honest. Most important, she was honest, spoke frankly, never tried to hide her feelings.

Or maybe this was not honesty, but foolishness, a lack of modesty, no understanding of when to hide herself. Yes, that's how she was. Show everything, doesn't matter!

Look how she was. When we washed together every evening, she sat on the stool with her legs wide open like this, scrubbing herself vigorously—her breasts, under her arms, under her legs, between her legs, her backside, the crease of her bottom—until her skin was covered with red streaks. And then she would get on her hands and knees, just like a dog, and naked like that, she would dip her hair into the basin of cloudy hot water left over from her bath.

I was embarrassed for her—and for myself, knowing this was the way I appeared to my husband every night. I tried not to look at her. I would pretend to be busy washing myself, my thin arms folded in front of my breasts, one large cloth over my lap, while I used another cloth to wash what was underneath without showing any obvious motions. But I could not stop myself from watching Hulan. How ugly she looked this way. And then I would see how she was thrashing her head back and forth in the basin like a crazy woman, how she lifted her head, squeezed her hair with her strong arms, twisting it like a mop. Then she would stand up, poke a towel in her ear, wipe her nose, and rub herself all over, laughing at me and saying, "Look at you! Your water is going to evaporate before you finish with your bath."

Soon after we met each other in the tea room bathhouse, Hulan and I began to take walks together. It was always Hulan's idea to look for the strangest things. She would mention she had heard about an interesting site, that she learned this from another wife, or a pilot, or a shopkeeper in town. She seemed to talk to everyone, asking what was unusual to see. One time she had heard about a magic spring.

"The water from this spring," she said, "is heavy as gold, sweet as honey, but clear as glass. If you look into the pool you can see your face, just like in a mirror. If you look another way, you can see the bottom of the pool, covered with black rocks. I heard you can fill a cup with this water, then drop the black rocks into the cup to try to make the water overflow. But not a drop will spill out, it is that thick! A monk told me this."

But when we reached that spring, it turned out to be only a teahouse that charged a lot of money for a strange-flavored drink. Hulan drank that tea and said it was truly magic. It ran through her blood, immediately entered her heart and her liver, then made her feel completely peaceful. But I think she was only sleepy for her usual noontime nap.

Another time, she said she knew of a place in town that served a noodle soup called "cat's ears," and in the window of this restaurant were half a dozen cats with their ears cut off—proof that the restaurant used only the best ingredients. But we could never find the place. And later I heard that "cat's ears" was only a local expression for wonton soup.

I began to think that people liked to fool Hulan, to watch her mouth drop open as they told her fantastic lies, to laugh behind her back. I felt sorry for her, so sorry that I did not want to be the first to tell her the truth, that somebody had only made a big joke on her. But later I became annoyed. I thought she was only pretending to be so innocent, so willing to believe when someone said, Go see the white snake with the figure of a lady. Go see the cave with the singing flutes. And when she invited me to see these things, I began to give her excuses, that I was tired, or my stomach did not feel well, or my feet were too swollen that day to walk so far. I said these same excuses so often they became true. *Daomei* thinking.

That is how it was between Hulan and me. She grew a field of hope from a little seed of imagination. And although I did not know this, from all my excuses, I began to grow a baby.

# IO

# LOYANG LUCK

And then the war began, and I did not know this either. Now you must think your mother is a stupid person—didn't even know a war had started.

But you should know, if I was this way, many people were this way—not stupid, only ignorant. Nobody told you anything back then. And you didn't know where to go for official information, who to ask. Our husbands didn't tell us. We could only overhear.

And if you read something in the newspaper, you couldn't trust it, not one hundred percent. The newspapers reported only what the government wanted you to hear, just a little bit, only good things about their side, bad things about the other. I am not just talking about what they do in China today. It was already this way during the war, even before that. Maybe it's always been that way, keeping people ignorant, like some kind of strange custom, although nobody calls it that.

So we got most of our information through gossip, passed from one mouth to another. We did not talk about the fighting so much. We talked about how we were directly affected, just like what you do here—if the stock market is up or down, if prices are up or down, what you can't buy anymore, that sort of thing.

Of course, now when I look back, I know what started the world war. You thought it started in Europe? You see, maybe you are ignorant too. It started in China, with a late-night shooting up north in Peking, a few people killed, but the Japanese were beaten back.

You didn't know that? Even I knew that. But of course, when I heard it, I didn't think too much about it. This kind of small fighting had been growing inside China for many years. So it seemed like it was only a small change, like the change within the summer season, when we all began to complain about the heat earlier in the morning than the day before. That is how I remember the start of the war, only the weather, the hot damp making my mind move as slowly as my legs.

During that time, Hulan and I could think of nothing but which dishes to eat to cool us inside out. We were busy fanning ourselves, or chasing away biting flies with a tassel. In the daytime we did nothing except drink hot tea, take cool baths and long naps, or sit on a veranda, moving our chairs farther back as the sun moved across the sky and ate up our shade.

I was often sick or too irritable to talk. Hulan chattered like a noisy bird. She said she knew exactly why I was not feeling well: "The food they serve, nothing is fresh, and all the same sour taste," she said.

And when I did not answer, she continued with other complaints. "Down there," she said, pointing toward the city, "it is worse, as steamy-filthy as a lice-infested bathhouse. Down there, the stink from the waterways can shrivel your nostrils." This kind of talking did not help my stomach.

In the evenings, the pilots and advisors would return to the monastery for dinner. We all ate in the same big hall. But the Americans would eat their own kind of food, perspiring into their plates. Too much heavy food, the rest of us always whispered, for such hot weather. I was sick just to see it.

Hulan and Jiaguo would eat with Wen Fu and me. We ate many dinners together like this, and I remember thinking how different Hulan's husband was from mine. He was older than Wen Fu, perhaps by ten years or more. And because he was Wen Fu's boss, the vice-captain, he was certainly more powerful. And yet he was not.

One night we heard Hulan scolding Jiaguo, telling him not to eat this or that because of his bowel condition. Another night she announced she had found the book that his absentminded self had misplaced. Still another time, she said she had washed his dirty laundry that day, but the stain on his pants did not come out.

And hearing all this, Wen Fu and I would look at Jiaguo to see what explosion would follow. Wen Fu had told me that Jiaguo had a boiling-point temper, that he once threw a chair at another pilot, missing him by only one hair. But each time Hulan scolded him, Jiaguo did not seem angry or embarrassed. He ignored her, that's what it looked like to me. He would continue to eat, answering, "Anh, anh, anh," as Hulan made one remark after another.

If Wen Fu could have forbidden me to see Hulan, he would have, I'm sure. But how could he tell me not to be friendly to his boss's wife? So instead, he often had bad words to say about Hulan. "A woman like that," he said, "is a whore and a fox-devil, all mixed into one. I would rather have a dead wife than a wife like that."

I said nothing. But secretly, I envied Hulan, that her husband was so lenient to her, even though she was not a very good wife. At the same time, I did not admire Jiaguo. I pitied him, all his weaknesses exposed in front of others like that. Of course, I did not know then the true story about their marriage, why he had to let her be this way.

After dinner, all the men, Americans and Chinese alike, would remain in the hall and play cards. If we women went outside to find a breeze, mosquitoes would immediately cry with joy to see us—*zzzs! zzzs!*—and chase us back inside. So Hulan and the other women and I usually remained inside. We would watch the men play, amid the smell of cigarettes and cigars, foreign sweat, and Chinese whiskey.

Watching like that, I learned that my husband was very popular with the other men. One man would always save him a seat at the table closest to a ceiling fan. Another would always offer him a drink or a cigarette. And Wen Fu would reward them by laughing out loud, very loud, while banging his hand on the table. The other men would begin laughing too, pounding too.

One time I saw Wen Fu jump up and announce, "Want to know what the American instructor taught me today?" And two other men cheered him on, then laughed with tears in their eyes as he puffed his chest out, hands on hips, and swayed back and forth, barking out nonsense.

I saw how his boldness, his recklessness, made other men want to be the same way. He acted as if he were already a hero: never can lose. no matter how dangerous. And the others must have believed that by being in his company, by laughing his big laugh, this feeling could swell in their lungs as well.

But he also scared them, made them feel his danger. I saw this too. One time he leapt up from the table, so angry, and everyone became alarmed. He was shouting at a young man opposite him, tapping the man's cards already showing on the table, and asking repeatedly, "Are you throwing tricks at me? Are these really your cards?" And the young man—in fact, all the men at that table—were unable to move or speak as my husband continued to shout. And then, while he was still standing, both hands leaning on the table, he suddenly smiled.

"Good, then." And he threw down his cards—"Wah!"—his winning hand. The men stared at each other, then roared with laughter and slapped the accused man on the back, while congratulating my husband on his good joke.

Hulan, Jiaguo, the other men in the room—they all thought Wen Fu was clever, so funny, so charming. I laughed out loud too, a nervous laugh. I saw that my husband did this laughing-scaring game not just with me, but with his friends. And I also began to see that what he did was wrong, cruel, but no one else seemed to see this.

So maybe I was not so ignorant. The other pilots—they were smart, they were nice people. But they didn't see what I could see: He accused and tormented, shouted and threatened. And just at that point when you did not know which way to move, he took the danger away, became kind and forgiving, laughing and happy. Back and forth, this way and that.

Of course, we were confused, fooled into thinking we always wanted to please him. And when we did not, we tried hard to win back his good nature, afraid we would be lost without it.

During the summer afternoons, the sky would often darken, then thunder would come. Whenever we heard this, Hulan and I would hurry and gather together a small hamper of food, our embroidery, that sort of thing. This was like an adventure!

We would walk quickly up the pathway behind the monastery,

up three terraces of steps, until we had reached the little outdoor pavilion sitting atop a mound with the wet-green hills in back, the lake below, and the festering city beyond that. And in that tiny heaven we would watch the world being washed down, until we could no longer see the city or the hills, only the soft gray curtain of rain surrounding us completely.

This pavilion reminded me of the greenhouse on the island. It made me homesick—although not for the house where Uncle, Old Aunt, and New Aunt lived. I was longing to be back at that place where I had hidden myself, where I pretended to be lost, where I imagined somebody would find me. I was remembering my poor little broken treasures: my mother's painting, the wings of a butterfly that crumbled into dust, a dried flower bulb that I once watered every day, thinking it would grow into a fairy maiden who could be my playmate.

Of course I did not tell Hulan these childish thoughts. We sat quietly in the pavilion, like two proper married ladies. But I also think we were both pulling from our own memories, trying to recall how it was that we had lost our girlhood so quickly.

I remember one afternoon in particular when we sat in that little world. The lightning came, and the rain fell, faster and stronger every minute as if it would never stop. It seemed unnatural for rain to fall so hard and for so long. When two hours had passed, we became nervous, although we tried not to show this.

"We have to go back soon," said Hulan, "even if the rain keeps falling."

"Well, what can we do, then? Can't worry it to stop, that's for certain," I said.

"Who said anything about worry? You are looking at someone who lived with floods all her life. The water used to come up to my waist before I'd think about moving my teacup off the table."

While waiting for the rain to stop, I searched through an old Shanghai newspaper I had found in the dining hall a few days before. So many good stories: A famous actress was involved in a big scandal. A Russian Jewish singer had just arrived from Manchukuo and was singing in a benefit play. Money had been stolen from a bank, the same one robbed just two weeks back. A British horse named Go the Extra Mile had won a race the week before.

An advertisement claimed a medicine called Yellow could cure the brain of confusion and bad-luck thinking, worries and slow-mindedness. Old Aunt had once bought Uncle a bottle.

There was not very much news about fighting anywhere, only a big declaration from Chiang Kai-shek, saying China would not give up anything to Japan, not even one more inch of land.

While reading, I would reach into my hamper of food, which had been quite full at the start. Perhaps it was my own nervousness about the war that had turned my appetite upside down. I often did not know what I could eat until the moment I was hungry. One minute I wanted one thing, the next minute I could not swallow another bite, and in another minute—hungry again for something completely different! So I had packed a little of everything. And I ate a little of everything, a taste at a time, according to the desires of my tongue and the moods of my stomach. A salty dried fish, a sweet beef jerky, a sour-sweet pickled vegetable, and even a spicy cabbage that punished my mouth and steamed my eyes until tears poured out. Snacks, you would call them here.

And when even these different foods did not seem enough, I asked Hulan what she had brought to eat, if she had anything crisp and salty. That's when Hulan told me I was carrying a baby.

"I know this," she said, as if she had sent a hundred babies into this world. "It's a sure sign when something inside you is hungering for all the tastes of life. Probably a boy, judging by the demands of your appetite."

When she told me this, I did not believe her. I was only nineteen, still growing myself. And Hulan was even younger than I was, so what did she know? I jumped up and put my hands over my hips, pressed them against my dress to see my stomach. Nothing, no baby's head pushing to come through my belly button. Yet I could feel something, so hungry for life it might devour me.

And then I thought, No, this is only my own unhappiness, always wanting something more, never happy with the life given me. Old Aunt had told me once that my mother had been this same way before she died: "Too strong inside here," and she had pointed to her stomach. "Never content, always looking for a pear when she already had ten plums to choose from."

"It is only a sour stomach," I said to Hulan. "All this waiting for something bad to happen."

"I'm telling you, it is a baby," said Hulan.

I shook my head.

"A baby," she said, nodding.

"Ai, you think I do not know my own body!"

"Tell me, then," she said. "When was your last bleeding?"

My face instantly became hot! She said that word aloud, the same as if talking about a cough, a headache, a bit of dust in the eye.

"What does this have to do with a baby!" I said, and Hulan folded her bottom lip into her mouth, trying not to laugh.

"Your mother, what did she tell you?" she asked.

And I was struggling to remember what Old Aunt had told me that morning I saw my first blood.

I had woken up, felt the stickiness, then pushed up my gown and looked at my legs. "Somebody chopped me off!" I murmured to Peanut, thinking this was a dream.

And Peanut saw the same blood and screamed. She leapt out of our bed and ran into the courtyard. "Hurry!" she cried. "Weiwei's been killed, same as her mother. She's already dead! Help me, help me!"

Old Aunt came running into the room, then New Aunt, two servants, my boy cousins, and after them the cook's helper, waving a cleaver in his hand. Old Aunt stepped close, took one look at me, but did not look concerned. She told everyone to leave, waving them out.

"Stop this crying," Old Aunt scolded when we were alone. New Aunt came back into the room with Peanut, who stared at me with big eyes.

"See, she's not dead," New Aunt said. She handed me some cloths.

"Listen carefully, both of you," said Old Aunt. "The bleeding is a sign. When a girl starts having unclean thoughts, her body must purge itself. That is why so much blood is coming out. Later, if a girl marries into the proper family chosen for her, if she becomes a good wife and loves her husband, this will stop." That's exactly what Old Aunt told me. And just as she predicted, once I became a good wife, the bleeding stopped.

"Pah!" Hulan said when I told her this, and then she spit on the ground. "Worthless words."

The rain kept pouring down around the pavilion. And that afternoon Hulan told me strange things that I did not believe. Why should I. She was the one who believed the most ridiculous ideas. She said that a woman-body built its own nest once a month. Impossible! She said that a baby came out from the same place a man-thing went in, not through the opening of the stomach. Nonsense talk!

And then she told me how she knew this. She said she had once helped a girl give birth to a baby. "I am telling you the truth," Hulan said. "I saw where the baby came out. Last year I saw this."

The girl, she said, had fallen in love with one of the pilots in Loyang, near the village where Hulan and her family lived.

"This poor girl was only looking for a chance to change her luck," said Hulan. "Lots of girls did that, hoping to catch a husband who would take them away. She was like every girl in that village, not very pretty, destined to marry an old farmer or the one-eyed pot-mender down the road, a life guaranteed with hard work, no hope for any kind of happiness. So when this girl met a pilot, of course she gave him her own body—for a chance, even a small chance, something to hold onto."

Hulan could tell I did not believe her. "Hard for you to imagine, I know," she said. "Your situation is so different. You always knew you would marry someone good, no worries like that." She said this as if she were accusing me. And that made me think, Maybe she did the same as that girl, gave her body to Jiaguo for a chance. Lucky for her, that chance turned into a husband.

"When the girl was about to have her baby," Hulan continued, "she asked me to walk with her to the pilot's house. She was hurting so much we had to stop often along the way. And then we arrived at the housing quarters. The pilot looked very angry to see her. He yelled at all the other men and told them to leave. I stood outside, but I heard everything.

"She begged the pilot to marry her. He would not. She promised his baby would be a son. He said he did not care. She said he could take her as a concubine, marry a real wife later. He refused again. Then she cried and became angry—had no shame left to hide. She shouted and told him she had no chances left in life. She had used them all up on him. She said she could never marry now. Everyone in the village knew she was bad merchandise. Her family would turn her out. And her baby would never have any chances in life, a future with no future.

"And then she became like a madwoman, screaming and wailing. I ran inside the house. She was hugging herself, cursing him. 'You might as well kill us both now. Better than letting us slowly starve. But after we die, we'll see you soon enough. We'll both pull you down from the sky!'

"That pilot got so angry hearing her death-curse. He slapped her hard, and she fell, hit her stomach against the arm of a chair, and rolled to the floor. That slap did not kill her. The arm of the chair did not kill her. But while she lay on the floor, her baby started to come. She screamed and groaned, tried to crawl backward like a crab. She was crying to the baby, 'Don't come out! No reason to come out!'

"The pilot and I ran to her. I pulled back her skirt and saw the top of the baby's head. And then the whole head popped out, with a rope wrapped around its neck. It looked as if it were covered with rice dust. The face was blue, the eyes squeezed shut. I tried to pull the baby out, to pull off the rope. I tried so hard. But the girl was moving too much. 'Lie still!' the pilot shouted to her. And she grabbed his hair, would not let go.

"Now all three of us were shouting and screaming, sharing so much misery. That baby was pulling her insides out. I was pulling that baby out. She was pulling the pilot's hair out. And after it seemed none of us could endure this any longer, she fell back and began to twitch. She rolled back and forth. Her whole body shook. She took a deep breath, sucking deep as if she could not drink enough of the air. She let her breath go. She breathed deeply once again, and then—nothing, no breath came out. How bad! Before one life could begin, the other ended. And that baby with his blue head sticking out of her body turned darker and then died."

Hulan stopped talking. She was squeezing the hem of her dress, biting her lips. I thought her story was over.

"Very sad," I said. "You're right, we are lucky."

But Hulan was not finished. She began to cry. "Boy or girl, I don't know which it was," she said. "My mother would not cut her open to find out. She refused to send her daughter to the next world with her womb cut open. She would not send her firstborn grandchild without a head. So that's how my parents buried her, with the baby half in, half out."

Hulan looked at my face. "That's right," she said, still crying. "My sister. And that pilot was Jiaguo, so scared of my sister's curse that he married me."

I watched her, not able to say anything. Finally, Hulan spoke again, this time more calmly. "I knew he was marrying me only to ease his fear, so she wouldn't come back and pull his plane down. But I married him anyway, thinking I could get some revenge for my sister. Of course, my parents were angry beyond belief. I kept telling them I was marrying him only to make him miserable every last day of his life, to always remind him of my sister and the tragedy he had caused.

"But how did I know Jiaguo would turn out to be a good man, such a good man? You know this, you see his character. He was so sorry, so sad. And he was kind to me, bought me nice clothes, corrected my manners, never laughing at me. How did I know he would be so kind?"

Hulan looked out at the rain still coming down. "Sometimes I'm still angry at him," she said quietly. "Sometimes I think about it another way. After all, he didn't kill her. She would have died anyway, giving birth, married or not. And sometimes I think my sister is angry at me, her baby hanging down from her limbs, cursing me for marrying the man who was supposed to be her husband."

So that's how Hulan and I started this telling and keeping of secrets. I told her the first, my ignorance about my own body. And she told me how she wished for revenge, and got happiness in return. And later that afternoon I told her about Peanut, how she was the one who should have married Wen Fu.

"So we both had our fate changed just in time! Lucky for us," cried Hulan. And I said nothing. I told her only half my secret, because I no longer knew whether I was lucky.

I waited until nighttime before I told Wen Fu about the baby. We were getting ready for bed. He reached for me.

"Now we have to be careful," I said. "I am going to have a baby."

He frowned. And just like me, he did not believe this news at first. So I told him about my appetite, my recent sickness, how these were all the signs of new life. Still he did not say anything.

Perhaps Wen Fu knew no words for the feeling he had. In any case, he did not show me what he was thinking. Maybe most men would have walked around like roosters, crowing to everyone. But Wen Fu only said, "It's true, eh?" and then he began to undress.

Suddenly he leaned forward and embraced me, pressed his mouth to my forehead, breathed in my ear. At that moment I thought he was telling me he really was happy, pleased about the baby. At that moment I truly felt I had finally pleased him, and I was content to be the nest of his future children.

But that feeling lasted only one more moment. Wen Fu was touching the back of my leg, pulling up my dress. How can he be thinking this? I protested softly, but this only made him hurry more. He was trying to part my legs.

I said, "I have a baby growing inside me now. We can't do this anymore."

Of course, I was ignorant saying this. But he had no understanding or sympathy for me. He only laughed and called me a silly country girl.

"I'm only making sure it comes out a boy," he said. And then he pushed me down on the bed and fell on top of me.

"Stop!" I said. And then I said it louder and louder. "Stop!" Stop!" Wen Fu stopped and frowned at me. I had never shouted at my husband that way. Maybe it was because of the baby inside me. Maybe that's what made me want to protect myself. But he kept looking at me with such a terrible eye that I finally said to him, "Sorry." And without another word, he finished what I had begged him to stop.

The next day, I confided in Hulan once again. I thought she would listen with a sisterly ear. So I told her that my husband had "unnatural desires," an "overabundance of maleness." He was this way every night, even after I told him I was carrying a baby. And I was worried, so unhappy—that was my pitiful excuse for burdening her again with my problems.

Hulan looked at me without any expression. Maybe she was shocked by my frank words. Finally she said, "Hnh! This is not a problem. You should be glad. That's how you got your baby, isn't it?" Her voice sounded mocking. "This kind of desire doesn't hurt a baby. It is only a small inconvenience to you. Why shouldn't you do this for your husband? You should be grateful he still wants you! And when he does lose interest in you, he'll just go somewhere else. And then you'll know what it truly means to be unhappy with a husband."

Now it was my turn to look shocked. I thought she would give me her sympathy. She gave me a scolding instead. And she wouldn't stop. "Why do you think something good is bad?" she said. "Eh, if you think a dish won't be cooked right, then of course, when you taste it, it won't be right."

You never saw this side in Auntie Helen? Now you know, she can be mean too! She saves it up only for me, I don't know why. Or maybe I'm the only one she can show this side to.

You know what I think? I think she does this when something else is bothering her and she can't say. She tries to hide this by becoming bossy. That day, when she said this to me, I was very hurt of course. She made me feel so small that I became nothing. And I did not find out until several years later why she really said that. I did not know she was holding a secret inside, and only letting her anger come out. But I will tell you about that later.

It was in that little pavilion, about a week later, that I knew for sure that the war had begun.

Hulan had fallen asleep after lunch. A rainstorm started and I decided to go to the pavilion alone to write Peanut a letter. I was writing about pleasant things: the interesting sights I had seen, the boats on the lake, the temples I had visited. I said maybe we would come home soon, perhaps in a few months. I said I hoped we were back in Shanghai by the new year, when I hoped to show everyone a little son.

And then I saw Hulan running toward the pavilion, her wet clothes pressed against her plump body in an immodest way.

"They're flying away! Already leaving!" she shouted even before she reached me. Chennault was at the air force base, other Chinese leaders from the north and south had come. All the pilots were already gathered. And everyone was saying the same thing: No more time to get ready. It's already time to go.

Soon Hulan and I were back at the monastery, still in our wet clothes, packing for our husbands. I carefully put Wen Fu's clean shirts and pants, his socks, and a good new blanket into a trunk.

My hands were shaking. My heart was pounding. China at war. Wen Fu could die. I might not see him again. I wondered whether I really did love Wen Fu and only now realized it.

A truck began sounding its horn, telling us it was time to leave for the air force base. I ran to Hulan's room to tell her. And I saw she was not ready. She was running her fingers through a bureau drawer, then her hair. She was crying, confused, and saying to herself: "What picture of me as a pretty wife? What good-luck charm? That book he always forgets, where is it?"

At the airport, nobody would tell us where our husbands were going. And yet we could see above the rain: the blue sky, the white clouds. We were excited, proud. And then someone led us into a damp little room with a small cracked window that made everything outside look small and dangerous. The rain poured down on a narrow runway. Pilots were standing underneath the airplane wings. Someone was pointing to the blade of a propeller. Another man ran by with a box of tools. Jiaguo was going from plane to plane, holding out a large piece of paper, perhaps a map, that flapped with a wind that now seemed to rise up from the ground.

And then we saw the blades were spinning, the engines roaring louder. And I fought hard not to look at the others, not to say anything, not to let any wrong words leap out of my throat that would bring everyone bad luck. I think everyone was the same way, quiet and still, now uncertain.

But as the planes moved away from us slowly, Hulan began to wave. Rain, steam, and smoke were swirling all around, so the planes looked as if they were moving forward in an uneasy dream. Hulan waved harder and harder, tears streaming. The planes raced down the runway. And then she was waving furiously, crazily, like a wounded bird, as if this effort and all her wishes and hopes could lift them up safely, one after the other, and send them to victory.

Of course, the next morning we heard what really happened.

# 11

# FOUR SPLITS, FIVE CRACKS

Do you remember the stuck-up girl, the one Hulan and I took baths with? She was the one who told us what happened in Shanghai, where the air force flew to save all of China.

She had come into the dining hall, where we were sitting in front of a radio. We had already heard our husbands were alive, and now we were listening to the victory report, our ears open, ready to catch every word of this good news.

"What you are listening to," she had said in a bitter voice, "is just empty noise." We turned to look at her. We saw her eyes, red as a demon's.

And then she told us. The man who always saved a chair by the ceiling fan for my husband, he died. The young one that my husband shouted at for playing tricks on him, he died too. And the stuck-up girl's husband, he was also killed.

"You think you are lucky because your husbands are alive," she said. "You are not."

And then she told us how the planes had flown late at night, toward the Shanghai harbor, swollen with Japanese boats. They were hoping to surprise them. But before they arrived, Japanese planes dropped from the darker sky above—already knew our planes were coming. And it was our pilots who had the surprise, became confused, then hurried to drop their bombs. Such a big hurry! Such a small distance from the sky to the ground. So the bombs fell on Shanghai that night, on the roofs of houses and stores, on streetcars, on hundreds of people, all Chinese. And the Japanese navy—their boats still floated on the water.

"Your husbands are not heroes. And all those people, those pilots, my husband—died for worse than nothing," the girl said, and then left the room. We were all quiet.

Hulan broke the silence. "How does she know what happened, what did not happen?" she said in an angry voice. And then she said she was still happy, because Jiaguo was alive. At least that was true, she said.

Can you imagine? In front of all of us she let her happiness show, didn't matter. How could she reveal such a selfish thought?

But I did not scold Hulan for her bad manners. I tried to correct her in a big-sister way: "If what that girl said is true, we should be thinking about this tragedy. We should be serious and not let our own happiness take over."

Hulan quickly took that happy look off her face. Her mouth dropped open to let this thought come in and nourish her brain. I was thinking, Good, even though she is uneducated, she is quick to learn something new.

But then her eyebrows drew close, her face became dark as clouds. "This kind of thinking—I don't understand," she said.

So I explained again: "We must have concern for the whole situation, not just our own husbands. Something worse could still be coming."

"*Ai-ya! Daomei!*" she cried, and covered her mouth. "How can you use these kinds of bad-luck words to poison everyone's future?"

"They are not bad-luck words," I insisted. "I am only saying we must be practical. This is wartime. We must feel with our hearts, but also think with our minds—clearly all the time. If we pretend the dangers are not there, how can we avoid them?"

But Hulan was no longer listening to me. She was crying and shouting. "I've never heard such poisonous words! What use is it to think this way, to use bad thoughts to attract only bad things?"

On and on she went, like a crazy woman. Now that I remember it, that was when our friendship took on four splits and five cracks. Hulan did it, broke harmony between us. I tell you, that day Hulan showed me her true character. She was not the soft melonhead she made everyone believe she was. That girl could throw out sharp words, slicing fast as any knife.

"You are saying tragedy will come to us too. You are saying a husband can still die," she shouted. "Why can't you be happy, holding onto what you have now?"

Can you imagine? She was accusing me in front of everyone! Throwing out a question that was looking only for a wrong answer. Making it seem as if I were the one who had said something bad.

"I did not say this," I answered right away.

"You are always wishing for the worst."

Again these lies! "No such meaning," I said. "Practical is not the same as bad-luck thinking."

"If there are five ways to see something," she said—and here she fanned out the fingers on one hand, then pulled up her thumb as if it were a rotten turnip—"you always pick the worst."

"No such thing. I am saying our own happiness is not enough during a war. It is nothing. It cannot stop the war." I was so angry I could no longer understand what I was saying.

"Chiang Kai-shek says he can stop the war," she was shouting. "You think your thoughts are stronger than Chiang Kai-shek's?"

Hulan and the other two women were staring at me. Not one of those women stepped forward to stop our fight. They did not say, "Sisters, sisters, you are both right. You only misunderstand each other." And I could see Hulan's strong words had already damaged their thinking, left big holes where understanding could drain out. No wonder they could not see how ridiculous Hulan's arguments were.

So I said, *"Suanle!"*—Forget this! And I left them to go to my room.

Remembering this, I still get mad. And that's because she has not changed. You can see this. She twists things around to her way of thinking. If something is bad, she makes it sound good. If something is good, she makes it sound bad. She contradicts everything I say. She makes me seem like the one who is always wrong. And then I have to argue with myself to know what is really true.

Anyway, after that fight, I was so mad I could only sit on my bed, thinking about Hulan's mocking words. I told myself she was the one who always said foolish things. She was the one people laughed at behind her back. And when I no longer wanted to hear her words in my head, I searched for something to do. I opened a drawer and took out some cloth given to me by New Aunt, a bolt of cotton made by one of our family's factories.

It was a pale green fabric covered with small gold circles, very light cotton, suitable for a summer dress. I had already thought up a pattern in my mind, fashioned it from my memory, a dress I had seen in Shanghai, worn by a carefree girl.

So with this picture in my head, I began to cut my cloth. I imagined myself as this girl floating by in a green dress, all her friends admiring her, whispering to themselves that her clothes were as fine as her manners. But then I saw Hulan criticizing the dress, saying in her too loud voice, "Too fancy to wear after a husband has just died."

Right away I made a mistake—cut a sleeve hole too big—that's how mad I still was. Look what she did! Affected my concentration. Worse!—twisted my thinking and put a very bad thought into my head.

Such a bad thought, a thought I never could have imagined on my own, never. But now it had jumped out and I was chasing it. I was imagining a time, not too far away, when Hulan would say to me, "Sorry, your husband was killed. Bad fate that he fell from the sky."

"Oh, no," I said to myself. "Goddess of Mercy, never let him die."

But the more I tried to push this thought out of my mind, the more it fought to stay. "He's dead," Hulan would say. She would probably smile when she told me this. And I would be angry and shouting like the stuck-up girl who had just lost her husband.

And then I thought: Maybe I should cry and look sad instead, lamenting about my fatherless child. Yes, that was more proper.

The next moment, my thoughts ran in another direction: Would I have to return to the island and live with Old Aunt and New Aunt? Perhaps not, not if I married someone new. And then I decided, Next time I will choose my own husband.

I stopped sewing. What was I thinking? That's when I realized that I truly was wishing Wen Fu might die. I wasn't thinking this because I hated him. I didn't. That was later, when he became much worse.

But that night, in my room, in my mind, I was arguing with Hulan, with myself: Sometimes a girl makes a mistake. Sometimes a mistake can be changed. A war could change it, and it would be nobody's fault, one unlucky thing exchanged for another. This could still happen.

And so I finished making that dress. I cut the loose threads. I drew the dress over my head. But by then, my belly and breasts had already begun to swell from the baby. I put only one arm in before I realized: I was stuck.

Oh, you think this was funny? Stuck in my dress, stuck in my marriage, stuck with Hulan as my friend. Sometimes I wonder why she's still my friend, how it is that we can do a business together.

Maybe it's because we fought so much in those early days. Maybe it's because we had no one else to turn to. So we always had to find reasons to be friends. Maybe those reasons are still there.

In any case, this is what happened after that big argument.

A few days later, the air force told us they would soon send us to Yangchow, where we would be reunited with our husbands.

We heard this news at breakfast and we were suspicious. We were thinking the bombs would soon start falling where we were sitting.

"A big danger must be coming here," I said. "That's why they are sending us away."

One of the other women, Lijun, said, "Then we should leave right away. Why must we delay two more days?"

And the other woman, Meili, said, "Why Yangchow? Bombs can fall there too."

"It must be that Yangchow is not a good place," I said, thinking aloud, "a city the Japanese would never want, so it will always be safe." You see how I was thinking in a logical way? I was not saying I did not like Yangchow. How could I? I had never seen it.

Right away Hulan contradicted me. "I heard Yangchow is very pretty, lots to see," she said, "famous for beautiful women and good-tasting noodles."

I already knew I would not see such women. I would not taste such noodles. "I am not saying it is not a pretty city," I explained carefully, "I am only saying it is not a good city for the Japanese. What Japanese want and what Chinese want are not the same thing."

So we left for Yangchow at the end of summer, only a few weeks after the war began. And we went by boat, because by then many roads and railways were already blocked. And when we arrived I saw that city was just as I had imagined it, a place the Japanese would never want.

Our new home was only one half-day northwest of Shanghai, the best city in the world, very modern. Yet Yangchow was completely different—an old-style place with no tall buildings, only one story for houses, maybe two stories only for more important buildings. Who knows why Du Fu and the old poets wrote about this place? To me, the city seemed to be made entirely out of dirt and mud. Under my two feet, it was dirt streets, dirt courtyards, dirt floors. Above, it was mud-brick walls, mud-tile roofs.

The air force found us a place just like that, mud and dirt, divided into four living quarters, two rooms each, and a shared kitchen with four old-fashioned coal stoves. When we first saw this, we were all shocked.

"This is wartime," I finally said to the others. "We all have to make sacrifices." Lijun and Meili immediately nodded and agreed. Hulan turned her face.

And then she began inspecting everything, criticizing what she saw. She poked her finger into a crumbling part of the wall. "Ai!" She pointed to another wall, where bugs were marching through a crack of sunlight. "Ai!" She stamped her feet on the floor: "Wah! Look how the dust rises up from the floor and chases my footsteps."

I was looking. We were all looking. I wanted to shout, "You see how she is. She's the complaining one, not I." But I saw I did not have to say one word. Meili, Lijun, they could see for themselves how Hulan was.

That afternoon a cook girl and a manservant also arrived. The air force provided only one of each, so we had to share. The cook was a local girl, very young, with a big, happy face. Her job was to keep the coal stoves burning at the right times throughout the day, to wash and chop the vegetables, to kill the chickens and gut the fish, to clean up everything before it began to stink.

The manservant belonged to the air force, a middle-aged man we called the *chin wubing*, which is the common word for a common soldier, the kind who fights only with broomsticks, only against flies. He was a small, thin man who looked as if his arms and legs would break if he carried anything too heavy. He was also a little crazy. When he worked, he often talked to himself, imagining himself to be a high-ranking officer who had been given bad orders: "Beat this bed cover! Wash this spot out!"

That's how I found out Hulan had ordered the *chin wubing* to mix six egg whites into a bucket of mud.

"Plucked this strange recipe from the air," I heard him say to himself. "That's what I think. Paint this sauce on the floor, she tells me. A wind is blowing through her brain! Thinks she is going to eat her floor. Thinks it looks like a big delicious pancake. Ha!"

I told Lijun and Meili what the *chin wubing* had said. I had to. What if Hulan was so crazy she decided to burn the house down? The other women also had strange facts to report over the next few days. Hulan had ordered the *chin wubing* to spill this egg soup on her floor every day for three days. And when the soup had cooked dry, she told him to spill some more. Worse, she made him cook a sticky porridge of rice and mud.

"Threw it on her wall. Said it was cooked just right," he said. And we all clucked our tongues. Poor Hulan.

But a few days later, the *chin wubing* said nothing. He did his chores quietly, complaining only about a shopkeeper who had cheated him, had sold him a roast duck so bloated with air the moment he went to cut its skin, the duck burst and shrank to half its size.

"Do not worry about the duck," I said. "This is not your fault." And because I could no longer keep my curiosity inside, I said, "Better than drinking mud soup, hanh?"

The *chin wubing* frowned at me. "Sorry, *tai-tai*," he said carefully. "I am not hearing well today."

I nodded toward Hulan's side of the house. "The mud soup she made," I said. "Probably it's not very good-tasting, hanh?"

"I'm sorry, *tai-tai*," he said again. "Today my ears are not opening the way to my brain."

So I had to find an excuse to visit Hulan, to see for myself how she had become crazy. I plucked my best embroidery needle from my basket.

"Is this your needle?" I said when she came to her door. "I found it on my floor, and now I am not sure if it is mine." And as Hulan stared at that needle, I saw what she had done with her egg mixture, her mud soup. Her floors had baked shiny-hard like porcelain, so no dust rose up. And her walls that once had been crumbly like ours—they were smooth and clean with new mud, not one insect marching across.

As I stared at this change, Hulan announced, "You're right. This is my needle. I've been looking for this same one for many days."

Later that afternoon, Hulan helped me fix my floors, my walls. I let her patch things between us that way: fix one thing so you can fix another. She knew I would let her do this. Because she took that needle, and we both knew it was mine.

I don't know why I am talking so much about Helen. This is not a story about her, although she is the reason why I have to tell you my story. If she told you this story, she might say I did not try hard enough to have a good marriage. Let me tell you, I tried.

Like that time in Yangchow. A week or two after we arrived, our husbands returned home, and I cooked Wen Fu a big celebration dinner. And not dinner just for him but for his pilot friends too, five or six men from the second and third class.

Those men liked Wen Fu for his generosity, the way he said, "Come to my place! Eat all you want!" He invited them over, and also Jiaguo. So of course, I invited Hulan, also Lijun and Meili, as well as their husbands. All together, I made dinner for fourteen people. Hulan offered to help me shop and cook. And with so much to do, I protested only a little, before agreeing I could use her extra hands.

It was my dowry money that bought all that food, the money my father gave me on my wedding day. No, Wen Fu's family had not taken that away from me, not yet. My father was smart. He deposited the money in a Shanghai bank under my name, four thousand yuan, Chinese dollars. And I had pulled out two hundred after my wedding. In Yangchow I still had maybe one hundred left.

Wen Fu earned seventy Chinese dollars a month. That was a

good salary, maybe twice as much as what a schoolteacher could earn. But Wen Fu used his money only for foolish things—to buy whiskey, to play mah jong, to bet that the weather would change when he said it would.

So I used my dowry money to buy the furniture we needed as we moved from place to place. I didn't have to. I used my money to buy food better than what the air force provided. I didn't have to. And for dinner that night I bought good pork, fresh clover for dumplings, many catties of sweet wine, all very expensive during wartime, over fifty yuan.

I didn't mind spending this money. As I bought this good food, I was thinking about those men, all the pilots, also Wen Fu. If their luck blew down, those men might not return for the next meal. And with that sad thought, my hand would hurry and reach for a thicker piece of pork, one with lots of good, rich fat.

And then I decided also to include a few dishes with names that sounded lucky. These were dishes I remembered Old Aunt had cooked during the New Year—sun-dried oysters for wealth; a fast-cooked shrimp for laughter and happiness; *fatsai*, the black-hair fungus that soaks up good fortune; and plenty of jellyfish, because the crunchy skin always made a lively sound to my ears.

Hulan saw me choose these things. Her mouth was watering as I picked out my ingredients. I don't think she had ever eaten food so fine.

Back home, I told the cook girl to boil enough pots of water and to chop enough pork and vegetables to make a thousand dumplings, both steamed and boiled, with plenty of fresh ginger, good soy sauce, and sweet vinegar for dipping. Hulan helped me knead the flour and roll out the dough into small circles.

I admit I was at first impressed by her cooking skills. She worked fast, pushing hard against her rolling stick. She was able to roll out three skins for every two that I made. And she always grabbed just the right amount of meat filling to dab in the middle of the skin, never having to add a little more or take a little off. With one pinch, she closed the dumpling off.

And I also admit I enjoyed Hulan's company during that after-noon. We were both happy. The pilots had returned. Everyone was excited. We all had smiles to give out. So on that day, Hulan and I did not criticize each other. We did not complain about others.

We did not have to be careful to make only polite conversation. All our words naturally spilled out from our good thoughts.

I told Hulan, "Look how fast you work. With your hands, we could make ten thousand dumplings if we wanted, no problem." Of course, I found out later that she was good at only those kinds of laborious cooking tasks: kneading, rolling, stuffing, pinching. As to her sense of taste and smell, I can only say my opinion may not be the same as others'.

Although maybe you can tell me. Be honest. Who is the better cook? You see! I am not boasting. It's true. I know how much soy sauce to put on a meat dish, so that a salty taste does not become a salty flavor. I know never to add more than a pinch of sugar; anything more and you may as well be eating Cantonese food. I know how to make each dish delicate-tasting, yet the flavor is clearly distinguished from other dishes—not everything bland or every-thing hot as the same roaring fire.

And others would tell you the same thing, if they were here today. The pilots, for instance, even Hulan's husband, they all praised my cooking that night, told Wen Fu how lucky he was. They said it was impossible that a man could have both a beautiful wife and a talented cook—yet their eyes and tongue told them differently. I watched them eat, encouraged them to eat more, teased that I would be in trouble with my husband if more than ten dumplings were left over. At the end of the meal—just four left! What a good dinner that was.

I cooked many other dinners like that. Whenever Wen Fu and the pilots returned home after many days' absence, they always wanted to eat my dumplings first thing—steamed, water-cooked, or fried—they always thought they were delicious.

In those days in China, it didn't matter what part of the country you came from. Everyone knew how to eat and play together. You found any kind of excuse to live life as full as your stomach could hold. And in those days, I was still trying to please Wen Fu, to act like a good wife, also trying hard to find my own happiness. I was always ready to cook a good meal, even though the men usually returned home without telling me ahead of time—and sometimes, with fewer pilots.

Oh, that was always very sad. Jiaguo was the one who had to gather the belongings of any pilot who had died. He would wrap them carefully in a soft cloth, then write a long note, explaining how this son or that husband had died a true hero's death. I would see the wrapped belongings sitting on Hulan's sewing table, waiting to be sent out. And I always wondered whose happy hands would open a package, thinking it was a gift, whose sad eyes would cry to see what was inside.

So our dinners became smaller each time. And I may have imagined this, but it seemed to me, when one pilot died, another took over his appetite. Those pilots ate as though they would never taste such good food again.

I remember one night each man ate thirty dumplings, loosened his belt and sighed, then ate thirty more. I was running back and forth, carrying big platters to them, also to Hulan, who knew how to eat plenty. And after more talking and laughing, the men loosened their belts once again, ate more and more—until one man finally said in a funny voice, "To pay any more respects to the cook, I have to drop my pants!"

The man who made that joke was a tall, thin man named Gan. He always laughed, but in a quiet way. And what he said was coarse, but I was not angry, not even embarrassed. He made good jokes, never pushing anyone else down to make somebody laugh. With his jokes, he was the foolish-looking one, the one we laughed at.

In fact, he reminded me of an American movie star. Not a loud, big hero kind like John Wayne. More like Danny Kaye, a quiet man everyone liked, someone who made people laugh without showing off.

Gan was that same way. When he smiled his mouth grew wider than most people's and one of his dogteeth stuck out. He walked in an awkward manner, like a boy who had grown too tall too fast. So when he rushed over to help me move a chair or carry a pot, he would stumble and fall before he had taken three steps forward. That's how he was—without even trying, he made people feel better about themselves.

When he was not laughing or talking with the others, he acted shy with me. I often felt him watching me, trying to think of what to say. And once, after thinking a long time, he told me with a quiet, sincere voice, "This dish—even my mother could not make it better."

I scolded him. "You can never say such things about your own mother!" His face turned red. "Sister," he said, "excuse my bad manners." Then he ate two more dumplings and said in the same quiet voice, "Better than my own mother's."

I remember when he said that, Wen Fu laughed out loud and said, "Is that why you are as skinny as a bamboo reed?" I could not tell whether this was an insult to his mother or to me. I thought to myself, Why couldn't my husband be more like Gan? And that put another thought in my mind: I could have married a good man. They were not all like Wen Fu. Why didn't I know I had a choice?

I saw that the other pilots were kind men, all nice. They treated me well. They never mentioned out loud that I was carrying a baby, but they knew. They rushed to help me carry my groceries when they saw my arms were full. One man, who had the use of an air force truck, offered to drive me anyplace I needed to go. And Gan, the shy man who liked my dumplings so much, played chicken-feather ball with me, while Wen Fu and the others played cards or mah jong in the evening.

I remember those nights. We played using only the moonlight and the glow from the nearby window, batting the feather ball back and forth over the net, laughing as we tried to hit each other. When I missed, Gan would insist on picking up the feather ball, so I would not give my full stomach "indigestion." Sometimes, when Wen Fu was out of town, Gan would invite me to eat with him, just a bowl of noodles. Maybe we would go to some cheap place for wonton, nothing too special. And then he would walk me home, always acting just like a proper family friend or a brother, apologizing if he accidentally bumped my elbow.

One time Hulan saw us talking at the kitchen table. And after Gan went home, she teased me: "Oyo! Be careful."

"What is your meaning?" I said.

"No meaning," said Hulan. "I am telling you to be careful now so there is no meaning later."

"What nonsense," I said, and she laughed.

It is so strange, remembering this now. I have not thought about Gan for over fifty years. So finding this memory is like accidentally discovering a hidden piece of my heart again, the happiness I could not show anyone, the sorrow I later could not tell anyone. How could I tell Hulan? I was the one who said we should not be carried away by happiness during the war. I said that before I knew what happiness could be.

So maybe I can confess this to you now. Gan had a special meaning to me. We did not know each other for very long. Yet I knew his heart better than my own husband's. And that made me feel less lonely.

He once told me how much he enjoyed walking with me in the evening. And before I could ask why, he answered me. He said he was afraid of being alone at night. And again, before I could ask him to explain, he explained: "You know how it is, how you can see things at night that you cannot see in the day." I nodded and told him I had always felt this way too.

And then he told me more about his nighttime fright. "I have never told this story to anyone else," he began, "what happened when I was a young boy, the last time it was a Tiger year. That's when I saw a ghost shining in the dark."

And I started to tell Gan how I had seen the same thing, many times as a child. A ghost that turned out to be the moon against a window. Or a ghost who was really Old Aunt getting up at night to cure her indigestion. Or a ghost that was really a dead plant stuck against the greenhouse window.

Gan said, "I've seen ghosts like that too, just bad imagination. But this ghost was different. This ghost said he would come back and get me before I reached the next Tiger year—before I reached the age of twenty-four."

"So much nonsense comes from dreams," I said. But Gan kept talking as if he were still in that bad dream.

" 'Don't worry too much,' the ghost said. 'Your death will be painless, it won't hurt. But when you see my ghost face calling to you in the dark, you must come with me and not argue, not even one word.' Of course, I didn't believe him. I shouted to him, 'You are only a bad dream. Go away!' "

"Then you woke up," I said, trying to calm him, or perhaps myself. "You were still frightened, but you never forgot that memory."

"Much worse," said Gan, his voice now very dry. "I woke up, this is true. I got up to convince myself I was no longer asleep. And when I stood at the door, I saw the ghost was still there. He said, 'You don't believe this is your fate? I have proof that it will be.' And the ghost named nine bad fates that would happen to me before my life was through. Nine, the number of completion. When the ghost left, I was still standing at the door.''

"Ai, Gan, this is a terrible story!" I said.

"For these past eleven years, I have tried to forget that dream. But now eight of those fates have already happened, come true, exactly as the ghost described them. Now I think the ninth is coming. In four months, the new Tiger year comes." He laughed nervously. "So much pain to wait for a painless death."

After Gan told me this story, he was trembling hard, as if it were winter-cold outside, and not the wet warmth of autumn. I could see he believed the story. Even I was scared. I was too frightened even to ask him, What were the eight fates that have already happened? I could only laugh and say, "What a bad dream you had in your little-boy days!"

At the time I did not know why I said that. That was not the feeling I had inside me. Just the opposite. Inside, I wanted to hold poor Gan against my heart and cry, My boy, my beautiful little boy! Are you sure about the eight bad fates? What were they? What is the ninth? Hurry, tell me!

But now that I remember my feelings, I know why I did not say this to Gan. I was afraid, not because of the ghost, but for another reason. I was a married woman, yet I had never felt love from a man, or for a man. And that night I almost did. I felt the danger, that this was how you love someone, one person letting out fears, the other drawing closer to soothe the pain. And then more would pour out, everything that has been hidden, more and more—sorrow, shame, loneliness, all the old aches, so much released until you overflowed with joy to be rid of it, until it was too late to stop this new joy from taking over your heart.

But I stopped myself. I kept myself hidden. I only laughed at Gan and made fun of his ghost dream to comfort him, to comfort myself. And perhaps I also did not pay more attention to his dream because we all felt something bad was coming. We just didn't talk about it openly the way Gan did.

If a pilot joked, "This is the last time I lose all my wages playing cards with you," the others would shout, "Wah! Don't say 'last time,' what bad luck! Now you have to keep playing to cancel out the meaning."

Those pilots knew their airplanes were not fast enough before they even left the ground. They knew they did not have enough training, enough clever tricks to avoid Japanese fighter planes, which were newer and faster. They used to stand around in a big circle before they had to fly off, shouting slogans as they spit onto a rock for a target. That's how they laughed about becoming heroes. That's how we knew they were brave. That's how we knew they were scared. How could they be true heroes when they had no choice? How could they not be when they knew they had no chance?

Two months later, half the pilots at that dinner were dead. The way we heard it, they all died as heroes, all of them shot and killed inside their fighter planes. But the way those planes fell from the sky—it was awful! You could not even find a body to bury. You didn't have to be religious to feel bad about that.

One pilot I knew, his airplane flew into the Henan city gate, ran right into an opening, and was stuck-crushed inside there. Meili's husband, his plane crashed on a high mountaintop. The pilot who used to drive me in a truck?—he burned up before his plane even hit the ground.

As for Wen Fu, he was not even wounded. Do you know why? He was a coward! Each time the fighting began, Wen Fu turned his plane around and flew the other way. "Oh," he would explain to Jiaguo, "I was chasing a Japanese fighter that ran off another way. You didn't see it. Too bad I didn't catch him." Hulan told me this, how Jiaguo was thinking he would have to court-martial my husband. You think she wouldn't find an opportunity to tell me this?

I learned this around the same time I found out Gan's plane had been shot down outside Nanking. They took him to a hospital, still alive. We all hurried to go see him, Wen Fu, Jiaguo, Hulan, the other pilots who had not yet died.

Oh, I saw! Gan's eyes were pointed to the ceiling, laughing and crying. "So, ghost, where are you?" he was shouting. "I am not refusing to die!"

"He's crazy," Wen Fu said. "His mind is already gone. Lucky for him, there's nothing left to feel the pain."

I remember the pain I felt. I couldn't say anything. I couldn't put my hand on Gan's forehead. But I wanted to cry and shout, He's not crazy! That ghost promised him: "Your death won't hurt. You just come when I call you at night."

And that ghost lied. Because Gan suffered hard, so hard, all his intestines fallen out. Two days, two nights, he had to live with so much pain before he could finally leave and chase after that ghost himself.

I grieved so much, and yet I could not show anything. My heart hurt the same way as when I lost my mother. Only, I was not aching for a love I once had. I was regretting I never took it.

So after Gan died, that's when I claimed his love. He became like a ghost lover. Whenever Wen Fu shouted at me, I would remember the last time Gan came to my house for dinner. He had watched me all evening, the way Wen Fu treated me. And when my husband went out of the room, Gan looked at me, then quietly said, "You see yourself only in a mirror. But I see you the way you can never see yourself, all the pure things, neither good nor bad."

I would recall this many times. When my husband had exhausted himself on top of me, after he had fallen asleep, I would get up quietly and look in the mirror. I would turn my face back and forth, trying to imagine Gan's eyes looking at me. I would cry to myself, "What did he see? What did he see?"

And sometimes when things were worse than that, when I wondered what I had done to deserve such a terrible life, I would remember our walks at night, the story Gan told me. And although I never knew what the eight bad fates were, I knew the ninth. I was the ninth.

# 12

# TAONAN MONEY

By the time winter came there were few planes left. So the only thing falling from the sky was rain. And then, one day, it grew so cold it snowed.

This was the week we moved from Yangchow to Nanking, which was only a few hours' ride by truck. And that day in Nanking was the first time I saw snow. It reminded me of little feathers, the ones that flew through the air when Gan and I used to play chicken-feather ball. That's how it felt to me.

In Nanking, we also had an air force servant, different from the one in Yangchow, not so crazy. And he was saying, "Don't worry, ladies. This won't last long. In Nanking, snow is like a high-level official—doesn't come too often, doesn't stay too long."

Hulan and I were watching from the first-floor window of a large house. The place had once been a fine-looking mansion, built for a foreign businessman, now used as temporary quarters for all kinds of people. It was two stories, with four pillars and tall windows running across the front. And all around the house were trees— the servant said they came from France. But the leaves had fallen off, so French or Chinese, you couldn't tell any difference. The house was in a good part of town, near the old West Wall, walking distance from Sorrowfree Lake. So it was not too far from the center, but also not too close.

But then if you looked at the inside of the house—that was a different matter. As you walked in, you could see right away: the sofas had been worn down by many people's bottoms, the rugs scraped thin by feet going in and out year after year. And in every room, the wallpaper was cracked and peeling. The kitchen had a leak coming from two corners. You could tell this house was like an orphan, no family to love it.

The same afternoon I first saw snow, I was showing the servant how to clean out the coal stove so it would not smoke so much the next time. At that moment, Wen Fu came home and said, "If you clean that, it is only for somebody else." And then he told us what the air force had announced. We would leave Nanking soon, maybe in two weeks, maybe less.

"We have not been here even one week," I started to say. Wen Fu was not smiling, and I knew his meaning: The Japanese were coming.

That day I went to the air force post office to send two telegrams to Shanghai, one to my bank instructing them to withdraw four hundred Chinese dollars and give it to Wen Fu's sister, the other to Wen Fu's sister telling her where to send the money. The telegraph operator girl helped me pick the right number of urgent words. At the end of the telegram to Wen Fu's sister, I added, "Hurry. We are soon *taonan*."

I added the word *taonan* myself to make my sister-in-law hurry, to take my request seriously. Perhaps I was exaggerating, maybe not. Anyway, I put it there because that was a word that made everyone jump.

This word, *taonan*? Oh, there is no American word I can think of that means the same thing. But in Chinese, we have lots of different words to describe all kinds of troubles. No, "refugee" is not the meaning, not exactly. Refugee is what you are after you have been *taonan* and are still alive. And if you are alive, you would never want to talk about what made you *taonan*.

You're lucky you have never had to experience this. It means terrible danger is coming, not just to you but to many people, so everyone is watching out only for himself. It is a fear that chases you, a sickness, exactly like a hot fever in your brain. So your only thoughts are, "Escape! Escape!"—nothing else, day and night. And the hair on your head stands straight up, because it's as though you can feel a knife pointed at your neck, and someone's hateful breath just two steps away. And if you hear a shout, or see someone's eyes grow big, that would be enough. The fever turns into a chill and runs down your back and into your legs, and you are running and stumbling, running and stumbling.

You are lucky you don't know what this means. But I will tell you what it's like, how it almost happened to me.

After I wrote my telegram, the operator girl said to me, "Do you really think we are soon *taonan*?"

I did not want to alarm her, so I said, "I only put that down because my sister-in-law is absentminded. This will make her hurry before she forgets."

The girl laughed and congratulated me for being so clever. I liked her very much. I didn't know her real Chinese name, but she was nicknamed Wan Betty, "Beautiful Betty," because she looked like that actress Bette Davis that everyone liked so much. She combed her black hair in the same style, her voice was husky, and her eyes were big—droopy down below, swollen on top—although I think she had some kind of thyroid or kidney disease that made her look this way.

She was a typical Nanking girl, who had caught a "lightning marriage"—met a pilot, then married him right away, that fast. The pilot was someone from Wen Fu's class, I didn't know him too well. He died maybe only two or three weeks after the marriage, but it was enough time for him to leave behind the start of a baby.

Four days later I went back to the post office. My sister-in-law—she was so bad—she sent the money immediately, two days later, not to me, but to Wen Fu! That's what Wan Betty said. Wen Fu had already come in to pick it up, and what could she do? His name was on the banknote.

"That was my money, money from my dowry!" I told Wan Betty. "And that was supposed to be our running-away money, money just in case we needed it to save our lives."

Betty offered me tea from her thermos. "Ai, this is terrible. This is always what happens to women, to wives. It's true. Me, I had no dowry, of course, not like you. Four hundred yuan, that's quite a lot of money."

"Four thousand all together," I corrected her, and her mouth

grew big. "And furniture too, heavy wood, many, many things—
but now it belongs to his family. They claimed it."

"Same thing happened to me," she said, shaking her head.
"When my husband died, the survivor money from the air force—
all of it went to his family! Nothing to me. So you see what I have
to do to earn food for myself and this child inside me." She tapped
the letters she was sorting. "Now the family is saying I should go
back to Nanchang, have the baby, give them their grandchild. After
that, they said, I can leave, do what I want. I ask you, why should
I go there and let them treat me so bad? Do they think I'm a duck—
laying eggs so they can eat them?"

I laughed. That's how Wan Betty was, always speaking honestly,
straight from her liver, the same bile in her words. And soon, I
found myself talking the same way.

"I'm going to ask him to give my money back," I said.

"That's right," she said. "Reason with him. The money is yours.
The money is for *taonan*."

"The money is mine, for *taonan*."

"No excuses."

"No excuses."

A lot of big words. I returned home to reason with Wen Fu. "We
need the money for *taonan*," I said. "You never know what is going
to happen to us."

"Who told you we are *taonan*?" he said, picking his teeth.

"Even so, this is my dowry money," I said firmly.

And Wen Fu turned his mouth down in an ugly way. "What
would you do with so much money—become a rich, happy widow?"

"Don't say such things!" I cried.

"Then you should not say such things," he shouted. And just
like that, all my big words no longer made any sense. It was as
though the worst part of his heart could see the worst part of mine.
Of course, I had not been thinking he might die. But once the
thought was out, once he put it there, my red face could not hide
my black heart. How do you reason with a husband like that?

Later that night, I found out how useless my words had truly
been. Wen Fu had already spent all the money. A Cantonese pilot
from the fourth class had left a car at the airport, then died in a
crash. Wen Fu now owned that car.

Oh, what bad luck! How could Wen Fu think about buying a

dead pilot's things! As if he were still running his family business, turning a dead person's tragedy into his joy.

"If we really are *taonan*," he said, "we can use the car to escape. Now you see what kind of smart husband you have."

I said nothing, of course.

"The car is very fast," he added, still dreaming about it.

"But if they send us inland?" I said. "Then we have to go with the others, by truck or boat."

"Don't be so stupid. If we cannot take the car, we can sell it— at twice what I paid for it, and for gold, not just paper money."

I started to think that maybe I was wrong. Maybe this was the best idea, and I should not be so stubborn.

"It must be a very good car," I said.

"Hunh! Of course it is very good," he said. "What do you think— that I don't know how to make a good business deal?"

But that afternoon I saw what he drove back, an old sports car, a Fiat, I think, with its top cut off. What is that word Americans have for such a bad car?—a jalopy, that's it. It was a little jalopy, dusty and dented, no top to keep the rain, snow, or cold air out. And the passenger-side door would not open. Of course, any kind of car was rare during the war, a luxury. So Wen Fu did not mind that he paid the dead pilot's family ten times what the car was worth. He was honking the horn, laughing and shouting, "Hanh? Now what do you think?"

I smiled back, letting him think I was proud that he had made such a good business deal with a dead man. And then he told me to climb in over the broken door. You have to imagine: I was already six months pregnant, and I had on many layers of clothing because of the bitter weather. So I was working hard to throw one leg over. Wen Fu was eager to go. He was grinning. He was honking the horn.

"Let's go, lazy!" he shouted, and then pushed down hard on the gas pedal so that the engine roared loud, making me think he would take off before I got my other leg in.

I let him take me for a drive, down the main boulevard, out the East Wall Gate, over narrow icy bridges, then down long dirt roads that took us into the foot of the Purple and Gold Mountains. My hair was whipping my cheeks. Cold air was blowing into my ears, numbing my brain.

"Watch this!" Wen Fu shouted, then made the car go faster. Just as I screamed and closed my eyes, he turned a corner fast, leaving big ruts where our wheels had twisted.

"This is a good car, very good!" he shouted.

He turned the wheel again, one way, then another, missed a muddy pothole, then a slow donkey cart. He honked at a young boy, sent him scrambling into a rain-filled gully. He ran over a line of six ducklings, too new in this world to know they should have been scared. And every time I pointed out some fast-coming danger or slow-moving calamity, when I screamed or covered my eyes, Wen Fu laughed. I think it was the best time he ever had with me.

The next day I told him I was too tired to go for a drive. So he asked Jiaguo, and they drove off like happy boys. Late at night, Wen Fu came home, a sulking look on his face.

"So you had a good time?" I said. He would not answer me. I asked him why he was angry. He still did not talk. He lit a cigarette, poured himself a glass of whiskey.

And then I thought, Strange, I did not hear that noisy car when he came back. I looked out the window, walked to the door. I looked down the dark pathway, toward the road. No car.

"The new car, where is it?" I asked him.

I sat at the table with him. I watched as he drank more and more whiskey, smoked more cigarettes. Then finally he announced: "That car is worthless." And he cursed its worthlessness: "May the dog-mother rut with a dead devil!"

The next morning Hulan told me what happened, what Jiaguo had told her.

They had driven the car out to the countryside just beyond the South Wall Gate. They went over a little hill, down a long narrow road, and into what Wen Fu thought was an open field. He drove fast to chase a rabbit, pretending the rabbit was a Japanese airplane. But the rabbit was faster, turning this way and that. It ran up a mound and the car followed. That's when the car's stomach landed hard—on a pile of rocks, balanced like one turtle on top of another.

He tried to drive the car off. Jiaguo got out. He tried to push it forward. And then Wen Fu pushed the gas pedal all the way down, making the wheels spin faster and faster, making the engine roar louder and louder until—wah!—black smoke poured out from under the hood and flames burst out.

Both of them jumped back and stood there, watching the car burning on top of a pile of rocks. The flames rose higher, so they backed away. And then, as they searched for a means to put out the fire, they saw the rough land all around them, lit up by the fire. They saw the field was covered with these same humps of rocks— hundreds of turtles stranded in a sea that had lost its water.

Before Hulan told me any more, I knew what Wen Fu had done— he had driven his car into a poor village cemetery!

Hulan crossed her arms. "Of course, I scolded Jiaguo. How careless he was, not guiding your husband more carefully."

I should have cried when she told me Wen Fu had ruined that car. I should have been crazy with anger that he wasted my four hundred yuan that way.

Instead I was laughing. Hulan thought I had gone crazy. I was laughing so hard, tears fell from my face. I had no breath for words.

So I could not explain how I felt. How I could see the look on my husband's face, standing in the cemetery, realizing where he was. How I could see the little car burning up on a pile of rocks, the same way mourners send gifts to the dead. How I was now so glad for that dead Cantonese pilot, riding off to heaven in his claimed-back car.

That same morning, Hulan and I went into town. I put on my long green coat and everyday shoes, because it was three or four *li* to get to the middle of the city. A *li*? That's maybe half of one of your American miles. And I had to walk that distance. I wasn't like you, getting into a car to go two blocks to the grocery store.

Along the way I stopped off at a post office to send another telegram, this time to Peanut, who was now married to a rich husband in Shanghai, the one the fortune-teller found for her. I told Wan Betty to write the same message as the last telegram: "We are soon *taonan*." This time, however, I added: "Send four hundred yuan direct to Jiang Weili only." Betty did not ask what had happened to the other four hundred. But I think she knew.

After I sent the telegram, Hulan and I headed to the market square to do our grocery shopping. It was very cold that morning, and I remember looking at the gray, cloudy sky, saying, "Maybe it will snow again."

Hulan looked up at the same sky. "Not enough clouds. In any case, I heard that snow comes here only once or twice all winter, not one day after the next."

We arrived at the marketplace. It was perhaps ten o'clock and the vendors had been at their stands since dawn. They were now eager to do a little bargaining to warm up their blood. On the outskirts of the marketplace, young boys crouched in front of vegetables, piled neatly on the ground. And in the marketplace itself were rows of tables, covered with buckets of tofu and weighing scales, piles of sweet potatoes and white turnips, baskets of dried mushrooms, pans of live fish, freshwater soft-shell crabs from the south, and wheat, egg, and rice noodles.

Already people in a stream as long as a dragon were pushing past the stands, puffing little clouds of cold breath. At that hour of the morning, everyone was happy, not yet tired from the day's work, already thinking about the evening meal's ingredients.

Hulan and I had followed the sweet smoke of roasting chestnuts, and we were now standing in front of a sidewalk vendor. He was stirring a basket filled with dark nuggets. It was three hours since we had eaten our breakfast, so Hulan and I agreed: A handful would be good for warming our hands.

"You've come just in time," the vendor said. "I added the honey just half an hour ago, when the shells cracked open." He poured six chestnuts each into two newspaper cones.

I had just peeled one open, was about to put the steaming chestnut into my mouth, when—a shout in the street: "Japanese planes! Disaster is coming!" And then we heard the airplanes, faraway sounds, like thunder coming.

All those people, all those vendors—they began to push and run. The basket of chestnuts tipped over. Chickens were squawking, beating against their cages. Hulan grabbed my hand and we were running too, as if we could go faster than those planes could fly. The airplane noise became louder, until they were over our backs, roaring like elephants. And we knew the bullets and bombs were coming. Then everyone around us began to fall at the same time, just like wheat in a field blown down by the same wind. I was falling too. Hulan was pushing me down. But because my stomach was so big, I had to lie curled up on my side. "Now we are dying!" Hulan cried.

My face was turned to the ground, my hands over my head. If people were screaming, we could not tell—the planes were roaring so loud above us. Hulan's hands were shaking as she held my shoulders. Or maybe it was my body that was making her shake.

And then the sounds seemed to be going away. I could feel my heart beating fast, so I knew I was still alive. I lifted my head just as others lifted theirs. I felt so lucky. I felt so grateful. I could hear people crying, "Thank you, Goddess of Mercy! Thank you!" Then we heard the airplanes coming back. And all those praises to the goddess turned into curses. We lowered our heads, and I thought that those curses would be my last memory. The planes flew back and forth, back and forth, and people's heads were going up and down, up and down, as if we were bowing to those Japanese planes.

I was so angry. I was so scared. I wanted to get up and run. But my body was too numb to rise. And although I was fierce in my desire to live, my thoughts were only of death, perhaps because people around me were now crying and chanting, "Amitaba, Amitaba"—already calling upon Buddha's guide to the next world.

I thought, Have we already died? How do I know? It seemed to me my breath had stopped, yet my thoughts were still racing, my hands could still feel the cold, hard ground. And I could still hear the airplane sounds, which now—eh?—now seemed to be moving farther and farther away.

The chanting stopped. But we all stayed down, so quiet, not moving. After many long minutes, I heard somebody whispering. I could feel people around me uncurling themselves. Someone was moaning. A baby was crying. I did not want to look up, to see what had happened. Hulan was shaking me. "Are you hurt? Get up!" I could not move. I could not trust my own senses.

"Get up!" cried Hulan. "What has happened to you?"

Hulan was helping me stand. We all rose slowly, the same field of wheat, now unbending. And we all whispered the same thought: "No blood." Then Hulan shouted: "No blood! Only snow!" At least that's what she thought it was at first. And because she said that, that's what I thought at first too. Big flakes of snow covered the street, lay on the backs of people crouched on the ground.

And when I looked up, I saw the snow falling from the sky, each flake as big as a sheet of paper. A pedicab driver in front of us picked up one of those flakes, and it was a sheet of thin paper. He handed it to me. "What does it say?"

The paper showed a happy drawing of a Japanese soldier with a little Chinese girl sitting on his shoulders. "Japanese government," I said. "If we do not resist, good treatment will be given to everyone, nothing to fear. If we resist, trouble follows for everyone."

And then I heard a Chinese soldier screaming in the street. He was kicking the paper snow, like a crazy man. "Lies! Lies!" he cried. "That's what they said in Shanghai. Look what they did to us! This is what is left of our army! Only rags to mop up China's blood!"

An old woman began to scold him. "Be quiet! Behave! You have to behave, or we will all be in trouble." But the soldier continued to shout. The old woman spit on his feet, picked up her bags, and hurried away. Now everyone began to talk, and then others began to shout, and soon the whole street was filled with frightened voices.

I tell you, that day, when this fear sickness spread, everyone became a different person. You don't know such a person exists inside of you until you become *taonan*. I saw people grabbing for food, stealing things. Vendors walked away from their steaming pots. I saw fights and arguments, children lost and crying, people pushing to get into a bus, then emptying out of the bus when they saw the streets were too full for anyone to move forward.

Hulan asked the pedicab driver in front of us to take us home. But as soon as he got off his seat to help us in, a bigger man knocked him down, jumped on the pedicab, and drove off. And before I could even say, "How terrible," a beggar boy ran up to me and tried to tear my purse from my hands. Hulan beat him off.

Suddenly someone cried, "Run! Run!" And everyone behind this voice began to move forward, a crowd of people coming toward us. A barrel of ice and fish was knocked over, as if it were a light vase. A woman fell down and cried—such a horrible cry, lasting for so long until it disappeared under hundreds of feet. Hulan twisted my arm, made me turn around, pushing me along in the same direction as the crowd. And then we were swallowed up in the wave, carried between other people's shoulders. I could feel elbows and knees punching into my back, into my big stomach.

And then the space around us grew even tighter, and we were squashed together, moving in one breath, one current.

Hulan had one hand on my shoulder and was pushing me forward. "Hurry-go, hurry-go," she murmured behind my back, as if she were praying. "Hurry-go, hurry-go," she said with each step. Suddenly the crowd burst onto a wide boulevard, and I was no longer crushed between people. People were now running in different directions.

"This way, this way," Hulan said. I felt her hand slip off my shoulder.

"Which way?" I called back to her. "Hulan!"

No answer.

"Hulan! Hulan!" I shouted. I turned around and people rushed by me, but there was no Hulan. I turned forward again. She was not there either.

And in that crowd, all alone, all the fears I had been holding inside fell out. I started swimming against all those people rushing toward me, looking right and left, down below. She was gone.

"Ma! Ma!" I was crying. And I was amazed that those were the words coming out of my throat. "Ma! Ma!" As if she could have saved me, the mother who had abandoned me so long ago.

I was so stupid that day. I could have been knocked over, stepped on, and killed like so many other people. Someone could have knocked the baby right out of my body. Yet I was walking through the crowd, calling for my mother, looking for Hulan.

If you asked me how many minutes, how many hours went by before I was found, I could not tell you. When my senses came back, this was all I knew: I was sitting on a bench, staring at a chestnut in my hand. I had found it in my hand, the same chestnut I had peeled before the airplanes came. I wanted to laugh and cry, that this was what I had held onto when I almost died. And I was about to throw it away, when I considered I should still hold onto it. These are the kinds of important thoughts you have when your world changes so suddenly. The city gone mad, Hulan disappeared—should you keep a cold chestnut or not?

"Eh, sister! I hope you have one for me!" It was like a voice waking me out of a bad dream.

I saw Hulan riding up to me on a pedicab. Can you imagine! She was joking after a terrible disaster, joking when I had thought she was dead! I ran to her with a happy cry.

"Get in fast," she said, and held out her arm to pull me in. I threw the chestnut away, then struggled into the little backseat. Hulan pedaled off. She handed a stick back to me, the leg of a stool or chair.

"If anyone tries to steal this pedicab from us, beat them away!" she shouted. "You have to do this, understand? Beat them away!"

"Beat them away," I repeated. My heart was pumping fast. I looked to the sides, behind me, raising the stick at a man who was eyeing me.

It was not until we were almost home that I thought to ask her how she had found the pedicab.

"What a bad world," she said. "When we ran into the boulevard, I could finally breathe and see again. Right away I saw the same man who robbed the pedicab from the driver who was standing next to us. He was pedaling by, just a few feet away. I didn't even think. I just ran over and pushed him off the seat as hard as I could. When he fell, I jumped on and pedaled away to get you. I saw your green coat, saw you were looking for me as well. But right before I called out to you, at that same moment, someone ran up to me. Wah! He was waving a stick, ready to strike me down and steal this pedicab, the same as I had done, and the man before me had done. But I was ready. When he swung, I grabbed the stick, then used it to beat him away."

She waved her hand at me. One of her fingers looked broken. "You see how bad the world has become," she said. "Now I'm that way too."

That day we left Nanking.

So you see, in some ways I have been lucky in my life. I was never really *taonan*, only the next level before that happens.

Of course, I was scared enough to forget all about the telegram I sent Peanut. I forgot all about my four hundred yuan, until it was too late.

# 13

# HEAVEN'S BREATH

A few years ago, I was talking to Helen about this same thing, what happened in Nanking. She was complaining about her finger, that's what reminded me.

I said, "Remember how you stole a pedicab the day the paper warnings fell from the sky?" You see, I had never thanked her for saving my life. We were so rushed back then, so anxious to leave, there was no time to be polite. And then fifty years went by, and I still had not thanked her. So I was going to thank her now.

Helen laughed. "I don't remember this," she said. "Anyway, how can you accuse me of stealing something? I never stole anything!"

I said, "But this was wartime. You pushed a man off and broke your finger, the same finger that now gives you arthritis problems. And then you found me and took me home. I was six months pregnant."

But Helen still didn't remember. She remembers only a little bit about living in Nanking, about duck kidneys she ate there once and has never had since, about a table she never wanted to leave behind. And of course, she remembers Wan Betty. She thinks Betty was *her* friend.

Isn't that strange? We were at the same place, at the same time. For me, this was one of the worst moments of my life. I remember everything. For Helen, except for those duck kidneys, it was nothing worthwhile to keep in her mind.

Why do you think this is? My happiest times, my worst times— they are things only I remember, nobody else remembers them. A very lonely feeling.

Anyway, when Helen complained about her arthritis that day, I told her I would finish twisting the wire on the wreaths. I didn't say this was to thank her for saving my life in Nanking. She wouldn't have understood. But I knew what I was doing.

And now I will tell you how we escaped with our lives and didn't even know it.

Only one suitcase each, that's all we could bring. And only one hour until we had to leave Nanking. That's how it was—we had to decide what we needed to survive, what we could not bear to leave behind, all in one hour. No time to sell anything. The whole city was *taonan*-crazy. I was scared.

But Wen Fu did not know how to comfort me. When I started to tell him what had happened in the marketplace, he waved me away.

"Don't you have eyes?" my husband shouted. "I have more important things to do than talk about your shopping." And then he walked over to speak to a man in a truck. He lit a cigarette, smoked two puffs, then looked at his watch and stamped the cigarette out before lighting another. So that's how I knew he was scared too.

Jiaguo was the one who told Hulan and me that we could pack only one suitcase each. "What about my new table? What about my two chairs?" Hulan cried. A few days after we arrived in Nanking, we had both bought a few extra pieces of furniture, thinking we would stay longer in the capital city. And while Hulan's table and chairs were cheap, not very good quality, they must have been fancier than anything she had ever owned.

"Don't worry about those things," Jiaguo said, and then he took Hulan to the side and whispered something to her. I could not hear, but I saw Hulan's face was like that of a little girl, pouting one moment, beaming the next.

"Hurry." Hulan said to me in her new bossy voice. "No time to sit around and feel sorry for ourselves."

I wanted to tell her, "I was not the one complaining." But we had no time to argue.

As we packed, our air force servant went in and out of the room, carrying in the things we asked him to find: Wen Fu's other air force uniform; my sewing basket, so I could take just the needles; two bowls and two pairs of chopsticks, a set each for Wen Fu and myself.

The servant chatted nervously to us the whole time. "If you listen to the radio, if you read the newspapers, you would know nothing about the Japanese coming, nothing," he said. "But all you have to do is look at people's faces in the city."

The more he talked the more urgent our packing became. He said that runaway soldiers were robbing, even killing people to steal their clothes and disguise themselves as civilians before the Japanese came into the capital. Anyone with money or connections was running away. Even the mayor—the one Chiang Kai-shek appointed because he promised he would protect Nanking forever—he was running away too, and with lots of money.

"We are not running away," Hulan said sharply to the servant. "The second and third class have a new assignment in Kunming, very important business there. That's why we're going."

I wondered if she really believed this. Is that what Jiaguo had told her? And what kind of important assignment was in Kunming? Long time ago Kunming used to be a place where they sent officials who fell into disgrace. If they didn't chop your head off, they sent you to Kunming, almost to the edge of China, a place filled with tribal people. Of course, that was not the case anymore, but still, I thought about an expression Uncle once used: *kunjing Kunming*— "stuck in a tight corner, just like living in Kunming," meaning you had been pushed out of the real world. Living in Kunming would be like hiding in a secret spot where no one could find us, a safe place. I was glad to go.

After I finished packing Wen Fu's clothes, I started to fill my own suitcase. At the bottom, under the lining, I could still feel the ten pairs of silver chopsticks I got from my wedding dowry. On top of this, I put a small biscuit tin containing all my jewelry and a little blue perfume bottle my mother had given me long ago. I covered these things up with some good clothes. And then I saw I had packed only winter clothes—as if I would not live through more than one season. What bad-luck thinking! So at the last minute, I took out a sweater and put in two summer dresses.

The pots and pans and some old shoes—those were given to the cook and her daughter. As to the other things I could not take, I saw immediately who I should give those to. Wan Betty was walking down the road and I called to her to stop a few minutes.

"Where will you go?" I asked her. "Back to Nanchang, to your husband's parents?"

She shook her head quickly. "They don't want me, I don't want them," she said, so strong, so brave. "I'm staying here."

"Help me take a few things, then," I said. And I called to the servant to bring over the rest of my clothes, Wen Fu's radio, and my little black sewing machine. I instructed him to put these things into the pedicab, still sitting in front of our house.

"You take those things home," I told Wan Betty. And then I saw Hulan biting her lips, watching the servant carrying out the sewing machine. I saw how much she wanted that machine for herself, even though we had no room for it.

Wan Betty started to protest, and I stopped her: "We have no time for this kind of polite argument."

So she smiled and said, "Fine, then. I will use the sewing machine to make a good living for myself and my baby." She took my hands and squeezed them. "This is a debt I will always owe you," she said. "Even if I can return ten times all this, I still have to repay you forever."

I knew this was her good-luck wish that both of us would be alive to meet again. And then she quickly pulled something out of her purse. It was a picture of herself as a bride, a cheap photograph. She was dressed in a wrinkled long white satin gown, her pilot husband in black pants, a white dinner jacket, and a crooked bow tie. They were the same clothes every couple borrowed from the photographer who did the Western wedding pictures.

I thanked her for the photograph. I thought she was very brave to stay, because I think she could have argued with the air force to take her along.

And now Jiaguo shouted, "We're going!" Then Wen Fu shouted the same thing, and the servants hurried us along. We threw our suitcases into the back of an open military truck, then climbed in after them. The back of the truck was so high Wen Fu had to pull me in as Hulan pushed me from behind.

"Hurry!" Jiaguo shouted in a higher-pitched voice. And suddenly my heart started to beat hard, thinking we were not escaping fast enough, that just as we started to leave, the Japanese would arrive. Everybody seemed to have the same fear.

"Hurry, we're going!" people were now shouting together. "Hurry, get in. Don't waste time!"

The back of the truck was quickly filled with nine people, all of us elbow-to-elbow crowded. Hulan and I were the only women. Besides us and our husbands, there were two pilots from the third class, two officials, one who acted much more important than the other, an old man who paid a lot of money to ride in the truck, and of course, the driver, a man we called "Old Mr. Ma." He wasn't really old. That was a term of respect. He was in charge of taking us all the way to Kunming.

And then Old Mr. Ma shouted a curse in his hoarse voice, the truck started with a big roar, and we were going down the street, past other houses that had lost their elegance like the one we had just left. We turned down another road and then drove out the West Wall Gate.

We made many turns, traveled down the small roads hidden on the sides by tall trees. And as we left the city, we passed Sorrowfree Lake. Even in the wintertime it was beautiful, calm and quiet, with willow trees hanging down, sweeping the banks. It looked as if it had not changed one leaf since the first emperor. I was sorry I had not come there for a walk to feel that kind of unchanging peace in my heart.

And then I saw a boy standing next to the lake. He was very far away but we could see him waving. He jumped up and down, shouted something. We thought he had seen the pilots' uniforms and was now cheering us as heroes, so we waved back. He started running toward us, then jumped up and down, waved both arms, crossing them above his head. He wanted us to stop. Of course, we could not stop. As we drove past him, he stamped his feet. And then we saw him pick up some rocks along the edge of the shore. He threw them into the still lake, and the water broke and shivered. He threw his arms up in the air, wide like an explosion. "Poom!"

he shouted. "Poom! Poom!" And then that bad boy picked up another rock and threw it at our truck. Although he didn't hit us, we now heard what he shouted. "Runaways! Cowards!"

We drove to the Yangtze River harbor just outside the city. We were told that once we were there we would catch a boat to our halfway stop, Hankow–Wuchang, in the central part of the country, a place nicknamed "Demon's Furnace"—so hot that people joked a native from this area would think bathing in a vat of boiling oil was a good way to escape the heat. But of course, it would not be that way now; this was wintertime, this was wartime, no joking around.

We were on the boat for maybe a few days, maybe as long as a week. I don't remember now how long it was, because I have taken other boat rides since then, and sometimes I confuse them all.

Anyway, after we got off the boat in Hankow–Wuchang, we rested one night in a hotel. The next morning, we found Old Mr. Ma had already loaded our suitcases into the back of an army-style truck, the same kind we jumped into when we were in Nanking. This one, however, had a big tank on wheels attached to the back for carrying gasoline. That was the only way to get to Kunming back then. We didn't have gas stations every ten miles, no such thing. And we did not travel on big highways, with seventy-mile-an-hour speed limits. When we left Hankow, we drove on narrow dirt roads, two lanes, sometimes only one. We went twenty miles an hour, because that's how fast that truck could go. So if there had been any Japanese along the road, all they would have had to do was run by our truck and pull us out.

The first day, I was worried we weren't escaping fast enough. The second day, I was still a little worried. But after that, I forgot about my fears. I was bored. We traveled inward, away from the fighting. It was like going backward, to another world, a place from long time ago, before the war. And none of us minded. We would be safe.

On the way west to Changsha, we drove alongside the river and through villages with lots of narrow streams running through. In one place we saw the water was thick with fish—Hulan said it looked like some kind of rich soup.

In those poor, backward places, you would not think China was in any kind of war with outsiders. People there did not get news-papers. They could not read. And in any case, it was the beginning of the war and those people did not think their one *mu* of land was worth fighting over. They had no time to worry about anything except the price of grain at the market, the cost of seed for next year's crops, and how they would eat when no money was left over.

. Along the way, we did not run into any Japanese. Our only enemies were a fallen-down tree blocking our way, a big hole in a tire that slowed us down, things like that.

One time it was a pig who would not get out of the way. Old Mr. Ma honked many times, drove forward very slowly, and nudged the pig with the truck bumper. And the pig just turned around and butted his head on the truck, attacking it as if it were another pig. Wah! We laughed so hard. But then Wen Fu said he knew how to solve our problem. He jumped out and pulled a gun from the holster strapped across his chest.

"Don't shoot him!" I shouted. "He'll move away soon." But Wen Fu was not listening to me. He walked over to the animal, who was now snorting around the truck's tires. Hulan closed her eyes. Jiaguo said, "He's only joking." And then Wen Fu pointed his gun at the pig. We all stood still, just like that pig, his ears now twitching, his tail stiff and pointed, watching Wen Fu with a wary eye.

Suddenly an old man came running up the side of the road, shouting, "So that's where you are, you stinky old thing!" Wen Fu turned to look. The old man was waving a little tassel for a whip. "Bad pig!" he cooed. "Come here, you bad thing."

I was so relieved! We all started to laugh. Just then, Wen Fu turned back to the pig and fired his gun, only once, hitting the pig in his stomach. And that poor pig was screaming, blood streaming out. He stumbled to the side of the road before falling into a ditch, his four legs pointed into the air.

The old man's mouth dropped wide open. He ran over and looked at his pig. He began to curse, slapping the tassel on the ground, before shaking it at Wen Fu. "Are you some kind of crazy demon?" the old man shouted. Wen Fu frowned, then pointed his gun at the old man, whose eyes grew big as coins.

This time Jiaguo stood up and shouted: "Stop!"

Wen Fu put his gun down, then smiled at Jiaguo. "Of course I was only joking," he said. He put his gun away, then quickly climbed back into the truck. But I could see how nervous everyone around me looked. We were quiet for the rest of the day.

Just beyond Changsha, we drove past hills with rice terraces cut into them. This is the kind of China you Americans always see in the movies—the poor countryside, people wearing big hats to protect themselves from the sun. No, I never wore a hat like that! I was from Shanghai. That's like thinking someone from San Francisco wears a cowboy hat and rides a horse. Ridiculous!

In any case, the people in those places were simple, also very honest and friendly. During the day, we would stop at little villages, and children would crowd around us, only staring, never touching or asking questions. The air force servant would buy things for us to eat at the food stands. It was all local food, already made: a bowl of spicy *dan-dan* noodles or fatty pork with cabbage. Once it was a bean curd fried with chili peppers—oh, very tasty, the best dish we ate in two hundred miles.

When nighttime came, we had to quickly find a place to stay. The roads were too dark to see, and a sleepy driver could easily drive into a field—the same way Wen Fu did with his little car in the cemetery. So when the sun stopped, we stopped. And that's when we learned what kind of luck we had.

One time it was a pleasant place, a simple hotel, with clean beds and a common bathroom. Another time it was a roof over our heads in a school or a hospital dug into a hill. And once, it was a plank of wood in a pig shed, and at night the animals would be grunting at us from the outside, trying to get back in.

We didn't complain too much. Chinese people know how to adapt to almost anything. It didn't matter what your background was, rich or poor. We always knew: Our situation could change any minute. You're lucky you were born in this country. You never had to think this way.

On our journey, we passed all kinds of places filled with tribal people, dirty hats on their heads. They ran to the truck and tried to sell us things, cigarettes and matches, a cup made out of a tin can, that kind of junk. And when they gave us their best food, their highest quality, all you could do was stare at the two pieces of dried-out meat lying on top of watery rice and wonder what kind of animal this meal had once been.

I remember when we finally arrived in a bigger city, Kweiyang. We were going to stay there for a few days, so the air force could fix the truck and get more gasoline before the long, hard drive into Kunming. Wen Fu knew a saying about Kweiyang, something like this: "The sky doesn't last three good days, the land isn't level for even three inches." That was because it rained all the time. And the city was very bumpy. The buildings and streets went up and down like the back of a dragon. And behind the city stood sharp rocky hills, looking like ancient men, too stiff to move.

Everyone got out of the truck, very tired from the day's drive. Old Mr. Ma pointed to a restaurant across the street and said we should eat there while he went to find us a hotel. So we walked across the street. And in front of the restaurant we saw a giant wooden tub. And when we looked inside the tub we saw many white eels—alive and still swimming! In Shanghai, this was a rare treat, very special. Here we learned the white eels were so plentiful you could order them as an everyday dish—morning, noon, and night.

The cook dipped a net into the tub and drew out the slippery eels, calling to us, "Fresh, see?" That night we ate plenty, big platters piled high with eels cooked whole, as thick as our fingers. We all agreed the meal was the best we had eaten. So when Old Mr. Ma said he had found us a hotel, the finest in town, first-class, we expected a palace!

Let me tell you, it was terrible—primitive, dirty. When I asked where the bathroom was, they said, "Outside." I went outside and there was no bathroom, no toilet, not even a curtain. When they said outside, that's what it was, outside!—a dirty spot on the ground where everybody's business was right in front of your eyes. I can laugh about this now, but back then, I said to myself, I'd rather not go. I went back to my room. I stayed there until I was about to burst, tears and sweat dropping from my face. It's true. I waited that long before I forced myself to go outside again.

The inside part of the hotel was just as bad. They used any kind of thing for a mattress—dirty straw with little rocks still clinging to it, old feathers and things you did not want to imagine. The cloth holding all this in was thin, had never had hot water poured over it to tighten the threads. So it was easy for bugs to hide inside the mattress—just walked right in as if the door were open. During the nighttime, they crawled back out to eat our blood while we were sleeping. This is true, I saw them on Wen Fu's back.

I said, "Hey, what's this? Here, there—like little red dots."

He reached around to touch them, then yelled, "Ai! Ai!" He was jumping up and down, slapping his back, trying to shake them off. And I was trying not to laugh. When he finally calmed down, I helped him pluck them off, and where that bug's mouth had been, there was now a bigger red spot underneath. And then Wen Fu shouted that I had one too—on the back of my neck! I started jumping and screaming too. He laughed, showed me what he pulled off, then crushed it in half with his fingernail. Stinkbugs! What an awful smell!

The next day, I heard everybody had the same stinkbug problem. Over breakfast we complained to Old Mr. Ma in a joking way. And then Jiaguo came into the room and told us the news. The Japanese army had invaded the capital city: Nanking was cut off completely. He could not tell us whether people there did not resist, whether good treatment was given as promised. Nobody knew yet what had happened.

I thought about Wan Betty, her strong words. Did she bow down to the Japanese? I was sure other people had the same kind of thoughts, although we did not discuss our feelings with one another. We were quiet. We no longer complained about our conditions in Kweiyang, not even in a joking manner.

After we left Kweiyang, we drove higher and higher into the hills, then into the mountains. Hulan and I were staring over the side of the truck, very quiet. Just to see that steep cliff made us feel as if we were already tumbling down. The road became skinnier and skinnier. And every time we hit a little bump or hole, we cried out—"Wah!"—and then laughed a little and covered our mouths. We were all sitting in the back, bouncing up and down on our suitcases, trying to hold onto something so we did not slide too much and rub our bottoms raw.

Sometimes Old Mr. Ma let me sit up front with him because I was pregnant. He didn't say that was the reason. He never gave anyone any kind of reason. He would look at all of us every morning when it was time to leave, and then he would nod at someone and that meant the person could sit up front.

On the road, Old Mr. Ma had become the most powerful man in our group, like an emperor. Our lives depended on him. And we all knew a seat up front was the same as a throne. The seat had a cushion, and if you were tired, you could stretch your legs forward, lean your head back and fall asleep. It was not like the back of the truck, where everyone was always fighting over two inches and someone else's rough knees. On that mountain road, we didn't own anything more than our own lives and a chance for the front seat, and everything else, even the things we had in our suitcases, was worthless out there.

Of course, we all had reasons why we should sit on the seat. We talked about those reasons during mealtimes, when we knew Old Mr. Ma was listening. One man was old and complained of arthritis. Another man had caught a bad sickness in Kweiyang, not contagious, but he was still very weak. Another mentioned many times what an important official he was. Jiaguo admitted he was the top-ranking pilot, a captain, recently promoted. Hulan paid many compliments to Old Mr. Ma for his quick thinking while driving. And Wen Fu gave him packets of cigarettes or challenged him to card games which Old Mr. Ma always happened to win.

During the daytime the mountain road was very busy, but not with motorcars. There were no cars out there, only children carrying heavy bags of rice on their backs, or a man walking next to his ox-drawn cart, or people with stands set up for trade. When they saw us coming, they would squeeze up against the side of the mountain to let us pass, staring at us the whole time, then looking back down the road from where we had come.

"The Japanese will be here soon," Wen Fu joked to them. And those poor villagers became frightened.

"How far behind?" an old man asked.

"Nothing to worry about!" Jiaguo shouted back. "He's only joking. No one is coming." But the villagers acted as if they did not hear him. They were still looking down the road.

And then one night Old Mr. Ma stopped the truck on the side of the road, jumped out, and told us no villages were coming up for many, many hours. "We'll sleep here," he said. And then he lay down on his front seat, no more discussion.

It was so black at night, you could not tell where the road ended and the cliff and sky began. Nobody dared walk too far from the truck. Soon the men had made a little table out of suitcases piled on top of each other, and they began to play cards by the light of a glass candle lamp.

The baby was now so heavy in my womb I often ached to let my bladder go. "I have to do some business," I said to Hulan. "How about you?" She nodded. And then I thought up a very smart plan. I took Hulan's hand and told her to follow me. I put my other hand against the side of the mountain, the part that stood away from the cliff. And as I moved my hand against the rocky side, we walked away from the men to a place just around a curve. And that's where we both did our business. I had changed so much since Hulan and I first met—I was no longer embarrassed over matters like this, not the way I was in the bathhouse in Hangchow.

Afterward, I realized I was very, very tired. I was not yet ready to walk back. So we both leaned against the mountain and looked up at the sky. We did not speak for several minutes, no need with a skyful of stars like that.

And then Hulan said, "My mother once showed me the patterns of gods and goddesses of the night sky. She said they look different, depending on what part of the cycle it is. Sometimes you can see the front of the face, sometimes the back of the head."

I had never heard of such a thing. But I was not sure whether this was true in her family's province, so I only asked, "What patterns?"

"Oh, I've already forgotten," she said sadly, and was quiet again. But after a few more minutes' silence, she spoke up. "I think maybe one was called the Snakegirl. Look there, doesn't that one seem like a snake with two pretty eyes at the top? And that one there with the big cloudy part going across, I think that's the Heavenly Cowherd Maiden."

Oh, I had heard of that old story before. "He was the cowherd, she was the weaving girl," I corrected her. "One of the seven daughters of Kitchen God."

"Perhaps, or perhaps I am thinking of the cowherd's sister," she said. I did not argue. It did not matter what Hulan remembered or forgot or was making up. I was so tired I let my mind wander away, and I too was looking for make-believe patterns in the sky. I found one that I called the Separated Goose Lovers, and then another that I named the Drowned Woman with Her Hair Unbound. And then we both made up stories to go along with them, and they always began, "Long time ago," followed by some made-up place from our childhoods: "in the Kingdom of the Lady with the Horse's Head," or "in the Eye of Heaven Mountain."

I don't remember the stories exactly. They were very silly, Hulan's more so than mine. Her stories always ended with some sort of hero popping up and marrying an ugly animal who then turned out to be a kind and beautiful princess. I think mine had to do with lessons learned too late—not to eat too much, not to talk too loud, not to wander out at night by yourself—in any case, always about people who fell off the earth and into the sky because of their willful ways. And although I can no longer see those bright patterns in my mind, I still remember that feeling of friendship as we looked at the whole sky.

We all clung to little things like that—a make-believe story, a faraway star that became something closer to our hearts. Along our journey, we looked for signs of contentment in the world, a peace that would never change. Nothing else to watch for. Once we saw a bird sitting on the back of a grazing cow. We imagined they had been little and big friends forever. Once we saw a skinny boy in a village who waved to us with a genuine smile, not at all like the boy at the lake outside Nanking. We talked about that good boy all day, how handsome he was, smart too—how much he reminded us of our boy cousins, who now, in our memories, were very well behaved.

And one day we felt something in our hearts that made us forget for the rest of the journey all the miseries we had already gone through, all the unknown troubles that still lay ahead.

We had stayed overnight in a village called the Twenty-four Turnarounds. That was the start of a winding pass in the mountains. Someone in the village said it was best to cross the pass that day, because the next day an army truck was going to come from the other direction, starting from a village at the very top of the pass, called Heaven's Breath. If we met them going up—what trouble! There was no room for two army-style trucks to squeeze by each other. Our truck, the downside one, would have to go backward a long ways until we found a wide spot. This was dangerous: if our driver lost control or made even a small mistake—over the cliff, gone!

"How many *li* before we are finished with these twenty-four turnarounds?" I asked a local man.

The villager laughed. "It is not twenty-four all together, young miss," he said. "Maybe twenty-four each *li*. Oh! A person must go forty-eight *li* before his head and stomach stop spinning. But watch out for Lady White Ghost up there. She likes to pull people off the road, make them stay longer and drink ten thousand rounds of tea with her. The tea of immortality, we call it. You drink one sip, you never want to leave her cloudy house. Maybe you forget to come back!"

What a terrible sense of humor this man had! Jokes that could attract disaster! I did not know why everyone was laughing, Hulan too.

When we started that day you could see the clouds blowing above. The wind cried in little gusts, "Hoo! Hoo!" and then got quiet again. We wrapped blankets tight around us. And then our truck began to climb. After the first twenty-four turns, we were inside the bottom of those thin clouds and the wind was blowing even stronger. After another twenty-four turns, we were in the middle of the clouds. It was growing much thicker. Suddenly our whole world turned white, and our driver shouted he could not see very far in front. The truck stopped. Everyone except me jumped out, murmuring, "How strange! How strange!"

I heard Wen Fu's voice shouting, "Why are we stopping? Didn't you hear what that man said? We have to keep going!"

I looked at Wen Fu, the dark hole of his mouth shouting into the wind. I looked at the others. Their faces wore swirling veils of mist. like ghosts, so beautiful yet frightening. Ai! I wondered if we had already died and only I knew this. I looked down and saw no road beneath us.

"What will become of us?" I called out. But my voice seemed to vanish as soon as the words came out. And again, I had this feeling we were dead. I imagined my voice soaking into a cloud filled with other ghosts' laments, until the clouds became so heavy they turned into tears and rained.

But then Hulan climbed back in the truck, stumbling over suit-cases. And I decided we could not be dead, because a real ghost would never be this clumsy.

"It is just like that story I told you about," she said, "the Heavenly Cowherd Maiden. This is heavenly cow's milk spilled from the sky." And I told myself, A real ghost would not have said such a silly thought.

She opened her suitcase, dipped her hands inside until she pulled out what looked like an old-fashioned red wedding skirt. What was she thinking? She threw this to Jiaguo, and he was very calm. He ordered everyone to hurry and get back into the truck.

And now I could see that Hulan had taken my idea from several nights before. Jiaguo ran one hand against the side of the mountain, the roughness letting him know he was still in touch with the world. In his other hand he held the red skirt so it flapped in the wind, a marker the driver could follow as Jiaguo walked forward. The truck began to move, very slowly, but at least we were moving again. After a half-hour, Jiaguo climbed back into the truck, completely wet with exhaustion from his uphill walk. Wen Fu took over, and after him another pilot, until, inch by inch, the sky above us became brighter, the clouds turned thin, light blue in color, and we no longer needed the red wedding skirt to see the dangers of the road.

We continued to turn and climb, turn and climb—so many curves you could not tell what lay ahead beyond yet another bend. Until finally we came out of the wind and the clouds entirely. And we all gasped out loud—the surprise of it—then sighed. Because where we now were was like a place you read about only in a story—the blue heavens above, the white clouds beneath, all the problems of the world forgotten.

For the rest of the afternoon we traveled along the tops of those mountains, above the clouds. We were so happy. We were like people who had truly died and come back as gods: happy, healthy, wise, and kind.

The man who had become sick in Kweiyang, now he said he felt strong. The old man with arthritis, he held up his wrists and claimed he too felt much better.

"This place is like a magic spring I once saw," said Hulan, "able to cure anything. It releases a power inside that you didn't know you had." It was that same silly story she had told me in Hangchow, but now everyone was agreeing with her, even I.

And just as Hulan described it, I found Wen Fu talking from a place in his heart I never knew he had.

"This is what it is like to fly," he told me. "This kind of joy. To look down and see the clouds beneath—that is the best. Sometimes I dip like this, up and down, into the tops of the clouds, then back up into the sunshine, like swimming in waves."

"Is that true? It's always like this?" I asked with an excited voice.

"Truly. Always," he said. "Sometimes I'm so happy, I sing out loud."

I laughed, and then he began to sing—it was the funny opera song he had sung when I first met him almost a year before at the village play. I was surprised how good his voice was to listen to. And now the whole world was hearing him sing, and he was singing for me.

That day on the mountain, I think you can guess what I was feeling. So lucky to be there. So lucky to have these friends. So lucky to have my husband. My heart filled up until it ached from having too much. And I forgot that I would ever have to leave this place.

We reached the village at the top, the one called Heaven's Breath. There we all agreed to stop early and stay the night. Why not make the scenery last longer?

And then we saw the army truck that had driven up from the other side. It was still there, ready to go down the same road we had taken. Why not brag to them about the magical sights we had just seen? We could give them something to look forward to!

We hurried to get out of the truck. Wen Fu lifted me off and joked that I was as big as two wives. And I didn't mind.

We found the soldiers sitting outside on the ground, quiet and still. And right away we saw by their faces: Those men had no ears for our happy talk. They told us they were on their way to Chung-king—to help set up a new capital city—because of what had happened to the old. And then we learned what we did not know in Kweiyang, the news about Nanking.

Who knows why the Japanese changed their minds about their

paper promises? Maybe someone threw a rock, maybe someone refused to bow down. Maybe an old woman tried to stop her neighbor, scolding him, "Behave! You want to get us all in trouble?"

"They lied," said one of the soldiers sitting on the ground. "Raped old women, married women, and little girls, taking turns with them, over and over again. Sliced them open with a sword when they were all used up. Cut off their fingers to take their rings. Shot all the little sons, no more generations. Raped ten thousand, chopped down twenty or thirty thousand, a number that is no longer a number, no longer people."

I was seeing this in my mind. The old woman who was our cook, Wan Betty, the little boy throwing rocks in the lake. I was thinking, This happened when we were having good times and bad times, while I was complaining as we traveled from there to here. I was hearing this with no danger to myself, yet I had so much terror in my heart I did not want to believe it.

I told the soldier, "This cannot be true. Only rumor."

"Believe what you want," the soldier said, and then spit on the ground.

I found out later I was right. What the soldier had said—that was only rumor. Because the real number of people who died was much, much worse. An official later told me it was maybe one hundred thousand, although how did he know? Who could ever count so many people all at once? Did they count the bodies they buried, each one they burned, those dumped into the river? What about all those poor people who never counted in anybody's mind even when they were alive?

I tried to imagine it. And then I fought to push it out of my thoughts. What happened in Nanking, I couldn't claim that as my tragedy. I was not affected. I was not killed.

And yet for many months afterward I had dreams, very bad dreams. I dreamt we returned to Nanking and we were telling the cook and Wan Betty about the beautiful scenery at Heaven's Breath, bragging about the good dishes we ate in Kweiyang. And the cook said to me, "You didn't have to leave Nanking to see such things, to taste such good food. We have the same, right here."

In front of me, she set down a dish, piled with white eels, thick as fingers. And they were still alive, struggling to swim off my plate.

Helen told me there's a restaurant—just opened—and they have this same kind of eels, cooked with chives in very hot oil. She wanted us to go try them, to see if that restaurant is any good. But I said no. I don't have an appetite anymore for that kind of eels.

My tongue doesn't taste things the same way anymore. Like celery, I can't eat celery anymore. All my life I loved celery. Now, as soon as I smell it, I tell myself no. And I don't even remember what made me not like it anymore. But with the eels, I know.

Do you know why that is? Why do some memories live only on your tongue or in your nose? Why do others always stay in your heart?

# 14

# BAD EYE

And now I will tell you when all my luck changed, from bad to worse. You tell me if this was my fault.

By the time we arrived in Kunming, I was almost eight months pregnant, so big with my baby I thought it would pop out with every bounce of the truck. Now that we were out of the mountain, our driver seemed to be in a big hurry. He was driving fast along the straight road, and I had to hold onto the sides of my stomach as we hit one bump after another.

"Eh!" Jiaguo shouted to him. "You drive any faster, you'll send us straight to the devil." Old Mr. Ma turned around. "Faster?" he shouted above the noise, then smiled. And before Jiaguo could answer, the truck roared ahead with more strength.

It didn't matter. We were all eager to get to our new homes. No more climbing into the truck every morning. No more small villages and bad food.

It was still wintertime. Yet the air blowing on our faces was not cold. It seemed to all of us that we had traveled to a land with a completely different kind of season, an eternal spring.

Hulan turned to me. "Look over there. Kunming is just like that expression about picturesque places—green hills and clear waters. And the sky is good too."

Of course, at the time we didn't know that we were only on the outskirts of the city. And as we continued to drive, we saw this good scenery disappear.

The truck slowed down, the driver was honking, and then we were passing hundreds of people, carrying sacks, looking tired. Wen Fu shouted at them, "Move to the side! Get over!" And when they did not jump to his orders, he cursed them—*"Louyi!"*—which was a very mean thing to say, calling those poor people crickets and ants, little nobodies.

Here and there we saw workers digging up rocks from the road and throwing them into wheelbarrows. And farther along, we passed another army truck, then another and another. Wen Fu waved to them each time, pointing to himself and shouting, "Air force, Hangchow, second class."

And then we entered the city itself. It was crowded and busy, a big city, bigger than I had imagined. We drove past a railway station, down a wide street with gray buildings, not too old, not too modern either. And then the streets became more narrow, more crooked, more congested with people, carts, and bicycles. The driver was honking his horn every few seconds. The air felt thick with bad smells. My head hurt. I saw mud-brick houses crowded together, some clean and whitewashed, others so rough and crumbly you didn't know why the building was still standing. And many of the faces looking back at us were not Chinese. They were tribal people, recently come down from the mountains. You could tell they were not local people. They did not wear the drab top and pants of poor-class Yunnanese, or the long gown of the merchant, or the Western shirt and pants of the educated. They wore colorful skirts, bright bands on their sleeves, turban scarves wrapped around their heads or hats that looked like tight-fitting straw bowls.

Chinese or not, the people we passed on the streets would stare at us with dark faces. They watched us so carefully, so quietly— all those signs of war now driving by their doorsteps. This city, which had been quiet for so many centuries, was now turning noisy from top to bottom.

We moved into a hotel for a few days, while some air force workers went to find proper housing for us. And then we finally moved to a two-story house halfway between the north and east gate. Jiaguo and Hulan lived there too, as well as another couple, people we met the day we moved in.

The woman was older than Hulan and I. She was very bossy. And her husband was also connected with the air force, although he was not a pilot, but an inspector of all sorts of transportation matters, bridges, roads, railways.

The first time we saw the house, Hulan said, "Look at its long wooden face. And those two big windows—like eyes looking out." All the houses on that street looked the same, two- or three-story wooden houses—*yangfang,* we called them, foreign-style houses.

There was no courtyard in front, nothing to separate the house from the street. You walked down three steps—boomp!—there you were, with everybody else on the sidewalk. But we did have a backyard, and this was closed off by a fence. It was not a pleasant place for visiting with friends, not that kind of yard. It was just concrete and dirt, a few bushes scattered about in no particular design. On one side of the fence was a water pump and long tub for washing clothes. Above that were ropes for hanging the wet laundry. Next to that, a large stone gourd for grinding rice and sesame seeds, that sort of thing.

The back fence had a gate that led into an alley, and this was wide enough for night-soil collectors to push their wheelbarrows through. Down this alley and one turn to the left was a pathway with bushes that led to a small city lake. I was told this lake was very pretty to see, and perhaps it had once been that way. But when I saw it, the poorest people of the city were doing their bathing, their washing, and other things too awful to talk about.

As I said, the house was foreign-looking on the outside. But inside, it was still Chinese in feeling and thinking. We had two large common rooms downstairs. One was a big kitchen with two coal-burning stoves made out of thick clay, with many burners for cooking. We also had a sink with a drain, but no running water, only running servants. That was the Chinese way. The cook and the servant had to go to the pump in the backyard and carry in the big, heavy buckets. Maybe they had to carry these upstairs as well. I don't remember now. When you have never had to do these things yourself, you do not think about what someone else has to do instead.

In any case, someone must have brought the water upstairs. Because every morning, every evening, I always had enough boiled-clean water for washing my face and taking a small half-bath to clean my upper body in the morning, my lower body at night. I was too big with the baby to do everything all at once. And every day, the servant had to empty the basins and tubs, as well as the chamber pots, so that they could be taken to the alleyway and cleaned.

The other common room was a large eating and sitting area. There we had a big table, lots of chairs, two cheap sofas, and an old windup phonograph Wen Fu had found soon after we arrived in the city. This windup machine did not mean we lacked electricity to run a newer phonograph. This was wartime. Where could you find a new phonograph? Of course, it is true that most people there did not have electricity; they lived in old-style mud or straw buildings. But in our house, on our street, everyone had electricity, upstairs and downstairs. And when the rest of the city turned dark and quiet at night, we turned on our radio, our fan, our lamps, and played mah jong late into the night.

We were always ready to squeeze out one more moment of fun. We liked to think we were just like those people in Berlin. We had heard it was a crazy kind of place, where people did not think about the war, only what pleasure they might find each day—gambling, eating, nightclubs. That's how we were, wanting to lead the same kind of crazy life. Of course, that was Berlin. We were in Kunming. And so, when we tired of listening to the scratchy music on the phonograph, when the radio ran out of music, when we had no more people to gossip about, when our hands were too tired to lift another mah jong tile, what else was there to do? We could not go to a nightclub. We went to bed.

Since Jiaguo was a captain, he and Hulan had the best part of the house, the two large rooms downstairs. The rest of us had rooms upstairs, which was very hard on me. I could not see my feet beyond my stomach. So once I went upstairs, I could come down only by thinking carefully how to place each foot on each stair, one at a time.

When we first moved there, Wen Fu and I received the worst rooms, both of them facing a bad-luck direction. The only way to make the bed face the right way would have been to push it against the closet door and block the door for going in and out. How could we do that?

So those were our rooms—but only because the wife of the inspector had already chosen the best upstairs rooms for herself, claiming her husband was higher-ranking than mine. This was true, but she didn't have to say it that way. She could have said, "Here, you choose first." I would have picked those unfortunate rooms, making it my generosity and not her punishment. I would have picked at least one.

So the first week in that house was very bad. I did not like those rooms. I did not like the inspector's wife. I especially did not like the way she played mah jong, the way she raised her eyebrows and said "Hnh!" every time I threw down a tile. On top of that, every night we had to listen to the inspector and his wife arguing through the walls.

At first it would be the husband's low voice, then her sharp one. The woman would begin to wail, and Wen Fu would pick up his shoes and throw them against the wall. But the couple would stay quiet for only five minutes before starting to fight again.

After three or four nights like this, Wen Fu complained to the woman, and then Hulan complained about the shoes thrown against the wall—"Like a bomb," she said, "almost scared us to death!" And soon everybody was arguing, all kinds of bad feelings coming out at once, until no one would speak to anyone, not one word. At night, when the radio programs went off the air, we did not choose to stay up late and socialize. We all went to our rooms, and it was quiet enough to hear a fly landing on the roof.

This problem lasted only a few more days. Because then the inspector went to look at the progress on the Burma Road. We were told later that the mosquitoes in that area were more dangerous than the Japanese. We heard the malaria ate up his brain in only three or four days, so he died in an awful kind of way. And then we had to listen to his wife moaning and crying for many days after that. Of course, this time we did not complain. Wen Fu did not throw his shoes. We were all very kind to her. And by the time she was ready to leave, we all agreed we had become friends for a lifetime. Although now I cannot remember her name, Liu or Low, something like that.

In any case, after she was gone, I took over their rooms, paid extra money of course, money from my dowry. Peanut sent me the money from my bank account, and that's how I found out she had also sent the other four hundred Chinese dollars to Nanking, the money I never received.

Actually, by then lots of things cost me extra. The air force could not afford to give us servants anymore. Even Hulan, a captain's wife, had none. So I had to pay for my own cook, who was an old widow, and I hired my own cleaning servant, who was a young girl. And I also had to pay for the small room just off the kitchen where they lived.

You should have seen Hulan's face when my servant girl did our laundry or cleaned our chamber pots. Hulan had changed lots by then, no longer a simple country girl, grateful to be married to an air force captain. You know what I think? When Jiaguo got his promotion, Hulan gave herself a promotion too! In her mind, she was more important than I was. And she was mad that I could afford servants and she had none.

Of course, my servant and cook did many tasks that helped Hulan too. They cleaned the common rooms. They brought water in from the well for making tea or washing—for everybody to use.

But Hulan was not grateful. She went looking for spots of grease on the floor, found them, then said, "Ayo! Look here." And when I invited her and Jiaguo to dinner, she would eat lots, then say, "Very good, but maybe the meat stayed in the pan too long." The next time, she would say, "Very good, but maybe the meat was not cooked long enough."

So it did not matter what I did, what favors I gave her. She was always unhappy until I was the same level of unhappy as she was.

By the ninth month, the baby inside me grew until it was the size of two babies. But still it would not come. I was not too worried, because I could feel it swimming inside of me, turning its body around, pushing with its feet, rolling its head. It moved when I sang. It moved as I walked in my dreams. It moved when I saw a vegetable at the market I wanted to eat. That baby had my same mind.

Every day I sewed baby blankets or knitted sweaters and clapped together their tiny sleeves. I remember one day, when I was sewing, the baby was kicking me harder than ever. I imagined this strong baby would soon be running up and down the stairs in the same way it ran up and down my womb.

"Come out, little treasure," I called. "Mama calls you to come out." And as I said this, the baby kicked me again and I dropped my scissors on the floor. They landed with their points stuck in the floor, just like a little soldier, waiting to take orders. At first I laughed, but then—eh!—I felt something very strange. The baby stopped moving inside me. I don't think I was only imagining this. That's how it happened: The scissors fell, the baby became very still.

I tried to pluck those scissors out of the floor, but I was too big to bend over. And then I remembered what Old Aunt had once said about the bad luck of dropping scissors. I could not remember the reasoning, only the stories: a woman who lost the sharpness of her mind, a woman whose hair fell out of her head overnight, a woman whose only son poked his eye out with a little twig, and she was so sorry she blinded her own eyes with the same stick.

What a terrible thing I had done, dropping my scissors. I called my servant right away and told her to throw those scissors into the lake.

That night the baby did not move even once. I sang. I walked up and down the hallway. It did not answer. The next day I went to the hospital, and the doctor did something to make the baby come out fast. But of course, it was already too late.

Hulan was there. After the doctor left, she was the one who said the baby was big, perhaps over ten pounds. What good was it to tell me how much the baby weighed, as if she were talking about so many pounds of fish taken from the sea? That baby girl never cried, never even took one breath of air.

Wen Fu patted my hand. "At least it was not a boy."

I don't know why, but right away, I told the nurse to bring me the baby. Hulan and Wen Fu stared at me.

"I want to see her so I can give her a proper name," I said in a firm voice. Hulan and Wen Fu looked at each other.

I sighed. "This is only being practical," I said, "to send a baby to the next world with a name. The baby will grow up there. And when we go to the next world ourselves, we can call her, maybe ask her to take care of us in our new life."

"This is being practical," Hulan agreed. And then she and Wen Fu both left. I'm sure they thought I would cry over that baby, and they did not want to be embarrassed watching me do this.

After the nurse brought her in, I did not get up to look at her. I lay in my bed without even turning my head. I wanted some memory of her, and I was thinking of those times we danced together, how she was so lively when I talked to her. And then finally I pulled myself up and went to look.

A big baby. So much hair. Ears that looked just like mine. A tiny mouth. But her skin—so sad!—it was the color of a stone. Her two hands were squeezed into tight little fists. I tried to uncurl one, and that's when I started to cry. If this baby had been born in Shanghai. If this baby had been born when it was not wartime. If I had not dropped those scissors.

But I quickly chased away those sad thoughts and made myself strong. People in the countryside were starving. People in the war were being killed. People died for any sort of reason, for no reason at all. So when a baby died, at least you could tell yourself it had no chance to suffer.

The next afternoon we drove to the western foothills, the place everyone called the Sleeping Beauties. The hills there look like sleeping maidens, resting on their sides. That's where we buried her. I said only a few words in her honor: "She was a good baby. She never cried." And that's when I named her after the lake in Nanking: Mochou, Sorrowfree, because she had never known even one sorrow.

I did not use any scissors for a long time. I waited more than one hundred days. And it was hard not sewing or knitting for so long. As I have already said, in Kunming there were not too many fun things to do, nothing to see, especially in the daytime. You could not say, I'm bored, let's go see a movie this afternoon. You could only stay bored. So after many days of doing nothing, I decided to buy a new pair of scissors and start sewing again.

Hulan told me, "I heard that Yunnan people make the best scissors, very sharp and sturdy. And it is true, I found some a few weeks ago."

She said there were many vendors who sold scissors, but the best could be found at a local shop on one of the side streets in the marketplace in the old part of the city. The scissors were the highest quality, also very cheap. There was no sign for the streets or shop, she said. But it was easy to find.

And then she gave me directions: "Take the northeast footbridge across the lake. On the other side, look for the old man with the soup stand. Then turn toward another place that sells dried fish. Keep walking and walking, until you see the girl who sells baskets filled with old foreigner shoes. Then turn again—only one way to turn—and keep going until you see a curve in the road. The houses become better here, whitewashed, sometimes a sign or two. Look for a place selling big rocks of brine. Go the opposite way. You'll see the marketplace after five more minutes of fast walking. The girl with the scissors is sitting outside at a table."

Of course, I got lost. What kind of directions were those? That part of the city was thousands of years old. And to walk through those streets you would think it had not changed one bit in all those years. The roads turned in and out and met up with one another here or ended there for no reason. They were crooked, paved with rough stones worn smooth down the middle by people's feet. Little houses were crowded in on both sides, and the streets were very narrow. No motorcar had ever driven through here, that was certain.

I was lost for more than an hour, wandering through a very bad part of town. Even though I was in a simple dress, other women stared at me, up and down, pointing at my shoes. Little children followed me, crying, "Hungry! Hungry" while holding out their palms. I looked for someone who could help me, but there was no one. Faces looked back at me, empty, no friendliness to be found there.

And so I walked and walked, with little children dancing at my heels, past windows with bad cooking smells. I saw a woman come to the door, naked to the waist, nursing her baby. An old man sitting on a plank looked up. He saw me and laughed a little, then started to cough in a choking kind of way, coughing so hard I thought he was going to die right there. My throat was tight from trying not to cry.

Finally I came into a larger street filled with people, the marketplace. The children crowded around me so I could not move. I dug into my purse and threw a few coins over their heads. And they shrieked, then fell to the ground, fighting over this small amount of luck.

I decided to ask someone right away how I could find a pedicab to take me home. I walked over to a young barefoot woman with a dirty face and messy thick braids. She was seated at a bamboo table. Before I could even ask my question, I saw the scissors lying on her table. This is true! Wouldn't that also make you feel someone was playing a big joke on you? Wouldn't that make you feel you only got things in life you didn't want?

The scissors were arranged in neat rows on a faded red cloth, smallest to largest with two styles. One was a plain kind, with sharp blades but no decoration on the handles. The other style was quite fancy, shaped like a crane bird, like something you would expect to find in a good Shanghai store. I was surprised to see them here. The blades were thin and tapered to look like a long beak. Where the blades connected with a metal pin, that was the eye. And the two holes for putting your fingers through, those were the wings.

I wondered how they made them, each one looking exactly the same, different only in size. I picked up one, opened the beak and closed it. It looked as if the crane were talking and flying at the same time. Wonderful, so clever!

"Who made these scissors?" I asked the young woman.

"Only members of our clan," she said, and when she smiled, I saw all her top-row teeth were missing. She instantly turned from young to old. I picked up a larger pair of scissors. She pulled out a dirty rag, inviting me to test the sharpness of the blades.

A naked little boy came to the doorway behind her. "Ma!" he cried. "Wait," she scolded him. "Can't you see, I have an important guest." The little boy went back inside.

"This is not just a boast," she said, now chattering in her toothless speech. "You try scissors anywhere else in the city and you can see they are not as sharp as ours, not nearly as sharp. That's because our family people have been scissors makers for many, many thousands of years, ten thousand years maybe. Here, you try this pair, best-made quality." She gave me the rag for cutting. The scissors felt very good the way they bit into the cloth.

The woman wiggled her fingers. "This skill runs through everyone in our family. We pass it on from generation to generation, in the blood, also through training. We teach the youngest ones to make big-eyed needles first, later smaller and smaller ones, then scissors."

"How much?" I asked, holding up a pair of the fancy scissors.

"How much do you think they are worth?" she said, pinching her mouth, staring at me directly. "How much for such fine scissors?—the best, a good strong metal, American steel."

This woman must have thought I was a fool. "How can this be American steel?" I said. "There are no American factories here."

"West of the city, that's where we get the metal, at the bottom of the Burma Road," she said. "Every once in a while, a foreign truck goes over—wah, a thousand feet down—they just leave it there at the bottom. Boys from different families climb down with ropes, bring back the bodies, also supplies if they're not broken to worthless pieces. The rest they let us keep. Ten families share. Two families take any wooden things. Another two take the seats and rubber parts. We share the metal with the others. With our portion, we cook the metal down and make scissors." She was smiling, very proud.

How bad to hear!—making scissors from a foreigner ghost truck. I was about to put the scissors down when she said, "Four yuan. How about it? This is my best price."

I shook my head. Oh, in American money that would be like two dollars. And I was thinking, Why should I pay so much for such bad-luck scissors?

"Three yuan, then. Don't tell my husband. Three is my best price."

I shook my head. But now the woman thought I was only trying to bargain her down.

The woman sighed. "If you like them, you only have to tell me how much, what price. Two and fifty, then. Don't tell anyone else. It is too cheap to believe. Two yuan fifty."

And that's when I thought to myself, What harm would it do? Two yuan fifty was a very good price. Where else could I find scissors like these? So I opened my purse and put the money in her hand.

"Next time you come I can't promise you the same price," she said, and then laughed.

I leaned over to pick up those wonderful scissors. And I was secretly congratulating myself for my bargaining skills, when my purse slipped down my arm and banged into the corner of the flimsy table. All of a sudden, the end of the table flew up, then crashed down, and forty pairs of scissors fell to the ground!

I stared at them, all their bird mouths flung open, all that bad luck pouring out.

"Ai! How terrible!" I cried. "How could I let this happen?"

"No problem, no damage," the woman said. She stooped to pick up the fallen scissors. But I was already hurrying away.

"Wait! Wait!" I heard her call after me. "Your scissors, you forgot them."

I was walking fast, and without thinking, I turned back into those crooked streets. And now every place looked the same, yet nothing was familiar. It was like wandering in a bad dream, not knowing where I was, or where I wanted to go, worried that if I stopped, something bad would catch me.

So you see, I made a bad deal, like a deal with the devil. And for what? I found out later you could buy those bird scissors from anybody, for even cheaper. Lots of people made them, and not just in China. Just the other day I saw them—at Standard Five and Ten. Yes, can you imagine? Of course, I did not buy them.

If you think I am only being superstitious saying this, then why did I drop all those scissors that day? Why did something terrible happen right after that?

Hulan was the one who told me. She was waiting for me at the house. She jumped up, put her hands to her mouth, and told me to hurry and go to the hospital. "Accident!" she cried. "Wen Fu is hurt very bad, maybe dying."

I gave a little shout of fear. "How can this be?" And then we were both running out the door to an air force car waiting to take us to the hospital.

On the way, Hulan told me what had happened. "He was driving an army jeep, heading toward the Sleeping Beauties Hills. But a wheel fell off, and the jeep turned over and threw him out."

"Ai-ya, this is my fault," I cried. "I made this happen."

"Don't say this," scolded Hulan. "How can this be your fault?"

And then she told me Jiaguo had ordered Wen Fu to be taken to the French Christian hospital run by Chinese and foreign nuns. Hulan said it was not the local hospital, which was very poor, filled with people who could give you more problems than what you already had. What a good man Jiaguo was!

As I walked down the hallway of the hospital, I could already hear Wen Fu moaning and screaming. It was the sound of a man being tortured, of someone who had already lost his mind. And then I saw him. His head was bandaged all around the top. His face was swollen and purple. This is terrible to admit, but if no one had told me this was Wen Fu, I would not have recognized him. I was staring at his face, trying to find his same eyes, nose, and chin. And then I thought, Maybe they made a mistake. Maybe this is not my husband.

"Wen Fu?" I said.

"He can't hear you," the doctor said. "He has a very bad injury to his brain. He was already dead from shock when they brought him here. But I gave him a shot of adrenaline, and his heartbeat came back." Of course, I thanked the doctor for saving my husband's life.

I turned to look at Wen Fu again, calling his name softly. And suddenly, one eye popped open! I gasped. I could not help myself. His eye was big and dark in the middle, yellow and bloody all around. It seemed to be looking out with so much anger, no good feelings behind it. He looked like a monster.

A few days later, when it was certain that Wen Fu would live, Jiaguo came to the hospital and said, "Weiwei-ah, now I have to give you bad news."

I listened to everything, never changing my expression, never crying out. That afternoon, Jiaguo told me he might have to dismiss Wen Fu from the air force, maybe even send him to jail. He told me my husband had not had permission to take the jeep. Instead he had bribed an army driver, who was now being punished. And he did not crash because of a bad wheel. He was driving too fast and when he almost ran into a truck coming the opposite way, he turned too fast and threw the jeep upside down. And then I heard Jiaguo talking about a girl. Who knows how that girl came to be in the jeep with him? In any case, she was killed, crushed underneath.

That was the first time I heard about my husband seeing other women, although I later found out she was not the first. But back then I didn't want to believe this. Maybe Wen Fu was going to the Sleeping Beauties Hills to visit Mochou's grave. Maybe the girl got in the jeep to give him directions. Maybe he was only being kind, because he saw she was poor. Maybe she had never been with him at all. Maybe she was standing on the hill where he crashed, that's how she came to be killed.

Of course, none of those excuses could find a place to rest in my head. And instead, I could see Wen Fu driving along the winding road, kissing someone who looked like Peanut. He was singing the opera song to her. And they were both laughing, as he drove up and down, up and down, swimming in the clouds.

I was still thinking this when I visited Wen Fu the next time. His face was not as swollen as before. He was sleeping and I wanted to shake him awake. I wanted to ask him, "Why did you do this? Now you are going to go to jail, disaster on all of us." But as soon as I thought that, he moaned, making that terrible sound that hurt my heart. And so I wiped his brow and forgave him before he even had a chance to say he was sorry.

When he finally woke up, Wen Fu was fussy and weak. He complained about everything: the pain, his bad eye, the food, the manners of the nurses, the delays of the doctor, the hardness of the bed. Everyone tried to comfort him. At that time, I did not think the accident had changed him, only that he was still suffering. That's why he was being so troublesome.

But then his strength came back, and he became angry and wild. He threw his food at the nurses and called them whores of the devil. He accused the doctors of being so stupid they should not even work on a dead dog. He threw a bedpan at the doctor who saved his life. He would not take his medicine, and when four nurses tried to hold him down to force him, all the strength they didn't know he had flew through his arm and he punched one of the nurses and knocked her teeth loose.

One night, he reached out and grabbed a nurse's breast. The next night, they assigned an old woman nurse. He grabbed her breast too, didn't matter.

Soon nobody wanted to take care of him. This was my shame too. He was getting better, but he was also getting worse. The doctor said he was still too weak to leave. His one eye was still blinded. They tied his arms and legs to the bed and told me I had to urge my husband to behave.

Every day I had to listen to him beg me to untie him. He begged me to climb into bed with him. He begged me to take off my clothes. And when I would not do any of these things, he cursed me at the top of his voice. He accused me of sleeping with other pilots. He said this loud enough for everyone in the hallway to hear.

I tried so hard to keep my sympathy for him. I tried to remember that it was the pain that made him act this way. But secretly, I was thinking how Wen Fu would soon go to jail. I was already planning a quiet life when I would no longer have to care for him.

But he did not go to jail. Jiaguo ended up not charging him with any kind of crime. I found out: Hulan was the one who persuaded him not to. She did this for my sake, she told me later.

"If you punish the husband, you punish the wife," she explained. "That's all I said."

I thanked her with many words. I told her I was ashamed she had to go to so much trouble to help my husband and me.

"I did nothing, Jiaguo did nothing," she said. "Now you should forget this ever happened." Even when she told me that, I knew she would never forget. I could never forget. I now had a big debt to pay.

Of course, Hulan did not know what she had really done, how sorry I was that she had done me this favor. I felt so bad, and yet I had to act grateful. It reminded me of that time when I was a little girl and Old Aunt had asked me on my birthday which chicken in the yard I liked best. I picked the one that let me feed her out of my hand. And that night, Old Aunt cooked her up.

Anyway, I showed Hulan my thanks over and over again. I had my cook make the dishes she liked, the way that she liked them, vegetables steamed until they were soft and tasteless. Hulan said nothing, and this was proper, not to call attention to my thanks. I told the servant girl to give Hulan and Jiaguo's rooms a thorough cleaning. Hulan said nothing. And several days later, I gave her many yards of very good cloth, telling her the color was not right for me.

This was not true, of course. I picked that cloth especially because it looked so nice against my skin. It was a very pretty fabric, peach-colored, hard to get during wartime and very expensive.

"This color does not suit me any better," Hulan said frowning, her fingers already stroking the cloth.

"Take it, take it," I said. "I have no time to sew anyway, now that I have to take care of my husband."

So Hulan took my gift without any more protest. She knew what kind of bad marriage I had, and she let me cover it up with a beautiful piece of cloth.

250

When my husband came home, I already had a special bedroom made up for him. He was still too weak to leave his bed, so I hired a special nurse servant to take care of him, to change his bandages, to bring him food, to listen to his complaints. That nurse stayed only one day. The next one lasted maybe two days. Finally I had to take care of him myself.

Jiaguo and Hulan visited him every day, of course, since they lived in the same house. And one day three pilots came over. I took them to Wen Fu's room and they treated him as if he were a hero. They said that as soon as Wen Fu could fly again, China would be certain to win the war very fast, polite lies like that.

But everyone already knew he would never fly again. How could he fly with only one eye? Still, the pilots were very generous to say that, and Wen Fu was glad to hear it.

They were so nice I invited them to stay afterward for dinner, thinking this was what Wen Fu would want me to say. He always liked to show his generosity to the other pilots that way. And in fact, Wen Fu did say, "Stay, please stay. My wife is an excellent cook." I think he was remembering those good dinners in Yangchow when I made a thousand dumplings. The pilots agreed immediately. And I went downstairs to tell the cook to go out and bring back a fresh-killed chicken.

After our dinner, the pilots, Hulan, Jiaguo, and I continued talking at the table, while the servant cleaned up. At first we were quiet, so we would not wake Wen Fu up. I remember we talked a little about the war in solemn voices, and yes, we were still certain we would win as soon as China could bring in more supplies.

One pilot said he had heard about a contract to buy American-made planes flown in from India, maybe a thousand, enough to fight evenly with the Japanese. Another said that airplane-making factories were being built in different parts of China. Maybe there would soon be one in Kunming. And we all agreed that would be best: to make the planes in China, so we knew they were properly built, not full of problems like the old Russian planes or the new Italian ones. Chinese-made was best, bombers and fighters, all very fast and able to fly at night.

But we all knew this was just talk, the same old talk. So after a while, we began to remember the villages we had come from, stories from there, very pleasant kind of talk. And then we were singing.

We took turns remembering silly village songs, the kind people sing when drinking or celebrating.

One of the pilots could make his voice sound almost like a woman's, and together we sang a very silly love song, then laughed and sang it again: "Ten thousand clouds, one thousand birds, one hundred tears, my two eyes look to heaven and see only you, my two eyes—"

Suddenly we heard heavy steps coming down. And then—bwang!—something was knocked down. I jumped out of my chair and saw Wen Fu, his head wrapped in a bandage. He was leaning on a stick. His face was pale and sweaty, looking like a ghost's. On top of his pajamas he wore his air force jacket.

"You are too sick to be up!" I cried, rushing over to help him back into bed. Jiaguo and the pilots started to get up too.

Wen Fu waved his stick in the air. "How can you sing that?" he roared. "I am a sick man, you are a healthy woman! I am a hero, you are a whore! Your two eyes see other men!"

I did not know what he was talking about. "You've had a bad dream." I tried to soothe him. "You are still dream-talking. Come back to bed."

"Liar!" he shouted. He marched over to us and used his stick to knock over the rest of the food on the table. "You are wrong. Kneel down. Bow your head and beg me to forgive you. Kneel down!" He slammed the stick on the table.

I looked at his face. His one good eye was wild, like a drunken man's. His face was so ugly—and I wondered how I could have married such a person. How could I have let this happen?

Wen Fu must have seen my thoughts with his bad eye, because right then he reached over and slapped me, gave me a real big slap in front of all those people. I gasped. I did not feel any pain. I thought the stinging was just my embarrassment. Everyone was staring, not moving.

"Kneel down!" he shouted again. He started to raise his stick, and that's when Hulan pushed me down by my shoulder.

"Kneel down, kneel down," she cried. And I found myself falling to my knees. "Just listen to him. Say you are sorry, what does it matter?"

I remember this: All those men, Hulan—nobody tried to stop him. They watched and did nothing as I lay with my head touching the floor. They said nothing when my husband ordered me to say, "Sorry, I am wrong, you are right. Please forgive me." They did not protest and tell Wen Fu, "This is enough," when he told me to beg for forgiveness, again and again.

And as I bowed and begged, cried and knocked my head on the floor, I was thinking, Why doesn't anyone help me? Why do they stand there, as if I were truly wrong?

I am not blaming Helen today for what she did back then. She was scared, same as the others. But I still can't forget: What she did, what the others did—it was wrong, it was dangerous. It fed Wen Fu's power, made him feel stronger.

But if I brought this up with her today, she would not remember what I was talking about. It's the same with that peach-colored cloth I gave her. We were at House of Fabrics recently, and I said, "Hey, doesn't this look like the same cloth I gave you in China?"

"What cloth?" she said.

"The cloth! The cloth! Peach-colored with red flowers," I reminded her. "I gave it to you because you told Jiaguo not to put Wen Fu in jail. You knew what he did, the girl he killed in the jeep. You took that cloth and made a summer dress. And you were so happy and then mad the day the war ended—remember?—because you tore that same dress jumping up and down."

"Oh, that cloth," she said, remembering at last. "You didn't give me that cloth. I bought it myself, went to the old part of the city before it was destroyed and bought it from a girl sitting at a table. That's right, I remember now. She wanted too much money, and I had to bargain her down."

So you see—how can I argue with Helen's memory? Her truth lives in a little confused part of her brain, all the good things she still wants to believe.

Sometimes I envy her. Sometimes I wish I never gave her that cloth.

# 15

# A FLEA
# ON A TIGER'S HEAD

One time your father gave a sermon called "Jesus Forgives, Can You?" I liked that sermon a lot. It gave me a peaceful feeling, letting go of my anger.

I remember right after that, the Italian man who owned the hardware store treated me mean, yelled at me just because I wanted money back for a light bulb already burnt out when I bought it. He pretended he could not understand me. My English wasn't good enough, so no money back.

I got mad. But then I said to myself, Forgive, forgive. I was thinking about what your father said, letting Jesus's tears from the cross wash all my anger away. And it worked. I was no longer angry.

So I tried to tell the hardware man how I put the light bulb in my socket. Right away he interrupted me, said, "You bought it, you broke it."

I got mad again. I said to myself, Forgive, forgive. Again it worked. I stopped my anger. But then the man said, "Lady, I got a business to run." And I said, "You should have no business!" I let myself get mad. I forgave and forgave, and that man didn't learn anything! Who was he to criticize me? His English wasn't so good either, Italian accent.

So you see, that's the way I am, easy to get mad, hard to forgive. I think it is because of Wen Fu. I can never forgive him. I can't excuse him because of that accident. I can't excuse what happened later. Why should I?

I only feel bad that maybe your father will think my heart is not big enough.

But then I also think, When Jesus was born, he was already the son of God. I was the daughter of someone who ran away, a big disgrace. And when Jesus suffered, everyone worshipped him. Nobody worshipped me for living with Wen Fu. I was like that wife of Kitchen God. Nobody worshipped her either. He got all the excuses. He got all the credit. She was forgotten.

About a year after Wen Fu's accident, at the start of 1939, I returned to that same hospital, this time to have another baby. Hulan was with me. She saw me pay one hundred Chinese dollars out of my dowry money for a first-class, private room. That was a lot of money back then, like paying one or two thousand American dollars today.

Wen Fu did not come to see me until two days later, after I had the baby, another girl. So the first time I saw my baby, I was by myself. When she opened her mouth and cried, I cried too. When she opened her eyes, I hoped she liked what she saw, her new, smiling mother. When she yawned, I told her, "Oh, how smart you are to learn this so quickly."

By the time Wen Fu came, his eyes were red-drunk from too much celebrating. He was wearing his air force uniform, and whiskey smells followed him into the room. The baby was asleep. He peered into her face and laughed, saying "My little thing, my little thing" over and over again. He tried to open her curled-up hand.

"Oh! She's very ugly!" he joked. "Bald as a monk, fat as a greedy one. How could I come to have such an ugly child? And so lazy too. Wake up, you little Buddha." Watching the way his eyebrows were dancing, I could tell he was happy. He was trying to charm his own daughter!

And then he picked her up in his drunken hands. And the baby flung her arms out and began to cry. He bounced her up and down in his arms, and she cried louder.

"What's this?" he said. "What is the matter now?"

"Softer, be gentle," I suggested, but he did not listen to me. He began to lift her up and down, as if she were a little airplane. He sang her a loud drinking song. Still she kept crying.

I held my arms out, and he gave her up. In a few moments, she was quiet. And then I saw Wen Fu's face. He was not relieved, smiling with joy. He was angry, as if this little baby had insulted him—as if a baby only one day old were choosing favorites. I was thinking to myself, What kind of person would blame a baby? What kind of man always puts himself first, even before his own child?

And then the nurse came into the room to give me some medicine. Right away, Wen Fu told her he wanted something to eat: a good hot soup—noodles and beef tendons. He ordered this dish, fast, like a customer in a restaurant. He told her not to be skimpy with the meat. That's what he always said in a restaurant. He also told her to bring him a good rice wine, not the cheap local brand, but the best.

Before he could continue, the nurse interrupted him: "Sorry, no food for visitors, only for patients."

Wen Fu stared silently for a moment. And then he banged his fist on the wall. "You're the one who still has two eyes!" he shouted at the nurse. "Don't you see I am a war hero?" He pointed to his eye, the one still drooping from the accident.

I wanted to tell the nurse, He's no hero! That was not the way it happened, how he got his bad eye. Just the opposite. But the nurse had already left the room.

And then I made a big mistake. I told Wen Fu not to be a nuisance. Actually, I did not say this word "nuisance." I could never have said something so directly like that to my husband. So what I probably said was this: "They are busy."

And because I was excusing them, Wen Fu became even more angry. He was cursing the hospital, shouting at the top of his voice. I was begging him to calm down. "For the baby," I said. "A baby has just come into the world. A baby should not hear such things." But already the baby was crying again. Wen Fu stopped shouting. He stared at his little daughter, so angry at her new outburst. Then he left.

Good, I thought, he's gone. Not even five minutes had passed before the nurse ran back into my room, trembling mad. "That man who is your husband, what kind of crazy person is he?"

And then she told me how Wen Fu had gone downstairs to the hospital kitchen. He had pushed the cooks out of the room. He had picked up a big cleaver, the kind you use to chop a large bone in half. And—pah!—he chopped up the table, the walls, the chairs. He knocked over jars and dishes. He smelled each pot, cursed its contents, and dumped out all the food they were cooking. Finally, when the blade broke, he threatened all the cooks and their helpers, who were watching from the door: "If you report that I did this, I will come back and chop your bones in half."

When I heard this, I was so ashamed. I could think of no excuses to offer. I asked the nurse to forgive me for bringing this trouble into the hospital. I promised to pay the hospital another one hundred yuan. I promised to later apologize myself to all the workers in the kitchen.

After the nurse left, I thought about this question she had asked: What kind of crazy person was my husband? This time I was not blaming myself for having married him. I blamed his mother!—for having given birth to him, for tending to all his desires as if she were his servant, for always feeding husband and son first, for allowing me to eat only after I had picked off bits of food stuck to my father-in-law's beard, for letting the meanness in her son grow like a strange appetite, so that he would always feel hungry to feed his own power.

And perhaps this was wrong of me, to blame another woman for my own miseries. But that was how I was raised—never to criticize men or the society they ruled, or Confucius, that awful man who made that society. I could blame only other women who were more afraid than I.

And now I began to cry, and my baby cried with me. I put her to my breast, she would not eat. I rocked her gently, no use. I sang her a soft song, she was not listening. She cried for so long, until she no longer had enough breath to cry out loud. She cried from down below, in her stomach. And I knew she was scared. A mother knows these things instantly about her own baby, whether she is hungry or tired, wet or in pain. My baby was scared. So I did something I thought was right. I lied.

"What a good life you will have," I murmured to her. "That man who was shouting? Nobody we know. Not your father, certainly not. Your father is a gentle man. Your real father will come see you soon, better not cry." And soon, she calmed down, she went to sleep.

That night I named her Yiku, "pleasure over bitterness," two opposite words, the good one first to cancel out the bad one second. This was when characters were written one on top of the other. In this way, I was wishing my daughter a life of comfort winning out over hardship.

I loved that baby right from the start. She had Mochou's same ears. But Yiku opened her eyes and searched for me. She would drink only my milk, refused that of her *sau nai-nai*, her milk nurse, so I sent the *sau nai-nai* away. You see, Yiku knew I was her mother. I would lift her high in the air, and we would laugh together. She was smart too—not even three months old and she already knew how to put her hands together and touch my hair, never grabbing.

But whenever Wen Fu began to shout, she always cried, cried all night long, and would not stop until I told her more lies. "Yiku, be good, and your life will be good too." How could I know that this is how a mother teaches her daughter to be afraid?

One day, perhaps six months after Yiku had been born, the servant girl came to me, telling me she had to leave. She was fourteen years old, a small girl, always obedient, so Hulan had no reason to scold her. When I asked why she wanted to leave, she excused herself and said she was not a good enough worker.

That was the Chinese way, to use yourself as an excuse, to say you are unworthy, when really you mean you are worth more. I could guess why she was unhappy. Over the last few months, Hulan had started asking the girl to do lots of little tasks that turned into big ones. And that poor girl, who never knew how to refuse anyone, soon had twice as much work for the same amount of money I paid her.

I did not want to lose her. So I told her, "You are an excellent servant, never lazy, deserving of even more money, I think."

She shook her head. She insisted she was unworthy. I said, "I have praised you often, don't you remember?"

She nodded.

And then I thought maybe Hulan had been treating her in a mean way, scolding her behind my back, and now this girl couldn't take it anymore. Oh, I was mad! "Has someone else been causing you problems?" I said to the girl. "Someone is giving you trouble, am I right? Don't be afraid, tell me."

She began to cry, nodding her head without looking at me.

"Someone is making it hard for you to work here? Is this so?"

She nodded again, more tears. And then she told me who. "*Tai-tai*, he is not well, very sick. I know this. So I am not blaming your husband."

"Blame? What is your meaning for bringing up this word?" I said. It was summertime, but a chill rushed over my body and I ordered the girl to speak. I listened from a faraway place as the servant girl begged me to forgive her, slapped her own face twice, and confessed she was the one who was wrong. She said she was the one who was weak for letting him touch her. She cried and prayed for me to not say anything to my husband.

And now I don't remember exactly how I got all her words out, how I pulled them out, one by one. But that afternoon I found out that my husband had started to put his hands on her while I was in the hospital, that she had struggled each time, and each time he had raped her. She did not say "rape," of course. A girl that young and innocent, how could she know such a word? She knew only how to blame herself.

I had to ask her many times: The bruise on her face that she claimed was her own clumsiness—was that the time he had tried once before? The times she claimed to be ill, always in the morning—was that after it happened?

Each time the girl confessed something, she cried and slapped her own face. I finally told her to stop hitting herself. I patted her arm and told her I would settle this problem for her.

Her face became scared. "What will you do, *tai-tai*?"

I said. "This is not your worry anymore." And then I felt so tired and confused I went upstairs to Yiku's room. I sat in a chair and watched my baby daughter sleeping, so peaceful in her bed.

What an evil man! How could I have known such an evil man existed on this earth! Last year's accident had taught him nothing!

And then I thought, What will people think when they find out? What will they think of me—if I take sides against my husband and defend a servant girl instead? I imagined Hulan scolding me, accusing me of seeing only the worst in everything and everybody. I saw others criticizing me for not managing my house better. I could imagine people laughing—a husband who chases after a servant girl because his own wife is not enough—the classic old story!

And then I thought to myself, What he did was wrong, maybe it was a crime, but not a big one. Many men did those kinds of things with servants. And who would believe a servant girl? My husband would say she lied, of course he would. He would claim that the girl seduced him, a big hero. Or he would say she had already slept with many pilots. He could say anything.

And what would I gain by accusing my husband? I would get a big fight from him in return, pitiful looks from Hulan and Jiaguo, all that shame. So what would it matter if I tried to help that girl? What would I gain? Only trouble in my own bed. And then what would I lose? I could not even begin to imagine that.

I sat down and remembered a saying Old Aunt used to tell me whenever I complained that I had been wrongly accused: "Don't strike a flea on a tiger's head." Don't settle one trouble only to make a bigger one.

So I decided to say nothing, do nothing. I made myself blind. I made myself deaf. I let myself become just like Hulan and Jiaguo, that time they said nothing when Wen Fu slapped me.

I gave the servant girl three months' wages. I wrote her a good recommendation. She went away, I don't know where. I think she was grateful she could quietly leave. And when Wen Fu asked two days later where the servant girl was, I said, "That girl? Oh, she got an offer from her mother to marry a village boy. So I sent her home."

Several weeks later I heard the servant girl was dead. Hulan told me while I was nursing Yiku. She said the girl had gone to someone else's house to work. And one morning, after the girl knew she was pregnant, she used the old country way. She took a piece of straw from a broom, poked her womb until she began to bleed, but the bleeding never stopped.

"So stupid, to use a piece of straw like that," said Hulan. "And that family who took her in—oyo!—so mad that she brought a ghost on them. Lucky for us she didn't die in our house."

While Hulan talked, I felt strange, as if I were feeling that slap to my face all over again, everyone in the room looking down on me, saying this was my fault. I could see that girl lying on the floor, her blood spilled all around, people lamenting only that she had left a big mess behind.

Of course, Hulan didn't know it was Wen Fu who got that girl in trouble. Or maybe she knew and wasn't saying anything. Still, how could she think this way! Criticizing a helpless servant girl, congratulating us for being rid of her before she turned into a ghost. Why was she not thinking of her own sister, the one who died almost the same way? And I was just as bad, because I had become almost like Hulan: no sympathy, only relief that I had avoided troubles for myself.

After Hulan left, I picked up Yiku and went upstairs. I told her, "Don't be like me. You see how helpless I am. Don't be like me."

When Wen Fu came home that night, I showed him my anger for the first time. I had waited until after the evening meal, after late rounds of tea and card games, gossip and laughter. "That little servant girl, you remember her," I said when we were up in our room. "Today she died."

Wen Fu was taking his shoes off. "My slippers, where are they?"

I could hear Hulan and Jiaguo, still talking downstairs in the kitchen. I closed the door to our room. I repeated what I had said, louder this time. "The servant girl is dead." And when he continued to ask for his slippers, I added, "She died trying to get rid of your baby, you fool!"

He stood up. "What's your meaning? Whose lies have you been listening to?" he said. He leaned toward me, staring, one eye droopy, the other large and wide open. I did not look down. I stared back at him, so strong. I had a new feeling, like having a secret weapon.

And suddenly—whang!—he knocked over a chair. He cursed. He was shouting at me. "Who are you to accuse me?"

Yiku was now crying in the next room, a scared kind of crying. I started to go toward her room, but Wen Fu shouted for me to stop. I did not listen, and I went to her and saw she was standing up in her crib, reaching with one arm to be comforted. I picked her up and soothed her. Wen Fu followed me, still shouting, knocking things over, but I was not afraid. This time he did not scare me. I put Yiku back in her crib.

"I know what happened!" I shouted back. "You pushed that girl down, ruined her life, who knows how many others. And now I'm telling you, you do your dirty business somewhere else. In the streets, I don't care, only not in my bed anymore."

He raised his fist. I did not look away or cover myself. "Hit me, I still won't change!" I shouted. "Hero, big hero! The only one you can scare is a baby."

He looked surprised. He looked toward Yiku standing behind me in her crib. She was crying hard. He put his hand down. He walked over to the crib very fast. And I thought he was sorry that he had made her cry. I thought he was going to pick her up and say he was sorry. And then, before I could even think to stop him, he slapped her—*kwah!*—hit her hard on the face, so hard half of her face turned red. "Quiet!" he shouted.

Her eyes were pinched closed. Her mouth was open, but no sounds came out. She could not breathe. So much pain! I can still see that look on her face, hurting worse than any slap to my own.

I rushed over to Yiku, but Wen Fu pushed me away and I fell. And then I heard her cry again. Her breath finally came back! And she cried even louder, higher. *Kwah!* Wen Fu hit her again— *kwah!*—again and again. And by the time I could get to my feet and push my body in between, I saw Yiku had rolled up into a little ball. She was making small animal sounds. And I was crying and begging Wen Fu, "Forgive me! I was wrong! Forgive me!"

After that, every time Yiku saw her father come into the room, she fell down and curled herself up small, just like the first time. She sucked her fingers, making little sounds. This is true, only six months old, and she had learned not to cry. Can you imagine—a baby who learned to be that scared before she even knew how to crawl away?

She became a strange baby. She never looked at people's faces. She pulled out hair from one side of her head. She banged her head on the wall. She waved her hands in front of her face and laughed. And when she learned how to walk, she stood on her toes, like a ballerina dancer. She tiptoed quickly across the floor, as if she could lift herself up into the air with each step. But each time she saw her father come into the room, she fell back down again, same as when she was a baby. She did not cry. She spoke no words, only the outside shapes of them, like the voice of a ghost.

Her voice sang up and down, high and pretty, sounding the way

I often called to her, "Yiku, look at me, look at me." And then her voice would become harsh, grunting the same way Wen Fu shouted, "Yiku, stupid thing. Go away!" Those were the only sounds she knew how to make.

She was strange all the time. I was worried, so worried. But Hulan kept telling me, "When she's older, she'll change. Now she's just nervous. Everyone's the same way. When the war is over, she'll change. You'll see."

I wanted to believe her. Why wouldn't I? I had never raised a baby. I didn't want to think my baby had lost her mind. I kept thinking the war would soon be over, then Yiku would get better. I believed that, one hope leading to the other.

The Double Seventh was supposed to be a lucky day. But it became a day full of regrets. I was already six or seven months pregnant with another baby. Yiku was maybe seventeen months old, so it must have been 1940, summertime and unusually warm, which made everyone irritable.

That day we learned the British were closing down the Burma Road to make the Japanese happy. That day Jiaguo invited the railway official to come to lunch, so he could discuss other ways to transport supplies. That day Hulan bought the food from the marketplace, and she found plenty of bad bargains.

The official brought his wife to lunch, a woman who reminded me of Old Aunt, the way she said, "Oh, you shouldn't eat spicy foods. Otherwise your new baby will be born with a bad temper." And then she proceeded to take another helping of the spicy noodle dish I liked so much, eating up my share.

When everyone had finished the meal, I was still feeding Yiku some leftover pieces of vegetables. Jiaguo, Wen Fu, and the official were drinking whiskey, talking about money values. Hulan was fanning herself, her eyes sleepy from the meal.

"Everything is falling down, down, down," said the official, with much authority. "Last year's money is worth half today. That's how you know if we are winning or losing the war. Look at the money. The enemy can control the country just by controlling the money."

"Then China should print more money," said Wen Fu, wearing his knows-everything look. I knew he was trying to match the official's arrogance. "Give everybody more money. They spend more. Everyone makes more. Or better yet, get the foreigners to give us more money."

Jiaguo shook his head. "Bad idea. Outside interference, that's what got China in trouble in the first place, divided us into little pieces too weak to fight together."

"That's why the foreigners should pay," Wen Fu insisted, "to clean up the mess they started. Tell them to give us enough money to win the war."

The official laughed. He turned to me and pointed his thumb at Wen Fu. "Eh, Mrs. Chiang Kai-shek, your husband finally knows how to solve all our problems. So simple, get foreign help. Hey, Mr. Roosevelt, Mr. Churchill, here's my begging bowl. Give me one hundred million dollars."

I thought the official was very rude. But I laughed too, just to be polite. I knew Wen Fu was not happy. So I tried to tease his humor back. "You'll need a big bowl," I said, and smiled. Big mistake!

Wen Fu's face got red. "Maybe I should give you a bowl and make you beg," he said in his angry voice. "How about it?" And right away, everyone became very quiet, embarrassed. I was trying to pinch back my tears.

Suddenly, Yiku started rocking back and forth, singing to herself. She shook her hands in front of her face, singing in her high little voice, then grunting loud and harsh, the same sounds she always made.

The official's wife rushed over and touched Yiku's forehead. "Ai, what's wrong with your baby? Is she sick?"

And this made Wen Fu even more angry. "Yiku!" he shouted. He slapped her hands down. "Stop that! Stupid girl, quiet!"

And Yiku started rocking faster, singing those shouting tones: "Yiku! Stop that! Stupid girl!" I was sick to hear it.

The official and his wife left soon after that. Jiaguo and Hulan went into their room to take a nap. And when we were alone, Wen Fu shouted for a long time about my being an improper mother, how I had not taught Yiku to be an obedient daughter. My stomach felt bad, very bad, and I thought this was because I was seeing Yiku clearly for the first time, the same way the official's wife saw her.

But the next morning, my stomach felt worse, and I knew it was the food from the day before. And then I said to myself, Oh, I hope Hulan didn't buy cheap vegetables from Burmese people. Those people had so many dirty habits—using their own night soil to fertilize the plants, spreading the germs they brought with them, cholera, dysentery, typhoid fever. And even as I worried about these things, I did notice Yiku was sick, too. She was not crying. She was only sleepy all the time. So how could I know?

But then her diarrhea started that afternoon. By evening, it still had not stopped and she refused to eat or take any water. And after Wen Fu had gone off to play mah jong at a friend's house, her eyes were half open, but she did not seem to see anything.

I was so stupid! I said to Hulan, "Maybe I should take her to the hospital. What do you think?"

Why did I ask Hulan what to do? I should have taken Yiku right away. But I believed Hulan when she said, "You need to have a doctor give his permission first. You can't go to the hospital by yourself."

I remembered that the doctor was playing mah jong at the same place as Wen Fu, a house maybe fifteen minutes' walking distance away. I ran.

"Your daughter is sick," I whispered when I arrived. "We need the doctor, so we can take her to the hospital."

He acted as if he did not hear me, only continued his betting. The doctor, who was sitting at Wen Fu's same table, looked at me. "What's the matter?" he said. I repeated what I had said, told him how sick Yiku was.

"She's become very weak from so much diarrhea. A little trouble breathing, her eyes bouncing back and forth from the fever. I'm afraid," I said. The other men stopped talking. The doctor stood up. "I'll go," he said.

Wen Fu jumped up. "Play! Keep playing! My wife is exaggerating." He laughed. "She sees an ant, thinks it's a lion. The baby sneezed once, she thinks it's pneumonia. Sit down, sit down, keep playing."

I would not leave. The doctor kept standing. "This time it is serious, not an exaggeration," I said quietly. "She could die."

And Wen Fu got so mad because I had contradicted him. "If she dies, I wouldn't care!" he shouted. He sat back down and took a mah jong tile. "Eh, she's only trying to chase me home before I lose all my winnings," he said with a big smile.

The other men laughed in a nervous way, then started to play again, too. The doctor sat down.

That's what happened. I'm not exaggerating. He said that in front of all those people: If she dies, I wouldn't care. Those exact words. Those men heard him. They did nothing. And I was standing there, my mouth wide open, thinking, Where did he get his power over these men? What did he do to scare them too?

I ran back home. "No use," I told Hulan. "The doctor won't come."

The next long hour that followed, Hulan and I ran up and down the stairs getting fresh water to keep Yiku bathed, to force clean water into her mouth. But Yiku would not take anything, only turned her head away.

Maybe another hour later, her little body began to shake, then stretched out stiff, before shaking again. I picked her up, ran downstairs and out the door, and stumbled down the dark road, Hulan following me.

They were still playing and laughing, drinking and smoking.

"You see! You see!" I cried to my husband, showing him Yiku. And now all the men stopped playing and stood up at once. The room was so quiet. Yiku's body was throwing itself up into the air, trying to jump out of my arms. The doctor ran to us immediately.

"You stupid woman!" Wen Fu shouted, then cursed. "Why didn't you tell me she was this way? What kind of mother are you!"

He acted as if he had forgotten everything! And not one person in that room said, "You're lying. Just one hour ago, she told you." The doctor said, "Hurry, hurry. Who has a car?"

On the way to the hospital, Wen Fu cursed me the whole way. I don't remember what he said. I wasn't listening, I was holding Yiku, holding her close to me. I tried to quiet her body down, tried to keep her with me. But I knew there was no hope.

"Now you're going to leave me," I said. "What am I going to do without you?" I was crazy with grief.

And then I saw her eyes looking at me. Perhaps it was the first time she had done this since she was a little baby, looked at me with such clear eyes, as if she were finally seeing me.

I thought I was imagining this only because her time left was so short. But then I looked again.

Her eyes were clear. She did not smile or cry. She did not turn away. She was watching me, listening to me. And I was remembering something I once heard: that right before children die, they become as they would have been had they lived a whole life. They understand their life, no matter how small it has been. And in her eyes I felt she was telling me, "This is my quick life, no worse, no better than a long one. I accept this, no blame."

In the morning, I watched Yiku die. Wen Fu had gone home earlier, after the doctor told him, "No hope, too late." But I was in the hospital room with her.

I thought about all the things I had done wrong, how I had not protected her better, how I had lied and told her she would have a good life. I watched her draining away from my life, growing smaller and smaller. I told her I was sorry. And then she pointed her toes like a ballerina dancer and was gone. I didn't cry. By then I had no tears left, no feeling.

I picked her up. And I knew I didn't have to lie to her anymore. "Good for you, little one," I told her. "You've escaped. Good for you."

Tell me. If you saw this happen to your own child, could you forgive?

## *16*

# *THE GREAT WORLD*

If I could have stopped another baby from coming into this world, that is what I would have done. But I was already six or seven months pregnant when Yiku died. And that is why I had to let the baby come, knowing already how bad its life would be. Boy or girl, I would name it Danru—"nonchalance"—a good Buddhist name, as if this baby would never be attached to anything in this life, not even its own mother.

That was what I thought before the baby was born. But then Danru came, and Hulan looked at him and said, "Oh! He's the same as his father." Wen Fu was grinning big. And right away, I wanted to fight for my baby, to protect him from this curse.

After everyone left, I examined Danru's small sleeping face. His hair stuck up straight, like new grass. I stroked its softness with the palm of my hand. And then he opened his eyes, not all the way, just a little, as if all the brightness of the world were a very bad thing. He stared at me and frowned, and it was not Wen Fu's mean expression, but a worried one. He poured all his worries onto me.

So you see, right away I loved Danru, even though I tried very hard not to. It is that feeling of protecting someone so trusting, and getting back a little of your own innocence.

I stayed in the hospital five days and Wen Fu came to visit only twice, telling me each time he was very busy with his new job.

Jiaguo had given him a position at the air force headquarters, training him to do radio communications.

When the doctor said I was ready to leave the hospital, I did not wait for Wen Fu to come get me that evening. I called for the milk nurse to gather all my things and find us transportation. And within two hours' time I arrived home.

It was still early afternoon. Hulan's door was closed. I told the milk nurse to put Danru upstairs in the crib. I stayed downstairs to ask the cook about supplies and to instruct her on what to make for our dinner. And then as I started to go upstairs, the milk nurse came down and whispered, "Oh, *tai-tai,* there's a ghost up there."

When servants tell you there's a ghost, it means something is wrong and they are not in the position to tell you why. I told the milk nurse to go into the kitchen. And then I walked up to my room to see what was the matter.

Right away, I saw a young woman sleeping on my bed, wearing one of my nightgowns, taking a nap! I quickly closed the door and stood in the hallway, trying to think what this could mean. How could Wen Fu bring a woman into our house—in front of everybody! I went downstairs and knocked on Hulan's door.

"Eh! Look at you, back already!" she said. "Where is the little treasure, sleeping? Come in, come in. You must meet someone from my family." She did not say anything about the woman sleeping in my room.

And then I saw another woman. She was sitting on the sofa, her face and hands as brown and cracked as parched earth. Hulan introduced me to her aunt, Du Ching, who had come from the north. To my young eyes, she looked as if she were already ninety years old. Although I found out later she was not even fifty.

Guess who this woman was? Auntie Du! That's right, Grand Auntie Du! That's when I met her.

She had arrived just that morning.

"How many days' journey was it coming here?" I asked her, making polite talk.

Auntie Du laughed big, as if I had told a joke. "Not days or even months—over seven years, starting in Jehol Province, just north of Peiping." Her face became soft and sad. She patted Hulan's hand. "Ai! That's when your father's brother died. What a good

269

husband he was to me. I am only glad he died before he could see
how changed our village has become."

Hulan nodded, and Auntie Du turned back to me. "He died
before the Japanese came down from Manchukuo and controlled
everything—what crops were planted, prices in the marketplace,
what was printed in the newspapers, even how many eggs the
scrawniest chicken should lay—everything! You cannot imagine
how bad it was. Of course, my daughter and I left before this
happened. I only heard about this recently. That's also when I found
out I have a niece in Kunming!" She smiled at Hulan. Hulan poured
more tea.

When Auntie Du mentioned her daughter, I suddenly realized
who the girl sleeping upstairs in my bed was. I was so relieved, able
to let go of my anger. "What luck that you left when there was still
time," I said.

"That's because when I lost my husband I lost my will to hold
onto things," said Auntie Du. "I sold everything. Why hold onto
our land and let the Japanese steal it later for nothing? I changed
all our money into four small sheets of gold. I used them all up on
four kinds of transportation, train, boat, truck, and now look—
shoes!"

She had on thick black shoes, the kind missionary teachers always
wore. "You should see the roads!" she said. "Some places, they
are building them very fast, using only their bare hands to make
them wider. Other places, they use dynamite to blow them up so
the Japanese can't get in. And the roads are like cities themselves,
very crowded, rich and poor alike, all trying to leave one place and
go to another."

As she said this, I thought again about the young woman sleeping
in my bed. She must be tired from her long journey. Of course, I
was also wondering why Hulan let her sleep in my bed. Why not
Hulan's? But I could not ask this. That would have been impolite.

After a few more minutes of polite talk, I excused myself to go
look after my baby.

"The little baby!" Hulan said, suddenly remembering. She turned
to Auntie Du. "Looks just like his father."

"Not too much," I said.

"His same eyes and nose, same kind of head shape," Hulan
insisted.

I invited Auntie Du to come see for herself. And as we walked upstairs I told her his name, how much he weighed, how strong his neck already was, how he urinated on the doctor's hands the minute he was born, that's what the nurses told me. So we were both laughing when we reached the top, and that's how we must have awakened the girl in my room. She opened the door and looked out with a sleepy face that quickly turned red with embarrassment. She closed the door again. I hoped for one second more that Auntie Du would say, "Oh, that's my daughter."

But instead Hulan said, "Who's that?" And Auntie Du asked, "Is she sick, sleeping so late in the day?"

I tell you, I almost fell down the stairs right then! Auntie Du and Hulan looked at me, still waiting for my answer.

"A guest," I said. That was all I could think to say.

I found out later that Auntie Du's daughter had joined the Communists in Yenan. Auntie Du did not agree or disagree with her daughter's choice. "As for myself," she said, "I was too accustomed to my old clothes, I could not change anymore and wear somebody else's new ideas."

When my husband came home that afternoon, I immediately asked him about the girl upstairs. I did not say this in an angry voice. I did not accuse him of sneaking a woman into my house while I was having a baby. I turned my face down toward Danru so Wen Fu could not see my expression.

And without even hesitating, Wen Fu said, "Oh, that person? A pilot in my class, that's his sister. Couldn't stay at his dormitory, so he asked if I would let her stay here a few days. Naturally, I could not refuse." Wen Fu was so calm saying this.

"Why is she in our bed?" I said.

And Wen Fu answered, "I don't know. Maybe she became tired." Right away I knew he was lying. If she had been a real guest, he would have jumped to his feet and roared, "Wah! In my bed? Kick her out!"

At first I was mad—the way he put his dirty business right under my nose. He was treating me like a stupid country woman! He let his woman use my nightgown!

But then I thought about it this way: Why should I let him see me angry, as if I were fighting for him? Why should I care if he sleeps with her? Better for me! Then perhaps he will leave me alone.

So when I finally spoke again, my voice sounded friendly. "Tell our guest she can sleep on the sofa in the other room." And I did not even turn around to see the surprise on his face.

That night, I went upstairs early and closed the door. When Wen Fu came to bed later, I pretended to be asleep. And in the morning I kept my eyes closed, pretended I was still asleep when he crawled off to the other room. Every night and morning I did that. And I slept so well! I did not have to worry, wondering when his hand would reach over to open up my legs.

So that was how I let a concubine come into our house. Of course, I did not introduce her that way to Hulan and Jiaguo. I said she was a guest, the sister of a pilot, the same lie Wen Fu told. And that girl, Min, treated herself as if she really were an honored guest! She stayed up late, slept in late, went downstairs and ate a lot of food, always taking seconds, never waiting to be invited to eat more. She was not educated. She could not read a newspaper, could not even write her name. She talked in a loud, too friendly way.

Soon enough Wen Fu began treating her just as badly as he treated me, no respect. He ignored her when she talked. He threw her ugly faces when she made mistakes in her manners. So that although I never intended it to be this way, I began to feel sorry for her.

I thought to myself, What kind of woman would be so desperate she would want to be a mistress to my husband? He was not sweet and tender. With his droopy eye and mean face, he could not be called handsome. He showed his bad temper all the time. And he was not so important, a former pilot from the second class, important enough, but now he was not even a real pilot. So what could he give her?—not even a bad marriage!

I decided the reason she stayed with him was not love, couldn't be that. It was something else: perhaps a way to give up her life slowly rather than all at once. Here she would have a place to sleep, food to eat. Everything else did not matter so much. The war had made many people that way, full of fear, desperate to live without knowing why.

In many ways Min and I were the same: pretty skin, foolish heart, strong will, scared bones. Of course, our backgrounds were different, not the same at all, but really, I was no better than she was.

We both dreamt the future would come, perhaps the next day, or the day after that. And when it did, we could then reclaim our happy past—one that never really existed.

So I can honestly say, I did not dislike her. Maybe I even liked her, because this was certain: She was good company.

Even though her manners were rough, you could tell she was sincere in a foolish way. She heaped great amounts of food in her bowl, praising its flavor to the skies. She admired my ring and my necklace, asking me if they were made out of real gold. She said my clothes were so pretty—how much did they cost? She did not ask these questions the way some people would, hoping you would then offer to give them what they admired so much.

And she never complained, never ordered the servants around, not like Hulan. She thanked them for the smallest favor. She offered to hold Danru when he was crying. She talked to him in her native dialect, which was northern-sounding. And when Wen Fu was away, she told me all kinds of things that no respectable girl would talk about—about old boyfriends, dance parties, and Shanghai night-clubs she had been to, some she had worked in. I can admit, I liked to hear her talk. I liked to watch the way she rolled her eyes and waved her hands, very dramatic to see.

"I'm a singer, a dancer, too," she told me one day when she had been with us for perhaps two weeks. "Someday, though, I'm going to be a movie actress."

I thought she was dreaming. "What name will you give yourself?" I asked, to be polite. I knew that many actresses took on new names, like Butterfly Hu and Songbird Lien, the ones I admired.

"Don't know yet," she said, and then she laughed. "Not that name they gave me in Shanghai, though. When I worked at the Great World—everyone called me the Rubber Fairy. The Great World, you know the place?"

I nodded. Peanut and I had once overheard Uncle and his friends in the porch talking about this place. It was an amusement arcade in the French concession, catering to foreign customers, a very wicked and dangerous place for women. Uncle said it was filled with all kinds of strange things: men with deformities playing games with beautiful girls, animals and acrobats tossing each other in the air, and every kind of old-fashioned superstition turned into a show.

No respectable Chinese person went there, and Uncle blamed the place for giving foreigners a peculiar idea about China, as if all Chinese men smoked opium and talked to the devil, as if all girls ran around their family households half naked, singing and dancing as they served tea. And now, to meet a person who had actually worked there!

Min stood up and walked to the other side of the room. "My show was very popular. I came out in a heavy headdress, a long robe, very classic, like a fairy queen, everything covering my limbs." She walked across the room.

"And then a Frenchman, my boss, would come out. He wore a round scholar's cap and gown, his eyes were taped in that manner that foreigners use to imitate Chinese, like this, very ugly. And glued to his face were whiskers that ran down to his knees like rat tails."

Min walked in the other direction, very slowly, stroking her imaginary whiskers. "Ah, little sister," she said in an old man's voice. "Where is the secret potion for immortality? Come on, talk now, tell me. Not talking? Then maybe I will have to torture this information out of you."

Min slowly slipped out of her imaginary robe, one arm at a time. "I had on a small blouse and short pants, cut off here, above the knees. My legs and arms were powdered to make them look white as ashes. And I had on bright red slippers and black gloves." She twirled her hands.

This was shocking, even to imagine it. What kind of girl would stand in front of foreigners in her underwear?

"And then the Frenchman took me behind a torture box, a wooden device, special-made, like a prison stockade, big as this room. Everyone saw him put my head in a hole, and my hands and feet in slits, slits that ran to the corners of the box." She pointed to the corners of the wall.

Min sat down on a chair to show me more. "From the audience, that's all you could see, my head, hands, and feet sticking out. I was shaking my head, wiggling my hands and feet, crying in a pitiful voice, 'Please, I beg for mercy, don't torture me.' And then I looked at the audience and begged them, 'Help me! Help me!' I was very good. I knew how to say this in French, German, English, and Japanese. Sometimes the customers got very excited and would tell the Frenchman to let me go. But lots of times men would call out, 'Come on, come on, hurry up and make her scream.'

"Then a man with a violin would start to play nervous music, the audience would lean forward, and the Frenchman would pull on a rope next to the torture box. And my hands and feet would be pulled farther and farther apart through the slits."

Here, Min started to move her hands apart. She moved her legs farther and farther apart, so that now only her bottom anchored her to the chair. Her eyes grew big and scared. I was scared, too.

"I would be screaming louder and louder," she whispered. "The violin sounds rose higher and higher, until my hands and feet were stretched up into each corner of the box—twelve feet apart from my head, still waving and struggling in pain! Finally, I cried to him in a hoarse whisper: 'I will tell you! I will tell!' And the Frenchman stroked his beard and said, 'What is it? What is the secret to immortality?' "

Min's eyes were pinched closed, her head tossing back and forth. "Finally," she said in a slow, pained voice, "I let the word bubble out of my mouth. 'Kindness!' I shouted, 'something you will never possess!' And then I collapsed and died."

Min's eyes were closed, her mouth hung wide open, just like a dead person. I stared at her, her twisted face. "Ai-ya!" I said. "How terrible. Every night you had to do this?"

Suddenly she opened her eyes, jumped up from the chair and was laughing, laughing hard. "It's just a trick, don't you see? Those weren't really my red-slippered feet, not my hands in those gloves. There were four other girls behind the box, and each had a hand or foot in there and had to move it along the slit as I screamed. Do you understand? I was only the actress, the face, the mouth with the screaming voice."

I nodded, still trying to make sense of this.

"Of course, I was a very good actress. At least once a week, someone fainted in the audience. But after a while, it was very boring work. And I didn't like it too much, so many people clapping and cheering when I finally died."

She sighed. "I quit when I got a better job. I went to sing at Sincere—you know, the department store on Nanking Road. I was one of the girls who sang to entertain the crowds in the open restaurants. But of course, that job ended right away, two months after I started. That's when the war started, when bombs fell on the store. I went and saw what happened."

When Min said this, I knew she was talking about those same bombs the air force dropped by mistake.

"Oh, you should have seen it," said Min. "I was standing across the street, in front of that other department store, with a big crowd. And from where we stood, it looked like hundreds of people had been killed, a terrible sight. And then some officials were telling the crowd to leave. 'Everything is under control!' they shouted. 'No one was killed! Those bodies? Not bodies at all—only men's and ladies' clothing.' That's what they said. Only clothes scattered by the bombs."

Min turned to me. "I saw one thing. I heard another. And I thought, Which should I believe, my eyes or my ears? In the end, I let my heart decide. I didn't want to think I had seen so many bodies. Better to think it was just an illusion, same as my acting at the Great World."

I was thinking, This girl Min is so much like me. Seeing one thing, hearing another, both of us following our foolish hearts.

"Wait a moment," Min said. "I know something your ears won't believe." And then she ran quickly up the stairs.

When she came back, she held a record in her hand. She wound up the old phonograph, wound it so hard that when she put the needle on, the music flew out very fast. She immediately started to swing her hips and click her fingers. "This is what I used to sing and dance," she said. "I sang this at Sincere before it was destroyed."

And then she began to sing and dance as if I were one hundred people in an audience. It was an American song about love, and I heard right away that she had a very sweet voice, the kind of voice that sounded as if her heart had been broken many times. Chinese people liked that kind of singing. Her arms swayed like branches blown by a soft wind, moving more and more slowly as the music came to an end. Really, she was quite good.

"Get up, lazy," she said suddenly. She wound the phonograph again and turned the record over. She pulled me up from my chair. "Now I'm going to show you how to dance tango."

"I can't do this!" I protested. But in truth, I was eager to learn. I had seen Ginger Rogers and Fred Astaire movie pictures. I liked the way Ginger twirled her body, landed into trouble, then danced away. I liked to watch the way she tapped her feet fast, like the wings of a bird.

But we didn't dance like that. She moved forward, I moved backward, quickly, then slowly. She dipped my head back one way, then another, and I screamed and laughed. That afternoon we played the record over and over again. And on other afternoons, she taught me other kinds of dances: waltz one-two-three, foxtrot, lindy hop-hop. The cook and the servant watched us both and clapped hands.

I taught her things too. How to write her name. How to make a stitch for a hole so it wouldn't show. How to say things in a proper sort of way. Actually, she was the one who asked me to instruct her on lady manners. This was after she got into a fight with Hulan.

Hulan had asked Min where she would live after she was through visiting us. And right away Min had said, "Not your business!" The whole evening Hulan would not look at Min, pretended her chair was empty. She made sniffing sounds with her nose so often I finally had to ask her, "Hulan, are you smelling something rotten?"

Later I told Min, "If someone asks you a question, you cannot say, 'Not your business.' This is not good manners, doesn't sound good."

"Why should I answer her? She's the one with bad manners to ask," she said.

"Even so, next time she asks, you smile and say, 'In this matter, you should not trouble yourself for my sake.' This is the same meaning as 'Not your business,' maybe even stronger."

She repeated the phrase several times. "Oh, this sounds good," she said, laughing big. "I sound like a lady."

"And when you laugh," I said, "put your hand over your mouth like this, so your teeth don't show. Laughing like a monkey doesn't look good, everything on the inside of your mouth showing."

She laughed again, this time covering her mouth.

"And your name, when you become an actress—I think it should be Miss Golden Throat. It has a nice sound, very cultivated." She nodded. And I then showed her how to write her new name.

One day, after Min had been with us for maybe three or four weeks, Auntie Du passed by my room and stood too long by my doorway. She asked about my health, my husband's health, Danru's health. So finally I had to invite her in to have tea with me.

We sat at the table for a very long time. At first we made polite talk about Auntie Du's health, Hulan's health, Jiaguo's health. And then she was quiet, although she sipped her tea very noisily.

"Now I have to tell you something," she said suddenly, then sighed and was quiet.

"You are a good person," she began again, then stopped, thought again.

"You really are too trusting." She stopped herself once more.

And then she moaned, "Ai-ya!" She shook her finger at me. "Look at you, so naive, naive to the point of being stupid. Do you know what your husband is doing with that girl Min?"

How could I admit that I knew this? I emptied my face of answers.

Auntie Du sighed again. "I see I have to tell you more clearly. So naive. Then listen, *syau ning*. They have been fooling around for a long, long time. You go outside, he goes to her bed. You go to sleep, he goes to her bed. You close your eyes, she opens her arms and legs. And now that girl is pregnant and you cannot even see this. She thinks he will make her a concubine. She says he has already made this promise. She's announced it to everyone except you. And what will you do, accept this when it is too late? Will you take care of your baby, as well as the baby of your husband's concubine? Don't be so foolish anymore. *Syau ning,* open your eyes."

"You tell me this," I said, "but what can I do? I can't stop my husband. You know the way he is."

"If you cannot stop your husband, you can stop that girl." She put her teacup on the table, stood up to leave. "And now I am sorry I told you this. But I am an old woman, so some things cannot wait until after I'm dead."

After Auntie Du left, I thought about this, how everyone knew. They would be expecting me to say something, do something, shout and tell Min, "This is a disgrace! Take your shame and leave my house!"

And then I thought, Maybe this is good, Min having a baby. Now I have an excuse to tell Wen Fu that I must leave him, leave this marriage. If he wants Min for his concubine, I will tell him, You can have her for your wife! Everyone can be happy that way.

That day I planned how I would tell Wen Fu. I would make no argument, no accusation. I would ask him to divorce me, to sign a paper in front of two witnesses that said we were finished as husband and wife. Then I would take Danru, and the rest of my dowry money. I would take the train south, catch a boat in Haiphong, then go home to Shanghai as soon as it was safe. Maybe that would not be such a terrible disgrace. The war had changed people's morals. No one questioned too closely why a woman who left one year with a husband now came back home without him. How lucky I was that Min had given me an excuse!

As soon as Wen Fu came home, I told him, "I must show you something on the other side of the lake." This was a phrase we used with one another when too many ears were listening.

We sat on a bench by the lake and I showed him the paper I had written, the document announcing he was divorcing me. I said right away, no explanation, "I will go. You stay here and marry her. Hulan and Jiaguo can sign the paper and be our two witnesses." That's all I said, no shouts, no fight.

I thought he would be grateful. I was giving him my permission to marry her. You know what he did? He sat down and looked at the divorce paper. "I did not write this," he said quietly. "I am not asking for a divorce." He tore the paper up and threw the pieces into the lake behind him. And I knew he did not do this to say that he loved me, that he was so sorry for what he had done. He did this to show me who was the boss. Because after he tore up my chance, he pointed his finger at me and said in a hoarse voice, "When I want to divorce you, I will tell you. You don't tell me what to do."

The next morning, Auntie Du congratulated me. She told me Min was already gone. She had heard her leave early that morning. I was so sorry to hear this! I wanted to run out and tell Min this was not my doing. I did not ask her to leave. I did not hate her. I sat in my room, so lonely, sad that she was gone, also sad for selfish reasons, that I had lost my chance.

In the afternoon, Hulan told me about the pattern for a dress she was making. Auntie Du talked about the cholera epidemic, how refugees were afraid to get the required vaccination, how a man died getting paid to take twenty people's shots. I sat in my chair, knitting, pretending to listen. But I had no ears for this kind of talk. I was looking at the phonograph, then at Min's record. Finally I said aloud, "That girl Min, she left some belongings behind. Too bad I don't know where she went."

And immediately Hulan let me know how fast gossip travels. "Zhang's wife at the market said that she went to that place near the railway station, Nine Dragon Guest House."

And that's where I found her the next day, in a boardinghouse, a very cheap place, with only a narrow hemp bed and a plank for a table. She was quiet, maybe a little embarrassed to see me. She apologized for the trouble she had caused, thanked me for bringing her record. And then she shrugged her shoulders and said, "Sometimes you think the situation might work out one way, but it goes the other."

I asked her how many months before her baby would come. She looked embarrassed. "In this matter, you should not trouble yourself anymore for my sake."

"I taught you those words," I said. "You don't have to use them on me."

I held some money out to her, and she said, "The problem is already gone. I did it this morning. It went well, no bleeding, everything clean." I still held the money out. She smiled, then took it, thanked me, and put it in a box right away. Before I left, I told her I had always liked her singing and dancing.

One week later, Hulan said to me, "You know that Min person? She's already left with another man, telling people they are brother and sister. That fast! What kind of girl is she? How many people does she think she's related to?"

When I heard that, I did not look down on Min. Of course, her morals were different from mine. But I was thinking, Good, now I don't have to worry about her anymore. Her heart heals fast.

So really, she was the lucky one. She left. And I was the one who stayed with Wen Fu. And sometimes I would dream it was the other way around. I was Min, and I had gone back to Shanghai to work at the Great World. It was the same life, the same kind of torture, pulling me apart, inch by inch, until I no longer recognized myself.

## 17

# THE FOUR GATES

Over the next year, Wen Fu did not change. But I did, little by little. To Hulan and the others, I probably seemed the same. But that was because I covered up my feelings. I pretended to be busy with my baby, no time to worry about anything else.

During the summertime in 1941, I liked to sit in the backyard with Danru in my lap, both of us waiting for the thunder and lightning to come. I would say to him, "Listen—boom—noise. Now wait, look, look there—wah! Pretty!" Only ten months old and he already knew how to clap his hands.

That summer it was always warm in the morning, but before it became too hot, thunder came, then rain fell, always in the afternoon, raising up the good smells of the earth, and sending the servant girl out to hurry and pluck the laundry off the line.

Maybe this sounds as if my life had become easy, everything quiet and lazy, nothing to do, like a happy summer vacation. But that was really the only kind of good time I had, playing with Danru. And I used that good feeling to help me forget about everything else.

Danru was so good, so smart. Maybe every mother claims this about her baby. But imagine this: When Danru was not even one year old, I could ask him, "Where's Mama?" And he would point to me and smile. "Where's Danru?" And he would pat his stomach and smile. "Where's Baba?" And he would point to Wen Fu, but he would not smile.

Danru trusted me, too, everything I said. If he woke up hungry and crying, I would come into his room and say, "Don't cry, don't cry. I'm going downstairs to get you something to eat." And when I came back into his room, he would be standing in his crib, still not crying.

So you see, I knew Danru would grow up to be a good person, someone kind, trusting, concerned for others. He was nothing like Wen Fu, nothing at all. It didn't matter that Wen Fu was his father.

After Wen Fu chased Min away, he came back to my bed. By then he was sleeping also with many different kinds of women: native girls, prostitutes, even a schoolteacher. I think we were all the same to him, like a piece of furniture to sit on, or a pair of chopsticks for everyday use. If I said one word against any of this—or against anything else he liked—a big fight would come, always during dinnertime. I tried to keep my mouth closed so our house would stay peaceful. But inside I would be fighting myself, no peace there. So finally I would say something.

One time it was only one little word. Wen Fu had asked the cook to prepare a dish he liked, pork with a kind of sweet cabbage. I liked this dish, too. But that summer the cabbage was bad, the flavor of the bad water it drank. When Wen Fu asked me how I liked the dish, I was honest. "Bitter," I said. The next night, he ordered the cook to make that same dish for me, nothing else.

He smiled and asked me again, "Now how do you like it?" I answered the same way as before. Night after night, it was the same question, the same answer, the same dish the next day. I had to eat that bitter cabbage or nothing. But I didn't give up. I waited for Wen Fu to grow tired of this cabbage game. And after two weeks' time, my stomach proved stronger than his temper.

Maybe this seems like a foolish thing, to be so stubborn over a bad-tasting cabbage. I could have lied and said, "Tonight the food is delicious." But if I didn't fight, wouldn't that be like admitting my life was finished?

So our marriage was becoming worse. But the way I remember it, everything was growing worse—all over the country. I heard the talk, during dinnertime, or when the pilots played their mah jong games late into the night. They talked about the war as if there were an epidemic, spreading around a sickness that made people lie and cheat and hate one another.

To my way of thinking, it had started the year before, when the Burma Road was suddenly cut off, so no more trucks could come through with war supplies. People were shouting, How can the air force fly planes without gasoline? How can the army protect us without guns? Everyone felt so helpless. And we were angry, too, because the Japanese didn't close that road—it was the British. They controlled it. They shut it off when they couldn't make up their minds which government to support—Chinese or Japanese, Japanese or Chinese. They took three months to decide. And when they finally said, We support you, China, who believed them? Of course we pretended to welcome them back. What choice did we have? We didn't want them to close that road again.

And the Americans were just as bad. One day they were bragging how they were our good friends—Our Chinese pals, they said. Chennault even came back in the summertime, saying he was going to bring in more airplanes to protect us. But the next day we heard the American companies were doing a big business with the Japanese, selling them gasoline and metal for airplanes—the same ones that were dropping bombs all over China. How would you feel hearing this? So many of our pilots were dying, so many of them were our friends. Half the third class was gone, almost everyone in the classes that came later was also dead—the sixth and the seventh class, all young men. At night the pilots told stories of each new death, every one a hero. Oh, how we cried, sadness and anger together.

But even that was not the worst. The worst came when our own Chinese leaders bowed to the Japanese. The number-two leader of the Kuomintang—he did that. He said China should give up and support the new Japanese government. This was like telling us to dig up our ancestors' graves and throw the bones to the dogs. Who could say such a thing? But many did. And each time it happened, we would lose a little hope, wonder if we had fought only for this kind of humiliation.

Of course, oftentimes big rallies were held in the market square, to curse the traitors, to keep everyone's spirits strong. I was in the square one day when a rally was held. An army captain was shouting over the loudspeaker that Chinese people should never give up. "We must be willing to fight the Japanese," he said, "even if we must sacrifice every last drop of our Han blood."

And this was a strange thing to say, because, except for me and Hulan, there was probably not one drop of Han blood in the crowd that was listening. They were all tribal people—Miao, Bai, Yi, Hui, as well as Burmese and other kinds of poor mountain people and refugees. They had been forced to come down from the mountains and the outskirts of the city to help with the war, to hand over their sons as soldiers and laborers. They had been treated like the lowest kind of person, just like animals made only to carry things. And yet they stood in the square, listening to patriotic words about Han Chinese, in a language that was not theirs—and they clapped and cheered.

I think those people must have had a very bad life up in the mountains. And this made me remember that common saying everyone in China was raised with: "If you can't change your fate, change your attitude." Maybe that's what those people did, no longer blaming bad fate, no longer looking at the bad things in their life, believing they had become Han too and now had something to fight for. I told myself, Look at these people. Learn from them.

After that day in the square, I changed my attitude little by little. I did not think I was ready to die, not yet. But I thought about it this way: If I have to die soon, then maybe I won't have to suffer too much longer in this marriage. And if I do not die soon, then maybe I can find a way to escape.

Around that time, Hulan started to change her attitude too. Or maybe it was not her attitude, only her appetite. She began to eat more and more every day.

At first I thought Hulan was going to have a baby and was keeping this a secret. I knew she was eager to have children. She did not hide this fact. Whenever I complained to her about Wen Fu, or the war, or my homesickness, she would say, "If I had a son like yours, I would be able to swallow anything, I would be that grateful."

No son came, but still she was swallowing everything, always hungry. I don't mean that she had a special hunger for a pungent tofu, or a delicious fatty pork, telling herself, "That's what I want to eat." Instead, she would see beggars, hundreds and thousands coming into the city every day. She saw how they were starving, how their mouths hung open ready to catch anything that flew in, how their skin clung to their bones. And I think she imagined she would soon look the same way if she didn't have something to eat.

I remember especially how she stared at a young beggar girl leaning against a wall that led into the old part of the city. Hulan looked at that girl, and the girl looked back, so strong and fierce. Hulan said, "Why is she staring at me? She looks like a starved animal hoping to eat me and save herself."

Each time we passed her after that, Hulan claimed that the girl's shadow against the wall was growing thinner and thinner. I think what Hulan was seeing was her old self back in her country village. I'm sure of it, because one time she told me about her family, how they almost starved to death when she was a young girl.

"Every year the river overflowed," Hulan had said. "Sometimes it spilled only a little, but one year, it was like a giant kettle over-turned. And when all that muddy water covered our fields, we had nothing to eat, except dried kaoliang cakes. We didn't even have enough clean water to steam them soft. We ate them hard and dry, wetting them only with our saliva. My mother was the one who divided everything up, gave a little to the boys, then half that to the girls. One day, I was so hungry I stole a whole cake and ate it myself. And when my mother found out, she beat me, shouting, 'That selfish! Eating a cake all by herself.' And then she gave me nothing to eat for three days. I cried so hard, my stomach hurt so much—for a little kaoliang cake hard enough to break my teeth."

You would think Hulan would remember those hard little cakes, and then put a few coins, or maybe some food, into the beggar girl's bowl, which is what I did. I'm not saying I did this all the time. But Hulan did not do this even once. Instead she put more food into her own mouth. She added fat onto her body the same way a person saves gold or puts money into a bank account, something she could use if worse came to worst. So that's what I meant when I said that Hulan changed her attitude. She had once acted so generous. But now, when she looked at the misery in other people, she saw what she once was—and what she still might become.

•

During that summer, Wen Fu and Jiaguo both left for Chungking. Jiaguo said they were training military people who had arrived to defend the new capital city. He did not know when they would return, perhaps in two or three months.

Before he left, my husband had bragged that his job was especially important, developing radio communications so the air force and army would know in advance when Japanese planes were coming. When he said that, I thought, How can the air force trust him to do all their important communications, a man who lies all the time? I was glad he was gone.

Right after they left, Hulan became worried, listening to every kind of rumor. "I heard the Japanese are going to do another big bombing raid on Chungking soon, maybe even Kunming," she said one day, and then she started to cook herself a big noontime meal. When she heard thunder sounds, she ran outside and looked up at the sky, waiting to see planes drop from the dark rainclouds.

I told her, "You have to use your ears before you use your eyes. The thunder always comes from the big Burma mountains to the west. If bombers come, that would be from the north or east."

"You cannot tell these things with the Japanese," she said in a smart voice. "They don't follow Chinese ways of thinking." And then she would run out and look at the sky as if she could find the proof that I was wrong.

I remember one time when she did this again. I was in the kitchen giving Danru a bath. And I heard her scream, "They're coming! We're dead people already!"

I picked up Danru, water splashing all over the front of my dress. And then I ran outside and looked to where she was pointing. It was a flock of black birds, soaring in the same arrow pattern as fighter planes.

I laughed with relief. "Birds," I told her. "The only thing they can drop on our heads is dirty stuff."

Hulan acted insulted. "Why are you laughing at me?" she said. "Not at you."

"I saw you laughing."

"Of course I was laughing. You tell me I'm dead already. I run out and see I'm not dead. I see birds. I'm laughing at that."

"They look just like planes, even now. You look. Anyone could make the same mistake."

To me, those birds looked like birds. That's when I started thinking Hulan's eyesight was getting worse. Now she was blaming me for seeing things wrong. In the beginning, she used to make a joke about it.

One time she put her knitting needles down and the next minute she lost them. When I found them for her, she laughed and said a ghost must have swallowed them, then spit them back up again. But the next time she lost her needles, she frowned and said, "It must be your son picked them up and put them in the wrong place."

I wondered how it was to live your life never seeing clearly enough, never seeing your own faults. And then I thought, Why should she blame my son for her own absentmindedness? Why should I be criticized when she was the one who confused birds with bombers? The next time Hulan, Danru, and I went to market, I took her to a place that sold glasses.

It was a small shop in the newer portion of the marketplace, the business section that sprang up after the war started. The shopkeeper had a few pairs of glasses on a small table, and many more were piled in different baskets. The glasses on the table, the shopkeeper told us, were only for demonstration, to test the eyes, to see which strength was best.

Hulan put the first pair on, looked at me and Danru, then laughed right away: "Oh, it's like that time in the clouds on the mountain road. This pair makes me very dizzy."

Danru was watching Hulan, quiet and worried. "Are you wondering where Auntie went?" I said. He smiled at me, then grabbed the glasses from Hulan's face.

We all laughed the same way, as Hulan tried on three more pairs of glasses. But after she put on the fourth pair, she was quiet. She did not let Danru pull them off. She looked up, then down, with the glasses on, then off. She walked to the doorway of the shop and looked out at the different vendors across the street. "I see a beautiful scarf," she announced. "I see some beans I want to buy."

The shopkeeper was very pleased. He showed Hulan which basket of glasses she should now choose from. Some had gold-colored frames. Others looked like they were made of cheap tin. And then

I saw that with some of them, the legs were missing from the frames, or the gold had worn off and I could see the gray metal underneath.

"These glasses are old," I said to the shopkeeper.

"Of course they're old," he said. "Where can you get new glasses nowadays? All the metal is being used for the war, not things like this." He turned to Hulan. "Here, Miss, this pair is especially good, British-made. Those you have on, they're cheaper, but I must be honest, they're Japanese."

This news did not seem to bother Hulan and Danru, who were now busy pulling out different pairs of glasses. But those baskets of dead people's glasses looked very bad to me. Hulan decided on a round pair, no frame, just a piece at the nose holding them together and gold legs to wrap around the ears. They were very old-fashioned, not attractive at all. I told her she looked like a scholar, and she seemed pleased to hear that.

As we walked through the streets, she kept taking her glasses off, looking at something or another, then putting her glasses on.

"Can you see that?" she said.

"Basket of red peppers," I said.

"Can you see that?" she asked, pointing farther down the road.

"A man selling charcoal."

"And beyond that?" She was acting as if she were giving me an eye exam!

"An army truck with soldiers standing outside."

She continued looking at all of the things in the marketplace, looking at them two different ways, with glasses, without. But now, as we walked closer, I saw Danru was staring at those soldiers standing by the truck. I wondered what a little baby could see.

They were young boys, just recruited, it seemed, by the way their new uniforms hung on them. Many of them looked proud and excited, eagerly inspecting their new shoes, the truck they would soon ride in, taking them to places they couldn't even imagine. They had Danru's same kind of young trust.

An older man shouted sharp orders, and the young soldiers all stood up straight, tried to look serious. In two seconds they all jumped into the back of the truck, and stood against the wooden rail, looking out as the truck engine started.

And now I saw the mothers, grandmothers, and sisters, crying and waving to them from across the road. They wore turbans, bright-colored patterns on their skirts, their best clothes. They had come down from the mountains to say good-bye. Some of those new soldiers were smiling and waving, still excited. But I also saw one soldier looking scared, his bottom lip trembling, trying not to cry, just like the little boy he still was. I was watching him as the truck moved away, wondering where he was going, what would happen to him. I think he was wondering the same thing.

"Can you see that?" Hulan asked again. She was pointing to a basket of mushrooms, my favorite. And soon, I too forgot about those soldiers.

That morning Hulan became a big expert on mushrooms. Now that she could see everything clearly, she was quick to find all the flaws: a bruise, a soggy part, a broken stem. But fortunately, there were plenty of mushrooms, many different kinds, all fresh. In Kunming they grew all year round, up in the shady creases of the wet hills surrounding the city. I picked out some with long stems and big caps. I don't remember what they were called, but I can still taste them, salted and cooked in hot oil, so tender and light you could eat the whole thing, cap and stem, nothing wasted. That day in the marketplace, I was hungry for them. I was thinking of cooking them that night with some hot peppers, the kind soaked a long, long time in oil until they turn black. I was still dreaming of those spicy fried mushrooms, reaching for a jar of peppers, when the sirens and loudspeakers cried out. *Dang! Dang! Dang!* Attention! Attention! It didn't stop.

Everyone acted the same as when Hulan and I were in Nanking, when the paper warnings fell from the sky. I held onto Danru, but dropped everything else—the mushrooms, the jar of peppers. And other people were doing the same, dumping their belongings on the ground. And then we were pushing and shouting, running in every direction, toward one of the city gates, because that's what the loudspeakers were telling us to do: Run to the nearest gate and go outside the city!

"The nearest! the nearest!—where is it?" people were crying.

Hulan pushed her glasses closer to her face. "This way!" she shouted, pointing to the south.

"This way is closest," I shouted back, pointing to the north.

"There's no time to argue."

"That's why I'm saying go north. If we hurry, there's still time."

And then I started running toward the north gate, not waiting to argue anymore.

A few minutes later, I saw Hulan was running next to me. We were still running when the Japanese planes arrived, bombers and fighters, both kinds. From the ground, we could see them coming. And we knew that those planes so high in the air could see us running. They could see how scared we were. They could decide which part of the city to bomb, which people to shoot.

I could see those planes coming closer. And if I had not been using up all my breath to keep running, I would have shouted to Hulan, "You see, they're coming from the east, just as I told you."

And then we both saw the planes turn, all at once. They flew off in another direction, and we stopped running. After a few seconds we heard a bomb explode, then another. The ground shook a little. And then—that was all. We didn't die. I saw smoke and dust rising up in the southeast part of the city. Danru was clapping his hands.

When the sirens stopped, we started to walk back. All around us, people were talking in excited voices, congratulating each other, "Lucky, lucky, lucky." Soon we were back at the market, which was busier than ever. Because now, all those people who didn't die had made up their minds—to buy an extra piece of meat, or a pair of shoes, or something they thought was no longer a luxury for a life that might end with the next siren.

Hulan and I went back to the same vendor to buy the mushrooms we had been dreaming about. The vendor told us he had lost nothing. All his goods were still there, nothing stolen, nothing destroyed. We congratulated him, and he offered us a special price. Everyone felt generous.

"Her son is so smart," Hulan said, pointing to Danru. "Not even one year old, but when the siren went off, he knew not to cry. And when the bombs fell, he thought this was just thunder. He turned his head, waited for the lightning to come, and when everyone shouted, he clapped his hands."

I was very proud to hear Hulan talking about Danru that way. I tossed him up in the air to hear his little laugh. "What a good little pilot you are."

"What a good baby!" said Hulan.

"So smart!"

"So smart!"

We walked home, agreeing all the way about Danru, how lucky we were to escape, what a good bargain we got at the marketplace after the bombing.

That night, we celebrated the first bombing with a big meal and lots of rich-smelling tea. Auntie Du and the servants all laughed loudly, recounting at least ten times where they were sitting or standing when the sirens came. By the tenth time, the stories had become ridiculous and we all laughed with tears in our eyes.

"I was carrying the chamber pot down the stairs," the servant said. "*Dang! dang! dang!*—then *bamp! bamp! bamp!* The whole floor, bombed with this smelly disaster!"

"You think you were scared?" Auntie Du exclaimed. "I was chasing a chicken with my cleaver—the next moment that chicken was chasing me!"

And Hulan said, "There we stood, Weiwei and I, arguing over which direction to run. I tell you, with a bomb over your head, your feet do not want to argue!"

Two days later, the planes with their bombs came again. And once again we ran to the gate. Once again we returned home unhurt, feeling lucky, but a different kind of lucky. And at night we celebrated, only this time not so loudly. Our stories were funny, but we did not laugh with tears in our eyes.

A few days after that, the bombs fell again. This time we had no jokes, no laughter. We talked quietly. Auntie Du heard that the wife of someone we knew had been hurt very badly. Hulan wondered why our own air force did not attack back. She hoped our husbands would return from Chungking soon. I mentioned how the Japanese planes always seemed to come from the east. And Auntie Du agreed: "Always from the east."

So that's how it was. The planes kept coming, maybe three times a week, always in the morning. I don't know why the Japanese chose the morning, no reason maybe. It was just a job for them: bomb Kunming in the morning, Chungking in the afternoon. And for us, the bombing became part of our lives, too.

Of course, we were still scared when we heard the sirens. But now we knew to let go of our things gently, remembering where we put them so we could find them later. Auntie Du would make sure no pots were left burning on the stove.

"No sense saving your life only to come back to a burnt-down house," she said.

Hulan would grab a bag filled with food, which she kept close to the door. Danru would lift his arms toward me, ready to go. And then we would walk fast, very serious, as if we were going to a funeral, hoping along the way it would not be ours when we arrived.

Sometimes we went toward the north gate, sometimes to the east gate. Sometimes we walked past places already destroyed from the week before: a few buildings smashed down, and all the other houses around them still standing, only their straw roofs gone, like hats blown off in a big wind.

After we reached the gate, we jumped into a pit, or stood behind a tree. We chatted with the same people we saw every few days, exchanging advice on where to find the best noodles, the best yarn, the best tonic for a cough.

I always chose the right gate. This is true. Three mornings a week we could have died. Yet all those times we never had bombs fall on us, not even close. I started to think I had a natural kind of luck for avoiding bombs. I always chose the right streets, the right gate to run to, the right place to hide.

And in that careless way, I stopped worrying.

One day, after our lunchtime nap, Hulan said we should go to the marketplace. Danru was still napping, so I left him with Auntie Du. We went first to the vegetable stands, searching for fresh *maodo*, sweet-tasting greens, very hard to find. They were expensive, but I bought some anyway.

I was lucky, of course, to have money to buy such things. So many people were poor and could not afford even the most ordinary kind of food. But during wartime, if you were lucky to have money, you didn't think about saving your luck. A chance to taste something rare or new was like your saying "Eat, drink, be married." You could still have something to look forward to, even if life ended tomorrow.

So I was using up my dowry money fast. Sometimes I did not even bother to bargain down the vendors too much. And they were always glad to see me. "Miss, Miss!" they called as soon as they saw me. "Look here, the freshest bean sprouts, the tastiest duck eggs."

As we walked to the section that sold fish, Hulan told me she had finally gotten a letter from Jiaguo. She pulled it out and showed me the envelope.

Although Jiaguo had been teaching her how to read and write, she did not study very hard. So that even after four years of marriage and reading lessons, she could make sense of nothing more than prices in the market, characters that stood for "fish" or "pork" or "noodles," all the foods she loved.

Of course, she had been careful to hide this from Jiaguo. She pretended she could read everything! If I was reading a notice pinned up in the marketplace, she would ask me what it said. Later in the evening, I would hear her say to Jiaguo, "Eh, what about this matter of the railway I read about in the marketplace to-day?"

So Jiaguo must have assumed he was a much better teacher than Hulan was a student. Because now he had written his wife a long letter, certain she would be able to read it by herself.

But of course, she could not. Hulan handed me the letter, ex-cusing herself by saying her glasses today were not strong enough to read such small characters. This was nonsense. Jiaguo had written everything with big careful strokes, the way a child is taught in school, the way he had taught Hulan.

" 'Dear Wife,' " I read out loud. " 'Such a long time has passed between my intentions to write and my doing so now. Today I was thinking about our talk at Green Lake, the painful words we had just before I left.' "

"Wah!" Hulan pulled the letter from my hand. "He doesn't say that!" She laughed as if the letter were a joke. She was looking at it, trying to see if her glasses helped her make out any of the meaning herself.

"You want me to read it or not?" I said.

She was slow to hand it back.

I glanced at the letter quickly, then started again, this time read-ing more slowly: " 'I hope your tears have long since dried. My heart and liver have been burning with misery, although it must seem less than the misery I have caused you as your worthless husband.' "

"No more! No more!" Hulan cried, one hand covering her mouth, the other reaching for the letter. I slowly handed the letter to her, and she turned her back to me, then quietly stuck the letter in her purse. When she turned around, her face was stern.

We walked a few minutes in silence. And now I could think of nothing natural to say. I was embarrassed—because I already knew what she did not want me to know. Before giving back the letter, I had quickly read those next few sentences. And now what secrets I knew: How Jiaguo regretted that he had not yet fulfilled his vow as husband to wife. How he now vowed to become a true husband to her, if he lived. By next year, he hoped, she would be the mother of his offspring.

I was shocked, of course, to know this about their marriage. I wondered what this meant. Was theirs a marriage like that of brother and sister, monk and nun? What else could it mean? Why else did Hulan have no children? Did this mean Jiaguo had no desire for her? Was he being faithful to the ghost of her sister? Or was he like Wen Fu, seeing other women?

At that moment, I understood her better. The time she scolded me for complaining about Wen Fu's appetite for sex. The times she looked at me jealously as I was bouncing Danru on my lap. I immediately forgave her and felt sorry for my mean thoughts about her.

But I also envied her, her sexless marriage over my loveless one. And now I wondered about her—this woman who had become a mystery to me, so many things kept hidden.

"You must not think Jiaguo did something wrong," Hulan was now saying in a firm voice. "It was only a little fight, over the most ordinary thing, so small now I've forgotten what it even was."

"Of course I was not thinking anything like that," I started to say. "I have always thought Jiaguo is too kind, too good—"

Right then the sirens went off.

Hulan frowned. "How can this be?" she said. "This is not the morning, it is already too late in the day." And then she started to walk in the direction of our house.

I called her back. "Don't be foolish! The others won't be home. They are already running out the door, hurrying to one of the gates."

I decided what we should do. Hulan would go to the north gate. I would go to the east. And later, we would all return home, looking for each other the whole time. And practical-thinking that I was,

I said that if it was not too late, we would come back to the marketplace and buy the fish, still in time for our evening meal. We parted with smiles.

I was hurrying along, still making good decisions. I turned down an alley, because that was faster. I kept one eye looking for Auntie Du and Danru, just in case. And then I was thinking about what I should buy when I returned to the marketplace: of course, some tofu skins to cook with the greens.

As I planned the evening meal, the planes became louder, making it harder for me to think. I wondered why they had not yet turned away to another part of the city. And when they grew even louder, I became more confused. I walked out into the middle of the street, and I was so mad to see the planes above me. I was thinking, How stupid they are. They must be lost.

Suddenly machine-gun bullets hit a whitewashed building in front of me—and a long line of holes instantly appeared, just like stitches when the thread is yanked out fast. The piece of the wall underneath those empty stitches crumbled away, and then the rest of the wall on top fell down, like a big pile of flour that had lost its sack. And in that small moment—it was that quick—all my smart thoughts flew out of my brain. I screamed, and dust instantly filled my mouth, burned my eyes.

I was choking and coughing. I was rubbing my eyes, trying to see again. The sirens were still ringing. I heard more gunfire, the booming sound of the airplanes circling above us. When I could finally open my eyes, the first thing I saw was a woman standing in front of me. She held a poor straw broom in her hand. She was staring up at the sky, her eyes as big as eggs. And then her mouth fell open, stretched bigger and bigger, a terrible look, as though her breath was stuck and she was trying to push it out.

Now I was looking up at the same sky. Two dark shadows the shape of fish were dropping, wobbling, and growing big. And before I could even say to myself, "Bombs," I was falling, the ground was shaking, then roaring in my ear, and from all sides I heard glass shattering.

When my senses came together, I was lying with my face to the ground. I did not know whether I had fallen or whether the explosion had pushed me down, whether one second had passed, or one day. And then I looked up. The world had changed. Sand was

raining down from the sky. I thought maybe I was dreaming, because people were walking slowly, as if they were still dreaming
too. Or perhaps we were dead and now waiting to go to the next
world. But then I coughed and felt stinging dust in my throat.

When the sirens stopped, I stood up and began to walk. To my
left, I saw smoke rising behind some rooftops. Maybe it was from
a fire one or two streets away. And lying on the rooftops and in
the road were all the things that had blown over the buildings. Bits
of blankets and stools, a bicycle wheel, a cookstove and pot, and
torn pieces of clothing—only it was not just clothing, but a sleeve
with a bent arm, a shoe with a foot, and things I did not want to
recognize.

I walked slowly past all this, unable to look away. And then I
saw the same woman with the broom, the one who had been screaming right before the bomb fell. She was sitting on the ground, lifting
her arms up and down, wailing to the sky. "Where are you? I told
you not to go outside. Now will you listen to your mother?"

That's when I thought to myself: Danru!—where is he?

I started running home. I ran by people who were limping, little
children who were crying, a smiling man with blood pouring out of
his ear. And then as I ran closer and closer to my house, I saw the
streets were filled with the usual happy people, chatting and gos-
siping in the way they always do after the sirens stop.

Hulan was already drinking tea when I arrived home, pushing
her glasses close to her face, inspecting a dried fish soaking in a
large bowl. "Oyo! Gone not even one-half hour and now look—
ten bugs at least are swimming in our dinner."

"Where are they?" I said.

"In this bowl, with the fish."

"Ai! Danru, Auntie Du—where are they?"

"Ah! ah! ah!" She laughed a little. "Not back yet. Or perhaps
they are coming just now."

The door opened and I was already leaping forward—but it was
only the cook and servant, the two of them laughing. I hurried to
the door to look down the road.

"Don't worry," Hulan called to me. "They'll come soon, soon
enough. Have some tea. You can't worry them into coming back
faster."

"How can I not worry?" I shouted back. "I saw a bomb fall,

almost on top of me. I saw lots of people dead, injured, terrible sights, shoes without feet, feet without legs—"

"What are you saying!" Hulan interrupted. "You saw this? Where?"

And then both of us were running down the road. Along the way, the thunder began. And just as we reached the place where the bombs fell, the rain started. Hulan had to wipe her glasses many times.

The streets were very busy. The civil police, the army, and American service people—everybody was already there. Fire trucks and ambulances blocked the road. And then we came upon a small hill covered with people, their backs soaked with sweat or rain, mud or blood, you couldn't tell which.

"What is it?" Hulan said, wiping her glasses with a finger. "What do you see?"

We walked closer. I could see many people kneeling on top of a little mountain that once must have been a building of some sort. They were all working hard, digging fast—with shovels, with kitchen pots, with broken boards.

And then I saw the same woman who was screaming in the street, the one with the broom. She turned and saw me too, a surprised look on her face. And for a moment, it was like looking in a mirror, seeing our same terror.

She turned away. "Not like that! You're being too rough!" she shouted to the others. But no one paid any attention to her.

"Gently, gently," she pleaded. "Like this." I saw her kneel on the ground. I saw her use her bloody fingertips to pull up a brick, a board, a rock. And after each dangerous object had been removed, she would bend her face close to the ground, looking, so tenderly, at what she had found.

I have always wondered what happened to that woman pulling away at that mountain of dirt, brick, and broken bone. Boy or girl, I don't know which she lost, because when they did find her child, I could no longer watch. She was screaming, "My fault! My fault!" And I did not want to see what child, all broken to pieces, she was now blaming herself for, because at that time we were still looking for Danru.

But we did not find Danru or Auntie Du in that pile. And we did not find them in any of the other broken buildings that lined the street. Hulan and I stayed for many hours in that part of the city, hearing other mothers calling for lost children, watching layer after layer of hope peeled away, hearing shouts, then screams, then moans of disbelief fading into whispers of regret.

Each time hope failed for someone else, I made a promise, promise after promise. I said them out loud, a vow to every god and goddess. To be a more watchful mother to my son, Danru. To be sincere and loyal to my friend, Hulan. To be kind and forgiving to my husband, Wen Fu. To respect and follow the advice of my elder, Auntie Du. To accept my life without complaint.

And after I made the last promise, I saw my servant running toward me, crying and shouting, "At last, I've found you," as if we were the ones who had been lost. Oh, how I cried when she told me!—big, big sobs, the ones I kept inside when I thought I had truly lost him. And now the servant was telling me that Auntie Du and Danru were at home, had arrived not even two minutes after we had left. And everyone felt so heartsick—to think we would worry ourselves to death, looking for them when they were not even lost.

So Danru was safe. And now I knew I had to keep my promises. Hulan heard me make them, especially the part about being her loyal friend. And of course, I could not even consider taking back even one. If I had promised one less, maybe Danru would have died. Maybe he would have been found, but with one eye or one leg missing. Who can say? Who knows how hopes are fulfilled?

Of course, later, much later, I remembered, lucky for me: I made those promises long after they were already home.

# *18*

# *AMERICAN DANCE*

I did not break my promises. I took back one, only one, the part about being a better wife to Wen Fu. That's different from breaking promises. That's like buying something at Macy's, then getting a refund. I did that last week, bought shoes on sale for Bao-bao's wedding. And two days later, I saw the same shoes were another twenty percent off. So I took them back, got my refund, then bought the shoes again, this time for cheaper.

I didn't hurt anyone by taking those shoes back. I bought the same ones all over again. See, they're right here in this box. The style is almost the same as shoes I once had during the war. They were also high heels, although not too high, and the color was more like a red-brown. They had the same kind of cutout toe, but they were not very well made.

I wore those shoes to the first American dance I went to. I was dancing in those shoes the first time I fell in love.

This happened when the Flying Tigers came to Kunming. Of course, back then they were not called the Flying Tigers. They were called the "ah-vuh-gee," the way we shortened the name for the American Volunteer Group. Although some people called them the Flying Sharks, because that's what they had painted on the front of their airplanes, shark teeth, very fierce. And later someone thought the shark teeth were tiger teeth. So now you know how they got their name, Flying Tigers. It was a mistake.

Anyway, we had been invited to an American victory dance. And the day we were supposed to go, Hulan was telling me there was a Chinese schoolteacher who went crazy, left her husband, and now wanted to sleep with the American air force, everyone, married or not, young or old, it didn't matter.

"She is openly saying this, a Chinese woman!" said Hulan. "This is true. Everybody is saying she came down with a sickness right after the American victory, then denounced her husband in public. What kind of sickness—who knows? But now she's crazy about sex, can't stop talking about it. She's old, too, maybe already thirty, and not even pretty."

Hulan said the crazy schoolteacher was going to be at the dance, the one that would be held at the American Club. The Americans invited the Chinese pilots to their party, wives and girlfriends could come too. Of course we wanted to go! At this dance, there would also be music—a phonograph and records—lots of food, and a whiskey punch that tasted like soda pop and made everyone dance wild.

I remember that dance party, Christmastime 1941. It was held three days after the Japanese planes had come once again to drop bombs on Kunming. But this time the American volunteers were there to chase the Japanese away. Our first big victory in so many years! Everyone had run into the streets, shouting and screaming, cheering the American fighter planes with their shark teeth painted on the front. Firecrackers were exploding, drums were banging, car horns honking, as if it were the New Year. So maybe we all went crazy for the Americans, just like that schoolteacher.

As soon as we walked into the American Club, we heard the music playing loud. It was the same lindy-hop song Min once taught me, "Air Mail Special," we called it, very lively. Wen Fu snapped his fingers, smiling at what he saw in front of him. People were already dancing, the girls with their high heels clicking, the Americans with big shoes sweeping the floor, making nice soft sounds.

If that schoolteacher was there, I could not tell. There were many crazy Chinese girls there: university students, teachers, nurses, and others who had fled from other parts of the country—all of them now eager to dance with the Americans. Who knows how they found out about the party. Who knows where they got their

Western-style party dresses—pink, green, yellow, some with flowers sewn on, many with big full skirts, almost nothing on top, their arms and shoulders all exposed. But there they were, dancing with the tall foreigners, putting the pilots' caps on their newly curled hair, all kinds of silly behavior.

Of course, the American Club was not really a nightclub. It was a large warehouse. During the day, the American volunteers used it as a big meeting hall. For the dance, the floor had been waxed many times, so that even though it was only concrete, it was as shiny as wet marble. The benches had been pushed to the side. And on top of long tables sat small buckets with burning candles, the kind used in the summertime to chase insects away; that was the only kind of candle you could get back then.

And from the rafters and all along the walls, the Americans had hung paper decorations—trees, candy canes, candles, and other shapes in bright colors. They were not very interesting. But then Jiaguo said these were special Christmas charms, made by the missionaries and Red Cross girls in Rangoon, and flown over the hump of the Burma mountains. We knew that such a journey was very dangerous to make, even for important wartime supplies, so we looked again to admire these American Christmas charms with new respect. The Red Cross had even sent a Christmas tree, which Wen Fu said was genuine American, recalling pictures he had once seen in a magazine. To me, that tree looked like some kind of local bush, only cut in the shape of a Christmas tree. It was decorated with greeting cards, red ribbons, white cotton balls, and something that looked like hardened white lotus seeds tied together in a long necklace. Underneath the tree were hundreds of big red socks, wool socks you could wear, and inside each was a piece of chocolate or a candy cane wrapped in shiny paper and tied with a ribbon. I knew what was inside only because Hulan took four socks, insisting each time that the Americans encouraged her to take more.

Wen Fu told me he had learned how to dance at nightclubs in Shanghai many years before. I could tell he was eager to show off what he knew. And I soon found out: He knew nothing! No rhythm, no technique, no regular footsteps. He did not dance at all like Min, who moved her arms and legs like branches caught by a soft wind. Wen Fu swung me so hard I thought my arms would pull away from my body. And finally he twirled me in such a clumsy way the heel on one of my high heels broke off, and suddenly I was dancing like a wounded person, one leg longer than the other. Wen Fu let me limp away.

From my chair, I watched my husband walk up to a group of girls, all wearing pretty dresses. He pointed to his uniform, and one girl began to giggle. I turned away. If he wanted to flirt, I didn't care.

And then I saw Hulan and Jiaguo dancing. Their shoulders were pressed together, but Hulan's feet were spread far apart, each foot going in the opposite direction of the other. Jiaguo would squeeze her thick waist closer to him, then shake her a little, as if this would make her feet cooperate. He seemed to be scolding her, but she was laughing. Watching them, I was wondering if finally Hulan had had her wishes fulfilled, if Jiaguo had become a true husband to her. And then she saw me, waved, and broke away from her husband.

"If I had to dance to save our lives—disaster on all of us!" she said, then sat down, fanning herself with a paper tree. "Did you see her?" she asked.

"Who?" I said. I was pounding the heel back into my shoe, then stamping my foot to make the nail go in.

Hulan leaned toward me. "The schoolteacher, of course, wearing a blue dress. She pulled all the hair out of her eyebrows, then painted them back on."

"Where is she?" I asked. I looked around the room.

"She was close to that table with the food, throwing herself at another American. Let's go see," Hulan said.

But we did not find a crazy woman at the table. Instead, Hulan found things she wanted to eat, American delicacies, also sent by missionaries from far away. I can admit this: I was curious to try them too, these foods that had to be sent such a dangerous long ways. So I tried them all, three kinds of taste. The first was a soft dumpling, named for its color, brownie—so sweet it made my teeth ache. The second was the necklace food lining the tree, popcorn. It was very dry and scratchy, and my mouth watered, trying to find a flavor. And then I ate a little cracker with something awful on top. Hulan ate one too, thinking that mine had been rotten by mistake. No mistake. That was the first time we ever ate cheese.

And then Hulan and I both noticed someone unusual. A Chinese man was walking around to each of the tables, talking to both the American and the Chinese pilots, shaking hands in the Western manner. He was almost as tall as the Americans. He had a very energetic and friendly manner. And this was even more strange, he was wearing an American-style uniform. When he came up to us, Hulan asked him in a rude manner, "Eh, where did you find the American uniform you are wearing?"—as if it were stolen!

But the man continued smiling. "I am an American," he said in Chinese. "American-born." And then he said something very fast in his American language, something about his mother and father and where he was born. Hulan laughed in astonishment, then re-marked that his English sounded genuine, just like a cowboy's. Of course, she said this in Chinese.

But I surprised this man, Hulan too, by speaking English. "Be-fore, in Shanghai, I study English lessons."

He started to ask me lots of questions in English.

"No, no," I said, going back to Chinese. " 'Study' does not mean able to speak. I was a very naughty girl, a bad student. The nuns had to pray hard for me."

He laughed. "And did God answer their prayers?" he asked in Chinese.

I smiled and shook my head. "Still I know enough English to tell. To my eyes, you look Chinese. To my ears, you sound exactly like a foreigner."

The man laughed again. "By golly," he said in English, then returned to speaking Mandarin to thank me. And after that— hah!—he switched to Cantonese, then to some sort of tribal dialect, then to Japanese.

"You change tongues as easily as a phonograph changing rec-ords!" I said.

"Oyo!" Hulan teased. "You are a spy perhaps, although for which side, it's hard to tell."

The man pulled out an identification card from his wallet, and then explained that he was with the United States Information Service, helping the American volunteers and Chinese air force with translation. "The work is not very difficult," he said modestly. "For example, one of your pilots wanted a way to say thank you to the Americans." He pointed to a poster on the wall in front of us. "I told him to write those words."

"What does it say?" asked Hulan.

" 'Hooray, Yanks.' "

"And what is the meaning?" I asked.

And then this man who was both Chinese and American looked at me. He did not say anything for a few seconds, as if he were thinking hard how to translate this carefully. Finally he said, "It means you are surprised by happiness, so much so you cannot express this feeling in ordinary words."

When he said that, I felt he had expressed the deepest wishes of my heart, that someday I too would be caught by happiness, like a fish in a net.

Suddenly I thought I was standing too close to him. The room was very crowded. I tried to lean back farther toward a wall, and that's when the heel on my bad shoe broke off once again, and this man had to catch me in his arms before I fell to the floor.

So that was how I met Jimmy Louie—yes, your father! Can you imagine? I went looking for a schoolteacher crazy for Americans. And instead I found an American man who was crazy for me.

Many years later your father would claim to his American friends, "I fell in love with her right from the beginning. As for Winnie— she only fell. But what matters is I caught her." He was charming and funny like that, remember? He was always like that, right from the start.

And it was true, what he said. I cannot claim I loved him right from the beginning. I had no such romantic thought. I was a married woman, trying to avoid troubles in my marriage, not looking for more.

Although I can admit I was interested in watching Jimmy Louie, his ease with the Americans. When those big men walked up to the food table, Hulan and I shrank away, trying to make room. But Jimmy Louie, without any hesitation, slapped them on the back, called them by name—"Hey, Smitty," "Hey, Johnny," "Hey, Hank."

And if I am to be honest, I should also confess that I grew more and more ashamed of the clothes I had chosen for that night, a plain brown dress with long sleeves. Worse, I had taken off both my shoes and was now standing barefoot. I must have looked no better than a local country girl. What would an American think!

And all around me were so many girls, all wearing fancy dresses, their hair pressed into shiny curls, no signs of war or unhappy marriages in their faces.

That night, it seemed all those pretty girls ran up to Jimmy Louie, five or six at a time. Of course, he was very handsome, but he did not encourage those girls the same way Wen Fu did. He was popular because of what he could give those girls: an American-sounding name, so they could introduce themselves to their new Yankee friends.

Jimmy Louie would examine their giggling faces, as if he could determine their character in a few seconds and the name that suited them best. For most of the girls, he gave out names that were easy to pronounce: Donna, Dotty, Patty, Peggy, Sally, Susie, Maggie, Mattie, Jeannie, Judy. But if a girl was too pushy, or too fussy, if she said she wanted a name that was prettier than her friend's, he would give her a twisty name that was impossible for the Chinese tongue to say: Gretchen, Faith, Theodora. "These are the finest American names," he would tell those girls, and then he would turn to us and wink.

"What about you two?" he finally asked. "You should have American names as well." He asked us what our Chinese names were. And then he squinted one eye, raised one corner of his mouth, pretending to look at us through an imaginary camera, as if he could capture exactly what he saw in a single word.

That's how Hulan became Helen. Jimmy Louie said Helen was a very elegant name, but I thought he chose it because it sounded like Hulan. And I became Winnie, which Jimmy Louie said was a lively and lucky-sounding name. "Win, win, win," he said. He wrote these names down on a piece of paper.

At that moment, our husbands found us. Jimmy Louie shook hands with Wen Fu and Jiaguo in the American fashion. He also bowed slightly in the Chinese manner. If he was disappointed to learn I was married, he did not show it then—although he soon found a way to let me know what he thought of my husband.

Hulan showed Jiaguo her new American name. She ran her finger across the piece of paper—as if she could already read English! "Hu-lan, Hu-lan," she said, pronouncing it slowly, the same as her Chinese name.

"Yours?" Wen Fu asked me.

"Winnie," I said.

"Not bad, not bad," Wen Fu said, then turned to Jimmy. "Since you are being so generous tonight, how about a name for my friend and me?" So Jimmy named them as well. To Jiaguo he gave the name Jack, "Jack like Jack London," Jimmy said. "An American famous for his struggles and adventure."

"Jock! Jock!" Jiaguo repeated several times. "I like this name very much." And without correcting him, Jimmy wrote down Jiaguo's new name as Jock. That was how Jimmy was, very polite, never embarrassing someone unnecessarily.

For Wen Fu, Jimmy suggested the name Victor. "A lucky name for a pilot, and one that matches your wife's," he explained.

But then Wen Fu demanded that his name be even more special than mine, that it should be unusual as well, not the same as everyone else's.

"Perhaps the name of a recent hero," said Jimmy.

"More important than that," said Wen Fu.

"Someone who changed history forever," Jimmy suggested.

"Exactly!" answered Wen Fu. "That would be the best."

"Judas," Jimmy said. "Your name is Judas. I know of no one else who has this name."

"Ju-dassa! Ju-dassa!" Wen Fu repeated, trying on his new name. "It is a good name, good-sounding to the ear, too." Jiaguo and Hulan agreed.

I was biting my lips, remembering what the nuns in school had taught me about this evil name. And now Jimmy Louie could see I was trying not to laugh. He smiled like a schoolboy, pleased that I knew what he had done.

He wrote Wen Fu's new name on a piece of paper, then said, "This song that just came on, it's 'Moonlight Serenade,' an American favorite. Would you be kind enough to let me dance it with your wife?"

Before Wen Fu could say anything against this idea, before I could protest that I had no shoes, I found myself whirling in the arms of Jimmy Louie, away from Wen Fu's frowning face, and into the crowd of happy dancers. He was a good dancer, almost as good as Min.

"That was very naughty, what you did, this name," I scolded him in a teasing voice. "Now I am in trouble with my husband."

Jimmy Louie laughed. "Doesn't he have a sense of humor?"

"Only for jokes he throws at someone else," I said.

"Of course, I was wrong to do it," said Jimmy Louie.

"Terrible," I said. And then I saw Jimmy Louie smile and wink. I slapped his shoulder. He bent my head back and laughed. Then I laughed too. This was not love, but the danger of it. And then Jimmy Louie twirled me out gently to the side, and I saw a terrible sight that left me without words.

It was the crazy schoolteacher in her blue dress, half an eyebrow smeared away, her eyes more closed than open. She was sleep-dancing in the arms of an American pilot. The pilot spun her into the arms of another pilot, and they both laughed, before spinning her away to someone else. I could not stop staring, to see this story Hulan had told me now in front of my eyes, to see my own self looking back from that woman's lost eyes. For there she was, a woman who had denounced her Chinese husband and was now worth less than all the words she had spit on him. And here I was, no better than she. I had let an American fool my husband. I was now dancing barefoot with this same American, letting him throw me this way and that, any way he pleased.

So I excused myself from dancing, telling Jimmy Louie I was a tired old married lady. I left him standing on the dance floor, and I did not think I would ever see him again.

By the time I found Wen Fu, it was already too late.

When we returned home, Wen Fu showed me his anger right away. He was not doing this because of the name Jimmy Louie had given him; it was not until many years later that he found out what Judas meant. That night he was angry because I had danced with an American. Another pilot had joked to Wen Fu that perhaps the Yankee volunteers had conquered the women, as well as the Japanese.

So I was not surprised he was angry. I was ready for this. In our room upstairs, he cursed and called me all kinds of bad names, the same ones he had used throughout our marriage: "Whore! Fox-devil! Traitor!" Whiskey smells poured out of his mouth. I did not protest. But I also did not act afraid. I let these insults roll over me.

Suddenly he grabbed my hair and threw me to the floor. "You

want to be a whore!" he shouted. "I will let you be a whore." He went to a table and pulled something out from the drawer. He threw down a piece of paper, and then a pen and a bottle of ink.

"Now I am divorcing you," he said. "Write that down. 'My husband is divorcing me.' "

When I looked up, I saw he was pointing a gun to my head, smiling crazily. "It's no use! Our marriage is finished," he said. "If you don't write this, I will kill you!"

What kind of fool did he think I was? He thought I was scared. I wasn't. He thought he was forcing me to divorce. He needed no such force. Instead, I felt I had just been given a crazy kind of luck. I was writing fast. Of course I was writing. My blood was rushing, my thoughts running fast, feeling I would soon be free. I quickly wrote down our names. I wrote the date. I signed my name. I left three spaces so he and two witnesses could also sign the paper. I checked everything twice, then handed the paper to him, trying to keep my anger and happiness in. "You sign here," I said, pointing to the bottom of the paper.

He read it, then looked at me with so much hate in his eyes. He signed the paper, almost tearing it with the force of his pen. He threw everything down on the floor. I picked up that piece of paper, so precious to me now.

"You see, you are divorced," he said in a strange voice. "Worth nothing. You have no husband. You have no home. You have no son."

I looked up, startled. I had not thought what would happen to Danru. How foolish I was! To think my body was my own, something to protect or lose only for myself. I could never leave him. I could never do what my mother did to me.

He waved the gun at me. "Now beg me not to divorce you," he said. "Beg me to tear up that divorce paper in your hand," he said. He moved the gun closer to my head. His mouth was ugly and wild, like a crazy person's, but his eyes were clear. "Do it!" he shouted. "Get down! Beg me!"

Right then, I knew he wanted to see me suffer. He would twist his mind this way and that, until I no longer had the strength to turn mine the other way. And he would not be satisfied until he proved over and over again that he had conquered me completely.

My mind broke. My will to fight was gone. My voice gave one

loud cry for myself. And then, with my face to the floor, I begged him.

"Louder!" he demanded. "Say you are sorry you are such a worthless whore." I said those words.

"Bow and say you promise to be an obedient wife." I bowed and said those words.

He laughed with delight. "Say you cannot live without me as your husband." I said those hated words.

Wen Fu began to laugh more. "I like this, I like this very much." And then he became quiet. He walked over and took the divorce paper from my hand. I thought the torture was over. He waited until I looked up. His face was sad. He was shaking his head, looking at me, looking at the paper.

"It is too late," he said. "I will not give you back the marriage. You are still divorced." And then he threw the paper on top of my head. "Get up!" he shouted. "Get in the bed."

"Kill me if you want," I begged.

"Of course I will kill you," he said. "You and everyone else in this house if you do not obey. Get in the bed."

That night, with a gun to my head, he raped me, telling me I had lost the privileges of a wife and now had only the duties of a whore. He made me do one terrible thing after another. He made me murmur thanks to him. He made me beg for more of his punishment. I did all these things until I was senseless, laughing and crying, all feeling in my body gone.

The next morning, after Wen Fu left for work, I picked up the divorce paper lying on the floor. I found my suitcase. And now I was hurrying. I packed only a few things. I took what money I could find, around two hundred Chinese dollars. I went to get Danru. Hulan and Auntie Du saw me as I came downstairs. I knew by their faces that they had heard our fight the night before.

"Every woman's husband has a bad temper," Hulan said, trying to reason with me. "Your situation is no different."

I showed them my divorce paper.

"What is this?" said Hulan.

"My divorce. Last night my husband divorced me. So you see, now I have to leave."

"Ai!" Auntie Du cried. "Disaster! Disaster!"

"Who were your witnesses?" Hulan asked, looking at the paper. She pressed her glasses closer to her face. "I see no name seals."

"No witnesses," I said. "Last night we had no time to get witnesses."

Hulan clapped her hands together with joy. "Then you have no divorce! He cannot make you leave. Now sit down, eat your morning meal. Calm down, no more worries. This is only a misunderstanding. Tonight he'll be sorry, tears of remorse pouring down his face, you'll see."

"You understand nothing!" I cried. "I am the one who wants this divorce. Why should I want to stay in this marriage!" I began to tremble hard. "It is not just his temper. He is a monster. He is more evil than you can imagine." And then I had an idea. "Here, you two can both be my witnesses," I said quickly. "Where are your name seals? If you do this, I am in your debt forever."

"How can I do this!" said Hulan, shrinking away.

"She is right, *syau ning,*" said Auntie Du. "How can you ask a friend to be witness to your tragedy? Reconsider. Think of your little son."

"Of course I am thinking of my son. That's why I am leaving. Divorce or no divorce, we are going."

Auntie Du began to wail. "Ai-ya! Ai-ya! Where can you go? Where can you stay? Use your head, *syau ning,* think. The Burma Road, the railway—both are cut off again. And in every corner dangers, each one worse than the other—bandits, mosquitoes, Japanese."

"I am glad to face those kinds of dangers rather than my husband," I said.

"It's no use!" said Auntie Du, and threw up her hands. "We cannot reason with her. A big angry wind is blowing through her head and she cannot hear anyone. She is going no matter what."

And that's when Hulan said in a quiet voice, "Then we must help her. Nothing else we can do." She turned to me. "I will not be witness to your divorce. Jiaguo, I'm sure, would be against that. But I can help you escape, if we both keep this a secret."

I threw my arms around Hulan, like a child against her mother. I cried with thanks and this embarrassed her. "We have no time for this," she said. "We must think about what you should do, where you should go." She walked over to her sewing basket and pushed her hand inside. She pulled out some money and put this in my purse. Auntie Du sighed, then went to the kitchen, found dried fish, mushrooms, noodles, and tea, then wrapped each of these things in clean paper.

That morning they helped me find a rooming house on the other side of the lake, close to the marketplace. It was a poor room in a straw house, as bad a place as I have ever been. But I did not complain, not one word, that's how happy I was to be there.

Hulan said I would be safe. She said she would come back when she had found me a ride on a truck.

In the afternoon, Danru and I played on the floor. I used my chopsticks to pluck bugs out of the mattress. Danru would chase them, smashing them flat with the bottom of a bowl. We did that until there were no more bugs, until we had changed our world, dirty to clean. And when we were done, I congratulated him for our victory. We ate a small meal; then together we fell asleep, his small self curled safely against my side.

We woke up, hearing Wen Fu's roaring voice. "Where is she?" He sounded like a bull, ready to crash through a gate. I sat up and pushed myself into the shadows of the corner.

"Be quiet, no sounds now," I whispered to Danru. And he was so good. He understood. He trusted me. He made no cry, no small whimper. He wrapped his arms around me and was quiet.

"Where is she?" we heard him shout again. Danru pushed his face against me harder.

And then I heard Hulan's small voice. "But you promised to be kind."

So you see, Hulan helped Wen Fu find me. Of course, she was very sorry later on. She saw his promise meant nothing. He was not kind. I don't have to tell you what happened.

So many years gone by, and still the anger can never come out completely. You can hear this in my voice. When I talk about him now, I am still angry. And if you think that was the worst part of my life, you are wrong. The worst was always what happened next, and then after that, and then after that. The worst was never knowing when it would stop.

One month after it happened, I found out I was pregnant. I went to the doctor and the baby came out before it could be born. Two months later, the same thing. Two months after that, the same thing. We had no birth control, not back then. Wen Fu didn't care, baby or no baby.

So now maybe you think I killed lots of babies, and I didn't care either. It did not mean I wanted to kill those babies. That bad man was using my body. Every night he used it, as if I were—what?— a machine!

Today you teach your daughters to say to a stranger, "My body is my body. Don't touch me." A little child can say this. I was a grown woman, and I could not say this. I could only stop those babies from coming.

I cried to myself, This is a sin—to give a baby such a bad life! Poor Danru. He trusted me. So I let those other babies die. In my heart, I was being kind.

Look at my face now. I was a young woman then. I had no more hope left, no trust, no innocence. There were many, many times when I almost killed myself, when I hated myself so much because finally I could not.

So I ask you: What do you see? What is still there? Why did I want to live so much?

# *19*

# *WEAK AND STRONG*

I have told you about the early days of my marriage so you can understand why I became weak and strong at the same time. Maybe, according to your American mind, you cannot be both, that would be a contradiction. But according to my life, I had to be both, that was the only way I could live.

It was like this: For the rest of the war, I lived a life without hope. But without hope, I no longer despaired. I no longer fought against my marriage. Yet I did not accept it either. That was my life, everything always in between—without hope, yet without despair; without resistance, but without acceptance. So you see, weak and strong.

I am not asking you to admire me. This was not harmony with nature, no such thing. I am saying this only so you will know how it is to become like a chicken in a cage, mindless, never dreaming of freedom, but never worrying when your neck might be chopped off.

But of course, even the stupidest chicken will fly away when the cage breaks open. And now I will tell you when that finally happened.

I had to wait until 1945, the middle of summer. I still remember that day, what I ate, what Auntie Du said, what Hulan was wearing. I wonder why that is, to remember the details of the moment right before everything changes. In any case, we were crowded around our little square table—Hulan and Jiaguo, Wen Fu and Auntie Du, and Danru, sitting on a little stool next to me. We were eating our morning meal—a very ordinary meal—a porridge made out of a tiny rice grain, a pickled vegetable that looks like a small snail, cold lettuce hearts, which were leftovers from dinner the night before, a stinky bean curd, and sweet boiled red beans, the kind that are as small as baby teeth. Our meal was so ordinary we did not even waste words criticizing or praising the dishes, which is what we always did when the meal was interesting, what was prepared well, what was not.

Of course, now that I am thinking of it, I would praise those dishes today—all those tastes you cannot get in America, what a pity. The lettuce heart, for example, it was thick like a turnip, crunchy but sweet, easy to cook. And the bean curd, we could buy that from a man who rolled his cart by our house every morning, calling, *"Cho tofu! Cho tofu!"* It was fried on the outside, and when you broke it open, inside you'd find a creamy-soft middle with such a good, stinky smell for waking up your nose.

But as I said, back then all those tastes were just everyday foods, like the cereal you buy at the store. Anyway, because it was summer—August by your calendar—we did not have an appetite to eat very much.

I remember something else about that breakfast. Hulan was eating one red bean at a time, very slowly, like this. She would pluck one from the plate, then wave it in the air as if it were the body of a fly, zigzagging into her mouth. By then she had grown quite fat, and the dress she was wearing, made from the peach-colored cloth I had given her, was too small across her chest.

"When I was a young girl," she said, "I was the only one in my village who could pick up one hundred of these beans, one at a time, never dropping any." She dropped another bean into her mouth.

Of course, I knew what she was talking about, the old silly custom of showing in front of prospective mothers-in-law how delicate, how elegant your manners. You were supposed to use your most slippery chopsticks to pick up the smallest bits of food—without making a big mess. "In your village," I teased her, "women had no other work than to count how many beans went into their mouth?"

"You don't believe this?" she said. She picked up another bean, swallowed it.

"I am not saying I don't believe you," I said. "Only that maybe there was no time to count how many you actually ate. Maybe it was only fifty—"

"I tell you, it was one hundred!" She ate another bean, then another and another, as if this would prove her right.

Auntie Du scolded us both. "What kind of nonsense are you two arguing about now? Maybe it was two hundred. In any case, why measure a girl's value by how many beans she can balance between her chopsticks?"

At that moment we heard a quick knock at our door. And then before we could even put our chopsticks down, the knock came again, this time harder and faster. A man burst into our house, a pilot, from the third class. He was grinning big, shouting, "It's over! It's over!" And even with this, we did not imagine—because we were told so many times not to expect this news for at least another year—we could not believe our ears when he said China had won the war, pushed the Japanese imperialists out forever!

Everyone was crying with joy—Hulan, Auntie Du, the cook, even our husbands. You should have seen the happy tears and heard the shouts. We could not sit down, we could not stand still. We were stamping our feet, jumping up and down. Hulan threw her arms in the air to thank the gods above, and of course, that's when she tore her dress, under both arms, although she didn't know it at the time. In a few moments, another pilot came into our house, and after him, another, and then another. Each time someone ran in the door, we made the first pilot repeat how he heard the news— who told him, how he couldn't believe it was true, how he finally came to believe it was true.

So you see, everyone was talking at once—except for me. I was laughing and crying as well, pretending to listen to all this good talk. But really, my heart was beating fast, my mind was dizzy, my feet were ready to run. Because I was remembering what it was like to dream again. I was thinking, Now I have a choice. I can go back to Shanghai. I would write a letter right away to my father. I would ask my uncle or Old Aunt or Peanut. Someone would help me, I was sure. And soon I could leave this marriage and start a new life.

By the afternoon everything was decided. We would leave Kunming immediately, the next morning. We would not spend even one extra day trying to sell our furniture. Better to dump everything! You see how excited we were? For seven years we had been stuck in Kunming. For eight years I had been stuck in my marriage.

And so that day we began to pack our things, sorting out belongings, what would stay, what would go, as quickly as saying, "This, not that." Danru was already five years old. Oh, how he cried when I said we could not take the little woven-hemp bed he had grown up with.

"Stop crying!" Wen Fu shouted. And Danru, so scared of his father, became quiet immediately. But Wen Fu was in such a good mood. This time he did not scold Danru anymore. He said, "In Shanghai, I will buy you a better bed, and not just a bed, but a little car made out of wood. Now smile." And Danru stretched his lips as wide as he could. Poor little Danru!

The next morning we left Kunming. This time we did not have to sit in the back of a truck. We got into a bus with Hulan and Jiaguo, along with other pilots. By then, only a few pilots were left in Kunming, so the bus was not too crowded. Wen Fu and I had our own bench to sit on. I sat by the window with Danru on my lap. And this time, we had brought with us many suitcases and boxes, not just the one trunk allowed us when we first arrived. We even had our own quilts with oilcloth bottoms, just in case we needed to spend the night in a place without proper bedding.

As the bus moved down the road, everyone but me looked back at our house one last time. Why would I want to see the place where I had lost my hopes? I was twenty-seven years old and I already wanted to forget everything that had happened in my life. I looked only ahead.

I saw that the streets were very crowded, filled with buses and trucks and people carrying their loads balanced on a stick. And then we were at the outskirts of the city, beyond the city wall, going past little villages, then climbing into the mountains. My heart was pounding, filled with a hurry-up anxiousness. It was the same kind of feeling I had when I thought the Japanese would catch up with us. Only this time I was scared that if we did not leave fast enough, someone would suddenly say, "This is a mistake. The war is not over. We must go back."

And then one of the pilots did shout, "Stop!" and ran down the aisle to give further instructions to the driver, pointing to the side of the road. Sure enough, the bus gave a big groan and stopped. I bit my hand to stop myself from crying out loud. Three pilots rushed out the door. I thought we were being attacked. I stood up and looked out the window. And I let out such a big laugh when I saw what they were really doing—taking pictures with a camera!

One of them was standing in a rather silly pose, proudly pointing to the sky—as if the sky here were different from everywhere else. I wanted to laugh. And then I too looked at that sky. And I remember I had a very strange feeling, the way you feel when you are coming out of a confusing dream. It was as if I had never seen Kunming before. Because what I saw was not just an ordinary sky, ordinary clouds. The color of the sky was shocking to the eye, such a bright blue, like a sapphire. And the clouds—three of them, one right after the other—were shaped just so, like gigantic cushions for the gods of the heavens. And then I saw a bird, a large bird, the color of its wings underneath like a rainbow. I saw green hills covered with trees, their arms sweeping down, brushing the ground. And running along the ground were flowers, so many different kinds, bursting wild from the earth. And beyond that I could see the old city itself, the peaceful winding streets, the whitewashed walls, now looking clean-bright from a distance.

I saw all this for the first time, and I was not happy to see it. I was bitter—that I had never felt this kind of beauty until now, too late.

Along the way to Wuchang, I saw what the war had done. In almost every village, it seemed, were rows of one-story clay houses, with their middles crushed in, or their roofs torn off, or the walls on one side all fallen down. Some houses were already fixed, holes patched here and there with the broken top of a table, or straw matting from a bed, or the door of a wrecked car. I once looked down into the mouth of a green valley. And scattered here and there in the tall wild grass were black clumps, a dozen or so. From that distance they looked like broken rounds of coal carelessly tossed away. I did not realize until after we had almost passed by that this had once been a village, and those black lumps had been small houses, burned down several years ago with no one left to build them back.

But mostly what I saw were poor and hungry faces, so many, many faces along the road, young and old, all wearing the same dry look of too much grief. They were poking through rubble, placing scraps in thin bags. And when their ears caught the sound of our bus, they dropped their bags, and their hands formed meager begging bowls. "Little Miss, look at our misery! Give us your pity!" their voices wailed, and then faded, as our bus kept driving, pushing all that misery to the side of the road. My stomach ached to see them.

Those of us in the bus had our own worries as well. We had heard that many poor people had become bandits and now roamed wild throughout China, especially in the mountain regions. And when we had to take a boat across Tungting Lake, we were warned that pirates had already seized many boats and would not hesitate to slice our throats. The Kuomintang insisted it was the Communists who were doing these crimes. And Auntie Du secretly told us this was not true. Her daughter had written her and told her Communists were now blamed for everything bad in China. So you see, the end of the war did not stop all the fights.

It was not until we safely reached Wuchang—where we would stay in a hotel only one night—that Hulan and I realized we would not see each other anymore. From here she and Auntie Du would go far north to Harbin, where Jiaguo was being sent to make sure Japanese troops and officials surrendered to the Kuomintang and not to the Communists. And Wen Fu, Danru, and I would go east by train to Nanking, where we would take a boat to Shanghai.

It's true that Hulan and I had had many fights, many disagreements those past eight years. But now we were sad to let each other go. That last night at the hotel, we talked for many hours, until our eyes could not stay open. The next morning we ate our breakfast slowly, the same kind of simple meal as I have described before: the same rice porridge, the small red beans. And after we ate, we exchanged addresses. I wrote down my father's, as well as Uncle's on the island. She copied the address in Harbin that Jiaguo had written for her. And then we both went to our rooms to search in our trunks so we could give each other a farewell gift.

Hulan handed me two good pairs of knitting needles, one for big stitches, one for small. I gave her my best sweater, a blue one with a clever design I had knitted myself. And we both laughed to think we had given each other the same thought, one the tools to knit, the other the result of the same tools. Jiaguo gave Wen Fu a fountain pen. Wen Fu gave him a bottle of American whiskey.

And then I saw Auntie Du playing with Danru. She had been like a grandmother to my son. I went back to my trunk, trying to find something special for her as well. And I remembered how much she admired the blue perfume bottle I sometimes let Danru play with. I held that bottle up once more to the light, and then I walked back and gave it to her. Auntie Du protested very loudly, saying, "Why would I want such a thing?" So I pressed it into her hand and she began to cry, telling me how much it embarrassed her to take it. "I have nothing to give you in return," she said.

So I told her, "What I give you is nothing also, just a color to look at, so you can remember a foolish woman and her son."

Before we left, Hulan and I held hands. I wanted to apologize for all our fights, but I did not know how. So I said, "I think it must have been one hundred red beans exactly." And right away, she knew I was talking about the last argument we had had, just before we left Kunming.

Hulan shook her head, crying and laughing at the same time. "No, you were probably right. Only fifty, no more."

"One hundred," I insisted.

"Fifty, maybe even less," she said firmly. And then she added, shyly now, "Our family was so very poor back then. I had to count that small mound of beans every morning, dividing them between my sister and me, one for her, one for me, one for her, one for me. So you see, I only wished there had been one hundred."

When we reached the Shanghai harbor, we did not go to see Wen Fu's parents right away. That would have been proper. But when the Japanese first occupied Shanghai, his parents had moved inland, and now it would take us another day by train to reach them. So Wen Fu insisted we should go to my father's house first. I think he was also dreaming we could live in that fancy house. And he had big ideas that he could do a better business in Shanghai than on the island or in little inland villages. What kind of business, he didn't say and I didn't ask.

"Of course, your father will want you to live with him, his own daughter," he said. He was wearing his air force uniform, and I suppose he thought everyone would be glad to see him, one of the great victors of the war.

I did not argue with him. I also wanted to see my father first. And I was not just thinking of his help. I was hoping my father would be glad to see me.

From the harbor, we hired a car to take us directly. Along the way, Wen Fu was humming a happy little song to himself. Danru was busy looking out the car window, his head turning in different directions to catch the sights of this strange, big city.

"Mama, look!" he cried, and I saw him pointing at an Indian man in a red turban, waving for cars to stop and go. When I was a child, I used to cry seeing these Indian traffic policemen. This was because one of my father's wives had told me that if I was disobedient, she would hand me over to the "red hats" and they would poke me with their sharp beards.

"Don't be scared," I told Danru. "You see that hat on top of his head? That's only laundry piled up to dry." Danru tried to get up on the car seat to see better.

"Don't feed the boy nonsense," said Wen Fu. And Danru sat back down.

The city was noisy and crowded in a wonderful way, as if nothing had been damaged, nothing had changed—at least not on the main roads. Cars and taxis honked, bicycles darted in between, and all along the sidewalks was every combination of life: rich merchants in their tailored suits, peasants pushing vegetable carts, schoolgirls walking arm in arm, and modern women wearing the latest hats, the highest shoes. They knew everyone was watching them, envying them. And of course, the foreigners were still there, although not as many as I remembered, very few, in fact. And those I saw seemed less proud, less sure in their walk, more cautious when they crossed the road, knowing now the world would not stop for them.

As we drove closer to my father's house, I tried to think how I would tell him about my marriage, why I needed to leave.

I forced myself to remember once again what happened to Yiku. "Father," I would cry, "he said that if she died, he wouldn't care. He let her die!" I thought about how Wen Fu had gambled away almost all my dowry money: "When there was no more money to steal from me, he used my own body like a gambling chip, laughing and telling the men they could sleep with me if he lost!" I remembered the many nights he used my body after he had already been with another woman: "He even brought a woman right to our bed and forced me to watch. Of course, I did not, but I could not shut my ears."

The more I thought about those things, the faster my breath came, filling my lungs with so much hate. How could my father refuse to help me? Of course he would help! What family would want such a terrible son-in-law?—no feelings, no morals, no shame. Those were my thoughts as we drove up to my father's house, the place on Julu Road. But I had not considered this: If my life had changed so much in eight years, then perhaps so had my father's.

As I passed through the archway of the gate, I saw immediately how strangely quiet the house looked. The outside shutters were closed on every window, as if the house had been shut down for the winter. But this was only September, and the weather that day was still quite warm.

"What a big house," Danru said. "Who lives here?"

"Quiet," Wen Fu said.

Because I did not know my father's house that well, I did not notice any other changes, the ones that were later pointed out to me: that the front gate had been smashed in and repaired in a clumsy way. That statues in the courtyard had been knocked down, then hauled away. That the walls on the lower part of the house had been quickly repainted in a color that did not match the rest of the house. That all the lower windows behind those shutters had been broken and not yet replaced.

After a long delay, a servant answered the door. She eyed us suspiciously until I told her who we were, Jiang Sao-yen's daughter, his son-in-law and grandson.

"Aiyi," I said, using the polite name for "Auntie," since I did not know this servant's position in the house. "I have come to see my father." She was a small, plump woman, rather old, and wearing plain working clothes. She was not at all like a servant who would answer the door of an important house. She looked more like someone who cleaned things when no one was looking.

"Anh!" she said. "Come in. Come in."

But she did not call to a head servant who could greet us properly. She led me herself to where my father was, sitting in his dark study, staring at nothing.

My father turned around in his armchair. He looked past me, past Danru, toward Wen Fu. Right away, one of his eyebrows flew up, not with delight, but with fear, like a man who had been caught. He rose quickly from his chair, and I saw that his back was curved. Oh, he had grown so old in these past eight years! I waited for him to greet us, but he said nothing. He only stared at Wen Fu.

"Father," I finally said. I gave Danru a little nudge and he stepped forward, whispering, "Grandfather, how are you?"

My father looked quickly at Danru, then at me, then at Wen Fu, then back at me. His eyebrow went back down. Relief poured over his face, and he sat down again, letting his body drop heavily back into the chair.

"Did you receive the letters I sent you? This is your grandson, already five years old." My father covered his face with one hand and said nothing. I was too scared to say anything else. But I was wondering to myself, Has somebody died? Where are the others?

But now the servant was calling us softly, "Come, come. Your father needs his rest." As soon as we left the room, she talked in a loud, friendly way that comforted me. "You must be tired to death yourself. Come in here, have some tea." She turned to Danru. "How about you, little boy? Is your belly hungry for a little something to eat?"

We went into the large sitting room. It was the same room I had sat in when Old Aunt and New Aunt came to ask permission for my marriage to Wen Fu. Only now the sofa cushions and curtains were worn-looking, papers were scattered everywhere, dust had gathered in every corner. The servant must have seen the shock on my face, Wen Fu's frown. She rushed ahead and swatted a sofa pillow, sending clouds of dust into the air. "I've been busy with so many other things," she said with a little laugh. She swept the hem of her sleeve across a dirty table.

"Don't worry, don't worry," I said. "After all, we suffered from the same war. Things are different, we know this."

The servant looked grateful. "Yes, yes, this is so, isn't it?" We all stared again at the messy room.

"Where are the others?" Wen Fu finally asked.

"How are they?" I said. "San Ma, Wu Ma—their health is good?"

"Good, very good," the servant said with a big smile. "Very healthy. Only now they are away, visiting friends." And then she looked at Wen Fu and became very nervous. "Although I cannot say where they have gone, exactly," she quickly explained. "That is, I don't know. That is, I am a stupid old woman, unable to keep anything in my head anymore." And she began to laugh, hoping we would join her.

So you see, our homecoming was very strange. And that first day I knew nothing of what had happened. I only assumed it was the war that had caused my father to become as broken as the house he lived in. It was not until the next morning, after Wen Fu had left to visit friends, that I learned about our family's new circumstances, and why my father was so scared to see Wen Fu in his Kuomintang uniform.

What the servant said was true: Our house had suffered from the war. But it was not bombs or bullets that had caused the damage. It was my father's weak will. This was a side of my father I had never known. He was always a person who controlled others with his strength. Even talking about it today, I find it hard to believe that he could have had such great opposites in his character. But I suppose these are things that come out in people during a war. That's what San Ma said when she came home and explained what had happened. And she was still angry when she told me.

"You see, after the war began, your father's factories began to do very poorly," she said. "This was the case with everybody, you know. One thing led to another, you had no control. One thing bumped into another and made the next thing fall down. Families lost their money and could no longer buy things. Stores that once sold fancy dresses closed their doors. So they did not buy cloth from us anymore. Overseas boats no longer went in and out of Shanghai. So your father could no longer ship his goods overseas.

"Still, we had plenty of money, so in the beginning none of us worried too much. But then the war continued one year into the next. And the turnipheads began to take over more and more businesses."

"Turnipheads?" I asked.

"Turnipheads!" said San Ma. "That's what we called the Japanese. Because you saw them everywhere—always eating their pickled turnips—then bbbbbttt!—leaving behind their long-lasting stink!

"Anyway, they would go to different businesses, pretending to do a safety check or a sanitary inspection. Hnh! Everyone knew they wanted to see if there was anything worth taking. And we knew that if a person did not cooperate, if a person raised any kind of objection, the Japanese would find a reason to take everything away, including one's own life! Everyone was very careful, of course, not to cause unnecessary trouble. But every now and then you heard about someone who had grown weak and had given in to the Japanese—flown to their side in exchange for holding onto their business with the hands of a traitor. They signed oaths of new patriotism to the turnipheads, and this made everyone suffer, because the Japanese only grew stronger. So people spit when they heard the names of those traitors. At night, they secretly went to the traitor families' cemeteries and destroyed their generations of graves.

"One day—this was perhaps 1941 or so, summer—a Japanese officer and several assistants came to our house. When the servant opened the door, she screamed, then fainted. The Japanese soldiers wanted to talk to Jiang Sao-yen. They went into his study. The other servants would not come out of the kitchen to serve the tea. So I had to do it, serve the Japanese officers tea, lukewarm and weak, of course.

"The officer admired your father's furniture, praising this and that for its antiquity and value. And then he turned to your father—as if he was eyeing another possession he wanted. He said, 'Jiang Sao-yen, I like your manners, your good sense. You know how to handle this new situation in Shanghai, how to help the city go back to normal.'

"Your father said nothing. He sat in his chair, very powerful, never moving one inch. The Japanese officer continued walking around the room, running his hand along your father's magistrate table, the backbones of great books, the scroll paintings on the walls. He hinted he would like to have valuables like these hanging in his own house.

" 'Jiang Sao-yen,' the Japanese said, 'we need your good sense to bring others to their senses, to behave in the same manner. Correct-thinking people like yourself can put an end to the war more quickly. This would be good for China. This would be patriotic. In this way, fewer families and businesses will have to suffer. Everything can stay intact.' And the officer swept his hand out toward the four scroll paintings on the wall. 'Like these,' he said.

"At this point, your father stood up and threw his cup of tea against one of those paintings! It's the truth. Those four paintings were over two hundred years old, and he ruined one of them with the toss of a cup!

"I was so proud of what he did.

"So I don't know what happened in that room. When I left, your father had just thrown tea on a painting as if to tell the Japanese, 'I would rather destroy my things than give them to you.'

"The next day, he looked worried. But I thought it was because we were now going to lose the house. Before I married, I had come from a poor family. So I was preparing myself to go back to my old way of life. I accepted this.

"And then, two days later, a banner went up along the front wall facing the street, and a big poster was nailed to the front gate. Both proclaimed that Jiang Sao-yen, owner of this house and the Five Phoenixes Textile Trading Companies, supported the new government in China, that of the Imperial Emperor Hirohito. This same news was announced in all the local newspapers as well. And in the article, it said that Jiang Sao-yen urged others to begin a new China, united with the Japanese in fighting off foreign imperialist influences.

"Almost all our servants left. So did my sons and their families. Wu Ma's sons and their wives and children stayed, but they have always been like chickens pecking the ground. They don't look up to see who's throwing the grain. Anyway, I tried to ask your father why he had done this. He would not answer. And then I shouted at him—the first time I ever did that! And afterward nobody was speaking to anyone.

"In a matter of weeks, the factories were operating full-time, they began to export textiles overseas, and this renewed business success was announced in the newspapers as well.

"Again I shouted at your father—'So this is why you became a traitor! For this all our family graves have been turned upside down. For this we will boil in a vat of oil for eternity.' Your father was shouting back, ready to strike me down. He tried to swing his arm out, but it dangled at his side like the wrung neck of a duck. And then he collapsed into his chair, unable to speak. He had suffered a stroke.

"After many months, he could move his arms and legs almost the same as before. There was no lasting damage there. But he still could not speak—although I always suspected this was because he did not want to talk about what he had done. He could still move one side of his mouth. But it was as if his face was divided in half, a different expression on each side. One side was the face he had always shown to the world. The other was the face he had lost and could no longer hide.

"When the war ended—well, you can guess what happened. Kuomintang soldiers marched to the houses and businesses of those who had collaborated with the Japanese. Our factories were immediately shut down, until it could be determined what should be done with this traitor to China. And then many people came with their anger and sacks of rocks. They painted slogans and smeared dirty things on the outside of our walls and the house: 'He who pats the horse's ass deserves the dung of a donkey.'

"Soon after that, the Kuomintang came to our house. Your father could say nothing, of course. So I explained what had happened. I told them your father hated the Japanese with all his heart. But he had already had a stroke when the Japanese took over his businesses. He was in no condition to fight back—as we all knew he would have. He was helpless, unable to speak, as they could

now see. And I said Jiang Sao-yen had done what he could to de-
nounce the Japanese. I showed them the painting with tea splashed
across it.

"The Kuomintang said it was still not a good excuse, because the
public would always believe he had been a traitor. But for now,
they would leave him be, they would not shoot him like the others.
Later they would decide what kind of punishment he deserved."

"What a good person you are," I told San Ma.

Upstairs in my mother's old room, I thought about San Ma's
story. I wondered what had caused my father to change his mind.
Was it fear? Was it a bribe of riches? Was it a mistaken idea that
he would have peace of mind?

But it did not matter what his reasons were. To other people,
there was no good reason. What my father had done was wrong,
a big mistake. And in my mind, I knew that he had done the worst
possible thing, throwing away honor, protecting himself by becoming a traitor.

But then I thought to myself, How can you blame a person for
his fears and weaknesses unless you have felt the same and done
differently? How can you think everyone can be a hero, choosing
death, when it is part of our nature to let go of brave thoughts at
the last moment and cling to hope and life?

When I said this, I was not excusing him. I was forgiving him
with my heart, feeling the same sorrow as when you believe you
truly have no choice. Because if I blamed my father, then I would
have to blame my mother for what she did as well, for leaving me
so she could find her own life. And later I would have to blame
myself, for all the choices I made, so I could do the same.

At first Wen Fu acted very angry when he learned what my father
had done. A collaborator with the Japanese! A traitor to Han
people! As if Wen Fu himself were not as bad. Didn't he turn his
plane around, scared of being shot down by the Japanese? Didn't
he save himself when other pilots were dying?

You should have seen Wen Fu, cursing my father as he sat silently
in his chair. "I should turn you over to the Kuomintang myself!"

My father's right eye grew round with fear. The other stared back
without expression, without care.

And then Wen Fu said, "But you're lucky your daughter married such a good-hearted person."

Right away I looked at Wen Fu. I was immediately suspicious.

"Your father needs my help now," he said to me. "Your father is in trouble with the Kuomintang. I am a Kuomintang hero. I can protect him."

I wanted to shout, "Father! Don't listen to him! He is all lies." But my father was already looking up at Wen Fu with half a grateful smile.

My father was so weak in his mind by then, he believed what Wen Fu said to him later that day, that his troubles would disappear if he allowed his son-in-law to take care of all the finances. Let me tell you, what disappeared was my father's money!

Right away we moved into my father's house, along with Wen Fu's mother and father and some of their relatives. A few of our old servants returned, but Wen Tai-tai hired new ones as well. San Ma and Wu Ma were not happy with this new arrangement. Because now Wen Fu's mother was in charge of the house, and she turned everything upside down.

She made the man who knew only how to garden beat rugs. She made the woman who knew only how to cook do laundry. She made the woman who emptied our chamber pots chop vegetables. She would give out an order, then contradict herself with the next. And when the servants were too confused to know what to do, she would fly into a terrible rage, threatening that she would cut off their heads and feed their bodies to the flies! So you see, maybe that mother passed her bad temper onto her son. After a short while, most of the servants left.

I think Wen Fu learned how to spend money fast from his mother as well. I have never known anyone so greedy. By this, I mean she not only knew how to buy fur coats and jewelry, but also knew how to keep her fist closed tight so that not even one extra coin rolled into someone else's pocket. I once saw her give something like a hundred-yuan note to a servant to buy some food. By then, a hundred yuan wasn't worth very much, maybe only a few dollars in today's money. And when the servant came back from the market, Wen Tai-tai made her list everything she had bought: "How much for this? Are you sure? How much for that? Are you sure?" She made the servant count over and over again, the amount spent, the amount to be returned, then questioned her for many minutes when she thought ten *fen* were missing—not even a tenth of a penny! That servant, who had been with my father's family for nearly forty years, left forever within the hour.

At the same time, Wen Fu and his father were losing lots of money at the horse races. And every night Wen Tai-tai invited people over to play mah jong. They were not even friends, just other people who liked to show off, acting as if they had no concern whether they won or lost the big stacks of money they piled in front of their noses.

And where do you think they got so much money to lose? From the house! That whole family had a sickness to steal as much as they could. Our house became like a bargain store, people coming in the front door, then furniture, rugs, and precious vases and clocks going out the back door. They had no feeling for what those things had meant to my family. I saw someone carrying out the dresser that belonged to my mother, the same one she used to hide English biscuits from me. The next day her stool was gone, the one she sat on while combing her hair.

And one time my father and I both watched a man carrying out a table from my father's study. It was the magistrate's table, both long and wide, with carved legs. It had been in my father's family for many generations, at least two hundred years. I could see my father trying hard not to cry out for that table to stay. And then we saw the table didn't want to leave either; it would not go through the door opening. The workers tried tilting it one way, then another. Finally, the man who bought the table told Wen Fu he wanted his money back. My father had a half-smile of relief on his face. But then a big argument broke out. Wen Fu refused to give back the money. The man said, "See for yourself, that table is stuck."

"That is for you to solve," said Wen Fu.

"No way to solve it!" shouted the man.

This continued for several minutes, until Wen Fu picked up a chair—and before anyone could shout to stop him—he cracked the table legs in half. "Now I have solved it for you," he said. You should have seen the tragedy on my father's face.

Nobody could stop Wen Fu's wild selling and spending—not my father's wives, not his other daughters and their husbands, nobody. They were all helpless. If someone tried to say one word against him, Wen Fu would shout: "Should I have all of you thrown into jail, along with this traitor? Is that what you are asking me to do?" And there would be no more protests after that.

Now I will tell you a secret. Maybe I was quiet, but I still found ways to fight back. And I am not proud to tell you what I did, because they were only mean things that made my heart glad.

Once I stole a mah jong tile from the set. The next time Wen Fu's mother and her friends sat down to play, they soon discovered they could not continue until they found the missing piece. I heard Wen Fu's mother shouting, "Are you sure? Stack them again! Count them again!" I had to hold my stomach in, trying not to laugh.

Another time I was so angry because Wen Fu refused to spend money to fix the broken windows all over the house. "Insects and diseases are coming in the house," I told him. He didn't care. So one day I took a little box and went into the garden and poked under rocks. And later, I went into Wen Fu's room, the one he had taken over from my father. I sprinkled little bugs in his dresser and under the padding of his bed. This was when I had my own room across from his, and at night I could hear him chasing those bugs with shouts, slapping them with his slippers. Of course, he still did not fix those windows.

Later I even found a way to get back my mother's room for my own. When Wen Fu's mother moved in, she picked this room for herself, and I was always angry to see her there. So I found my chance when I heard her complain, "Last night was so cold, as if a wind were blowing right through the walls." Right away I said, "Ai, I heard that a woman died in that room." I turned to San Ma. "Isn't this true?" And San Ma was glad to help.

"Murder or suicide," San Ma said, "nobody knew, the circumstances were never clear. Of course, that was a long time ago, nothing to worry about now." That day Wen Fu's mother forced me to change rooms with her.

But even my mother's ghost could not prevent Wen Fu from coming into my room late at night, smelling of nightclubs: cigarettes, whiskey, and perfume. He would roll me over, unbend my arms, unbend my legs, as if I were a folding chair. And when he was done satisfying himself, he would get up and go to his room, not one word spoken between us.

I would get up too. I always kept a basin of water in my room for just this reason. I would wet a rough cloth, then wash myself, rubbing hard wherever he had touched my skin, over and over again. And when I was done, I would throw this dirty water out the window. Pwah!

## 20

# FOUR DAUGHTERS
# ON THE TABLE

Do you remember Edna Fong? She goes to our church, three daughters, two sons, one became a doctor. She was at Bao-bao's engagement party in a red dress.

Helen said Edna just found out that one of her sons has a mental problem. Edna's son has a problem, not Helen's. Although Helen was saying how she always worried about Frank, no secure future. But when she heard about Edna's son, she became grateful. About Frank, that is, not about Edna's son. She said, "At least I should be grateful I don't have this kind of worry in my family."

I thought to myself, This is not being grateful, this is an excuse! The same kind of reasoning people used in China. Looking at someone else's misery so you would no longer have to think about your own problems.

Why should you compare your life that way? This kind of thinking only makes you feel afraid. You are only thinking about what more you can lose, not hoping for something better.

If I had thought this way in China, then I would still be there. Because I saw many, many people with lives worse than my own.

In Shanghai, for example, after the war, you could see all kinds of beggars, many of them women, sitting on the side of the street. Some had signs printed with their story, like advertisements: This one's husband left her. This one had her whole family wiped out during the war. This one's husband became an opium addict and sold everything, including the children.

Maybe some of these stories were exaggerations. But you can imagine what I was thinking. I had once told myself I would rather leave my marriage and become a beggar!

I was scared. If I had known I was running away to something better, that would have been different. But I had no such hope to run to.

I thought about this for a long time. And then you know what I decided? I still wanted to leave! It's true. I was lying in my bed one night and I vowed this to myself, with the full moon as my witness.

I don't know what this was, stubbornness maybe. I only knew I could not survive living with Wen Fu that way. So you see, my mind was made up long before I found something to hope for.

I was going to leave after I paid a visit to Old Aunt and New Aunt on Tsungming Island. That was only proper.

But before I could go to the island, Danru got sick with a high fever, then turned yellow with jaundice. And then I became sick with the same thing. I think it was a disease we picked up from that time we were on the road with Hulan and Jiaguo—after we left Kunming. I know this, because Jiaguo wrote us a letter, told us about their apartment and all the progress he was making in his new job. At the bottom, Hulan wrote a few words in her childish handwriting. She talked about Jiaguo's parents, very nice people, about a new table she had bought, beautiful beyond words. And at the end, she said her health was good, although recently she had been sick. Jiaguo added that she had turned as yellow as a field of wheat and as skinny as the blade that cut the wheat down.

So you see, I think it was some little river crabs Hulan wanted to eat in Changsha. That's what made us sick. It stayed in our bodies and broke out one day.

Anyway, after Danru became sick, I had to send a messenger to the island to tell Old Aunt why we were not coming. After the war, there still were no telephones connecting Shanghai to the island.

One week later, I received a letter back from Old Aunt, written in her bad Chinese. Like Hulan, Old Aunt had never gone to school.

She learned to write only after she was already grown up. So her Chinese was not the formal kind you learned for writing. She did not know the proper expressions to use to show you are from a refined background. Instead, she put down whatever popped into her mind.

"This old aunt of yours," she wrote, "nearly tore the letter in half, I was so anxious when I saw the man standing at my door. How can you say it is only a little illness, nothing important? Health is always the most important thing, everybody healthy, not like Miao Tai-tai. You remember her, made your wedding with the Wen family? Only last week this happened. One minute she was standing, complaining about a fly chasing her, next minute, lying on the floor. What a calamity. So then, the Miao husband ran down the street to telephone the local doctor. He was calling, calling, calling, couldn't get through! All the lines were being used! So then he tried calling, calling, calling again. No use. So then he ran outside, shouted to a boy, Hey, go get the doctor, hurry, here's some money. So then that boy ran off, fast as a racehorse, that's what a neighbor woman said. So who knows why the doctor took so long? Who knows who he was treating, not me. Two three hours later, the doctor went to the Miao house, guess what he found? The Miao wife crying over the Miao husband, cold as the floor he was lying on. Dead. Let your heart think about this. Scared himself to death just thinking she was dead. She didn't die, he died, died for nothing. I told your uncle, Now do you believe me, we should fix the telephone. During the war, it stopped working, this was when I was trying to call Uncle at the factory and could not get through. Now your uncle says, Who needs a telephone? My health is not good, he knows this. If I fall on the floor, then what happens? Weiwei, do not worry too much about me, but when you come here, you must tell your uncle, Auntie is right, fix the telephone. You must ask him, What is most important, no telephone or no wife? As I said, health is important. You get well fast. Drink lots of hot things if the sickness runs cold, cold things if the sickness runs hot. You write and tell me when you can come. Now I have to stop writing and go to the Miao husband's funeral. Give greetings to everybody."

When Danru and I finally went to Tsungming Island, it was already past the New Year, 1946.

•

I have already told you how my aunties treated me when I was a child. So I had always thought they did not care about me very much, that they saw me as a nuisance, a burden. And I always thought I had no strong feelings for them in return. Why should I?

So you can imagine how surprised I was to find my eyes stinging with tears as our flatboat drew close to the island. I tried to tell myself it was only the sharp cold wind, hurting my eyes. But then I saw them—Uncle, Old Aunt, New Aunt—waving to me from the harbor, screaming and shouting, "There she is!" And I knew it was not the wind.

They all looked old and worn, Old Aunt especially. She had lost the sharpness of her features. Even her eyes, which had once been a very dark black-brown, had faded in color. New Aunt had sprouted many white hairs, and fine wrinkles lined each smiling cheek, just like a spider's web. And Uncle was a man walking in his dreams, waking up only when someone shouted at him, "Be careful! Come this way!"

In fact, it was seeing Uncle this way that made me realize: He and my father were alike. They shared the same lost mind, the same weak spirit. Their eyes moved slowly back and forth, as they took in everyone else's opinions, unable to make up their own minds. And this made me think how both had always been this way. All those years, they only pretended to lead, shouted when they did not know how to speak, frightened people when they were afraid themselves.

Old Aunt stroked my cheek many times, telling me, "Ai! Ai! Look at you, pale and thin! And this little boy, it can't be—your son, so big already?"

Danru stepped forward and gave Old Aunt the present I had bought, a few ounces of precious ginseng root. "For you," Danru said. He frowned, then remembered what he was supposed to say: "So you will live forever." He frowned again. "Always in good health," he added. He frowned again, turned to me: "Is that all?" I nodded.

Old Aunt and New Aunt patted his head and laughed. "In your last letter, it seems you were saying he was only six years old this new year. Can this be? He's so smart. Look at his eyes, the same as Little Gong's."

I did not know if the years in between had softened her into someone more kind, or if I was only seeing this for the first time because I had been through so much hardness in my life.

"Where are Little Gong and Little Gao?" I asked. "They must be—how old—fifteen, sixteen?"

"Nineteen and twenty!" said New Aunt.

"That old already! And what are they doing? Are they in a good university?"

Old Aunt and New Aunt looked at each other, as if to decide what to say. "They work at the dockyard now, just down the road," said New Aunt at last.

"Fixing ships," added Old Aunt. "Although soon they will be returning to their studies, going to college."

"Actually, they do not fix the ships themselves," said New Aunt. "They bring the metal to the other workers. One loads, the other pushes the wheelbarrow, terrible work."

I tried to imagine this, those two spoiled boys now grown up and working so bitterly hard.

"Ai, Weiwei, you see how it is," New Aunt tried to explain. "Your uncle's business did very poorly during the war. Many of the machines rusted. There was no money to fix them and keep the factory going strong. So you see what has also happened to the house and our family," she said. "When the tree dies, the grass underneath withers."

"Ai," I said. "This is very sad to hear."

"Even sadder than you can imagine," Old Aunt said. And they walked with me and Danru around the house, to Old East and New West, to show me what they meant.

The big house had grown shabby. Paint was peeling everywhere, tiles on the floor were cracked, so that dirt underneath showed. And the beds all sagged deeply in the middle, not even enough money to tighten the rope lattice frames. But what saddened me most was the greenhouse.

All the little windows were cracked or broken, and the paint on the wooden frame was raised up in splintery leaves. And after many seasons of rain and heat, everything inside had turned black with decay or mold. So many changes.

Seeing all this, hearing what had happened to them, how could

I accuse Old Aunt and New Aunt of giving me a bad marriage? How could I ask them to help me out of my miserable life? No, I could not ask them.

We were still standing outside the greenhouse when I asked them about Peanut. "And what about your daughter?" I said to New Aunt. "Is she still living at the house on He De Road? The last letter I had from her was maybe two years ago. Every letter, she apologized for not writing sooner, then said nothing after that. Peanut! What a silly girl!"

Hearing Peanut's name, Uncle seemed to wake up. He huffed in a disgusted tone, then stood up and walked away, back toward the house. "Peanut is already dead!" he shouted back to us. Danru and I both jumped a little.

"What! Is this true?" I cried. "Peanut—dead?"

"Uncle is still very angry with her," explained New Aunt.

"Danru," Old Aunt said. "Are you hungry?"

Danru shook his head.

"Go follow Grand Uncle back to the house," said Old Aunt. "Go ask Old Cook to give you a bowl of noodles."

Danru looked at me. "Listen to Grand Auntie," I said.

After Danru left, New Aunt said, "Peanut ran away from her marriage. She went to a bad group of people who claimed they helped women escape feudal marriages."

"Hnh! She didn't have a feudal marriage!" said Old Aunt. "She agreed! She wanted to marry! And those people who helped her, they didn't tell her the truth, at least not in the beginning. I should have slapped her more often when she was a child."

"They deceived her," said New Aunt. "They didn't tell her the truth until it was too late. They're Communists, that's what we think. Yes, can you imagine?"

"Of course, her husband divorced her. Hnh! Why would he want her back?" said Old Aunt. "And then he put an announcement in all the big and little newspapers in Shanghai. It said: 'I am divorcing from Jiang Huazheng, deserter wife.' Your poor uncle, he read this while eating his midday meal—almost choked to death on a piece of radish."

"So now Uncle thinks she did this on purpose to kill all of us as well," said New Aunt. "This is not true, she has a good heart. It's only her mind that is rotten. But still, now we are all in danger. You see how things are. All this talk about unity among all the parties—nonsense. If the Kuomintang find out we have a daughter who is a Communist—ssst!—all of our heads could be rolling down the street."

"What a stupid girl!" said Old Aunt. "What happened to all the things I taught her? No firm ideas in her head. I should have beat her harder."

"She lost her marriage?" I said. "I'm sorry to hear this."

That's what I said, but guess what I was thinking? Of course! I was wondering how Peanut had done this—left her marriage. I was wondering when I could ask her how I could do the same.

To be polite, Danru and I stayed two weeks at my uncle's house. Less time and they would have thought I did not consider them important enough. Before coming to the island, I had gone to the bank and withdrawn the last of my dowry money. As I already told you, Chinese money was not worth too much after the war. By my memory, I had maybe two thousand left. By then, it was worth only a couple hundred dollars American. And I used some of that money to treat my relatives well.

Every day I walked to the market with New Aunt and Old Aunt. Every day I would pick out the vegetables and meat, expensive things I knew they had not tasted in a long time. Every day New Aunt and I got into loud arguments in front of the shopkeepers over who would pay. Every day I would pay.

During one of those walks to the market I finally told my aunties I wanted to see Peanut.

"Impossible," New Aunt said right away. "Too dangerous."

"I would not allow you," said Old Aunt. "That girl does not deserve to see anyone."

On the morning when Danru and I were supposed to leave, New Aunt came into our room early. She ordered Danru to go say good-bye to his grand-uncle.

When we were alone, she started to give me a long lecture on Peanut, as if I still wanted to see her, as if all her faults were mine.

"Maybe no one knows she is a Communist," New Aunt explained. "But she is still a bad influence, like a diseased person.

338

She should not be allowed to contaminate anyone else. That's why you cannot see her."

I listened, not saying anything. At the end of her speech, New Aunt sighed and said, "I can see there's no use arguing with you. Well then, if I cannot stop you, at least you cannot hold me responsible!" She threw a piece of paper down on the bed and left. It was an address, as well as instructions on what bus to take, what alleys to look for.

Suddenly, New Aunt appeared again at the door. "You should not let Old Aunt know I gave you this," she whispered, then left again. And in that way, I knew that she had secretly visited Peanut herself.

A few minutes later, it was Old Aunt who walked into my room. "And now I must ask you for a favor," she said. She set a small wrapped package on the bed. "This is something I borrowed from a friend long time ago. I feel so ashamed I never returned it. When you find time, maybe you can take it to her." On top of the package was the same address New Aunt had given me and the name "Mrs. Li."

"I feel so ashamed," said Old Aunt, tears now coming to her eyes. "Don't tell anyone."

After I returned to Shanghai, I waited a week before I went to see Peanut. I did not tell anyone about this, however. I walked out the door in everyday clothes, as if I might be going to the market to shop for food, or maybe to take a little walk in the park. When I was two blocks away, I jumped onto a bus.

I have already told you a little bit about Peanut. She was a girl who loved every kind of comfort. She cared only about pretty clothes and powder on her face. She always followed what was fashionable but had no ideas of her own. So you can imagine what I was thinking as that bus took me farther and farther into a bad part of the city.

I got off at San Ying Road, and from there I had to walk down streets too narrow for cars but filled with bicycles and pedicabs and carts. She lived in the Japanese section, where buildings curved around corners just like the long body of a dragon. The buildings all looked alike, two-story brick buildings with steep tiled roofs.

Along those alleys there were no sidewalks, just rough roads covered with coal dust and spit.

You might think this should have been the best part of town, since the Japanese had occupied Shanghai for so many years. Certainly there were some good parts. But most of that section had been built long before the war, and I thought it had an awful smell and was dirty and crowded. If you ask my opinion, maybe it was only a little bit better than the Chinese section.

I don't know why so many students, writers, and artists liked to live here. Maybe they thought it was romantic—if you had no food, you could eat each other's ideas. And there were many, many prostitutes, although not the high-class kind who lived in nightclub houses on Nanking Road. These girls were called "roadside wives," and every few steps, it seemed, I passed one standing in front of a three-stool restaurant, or a wine shop only as wide as a door, or a steep stairway leading to a second-story teahouse.

And then I came to a street filled with bargain stalls, so many of them, all selling used books, used maps, used magazines—history, romance, poetry, politics.

"Forbidden stories!" a man called out to me. From underneath his table he brought out a magazine. It had an illustration of a crying young woman being held by the ghost shadow of a man. I stopped to look. They were just like those stories Peanut and I used to read in the greenhouse. And standing in the street, I remembered those stories about girls who disregarded their parents' advice and then married for love, that sort of thing. And the endings were always sad, with scary morals given at the end: "Lose control, lose your life!" "Fall in love, fall into disgrace!" "Throw away family values, throw your face away!" I remembered the ones that made me cry the most—I used to think they were like my mother's own life, as sad as a story.

At that moment, and not until then, did I consider that all these stories were false—only stories. Like Peanut and everyone else, I had imagined an unhappy ending to my mother's life. Like Peanut, I had allowed myself to be scared by those sad tales. And look what happened. It did not prevent disaster from coming into my life. Just the opposite. And then I thought about it this way: Perhaps my mother's life was now filled with joy! Perhaps I too could still find the same thing. This was my hope.

I can honestly tell you, that is exactly what I was thinking. This is why I have always thought that what followed next was not just coincidence. It was a sign that I had finally come to a true thought of my own. Because this is what happened.

I felt someone tapping my shoulder. I turned around. I did not recognize him at first, this smiling man. "Winnie?" he said. "Do you remember?"

I thought to myself, That name, Winnie, it sounds familiar. You see, I thought he was saying that was *his* name. I was struggling to remember.

And then he said, "I've never forgotten the trouble I caused you."

What? What was this man talking about?

And then I recognized his voice, the Chinese-American soldier, Jimmy Louie, the one who had named me Winnie.

Yes, yes, your father! Just like that, five years later, our past and future bumping into one another on a strange street in Shanghai. Can you imagine? If I had not gone to see Peanut, if I had not stopped to read a silly magazine, if he had not been looking for a newspaper—one minute later, and our lifetimes would have missed each other. I ask you, isn't that fate meant to be?

That's what I said to your father many years later, after we were married. How lucky we were that fate brought us together. But your father did not think it was fate, at least not the Chinese idea of *ming yuan*.

"Fate," he told me, "is somebody else deciding your life for you. Our love was greater than that." And here he used the American word "destiny," something that could not be prevented.

Well, that sounded the same as fate to me. He insisted it was different, an important difference. So I told him, "Maybe you see things in an American way, and I see the same things in a Chinese way. You are saying, 'Look at the pretty fish in the bowl.' And I say, 'Look at the pretty bowl with the fish.' And it does not matter what words we use. It is the same pretty bowl, the same pretty fish."

But your father still insisted, "We loved each other from the moment we met, that's why our two wills joined together to find each other."

After that, I didn't say anything. How could I tell your father that I did not love him from the moment we met? Not in Kunming, not at that dance. I did not know such an instant feeling existed, so how could I feel it? Of course, after I bumped into him that second time, my love for him happened very, very quickly.

So maybe we were both right, and it was my fate, and his destiny. But later your father became a minister, and he decided it was God's will that brought us together. So now I can no longer explain how we found each other. All I can say is this: I was on a small road in Shanghai. Your father was at that same place.

After we bumped into one another, we stood there making polite conversation for a few minutes. And then Jimmy Louie—I still called him Jimmy Louie in those early days, both names, like the Chinese way—Jimmy Louie asked me to have some tea at a place just across the road, to sit down and rest awhile. I agreed, but only to be polite. Really, I had no intention of starting something.

We found ourselves sitting in a small upstairs teahouse, a place I thought was very dirty. I saw the waitress take away cups from one table and rinse them in cold dirty water before she filled them with tea and gave them to us. I had to wash those cups twice with hot tea before I would drink any. I did the same with Jimmy Louie's cup. You see, even back then, I was already worrying about his stomach.

We drank our tea quietly for a few minutes. And then he asked me about Wen Fu. "Does he still use the name Judas?"

I laughed, then pretended to scold him. "That was bad, what you did. My husband was very angry with me."

"But I was the one who gave him that name, not you."

I was too embarrassed to remind him of our dance together, how friends had teased Wen Fu that I had already been conquered by an American. And I could not tell him about the fight Wen Fu and I had afterward, although my face burned with anger just thinking about it. Jimmy Louie must have seen the look on my face, because right away he said, "It was terrible, what I did. I'm sorry."

"No, no," I said. "I am thinking about other matters, how so many years have gone by, how everything has changed, but nothing has become better." Jimmy Louie knew we should not talk about this further. So instead we talked about other people. I told him about Jiaguo and his new job in Harbin, how Hulan did not yet have a child. He told me that most of his friends in the American air force had been sent north to Peking to help with the Japanese surrender. He was still with the U.S. Information Service, press relations for the American consulate general.

"A very big job," I said.

"Only a big name," he said. "I read different newspapers every day. I keep an eye on what is reported." And then he said. "You see. I'm a spy." Of course, he was only joking! He always liked to tease people, you remember this about your father. I don't know why Helen still thinks he really was a spy. He wasn't! Don't listen to her. If he really was, why would he joke so openly?

In any case, we had more tea, more and more. Soon I found myself telling him about my uncle's factory, how poor they now were, how hard my boy cousins now had to work. And Jimmy Louie did not look down on them or pity my family. He had sympathy. He said the war was like a bad illness, and when it was over, it did not mean everyone suddenly became healthy again.

I told Jimmy Louie about Peanut. I did not say she was a Communist—I only said she was divorced. And Jimmy Louie did not say, "What a bad woman that Peanut is." He said many marriages could not survive a war.

So finally I told him about my father, what trouble he was in for cooperating with the Japanese. He said this was a terrible tragedy, that wartime had led people to mistakes they otherwise would not have walked into.

You see how he was? I felt I could tell him almost anything and find some sort of comfort. For an American, he had a lot of sympathy. And yet I still did not tell him about my marriage, not yet.

"How about you?" I asked. "Back home, how is your family? Do your wife and children miss you?"

"No wife, no children," he said. "No such luck." And then he brought out a little photograph. It showed four young women sitting in a row, youngest to oldest, wearing modern dresses and hairstyles. They were the daughters of Mrs. Liang, a schoolmate of his aunt's. And this Mrs. Liang, he told me, said he could pick any one of her

343

daughters for his wife. "Each daughter is educated," said Jimmy Louie. "Each one plays the piano. Each one can read the Bible in English."

"Very attractive, and stylish too," I said. "So many choices, so hard to decide. Which one are you thinking of marrying?"

He laughed, then became serious. "You," he said. "But you are already married."

This is true! He said exactly that. He could have chosen any one of those four beautiful girls, all of them innocent and young, none of them married before. But he picked me. Why do you think he did that?

In any case, at the time, I did not know if he was teasing or truly being sincere. My face was red. And because I could not look at him, I looked at my watch instead.

"Oyo!" I said. "If I go see Peanut now, I will have to leave as soon as I arrive."

"Better come back tomorrow to see her," suggested Jimmy Louie.

"There's no other way," I agreed.

"Tomorrow, then, I will meet you at the bookshop across the street and walk with you, to make sure you are safe," he said.

"No, no, too much trouble," I said.

"No trouble. I come here every day for the newspapers."

"Every day?"

"This is my job."

"I was thinking I might come at ten-thirty. Perhaps that is too early for you."

"I will be here even earlier, in case you are early too." And as we both stood up and walked down the stairs, I saw what he did. He left the photograph of four beautiful girls on the table.

The next morning I woke up very early, happy and excited. I was thinking about my life, that it was about to change. I did not know exactly how this would happen, but I was certain that it would.

But all these thoughts soon disappeared. Danru's screams rang through the house, and a servant brought him to me, reporting how he had fallen and bumped his head down a whole flight of stairs. While I was comforting my son, San Ma came crying to me, telling me that my father had woken up with a fever and a confused mind.

So I rushed to my father's room. A few minutes later, the cook came running in, declaring she was leaving for good, she would not tolerate any more of Wen Tai-tai's insults to her cooking. And from where I stood, I could hear Wen Fu shouting at the top of his voice and then the sound of something breaking on the floor. I went downstairs and saw the breakfast dishes scattered everywhere, noodles spilled all over the chairs.

I wanted to cry. My life would never change, it seemed to me. I was forever worrying over other people's problems, with no time to take care of my own. And I was sure all these small disasters were a sign that I would not be able to leave the house that day.

But life is so strange, the way it can fool you into thinking one way, then another. Because as soon as I gave up my plans for the day, my chance came back again. When I went upstairs to nurse my father, he was reading a newspaper and was irritated only that I had disturbed him. "He must have been fighting with himself in a bad dream," said San Ma.

When I went back downstairs, Wen Fu had already left for the horse racetrack. And the cook who was mad? She had already cleaned up the mess and had gone to the market to buy food for our evening meal. Little Danru shouted to me from his bed that he wanted to get up. He had forgotten his bump and was now remembering that Wen Fu's mother had promised that today he could go visit a family friend who had a little grandson just his age.

Finally I could leave the house! But I saw it was too late to change my life, almost eleven o'clock already. I tried to keep all my thoughts on seeing Peanut, what a happy reunion this would be. I was carrying the little package Old Aunt had asked me to bring. To that I had added five pairs of imported stockings. How happy Peanut would be to see this.

But of course, my mind kept turning to that little bookshop across from the teahouse. I pictured Jimmy Louie browsing through books, impatiently looking at his watch. I thought about hiring a taxi. And then I imagined Jimmy Louie looking at his watch once again, then leaving the store. I decided not to hurry myself to what would surely be an empty disappointment. So I pushed my hopes down and waited for the bus.

When I arrived at San Ying Road, it was already almost noon.

I had to force myself to walk slowly, calmly. And as I drew close to that bookshop, I had to force myself not to look. Keep walking, keep walking.

I could not breathe. I told myself, Don't fool yourself. He isn't there. Keep walking.

I did not allow myself to look to the side. My eyes faced the center of the road. Don't look. Keep walking.

I passed the bookshop. I didn't look. I kept walking, until I was one block away. I stopped. I let out a big sigh. And I had a little ache in my heart and realized I had let some hope leak out of there. And then I sighed again, this one very sad. And another sigh followed, one of relief, only it did not come from me. I turned around.

To see his face! The joy on his face!

We said no words. He took my hands and held them firmly. And we both stood in the road, our eyes wet with happiness, knowing without speaking that we both felt the same way.

And now I have to stop. Because every time I remember this, I have to cry a little by myself. I don't know why something that made me so happy then feels so sad now. Maybe that is the way it is with the best memories.

# 21

# LITTLE YU'S MOTHER

Peanut's place was just a short distance away. So during that brief walk, we had enough time to say only a few things.

"Why did you wait?" I asked. "I was so late."

"I thought it must have been your shoes," he said. "I was guessing you broke your shoes the same way you did at the dance in Kunming."

I laughed, and so did Jimmy. Then he became serious. "I have always loved you since that day, the way you could do anything, dance with broken shoes or in your bare feet. Fragile-looking, yet strong and brave, the kind of person nothing could stop."

This is true, your father said that. He thought I was a strong person. I had never thought about myself that way. I don't know why he believed that. The rest of his life he believed that about me. Isn't that strange?

Anyway, I told Jimmy Louie how much I had suffered in my marriage, how I had tried to leave Wen Fu during the war but could not because of Danru.

"But now I'm going to ask my cousin what she did," I said. "I'm going to get a divorce too."

And Jimmy Louie said, "You see how strong you are?"

I said, "This is not being strong. I have no more strength to fight him. Sometimes I don't know how I can live another day with him."

And Jimmy Louie said, "This is your strength." And then we

347

were in front of Peanut's place, a rooming house. Jimmy Louie said he would wait at the bookshop.

"I may be gone a very long time," I said.

"Two, three, four hours, it doesn't matter," he said. "I will wait. I have already waited almost five years."

You see how romantic he was? It was hard to leave him there when I had just found him.

I walked into a small common kitchen. On the floor were two little babies. I asked the woman frying her noontime meal if Jiang Huazheng lived in the house. "Anh?" she shouted. "Who do you want?" I stepped closer to her frying pan and shouted above the hissing oil. She smiled, wiped another stain onto her dress, took my elbow, and pointed me toward the stairs. "Up there, little sister. Third floor, room number two. Better knock, she already has a visitor." She went back to her cooking, laughing to herself. "So many visitors!"

I walked up those dark stairs, and with each step I took, I became more and more worried, wondering what I would find at the top. What if Peanut had become one of those roadside wives? Wasn't this what happened to women who lost their husbands and their families? How else could a woman support herself when she had no husband, no family?

I stood outside the door of room number two. I could hear a voice, a man's voice, it seemed to me. And then I heard a woman's voice, and this one sounded like Peanut, the same impatient tone, ending in a complaint. I knocked and the voices stopped.

"Who's there?" Peanut called out in a rough way.

"Jiang Weili!" I shouted back. "Your Jiang cousin!"

And before I could say anything else, the door flew open and Peanut pulled me inside the room, slammed the door. She was pulling my hair, pinching my cheek, shouting, "Look at you! Finally you've come! Why did you wait so long?"

She looked the same. That was my first thought. The same pouting smile, the same mischievous eyes. I was relieved.

But my second thought was that she looked entirely different, someone I would have passed on the street without recognizing. Her hair was cut short, parted no particular way. She wore a plain buttoned jacket of poor quality, and so shapeless I could not tell if she had grown fat or thin. And her face—there was no white powder on it—just her plain skin. You should have seen her. Here was a girl who used to pride herself on the paleness of her skin. And now she was almost as dark as a Cantonese!

"Hey! Meet my friend Wu," she said, and spun me around. I saw a young man with round glasses, with very thick black hair, swept back. He held a paintbrush in his hand. Large sheets of paper covered the room—scattered on the floor, dangling from the chair, lying across her small bed. They were all about the same thing, a student meeting of some kind, protests about the new land reforms. So it must be true. Peanut was a Communist.

"These ones that are already dry," she said to the young man, pointing, "take them. We'll finish the others in the evening." She said this in a bossy way, but the man did not seem to mind. He quickly rolled up several posters, told me he was happy to meet me, then left.

I did not know what to say, so I gave her the gifts, both of them covered in paper. She looked annoyed, then sighed and took them. I thought she would put them away and open them in private. That was the polite thing to do. Chinese people always do that, so if you don't like the gift, nobody has to see the disappointment in your face. But she didn't wait.

She opened Old Aunt's first. It was a small old-fashioned mirror, silver, with carvings on the back and on the handle.

"Ai! Look at this," said Peanut, frowning. "The last time I saw her, she said to me, 'The pretty girl I once knew, does she still exist?' I told her I did not have a mirror to see myself, but pretty or not, I did know I existed. So now you see what she's given me. Hnh! She thinks this silly thing will convince me to come back to my old life."

Peanut looked in the mirror. It seemed to me she still had her old vanity. She patted her cheeks, widened her eyes, smiled at what she saw. And it's true, she was pretty in a way. Her skin was smooth, her eyes were big. Although her face was too broad. Of course, this fault had nothing to do with her becoming a Communist. It was that way even when she was a spoiled girl with no sympathy for a person with a poor background. She put the mirror down and turned to the next package.

"I'm afraid my gift is not suitable either," I said.

She tore open the package, just like a child. When she held up the stockings, she started to laugh, a big, long laugh.

"I can take them back," I said. I was very embarrassed. "Here, give them to me."

"No, no," she cried, holding them close to her body. "These are very valuable. I can sell them on the black market for a good price. It's a good gift." She looked at me, then said in a very frank voice, no apologies, "I have nothing for you. I have no time these days to keep up with all the polite customs."

"Of course," I said. "You did not even know I was coming. How could you—"

"No," she stopped me with a firm voice. "I am saying, even if I knew, even if I had the money, I would not bother with these customs anymore. It is too much bother—and to what purpose?"

I was worried Peanut had grown bitter. She put the stockings on a shelf. But when she turned around, she held out her hand to me and said, *"Tang jie"*—sugar sister, the friendly name we sometimes used for one another when we were younger.

*"Tang jie,"* she said again, holding my hand and squeezing it hard, "I'm so glad you came. And now you know, these are not just polite words."

That afternoon, we had such a good talk. We sat on the bed and told each other secrets, in the same way as when we were girls, only this time we did not have to whisper. We talked openly about everything. Nine years before, we had argued over who had found the best marriage. Now, nine years later, we argued over who had the worst.

"Just think," I said. "You were once so mad that Wen Fu married me instead of you. Now you know what regrets you avoided."

"Even so, you got the better marriage," said Peanut. "Mine was the worst!"

"You don't know," I said. "You cannot imagine a husband that evil, that selfish, that mean—"

And Peanut broke in: "My husband was *zibuyong*."

When Peanut said that, I didn't believe her. I don't know how you say it in English, but in Shanghainese, *zibuyong* means something like "hens-chicks-and-roosters," all the male and female ingredients needed to make an egg that turns into a chick. We had heard Old Aunt tell a story once about a distant relative who gave birth to a *zibuyong*, a baby with two organs, male and female. Old Aunt said the mother of that baby did not know whether to raise it as a son or a daughter. Later she did not have to decide, because the baby died. Old Aunt thought the mother killed it, because even if she had raised the *zibuyong* as a son, he could never have had children.

"How could your husband be a *zibuyong*?" I asked Peanut. "I remember your letter saying he had five sons by the first wife, who died."

"The family went to little villages and bought a new baby son every year. You should see them—none of them look alike. One is dark-skinned, another very light. Another is lively and chubby, another thin and quiet. Anyone with eyes and brains can see the sons were bought."

"But how could Miao-miao marry you off to such a person?"

"She didn't know. The mother had always raised the child as a son. And for many months after my marriage, I didn't know either. He didn't touch me. I thought he was unhappy with me."

"And then you saw the two organs?"

"I saw him in our bed with another man! The female side of him had enticed a male. I ran to his mother and told her what I saw. And do you know what she did? She slapped me, told me never to repeat such lies about her son again."

"If you never saw the two organs," I said, "how can you be sure he was *zibuyong*?"

Peanut sighed. "Because I told the mother her son was *zibuyong*, and she slapped me again and again, as if she could change this fact by making me believe otherwise."

I am telling you this story the way Peanut told it to me. So I cannot tell you if her husband truly was as she said. Maybe she said that only because we had no word back then for "homosexual." If a man never married, people whispered, "Maybe he is *zibuyong*." They did not say this about women who did not marry. They had another word for that. But now I forget what it was.

Anyway, Peanut said she became a mock wife. "After a year, the mother forced me to go into hiding for five months," she said.

"I could see no one. And at the end, the mother presented a new baby boy to the world. I had to pretend that baby was my own. I tell you, I took no interest in that baby. I lost interest in everything, all my pretty clothes. They meant nothing. My life was just like a saying I read the other day: how we are living in a world where everything is false. The society is like bright paint applied on top of rotten wood."

Oyo! When she said that, she sounded just like a revolutionary. And yet she was also the same Peanut I knew when we were growing up: full of pride, headstrong about getting her own way, using words fashioned by somebody else's ideas.

"How did you finally leave?" I asked.

"Do you remember that girl Little Yu, who went to our school?"

I nodded. "Of course I remember, the naughty one who switched everyone's shoes when we were sleeping. What chaos the next morning! Each girl had a big right shoe and a small left shoe, or two right shoes, or two left shoes. We were late to classes, trying to sort them out. What a bad girl."

"She helped me leave my marriage," said Peanut.

"Little Yu?"

"In a manner of speaking," said Peanut. "It was after I had been married for four years to that hen-and-rooster, and his mother always pecking at my feet. I was thinking how easy it is to ruin your life with no chance of ever fixing it."

"I have felt the same way," I said. "Exactly the same."

Peanut continued. "I thought about my youth, things I once dreamt."

"All your hopes, your innocence," I added.

"Let me finish," Peanut said. "Anyway, with that feeling in my heart, I decided to pay a visit to the school, to see our old teachers. So I went, and Sister Momo—you remember her, the one with one big nostril, one small."

I nodded. "She was always very strict."

"Sister Momo had become director of the school by then. And she wanted to show me how much money had been donated to the school. She showed me the new library, the chapel with the new Baby Jesus window.

"And then she took me to the back, to the little cemetery. Remember how Sister Momo would send us to the cemetery when we were bad? She thought this would scare us into being good for the next world. The cemetery had a new fountain, water coming out of a baby's mouth. I was admiring this, and that's when I saw a memorial with Little Yu's name. I was so shocked. It was like seeing Little Yu turned to stone.

" 'What happened? What happened?' I asked Sister Momo. And she said, 'Oh, this is a sad story. Only one year into her marriage, and then she died very suddenly, an accident.'

"Sister Momo did not say what kind of accident. But right away I was suspicious. Why was she buried here in the school cemetery? Her husband's family should have buried her body in their family grave. I said this to Sister Momo. And she said, 'She was happy here for so many years. That's why her mother thought she should be surrounded by other happy girls.'

"And I thought to myself, This is a wish, not a reason. And as I puzzled over this, I heard a voice whispering in my ear. 'Go find out,' it was saying. Right away I found myself asking Sister Momo for the address of Little Yu's family, so I could pay my respects. I don't know why I did that. I was no longer myself. Something was pulling me.

"I left the school and went to the Yu family house immediately. This is when I had my second shock. Little Yu was not from a rich family like most of the girls at that school. The family house turned out to be a two-room flat on the second floor of an old building. One level above poor. And the family turned out to be only one widowed mother. That poor mother had taken a small inheritance from her uncle and stretched it into tuition for Little Yu, with enough put aside for a modest dowry. So you see, all her life's hopes went for that daughter, now dead after one year of marriage."

"Ai-ya!" I cried. "This is too sad."

"Even sadder than that," said Peanut. "The mother was so glad to see me. Nobody, it seemed, ever mentioned her daughter's name anymore. And this was because her daughter did not die from an accident. She committed suicide."

"Suicide!"

"She said the husband's family drove her to killing herself. My body shook when I heard this. Only that morning I had been thinking I might kill myself if I did not find a way out of my marriage soon."

"I have had these same thoughts," I whispered to Peanut.

"The mother blamed herself as well," said Peanut, "because she had helped to set up the marriage—to a nephew of a cousin's friend in a village outside of Soochow. The future husband, she was told, had a high position with his father's noodle business.

"Little Yu's mother had never met the nephew. She saw him for the first time at the wedding. He seemed nervous, she said. People had to keep reminding him which direction to walk in, what to say. He giggled and laughed out loud at all the wrong times, making Little Yu's mother think that he was drunk. He wasn't drunk. He had the mind of a little child! He still wet the bed. He cried when the wind blew too hard. He thought Little Yu was his big sister.

"When Little Yu came to her mother, asking for help to end the marriage, her mother said her life could be worse. At least the family was good to her, gave her plenty to eat. And even though the husband was simple-minded, she had heard he could still father children. He had done this with a girl in the village. So the mother told Little Yu, 'Be good, try harder.' And Little Yu returned to her husband's house. She climbed the tree in the courtyard, tied one end of a rope to a branch, the other to her neck, then jumped.

" 'For one year,' the mother said, 'my only thought was to do the same thing.' Little Yu's mother was crying when she told me this, and I was crying, too. I was feeling my own neck when she told me that. I was talking as if in a dream: 'So this is how a girl ends her marriage.'

"And Little Yu's mother cried, 'No, this was wrong, what happened to her, that she could find no other way, that she had no one to help her.'

"That afternoon, at last, I had a sympathetic heart to listen to my troubles. I now think it was Little Yu's voice guiding me to her mother. Because later that year it was Little Yu's mother who helped me escape from my marriage."

"How did she do this?" I said. I thought I was a few words away from hearing the answer to all my unhappiness.

Peanut stood up. "Why don't you ask her yourself?"

"What?"

"Ask her," Peanut said. "Ask Little Yu's mother. She's downstairs, cooking the noonday meal for all the women of this house who have already left their marriages."

So that's how I found out that whole house was an underground hiding place, filled with women and children. Can you imagine? I was scared and excited at the same time. I'm not saying I wanted to become a Communist, no such thing. I was excited because I was in a house with nine women who had once had awful marriages, nine women who no longer had to obey their husbands and mothers-in-law.

Little Yu's Mother was still cooking when we went downstairs. That's what everyone still called her, Little Yu's Mother. To look at her, you would not think this small woman, frying her dried fish and bittermelon, was an underground worker. But then again, most Communist people did not wear uniforms openly back then. You would be crazy or dead if you told someone you were a revolutionary.

The other women were coming home for lunch, one at a time, from their different workplaces. One tutored students in French. Another worked in a shoe factory. Another made straw brooms and sold them on the street. They came from many different backgrounds. Really, they were like any kind of people you might meet in Shanghai.

So nobody said to me, "I'm a Communist. How about you?" But you could tell by the things they said. When we all sat down to eat, for example, Little Yu's Mother said to me, "I hope bittermelon doesn't disagree with you too much. I don't eat it very often myself. But when I do, I remind myself how grateful I am to have other things to eat." She laughed, and Peanut and the other women laughed with her.

They all liked that bittermelon, not for the taste, but for the conversation that went with it. "Oh, you haven't tasted bitterness," one of those women said, "until you have lived a whole winter with only one coal brick for heating and cooking." And another said, "This melon is sweet compared to what I have had to swallow as a slave to a rich family."

I can tell you this. I did not like bittermelon, not before, not after, not now. And I was not revolutionary in my thinking. But I would have joined them if they had told me I had to. I would have eaten bittermelon every day, every meal, if it had meant I could leave my marriage. If I had had to change the whole world to change my own life, I would have done that. I think many of the women at that house felt this way about their lives.

After we finished eating our simple meal, they all asked me questions. And even though they were strangers, I told them everything, about Wen Fu's family, about my family, about how Wen Fu now controlled everything.

"He will not agree easily to a divorce, then," said one of the women at the table. "I too came from a rich family. My husband did not want to give me up, because that meant giving up my family's riches."

"How about your son? Do you want him to come with you?" Little Yu's Mother asked.

"Of course. My husband cares nothing about our son. He only uses him as a weapon to stop me from leaving."

"Money?" said another. "Do you have money of your own?"

"Only a little bit left from my dowry. Just spending money for everyday shopping."

"Don't forget your jewelry," said Peanut. "The two gold bracelets you received for your wedding—do you still have them?"

I nodded. "And two necklaces, two pairs of earrings, one ring."

"Does your husband have a mistress?" Little Yu's Mother asked.

"Many!" I said. "He's like a dog, sniffing from one bottom to another."

"But is there a special woman, someone he sees all the time?" asked another woman at the table. "Sometimes a mistress can force a man to divorce his wife, if his desire for the woman is strong enough." She gave out a hollow laugh.

"He cares for nobody that way," I said. "In the past, his habit was to pick up a woman, use her for a few weeks, then throw her away. Now we are living in my father's house, also with his own mother and father. There are too many eyes on him. So he does not bring his dirty business into the house anymore. I don't know who he is seeing."

"And what about you? Do you have a lover?" said a woman with a front tooth missing.

"Of course not!" I said in an angry way. "My husband's morals are the ones that are bad, not mine! How can you think—" And then I became confused, then embarrassed by my confusion. Because, of course, I was thinking of Jimmy Louie. We were not lovers, and yet I felt for the first time the secret feelings that lovers must have, shame and the need to protect that shame.

Little Yu's Mother patted my hand to soothe me. "This question is not meant to insult you," she explained. "Sometimes it's useful for a woman to pretend to have a lover."

"Especially if the husband has a big face he doesn't want to lose," said Peanut.

"That's what we did in your cousin's case," said Little Yu's Mother. "Made up a lover. She got her divorce very fast after that."

"But why should I make this my fault?" I said.

"Fine," said the woman with the missing tooth. "Save your face and keep your miserable marriage! So pretty and proud—it's women like you who can't give up the old customs. In that case, you have only yourself to blame."

"Stop fighting, stop fighting," said Little Yu's Mother. "We are only trying to find out as much as we can to determine the best way."

She turned to me. "In the meantime, you must put together all your jewelry, whatever money you can find. And when you are ready, you and your son must run away to here without anyone following you. When you come, we'll know what to do next. Can you do this first part by yourself, or do you need help?"

"I can do this," I said right away. And I said those words without knowing how I would make them true.

# 22

# ONE SEASON LEFT

By the time I left Peanut's place, it was already late in the afternoon. I had to hurry to the bookshop to find your father. The whole way there I was smiling big, I could not stop myself. And it seemed to me other people on the road saw my happiness and smiled back to congratulate me.

As soon as I saw your father, I told him: "In a week or two, I am leaving my marriage." I was trembling, both proud and nervous.

"Is this really so?" he said. He was trembling too.

"Really so," I said. He held my hands, and we were laughing with tears in our eyes.

If your father were still alive today, I think he would agree. We knew then we would always be together. I do not know how two strangers knew this, how we could be so sure. But maybe it was like this: When he put that photo of four daughters on the table, that was like asking me to marry him. And when I ran back and said I was leaving my marriage, that was like saying I accepted. And from that moment on, we were together, two people talking with one heart.

"And next?" he was asking me. "What must we do next?"

"We must wait awhile," I said. "We must wait until the right moment when I can leave."

And then we made a plan. When I was ready to run away, I

would call him by telephone late at night when everybody was sleeping. I would say something very quick and simple, such as, "Tomorrow I'm coming."

But then your father, he was so romantic, he suggested something else, a secret code. So this is what we decided I would say: "Open the door, you can already see the mountain," which is a classical saying, meaning you're ready to grab all opportunities and turn them into something big. Your father would answer me this way: "Let's go beyond the mountain." And then he would meet me and Danru the next day at the harbor, in front of the booth that sold tickets to Tsungming Island. And there we would get into a car that would take us to Peanut's place.

When I returned home that day, I saw my life as if I already knew the happy ending of a story. I looked around the house and thought, Soon I will no longer have to see these walls and all the unhappiness they keep inside.

I heard Wen Fu's mother shouting at the cook, and I imagined myself eating a simple, quiet meal without having my stomach turn itself inside out. I saw Wen Fu walk in the door, and I thought, Soon I will no longer have to rub my skin off, trying to remove his stain from my body. I saw Danru watching his father out of the corner of his eye, and I thought, Soon my son can laugh and play without any fears.

And then I saw my father, his back bent, shuffling into his study. It seemed as if I had never seen my father look so weak.

And that's when I remembered, My father! If I leave, Wen Fu will have him killed as a traitor. He would use my father just like a weapon.

I quickly went upstairs to my room. I began to argue with myself. I should let my father go to prison, I thought. After all, he brought this on himself. Let him see what it is like to suffer.

And then I thought of more reasons. He was the one who mistreated my own mother! He was the one who refused to see me when I was growing up. He was the one who let me marry a bad man. He did not care that he was giving me an unhappy future. Why should I sacrifice my happiness for him? There had never been love between us, father to daughter, daughter to father.

But all those angry reasons only made me feel I was as evil as

Wen Fu. So I emptied those feelings from my heart. I quietly excused myself: He is old. His mind is already gone. How can I be responsible for what Wen Fu does to him?

And still I knew: Those excuses would not cover anything up, the real reason. So in the end, all the excuses fell away, and I saw only one thing: Jimmy Louie.

I no longer denied I was betraying my father. I no longer looked for excuses. I knew what I was doing was both true and wrong. I could not make just one choice, I had to make two: Let me live. Let my father die.

Isn't that how it is when you must decide with your heart? You are not just choosing one thing over another. You are choosing what you want. And you are also choosing what somebody else does not want, and all the consequences that follow. You can tell yourself, That's not my problem, but those words do not wash the trouble away. Maybe it is no longer a problem in your life. But it is always a problem in your heart. And I can tell you, that afternoon, when I knew what I wanted, I cried, just like a child who cannot explain why she is crying.

The next week I was a person in mourning. I felt I had already lost my father, also a part of myself. I wanted to be comforted. I wanted to be miserable. And then one afternoon, without thinking, I found myself following my father into his study. I don't know why, maybe I wanted to let him know in some way that I was sorry.

"Father," I called to him. He looked up at me, without expression. I sat down in a chair opposite him. "Father," I said again. "Do you know who I am?"

This time he did not look at me. He was staring at the wall, at the same ancient scroll painting he had ruined with a cup of tea that afternoon the Japanese came.

The painting showed the springtime, pink flowers blossoming on trees, the trees growing on a mountain, the mountain rising up out of a misty lake. At the bottom was a black lacquer rod, weighing it down. You could tell the scroll had once been part of a set, the four seasons. But now the three other seasons were gone, sold by Wen Fu, and only their empty spots hung on the wall, like ghost paintings. And you could also tell why this scroll had been left behind—the big tea stain at the center, as if the painted lake had flooded itself.

"Isn't that strange," I said to my father, "that someone would want only three seasons? Like a life that will never be completed."

Of course, my father did not answer. And because I thought my father could not understand anything, I continued to talk nonsense. "My life has been like that painting nobody wants, the same season, every day the same misery, no hope of changing."

And now I was crying. "That's why I must find a way to leave my marriage. I do not expect you to forgive me."

My father sat up straight. He stared at me with one sad eye, one angry eye. I was startled to see this, that he had heard what I said. He stood up. His mouth moved up and down. But no words would come out, he could only chew the air with "uh! uh!" sounds. A terrible expression grew on his face. He waved his hands in front of his face, as if the words stuck in his throat were choking him.

My father reached out with one shaky hand. He grabbed my arm, and I was surprised how strong he still was. He was pulling me out of my chair, toward the scroll. "I must," I whispered to him. "You don't know how much I have suffered." He waved my words away.

And then he let go of my arm. His two trembly hands were now fighting with the black lacquer rod. I thought he wanted to pick up that rod and strike me over the head. But instead, he suddenly pulled the knob off the rod, and out poured three little gold ingots into his waiting palm.

He pressed them into my hand, then stared at me. I was struggling so hard to know his meaning. And I can still see the two expressions on his face when I finally understood. One side was agony, the other relief, as if he wanted to say to me, "You foolish, foolish girl, finally you've made the right decision."

"I cannot take them now," I whispered. "Wen Fu would find them. Later I will get them, right before I leave." My father nodded once, then quickly put the gold ingots back into their hiding place.

I have thought about this many times. I do not think my father was saying he loved me. I think he was telling me that if I left this terrible man, then maybe this terrible man would leave his house too. Maybe my father and his wives would no longer have to suffer. My leaving was their only chance. Of course, maybe he was telling me he loved me a little, too.

The next morning was very strange for me. Everyone came downstairs for the morning meal: Wen Fu, Danru, Wen Fu's mother and father, San Ma and Wu Ma. The servant brought in a bowl of steaming soup.

If you had been there, you would think nothing had changed. My father did not seem to recognize me. Once again, his mind seemed as cloudy as the soup he stared at. Wen Fu's mother had only complaints: The soup was not hot enough, the soup was too salty. Wen Fu ate without speaking. I wondered if I had dreamt what happened the day before, if I had only imagined the gold ingots. I was nervous, but I vowed to go ahead with my plans, what I had decided the night before.

I poured Wen Fu's mother more soup. "Mother," I said to her, "eat more, take care of your health." As she drank, I continued my conversation. "Poor Old Aunt. Her health is not so good. I had a letter from her yesterday."

This was true. I had received a letter, and as usual, Old Aunt complained about her health. She could be counted on for that.

"What's the matter with her?" asked Wu Ma. She worried a lot about her own health.

"A coldness in her bones, a lack of force at the end of each breath. She feels she might die any day."

"That old woman never feels well," said Wen Fu's mother in an unkind voice. "She has an ailment to match every herb grown on this earth."

Wen Fu laughed in agreement.

"This time I really think she is sick," I said. And then I added in a quiet voice, "Her color was very bad the last time I saw her. No heat. Now she says she is worse."

"Perhaps you better go see her," said San Ma.

"Mmmm," I murmured, as if I had not considered this before. "Perhaps you are right."

"The girl just got back!" exclaimed Wen Fu's mother.

"Maybe I could go for a short visit. If she is not too sick, I'll come home in a day or two."

And Wen Fu's mother only said, "Hnnh!"

"Of course, if she is really sick, I may have to stay longer."

But now the cook had brought in the steamed dumplings, and

Wen Fu's mother was too busy inspecting and criticizing the food to give me any more trouble.

So you see, she did not say yes, but she did not say no, either. I knew then that if I left the next day holding a suitcase with one hand and Danru with the other, nobody would think anything of it. And if I did not return home after three or four days, no one would go looking for me. They would only say, "Poor Old Aunt, sicker than we thought."

That afternoon, while everyone slept, I walked quickly into my father's study and shut the door. I went over to the scroll of spring-time. I shook the rod. Sure enough, the weight of those three ingots slid back and forth. Then bright gold fell into my hand. And I saw that what had happened the day before was true, not my imagination.

# 23

# SINCERELY YOURS TRULY

I have no pictures of myself as a young woman, from that time I was married to Wen Fu. I threw those pictures away. But your father kept this scrapbook. And he took pictures of me, many, many pictures. See how heavy?

These pictures at the beginning, these are American pilots he knew. And these women, they are not girlfriends. I think they are just people your father knew before he met me. I don't know why he put their pictures in the book. I never asked. Maybe he gave those girls American names, so they gave him pictures in return. Like this one here: "Sincerely yours truly, Peddy." What kind of name is Peddy? She could not even spell her name right. My English is not so good, but I know you can be sincerely or truly, one or the other, not both at the same time. Anyway, you can see this, she is not even very pretty.

Turn to this page. Here is where I begin. Here is where I sometimes think my whole life began.

Look at this picture, this one, and this one. See, I was once young. You didn't know this about your mother? This was how your father always saw me, young and fair, he said. Even when white hairs started to come out, your father said I looked the same. And in my dreams, I would always look the same as in these pictures, young and fair. Always, until recently.

But then on my last birthday I had a dream that your father did not really die. He lived around the corner and he just forgot to tell me. I was mad at first. How could he let me grieve for nothing? But then I forgot to be mad, and I was excited. I was getting ready to see him. And then I looked in the mirror. I said to the mirror, Ai-ya! What happened? How did you get so old? And my self looking back at me said, "This is your fault. You forgot." And suddenly I felt old. Suddenly I realized everyone saw me this way, older than I thought, seventy-five years old.

In any case, in 1946, I was young, pretty too.

See this picture, my smile, my puffy eyes. This picture is not so good, but it has special meaning. Your father took that picture maybe one month after I ran away from Wen Fu. That day, we had been walking in a park, arguing. This was because Little Yu's Mother wanted to send me and Danru away from Shanghai. She knew people in Tientsin, good people who could hide me until I got my divorce.

Your father was saying, "Don't go, don't go."

And I said, "How can we not go? Where would we go instead?"

"You two stay with me," he said.

That's what I was hoping he would say. Living in that house with Peanut and all those other women was no fun. Do you think just because they were Communists they never argued? No such thing. But I didn't let Jimmy know.

When he asked me to live with him, I said, "How can we do that?" I let him argue with me for two hours. If someone offers to take your burden, you need to know he is serious, not just being polite and kind. Polite and kind do not last.

After I knew your father was serious no matter what, he took this picture.

Oh, I don't know why your father put this picture in the book. I told him many times to take it out, this picture doesn't look nice. Why take a picture of me in a nightgown, my hair all messy like that? Your father said it was his favorite picture. "Winnie and the sunshine wake up together," he used to say. Every morning when I woke up, he was already awake, looking at me, telling me that. There was a song he sang to me. "You Are My Sunshine." He sang it many times, every morning.

Maybe this is not proper for me to say to you. But now I will tell you something about your father. He was—how do I say this?—he loved me with a true heart. Do you know why? When I went to live with him, from the beginning he never forced me. He did not demand anything. He was gentle. He knew I was scared of sex.

So for the first few nights he kissed my forehead, he smoothed my hair, he talked to me, told me he loved me so many times, until I felt I was floating happily in a dream. And a week later, I told him I was ready. I was willing to make the sacrifice to make him happy as well. I did not say it this way, of course, but that's what I was thinking. And I closed my eyes, waiting for the shameful feelings to begin. But he did not jump on top of me right away. Instead, he did what he had always done. He kissed my hands, my cheeks, my forehead. And he would not stop kissing my forehead. He did not stop stroking my back, until I forgot all my fears, until I was again floating in a dream. And suddenly, I recognized what he was doing, only it was not the same, but a completely different feeling. And I opened my eyes. I cried with joy to see his face, his face watching mine. And he was crying too, the same joy. And afterward he kept his arms around me, afraid to let me go.

So that's why your father liked this picture. In the morning, I was still there. I was his sunshine.

The picture on this page was three months after Danru and I went to live with your father. That's the front of the building, the door. And that woman next to me, she's the landlady who rented us two rooms upstairs. Your father called her Lau Tai Po, "Old Lady." In China, if you called someone Old Lady, you were being respectful, very polite. In this country, people say, "Hey, old lady! Watch where you're going!" They're not being respectful. I see the looks on their faces, mean.

But in this picture I am the happiest I have ever been in my life. See how my eyes look as though they can't stop smiling. Your father was the same way, laughing all the time. Every day we were happy. Every day when he came home from work, he lifted me high in the air, just like people in the movies. And Danru would run to him and say, "Lift me too, me too." Your father would try to lift him, and then say, "Oh! Too heavy. How did you get so heavy?" He told Danru to take a deep breath and fill himself with air, just like a balloon. And then your father would lift him high, high, high.

During that time, I wasn't too worried about Wen Fu. Peanut had already told New Aunt and Old Aunt I was living with another man. And of course, they told Uncle, and Uncle told Wen Fu. And by then Wen Fu had another woman living in the house with him, a woman who was going to have a baby. So I was sure Wen Fu would soon divorce me. Even his mother and father were telling him to do that. As for my father's money, there was not too much left to fight over. Wen Fu had followed government orders and exchanged all the gold and certificates for new paper money. And every week, it seemed, the new paper money was worth one-half what it was before.

Lucky for us, your father was paid in U.S. dollars. But even if we had had no money, we would have been happy. That's how happy we were.

Here is another picture from that same day. I made an extra copy, wallet-size, and sent it to Hulan. She and Jiaguo were still living in Harbin. I wrote to her: "Guess who we met? Guess who we are living with? Someone who speaks English and calls me Winnie. Guess and I'll tell you in the next letter if you are right."

In this picture you can see: Danru is playing with the landlady's dog. Doesn't that dog look just like a lamb? The curly hair, the little ears. Later he turned out to be a bad dog, he ate my slippers. Oh, I was mad! The landlady gave me her own slippers to replace mine. But she had some kind of rotten foot disease, so I was not eager to wear them, not even to be polite.

Of course, I still thought she was very nice. I remember one day, when she and I were alone, she told me about her life. That's how I found out she was married to a Chinese man from the United States. The husband had deserted her, left the dog behind too. He went back to America and married someone else, didn't even bother to divorce the landlady first. But he still sent her money. So she didn't care.

"That's fate," she said. I thought she didn't feel anything, just accepted her life that way, very old-fashioned. But then she told me, "You be careful. Don't you get my same fate." So you see.

•

367

This next picture looks like springtime. See the flowers on the trees in back. And now my hair is shorter, more stylish. Oh, I remember this picture. I look happy, but only because your father said, "Smile."

Actually, in this picture I am worried. I had already used two of my gold ingots to hire a good lawyer, a famous lawyer on Nanking Road, known for being smart and clever. He put an advertisement in the newspaper, saying I was already divorced, divorced since that time Wen Fu had put a gun to my head in Kunming and made me write, "My husband is divorcing me." The day after this came out in the newspaper, two men went to the lawyer's office and smashed everything to pieces and tore up my divorce papers. The lawyer was scared, mad too. "Is your husband some kind of gangster?" he asked. He wouldn't help me after that.

I started thinking, Maybe my husband is a gangster. Auntie Du thought this, too. I don't know why. Now it is too late to ask her.

This is a funny picture. See the apron I wore. I am at our new place, a two-room flat in Chiao Chow Road. Your father and I registered ourselves as husband and wife. That was like signing "Mr. and Mrs. James Louie." But I still used my real name seal, the one that said "Jiang Weili," my legal name.

Your father took that picture in the morning, just before he went to work. I probably went to the movie theater later with Danru. We went almost every day because I did not want to be in the house all day, just in case. Meaning just in case Wen Fu found us.

Actually, in this picture I am not really cooking anything, only pretending. Your father liked to take natural pictures, not just posed. "Baby-ah," your father said to me—he always called me by that American nickname. "Baby-ah, smile but don't look at the camera." So you see, this picture is natural.

Here is another picture with me and Danru. And another, and another. See how many? See how happy he looks? His face is fuzzy, because he started to move when your father took the picture. You cannot keep a six-year-old boy still when he wants to throw rocks in a pond.

In this one we were in a temple garden. In this one we were at a park with a small merry-go-round with animals shaped like cartoon figures. In this one we were leaning against a tree near a lake. You can't see the lake. But I remember it was there.

I also remember we took these pictures before we sent Danru up north—to Harbin, to stay with Jiaguo, Hulan, and Auntie Du. This was after the landlady told us two men had come by, looking for Danru and me. I wanted to go with him. Jimmy would have gone too. But I decided to stay a few extra weeks, because I had found another lawyer, the one who took my last gold ingot. He said I was very close to getting my divorce, but I had to be in Shanghai when it happened. So I stayed. I told Danru I would follow soon. Of course, he believed me. And I too believed I was doing the right thing. I was saving him.

Late at night, when Danru was already asleep, we took him to the train station with the landlady. She had agreed to take Danru up north, where she had a cousin she could visit. But just before they got on the train, Danru woke up. He began to shout. "Where's my mother? I changed my mind! Now I don't want to go!" He cried loud, in a pitiful way.

I rushed over. "How can you do this?" I said. "Embarrassing your mother in front of so many people?" Still he cried, his little heart breaking to pieces, piercing mine. I scolded him, "Don't cry, don't cry. I am coming to get you as soon as I am free."

Of course, I did this in a gentle way. But I still regret it. I should have held him. I should have praised him for shouting that he never wanted to leave me. I should have never let him go.

But look: In this picture, and this one, and this one, he is happy. You can see this, even in a fuzzy picture. Most of the time, I made him happy.

Here is a picture of me with Auntie Du. This was taken a few weeks after she came to see me in Shanghai. Whenever I look at this picture, I become very sad. Because I remember that day she arrived, how she waited patiently in the hallway until we came home.

I saw an old woman stand up slowly. *"Syau ning"*—little person—she said. I was so surprised, so happy. Auntie Du—all the way from Harbin! I ran to greet her, to scold her for not writing so we could pick her up at the train station. And then I saw her face, her mouth pushed tight, water at the edges of her eyes. When you see a face like that, you know, you know.

I tried to push her away. I was screaming, "Go back! Go back!" Jimmy had to hold his arms around me to keep me from pushing her away. And when she told me why she had come, I shouted, "How can you say this? Do you think this is some kind of joke? How can you ever tell a mother her little son is dead? He's not dead. I saved him! I sent him to Harbin!"

But she never blamed me. She made that long journey, knowing I would hate her. And she told me how the Japanese had raised thousands of rats with a bad disease. And after the war, they didn't kill the rats, they let them go. More than one year later, disaster—lots of people sick, no chance to escape, then dead from a fast-moving epidemic carried by rats and fleas. Poor little Danru, gone in one day.

Oh, and it was even worse than that. Jiaguo was dead too.

I wanted to rush to Harbin to hold my little son one more time, to make sure they had not made a mistake. After all, he never cried much. He did not wake easily from sleep. They didn't know these things about Danru, how much he trusted me.

But Auntie Du said they put Danru and Jiaguo in the ground the same day they died, before a person could even think, How did this happen? She said they had to burn everything in the house, Danru's clothes, his toys, everything, in case a flea was still hiding. So you see, I didn't have one thing left to hold for a hope or a memory. He was gone forever.

It was not until the next day that I asked Auntie Du about Hulan. "Where is she? Why didn't she come, too?"

And Auntie Du said Hulan was in Harbin, tending the graves. She brought food every day, telling Jiaguo and Danru that she hoped they were growing fat on the other side. "She insists on doing this," said Auntie Du. "She says she'll come to Shanghai later and meet me here. She has no reasons to live in Harbin anymore. At least she is making sense now. But right after they died—it was terrible. For two days she could not cry, she was so confused. She kept arguing, 'How can they be dead? The war is already over.' For two days she could not stop saying this. And then she became very busy cleaning her house, washing the walls and the floors with turpentine. And when she was done with that, she sat down to write you a letter, telling you as gently as she could what had happened to Danru.

"But she got stuck on an expression she did not know how to write 'your beloved son.' She went to ask Jiaguo. She could not find him. She called for him. I found her standing in her bedroom, shouting for him, angry tears running down her face. 'Jiaguo! Jiaguo!' she was screaming. 'Don't die now. What will I do without you? How will I know how to write "your beloved son"?' "

Now you see how skinny I've become in this picture. See how the sweater droops on my shoulders. You cannot tell, but the sweater is a dark red color, and the curly pattern on the chest and pocket was embroidered with threads twisted with real gold. Your father asked me to put that on for the picture. He bought it for me when I turned twenty-nine, so this was early spring 1947. I had never received a birthday present before. Americans give gifts on birthdays, Chinese do not. I should have been happy, but I was still very sad, because of Danru. I was still blaming myself. So your father did not ask me to smile. And I didn't. This picture is natural.

And now you see there are no more pictures of me here. Because soon after that, someone saw me walk into a beauty parlor, and when I came out, two policemen took me to jail.

Nobody would tell me why I had been arrested. They took me to a women's prison with a thick wooden gate and a big high wall. As soon as they brought me inside, I became sick. Such a terrible smell—just like sticking your nose into a toilet! A woman guard walked me down a long dark hallway, past long wooden tables and benches. On the other side were rooms, one after the other. And in each room were five women, people you would be afraid to look at on the street, a sad story on each face. And that's where they put me, in one of those stinky rooms with four other women.

I think those women knew I was there by mistake. They looked at me not with pity but with curiosity. Four pairs of eyes stared quietly at my *chipao,* the ordinary summer dress of a lady. They stared at my hair, the shiny curls, just fixed by the beauty parlor.

Most of the women there had on dirty long pants and tops. They had rough faces and oily hair.

And then one woman with a hoarse voice said, "Eh, little sister, sit down, sit down, stay and visit us awhile!" And everybody laughed, although not in a mean way. I think they thought a little joke would make me feel more comfortable. And then another young woman jumped up from her wooden stool and said, "Sit here," and everyone laughed again as she quickly pulled up her pants. And then I saw her seat was a wooden toilet in a corner of the room. That toilet was used for everything, no privacy at all! And you could not flush the toilet, you could not put a top over it, no such thing. Everybody's business just sat there, like one big ugly soup.

In another corner of the room was a thin padding on the floor, big enough for three people squeezed together. We were supposed to take turns sleeping, three people on the mattress, the two leftover people sitting on the concrete floor.

All night long I stood up. All night long I worried, not about myself but about Jimmy. I imagined him looking for me, running through the park, looking in the movie theaters. He was a good man, considerate and kind, but he was not strong. He had never been through any kind of bad hardship before. So I worried. I was hoping Auntie Du would help him find me.

By morning, my legs were shaky with exhaustion. A prison guard came to get me. She shouted my name: "Jiang Weili!" I shouted back, "Here! Here!" I thought they were releasing me. But instead, the guard put handcuffs on me, as if I were a dangerous criminal. And then I was put in the back of a truck with other handcuffed women, all rough-looking, like people who steal things. Maybe they were driving us to the countryside to be shot, we didn't know. We were just like tied-up animals being driven to market, bumping into each other whenever the truck made a turn.

But then the truck stopped at a place that turned out to be a provincial court building. When I walked into the courtroom, I saw him right away: Wen Fu, smiling like a victor, so glad to see me humiliated. My hair was messy. My dress was wrinkled. My skin was covered with the smells of the night before.

And then I heard someone whisper loudly, "There she is!" And I saw Auntie Du, Peanut, then Jimmy, his happy, painful face. I found out later it was just as I had hoped. Auntie Du was the one who went to my father's house, demanding to know where I was. That's how she learned what Wen Fu had done.

The judge told me what my crime was. I was being sued for stealing my husband's son and letting him die, for stealing valuables from my husband's family, for deserting my Chinese husband to run off with an American soldier I had met during the war.

I was so shaky with anger I almost could not speak. "These are all lies," I said in a quiet voice. I told the judge, "My husband divorced me a long time ago, during the war, when he put a gun to my head and forced me to sign a divorce paper." I said I did not steal anything from my own father's house, I took only what was mine to take. I said, How could I be accused of deserting my husband for another man, when my husband had divorced me and was now living with another woman? I said the other man was now my husband. We had already registered as husband and wife.

I saw Jimmy nodding, and someone took his picture. And then I heard whispering in the room. I saw there were other people there—just like an audience in a movie theater, people who came to watch because they had nothing better to do. And they were pointing to me, then Jimmy, whispering back and forth. Auntie Du later told me they were saying, "Look how beautiful she is, just like a movie actress." "Listen to the way she talks, you can tell by her character she's a nice girl." "That man she ran away with, he's no foreigner, anyone can tell he's Chinese."

But now Wen Fu was smiling and speaking to the judge. "There was no divorce. My wife is confused. Maybe we had a fight long ago and I said I might divorce her if she didn't behave."

He was making me sound like a silly woman, someone who could not remember if she was really divorced or not!

"If we are truly divorced," Wen Fu said, "where is the paper? Where are the witnesses?"

Right away, Auntie Du jumped up. "Here! I was a witness. And my niece, now living up north, she was another witness." What a good woman Auntie Du was! And so quick to think of this. This was not a lie, not really. She heard our fight, she saw the paper. The people in the room were excited to hear Auntie Du say this. They were talking in a happy way.

Wen Fu threw Auntie Du an ugly face. He turned back to the

judge. "This woman is not telling the truth. How could she be a witness and sign papers? I know this woman, and she cannot even read or write." And the judge could see by Auntie Du's unhappy face that this was true.

"Do you still have this divorce paper?" the judge asked me.

"I gave it to a lawyer last year," I said. "But after we made an announcement in the newspaper, this man, Wen Fu, destroyed the lawyer's office, tore up all his papers, mine too."

"This is a lie!" Wen Fu roared. And everyone started talking at once. I insisted again that Wen Fu had forced me to sign the paper. Auntie Du claimed that even though she could not read the paper, she knew what it said. "I marked it with my name seal!"

But now the judge was telling everyone to be quiet. "In matters like these," he said, "where everyone disagrees, I must go by the evidence. No one can show me a divorce paper. So there is no divorce. And with no divorce, a husband has the right to sue a wife for taking his property and his son. The wife does not deny she took both. Therefore, I sentence Jiang Weili to two years in jail."

The judge began to write this down on a document. People started shouting. Wen Fu was smiling. Auntie Du was wailing. And Jimmy and I were looking at each other, numb. I was dizzy, unable to think clearly. I had never considered I might go back to jail for Wen Fu's lies. I thought he only wanted to humiliate me, to send me to jail for one night to make me mad. I thought I was dreaming everything: the guard putting handcuffs on me, someone running up to take my picture, the judge marking his paper with a red seal.

All of a sudden, Wen Fu walked up to the judge and said in a loud voice, "Maybe my wife has now learned her lesson. If she says she is sorry, I will forgive everything, and she can come home with me." He smiled at me like a generous man.

All eyes were watching me, to see what I would say. I think they were waiting for me to fall to my knees and beg for forgiveness. I think even Jimmy and Auntie Du were hoping this. But I had so much hate in my heart I had no room for their hopes. I was blind to everything except Wen Fu's smiling face, waiting for my answer. And I could imagine how he would laugh at me, how he would later force his way into my bed, how he would make me miserable every day until my mind was completely broken.

"I would rather sleep on the concrete floor of a jail," I heard myself say in a loud voice, "than go to that man's house!" And the room roared with surprise and laughter. So you see, in the end, Wen Fu was the one who was humiliated. And when they took me away, I was smiling.

Three days later, Auntie Du came to visit me in the jail. We were sitting in a small visitors' room, with a woman guard in a corner, listening to everything.

Auntie Du put a package wrapped in cloth on the table. Inside I found two pairs of underpants, a wrapper to put over my dress and keep it clean, a comb, soap, a toothbrush, chopsticks, and a little Goddess of Mercy charm.

"Put the cloth down," Auntie Du explained, "to make a clean place on the bed. Put the charm on to make a clean place in your heart."

And then she reached into the sleeve of her shirt and pulled out a page of the newspaper, folded into a square. "Look what they did," she whispered. "It is in all the big newspapers. Jimmy Louie says it is very, very bad, what they wrote."

I opened up the newspaper and began to read. What Jimmy said was true. It was terrible, written just like some kind of cheap scandal. My face was burning with anger.

"American Romance Ends in Death and Tragedy," I read. I saw a picture of myself, looking strong, like a revolutionary. " 'I would rather go to jail!' lovesick wife shouts."

Next to that was a picture of Wen Fu, and his eyes were turned to the side, as if he were looking at my picture, angry and victorious at the same time. " 'Her selfishness killed my son!' claims Kuomintang hero."

And at the bottom was a small picture of Jimmy Louie, his face turned down, as if he were ashamed. "American GI says, 'I still want her back.' "

I read more, all lies from Wen Fu, saying I had given up a respectable life, turned my back on my own father, let my own son die—all because I was crazy for American sex. Wen Fu knew what the newspapers wanted to hear.

Auntie Du looked at the guard, whose eyes were rolling toward sleep. "Little person," she whispered. "I'm a stupid woman. I should have signed that paper long time ago. I'm sorry." We both sighed, we understood one another.

"Where is Jimmy Louie?" I finally asked. "When is he coming?" And Auntie Du looked down. "Ai, little person," she said. "Why am I always the one to bring you bad news?"

Here is a picture of the boat your father took to go back to America. See what it says at the bottom? SS *Marine Lynx*. See the bottom window circled here? That's where he stayed, dormitory class.

See how many people signed the picture for him? "Best wishes, Lee Wing Chin." "Best wishes, Mary Imagawa." "Best wishes, Raisa Hamsson." "Kindest regards, Johnnie Ow." "In Christ's love, Maxima Aspira."

This one is the best: "Dear Jimmy, When I first met you I thought of you as a big flirt. But after getting to know you I was sorry for thinking so, because you're one of the nicest swellest guys on the boat, I like you very much and your little 'Winnie' is a very fortunate girl to have a husband like you. Loads of luck from a friend indeed, Mary Moy."

Your father told everyone, even strangers on a boat, that he was my husband, I was his wife. He put that down on his passport papers going back home: Married. Auntie Du told me that. She was also the one who told me your father could not stay any longer in Shanghai.

After I was locked in jail, Wen Fu ran to the American consulate to cause Jimmy some trouble: "See what you Americans did? Ruined my family!" He ran to the newspapers and said the same thing. This was when lots of stories were coming out about American GIs raping Chinese girls, seducing Chinese women before going home to their wives.

So the consulate people told Jimmy not to see me anymore until everything quieted down. But instead, everything became worse. The newspaper stories went on for many weeks. Every few days a new part of the story came out, what Wen Fu said, what I said, what he said after that, what I said after that. And there were pictures—pictures of me in jail, sitting at a long table with twenty women; pictures of Wen Fu and his woman, the two of them looking so proud, walking a little Pekingese dog; pictures of Jimmy from the war, standing next to American pilots; a picture of Danru from when he was a baby.

Sometimes the newspaper made me sound glamorous and bad at the same time. Sometimes I sounded innocent, put in jail for no reason. Auntie Du told me I was like a celebrity to young girls in Shanghai. One time she heard two girls talking about me on a bus. How pretty, how tragic, they said.

But the consulate people did not care if I was pretty, if I had a tragic life. After a while, your father lost his job and people there told him, Go home, don't make any more trouble. He couldn't see me, he couldn't stay. So what could he do? He went home to San Francisco.

Of course, he wrote letters to me and sent them to Auntie Du, along with U.S. dollars so she would stay in Shanghai and take care of me. Auntie Du would have stayed anyway, money or not. But still, we were glad he did that, because Chinese money was so unstable.

So every month, Auntie Du came to see me, bringing me three or four letters from Jimmy each time. He always said the same thing: How he would come to get me in two years, no matter what. How he would always love me, nothing could stop his kind of love. How he was praying every day, every minute, that I would come home to him soon. I think he prayed so much he became like a religious person. I think that's why he joined the ministry. But I don't think he told anyone that his wife was in jail, that her other husband put her there. That didn't sound too good.

People in jail treated me nice. I think the guards and the other women prisoners believed me when I explained why I was there, why I shouldn't be there. I think they looked up to me, because I didn't look down on them. I was an educated person and now I was just like them. One girl said, "If I had your character, I would not be here." Another girl always washed my laundry for me. I didn't ask, she offered.

And I did things for them too. I asked Auntie Du to bring me a piece of wood so we could cover up our toilet smells. I found ways to keep our room clean, no bugs in the bed. When two girls asked me to teach them how to read and write, I asked Auntie Du to bring me old newspapers and a piece of charcoal so we could copy characters. And when we were done with our lessons, we tore the sheets into strips to use for toilet paper.

I also taught them manners, how to speak properly, just as I had taught that dancer-singer, that girl Min back in Kunming. Did I tell you I found out what happened to her? Oh, this is very sad. I was tearing newspapers one day, and I saw her picture. "Miss Golden Throat," it said, "dead at age thirty-three." I was surprised to see her picture. I was surprised she took the name Miss Golden Throat, the same one I suggested. I was surprised to see how old she was. And now that I had found her again, I was sorry she was dead.

She had become a famous nightclub singer in Shanghai—not a big kind of fame, maybe a little kind. I think they put her picture in the paper because she died in a terrible way. This happened during the wintertime, on a very cold night.

She was walking along the river harbor, wearing a fancy ball gown, no sleeves, no jacket. People were staring at her, dock-workers and fishermen probably. And then she started to sing. They thought she was very strange, but at the end, they clapped to be polite. She bowed and waved, backing away as if she were headed for a nightclub curtain. She smiled, said, Thank you, thank you. And then she jumped over the rail and into the cold river.

The newspaper said she was heartbroken, according to someone who knew her, but it didn't say why. Reading this, I saw myself. I once thought she was just like me, only stronger. If that were true, what could happen to me? I considered this for many days.

Actually, I thought about many things. I had plenty of time to think. Every day I sat on a workbench with the other women. We worked eight hours a day, no excuses. We made little matchboxes, cutting, folding, gluing, the same thing over and over again. Before I went to jail, I never thought someone had to make those little boxes matches go in. I never considered this little piece of nothing was someone's misery. It was boring!

So I would try to think of a different way to do it, folding all the tops first before gluing them, or maybe stacking them in a pattern, anything to keep my mind busy. When your mind stands still, all kinds of bad thoughts can come in.

I remember one time I got a letter from Jimmy. I stopped working for a few minutes so I could read it out loud to the women working at my same bench. They always became very excited when I got an air mail special, because they never received even regular letters. Of course, that was because they could not read.

" 'Dear Little Wife,' " I read. And all the girls sighed. Little Wife! And then I read them the usual things.

How much he loved me. And everyone giggled.

How he prayed for me all the time. And they sighed.

How he thought his head might burst from studying so hard. They laughed.

How much fun it was taking folk-dancing lessons at the YMCA. I stopped. Dancing lessons!

Those girls said nothing, they went back to their work. I was looking at my rough fingertips. I was imagining Jimmy holding the soft hands of a pretty girl. How could he love me and dance with another girl at the same time? How could he close his eyes and pray for me when he was too busy clapping his hands and stamping his feet? And then I imagined that if he said he was married on his passport papers, maybe he meant he was married to someone else, not to me. Pretty soon, Jimmy was dancing faster and faster in my mind—one-two-three—down a church aisle, into the arms of a new wife!

Those were the kinds of thoughts that crawled into my head. And I was stuck inside with them, nowhere else to chase them away. I could do nothing but wait and see, wait and see. And I would think, Maybe I am waiting for nothing. But then I would fight that thought and cling to a happy memory, Jimmy holding me at night, never wanting to let me go.

I did not have too many visitors besides Auntie Du. Old Aunt and New Aunt could not afford to come too often. Peanut came only once, and then she and Little Yu's Mother ran away from the house one night and disappeared. My father, of course, did not come. Maybe he did not even know where I was. I heard he could not stop dreaming now. His mind was somewhere else. He lay in his bed, eyes open, eyes closed, it did not seem to matter.

But one day, San Ma and Wu Ma both came. I was surprised to see them. But then I saw they were wearing white and I knew why my father's wives had come.

"Dead?" I said.

San Ma nodded her head, and Wu Ma looked away. And they

both began to cry. I did too. I was remembering the day my father gave me the gold ingots.

"He died with a clear mind," said Wu Ma. "He was very strong at the end."

I nodded. Those were the usual noble words. I thanked them for coming and telling me.

But then San Ma said, "It's true. It was very strange what happened just before he died. His mind so clear."

"It was like a miracle," said Wu Ma.

"Or maybe he was fooling us all these years," said San Ma, "pretending not to talk. Your father could be very stubborn that way."

"A miracle," said Wu Ma. "That's what I think."

"It was like this," said San Ma. "I went into his room five mornings ago, same as always. I tried to feed him a little rice porridge, same as always. He was not eating very much at the end. Every day I had to fight to open his mouth and pour something down his throat. Really, he was more trouble than a baby, wouldn't eat, always soiling his bed. That morning I was so exasperated I shouted, 'Goddess of Mercy, open his mouth!' Suddenly, he was staring at me with clear eyes. I thought, Hnh? Can he hear me? I said to him, 'Eat a little, eat, eat.' And he looked at me and said, 'Then give me something proper to eat.' Just like that—those words popped out! For almost seven years he says not one word—now, 'Give me something proper to eat.' I ran down the stairs as fast as these old legs could carry me."

Wu Ma nodded. "She told me what happened. I wouldn't believe it. 'You're dreaming,' I said, 'just like him.' That's what I said, those words exactly."

"I told the cook," said San Ma. "And Wen Tai-tai heard and she wanted to see, too. So everyone went upstairs, carrying a dumpling, a bun, a bowl of noodles, just in case he really would eat. When I went into his room—nnh!—he was asleep."

"I told her again," Wu Ma said, " 'You were only dreaming.' And then I saw the window was wide open, a big wind blowing from outside to inside. 'Why is this open?' I said. I went to close it—and he woke up and said, 'Leave it open!' "

"Our mouths flew wide open just like that window," said San Ma. "And then I gave him a dumpling. He ate it. The cook gave him a piece of *da bing*. He ate it. Then Wen Tai-tai ran down the stairs to call her husband and son to come see. They came to see."

"We all saw," said Wu Ma. "Your father looked around the room and frowned at everybody standing there. He said, 'What's become of this room? Why is it so shabby-looking? Where are my paintings, my rugs?' "

"He was just like his old self," said San Ma. "Very arrogant, lots of opinions."

Wu Ma nodded. "I told him, 'All those things are gone now. There's not much money left to fix such things.' He said, 'How can there be no money?' I said, 'The money situation is very bad now. It's the same everywhere, not just with us. Paper money has become worthless. The rags a bed is stuffed with are worth more.'

"He said, 'I'm not talking about paper money. The gold, the gold, you fool!' "

San Ma clapped her hands together. "And then guess what happened? Right away, Wen Fu said, 'What gold? Where is it?' And your father looked at Wen Fu, as if his son-in-law had a wooden head. 'Here!' he said, 'in this house, of course. Gold ingots as thick as your fingers, as much as you weigh.'

" 'Pah! There's no gold in this house,' said Wen Fu.

"And your father said with a big smile, 'That's because you do not know where I put it. Many years ago, I hid it.' And then your father scratched his cheek. 'Let me think—behind which wall? under which floor?' "

"Oyo!" said Wu Ma. "Right then we knew what your father was doing. We saw this behavior many times before, very mean. He was pulling a little string—pulling, pulling, pulling—and Wen Fu was the cat chasing it, pouncing onto empty air! When Wen Fu said, 'Where? Where?' your father waved him away. 'I'm tired now,' he said. 'Come back in a few hours, and I will tell you.' And then your father closed his eyes and went back to dreaming."

"What could Wen Fu do?" said Wu Ma. "He said, 'Pah! That old man is crazy!' But we saw Wen Fu and his father go downstairs. We heard them tapping the walls, tapping the floors, already looking."

"Three hours later," San Ma said in a trembly voice, "we went upstairs again, but your father was already dead. What a pity! I shook him a little and said, 'What? You come for only a short visit, then leave so quickly, no consideration for this old wife of yours?' "

"We were crying, crying so hard," said Wu Ma. "And that Wen Fu, he was so evil, evil beyond belief! Your father was still lying there, not even cold, and Wen Fu started to tear open a hole in the wall right next to the bed. That bad!"

"And now," said San Ma, "five days later, the walls and floors in your father's bedroom are completely torn apart, and Wen Fu is ready to pry open another room."

"As for us," said Wu Ma, "we do not care what happens to the rest of the house. He can pull the whole house down, we don't care. Tomorrow we are leaving, going to Yentai to live at my brother's place. He has already asked us, we have accepted." She had a satisfied look on her face.

And now San Ma and Wu Ma were looking at me to see what I would say. I had so many feelings running through me: grief that my father had died, anger at Wen Fu, sadness that San Ma and Wu Ma were leaving—all of us helpless, hopeless.

"Ai!" I said. "This is too bitter to swallow. To have nothing left in your old age. Terrible! To see all our gold go to such a bad man. Awful!"

San Ma frowned. "There's no gold in that house. Haven't you heard anything we said? We knew your father. Why would he leave gold to a man he hated? He woke up one last time to leave us a little joke, to leave Wen Fu a curse."

"Then the house is being destroyed for nothing!" I cried.

"For nothing?" said San Ma. "Do you think we did not suffer as well living with Wen Fu? Do you think you were the only one pressed under Wen Fu's thumb? Now your father is ordering Wen Fu around. Now Wen Fu is chasing your father's dreams. Now that house is falling down on top of him. Not for nothing!"

And now here is the telegram I sent your father, asking him if I could come to America and be his wife. You can see he saved it, how happy he was to receive it. But his telegram answering me back is not in here.

And now I will tell you why. This is the part I have been afraid to tell you. This is the part I always wanted to forget.

# 24

# *FAVOR*

One day Auntie Du brought me a surprise—Hulan, with a baby in her stomach! I cried, so happy to see her. She cried, so sad to see me in jail. This was February 1949, after I had been in prison more than one year.

We had written back and forth, five times on my part, maybe only three times on hers. She always excused herself, saying her writing was not very good now that Jiaguo had died. And remembering what Auntie Du had told me about Hulan's grief, I did not complain that her letters were slow to come, confusing to read. In her last letter, she mentioned she had something important to tell me—she did not say what—only that she was happy, and she hoped I would be too.

So this was her news: She had remarried—to a nice man, Kuang An. That was Uncle Henry's name before he changed it to Henry Kwong. Oh, he looked very different back then: skinny where he now has a big stomach, lots of black hair on his head. And his glasses were not so thick. I would not call him handsome, but he was pleasant and had good speaking manners. Helen can tell you how they met, only six months after Jiaguo died. She will probably tell you it was instant true love. Maybe for him. But I think she was being practical. She saw a chance, she took it, nothing wrong with that.

I am saying this only because I know how much Hulan loved

Jiaguo. It was a sweetheart kind of love she had for him, the same kind I had with your father. I think she was only sorry Jiaguo did not feel that way about her. She had a fall-in-love feeling for him. He had a grow-in-love feeling for her.

But Kuang An—he was crazy for Hulan! Anything she wanted, he would do. And she told him to help me out of jail. He had been some kind of military official up north, but then the Communists took over the north and chased all the old military people out. So he and Hulan went to Tientsin, and when that city was captured as well, they came to Shanghai. He had a schoolmate friend in Shanghai who had a very important position, the head of education for the whole province. And this person had connections to other people, lawyers, judges, police. Hulan said that Kuang An had to say only one word to this education chief, and the word would pass along, one person to the next, until I was let out of jail.

I believed her. I didn't ask, Is Kuang An really that important? Will his friend really listen? When you are in jail and someone throws you a little hope, you grab it. You don't care where it comes from.

I was in jail maybe another two months, and then one day someone came to me and said, "Jiang Weili, you can leave." That was all. I did not ask any questions, nobody gave me an explanation. I held hands with each of my roommates. I wished them a better life. And as I started to say more, they shooed me away, told me to hurry and go before my chance disappeared.

Before I walked out the front gate, a prison official gave me a document to sign, saying I was free. And on that document, in a section saying why I could go, somebody had already written: "Court error." Can you imagine how I was feeling? More than one year of my life in jail because of a mistake! I was happy and crying to be free. I was angry at the same time.

Auntie Du was outside the jail, waiting for me. We got on a bus. We were going home—to the apartment I had once shared with Jimmy. Along the way, I saw how much the city had changed. Banks, shops, schools, restaurants—so many places were closed. There were many cars on the streets, filled with people and their belongings, packed so full that clothes were spilling out of the windows.

People used to say that one hundred thousand people walk up and down Nanking Road every day. That day I came out of jail, it must have been one hundred thousand all pushing carts filled with strange combinations of things, sacks of rice and mink coats, that sort of thing. Auntie Du said they were all running to the train station and the boat harbor, to leave for Canton and Hong Kong before the Communists came.

Hulan was cooking when I arrived home. She ran to me, pinched my thin cheek, and said, "Maybe my cooking will never be as good as yours. But today I think you will like it better than what you have been eating." Her new husband guided me to the sofa, telling me to rest my feet, rest my head. I started to thank him with all my heart.

"Kuang An," I said, "without your help—"

He brushed my thanks away. "No need to say anything."

"It's true," I said. "Maybe I would not have lasted another six months in there."

"You're here," he said. "That's what matters. Everything else is past."

Really, he was being too polite. So I became too polite in a ridiculous way as well. "I know it was a lot of trouble," I said. "Maybe you had to pay some money. In any case, I will always be in your debt. If you ever need a favor from your friend Jiang Weili, you must ask. And each time I can do this, it will only add to my happiness."

His face turned red. Such modesty, I thought.

And now Hulan was chatting like a happy bird. "Didn't I tell you? Just one word, that's all Kuang An had to say. He knows everybody, many important people. Of course, I was after him many times. Why the delay, I said. Get her out faster."

"No more talk," Auntie Du said. "This poor little person is so thin she is about to blow away." And this was true. I was probably ten pounds less than I was the year before, and back then I had been quite thin.

My homecoming meal was very simple: spinach with one little black mushroom chopped up for taste, an egg custard with pork, fried strips of yellow fish, and a fish-head soup. That was all, three dishes and a soup, for four people. The portions were very small, too. I think Auntie Du saw me examining the last dish, knowing I was surprised there was nothing more coming.

"This meal is very special," she explained.

"Oh!" I assured her. "It is too good to be true, everything."

"Yes, but you should know anyway. We have not eaten anything like it in many months."

"The new paper money is worthless," said Hulan. "If you want a bag of rice—maybe you have to pay six million yuan in new money. Ridiculous! The money weighs more than the rice!"

"Then how did you pay for tonight's food?" I asked.

"I sold a little jade bracelet," said Auntie Du, and when she saw the shock on my face, she added, "It's the only way. That's all we can keep. Those are the only things you can use for trading. If they find you with gold or U.S. dollars on the street, you can be killed. The Kuomintang will shoot you in the head. And when the Communists come, maybe they will do the same."

"We have no money?' I asked Auntie Du.

"I didn't say this. I said they must not find you on the streets with gold or dollars. We still have one little gold bar from when you cashed in your bank account. And we have almost two hundred U.S. dollars, given to us by Jimmy Louie. Also there are still your gold bracelets, a ring, and some other little things, earrings and such. So really, we are quite lucky."

And then I remembered. "Maybe we are even luckier," I said. "Where is my suitcase?" We went into the bedroom. I opened the suitcase and pulled up the bottom. I had hidden them so well I had almost forgotten. But there they were: ten pairs of silver chopsticks, their chains still connected.

Hulan and Kuang An lived with us now—in the apartment Jimmy and I once shared. They slept in the living room. I took the bed with Auntie Du. That first night, I did not think I would sleep. I was remembering my life in the apartment just two years before, all those happy times with Jimmy Louie and Danru. But a moment later, it seemed to me, Auntie Du was shaking me awake. It was morning, and she was laughing, because I had squeezed myself flat against the wall, the same way I was used to sleeping in jail.

After breakfast, I gave Hulan a present, a pair of earrings. I put them down next to her plate. Her husband tried to refuse them for her.

"No, no!" he said. "There is no more need for thanks. Take the earrings back. No more arguing about this."

I pretended not to hear him. "Try them on," I said to Hulan. "I

only want to see how they look on your ears." And she hesitated—
maybe five seconds—then tightened one earring on, then the other.

You know the earrings I am talking about? The ones Auntie
Helen wears all the time to fancy occasions? They have a nice shape,
two thick half-circles with gold bands at each end. We call it imperial
green jade. You cannot find this color jade so easily anymore, very
rare, very expensive now. I gave her those earrings for helping me
get out of jail.

And then guess what I found out? When Auntie Du and I were
walking to the market that day, she said to me, "Don't give Hulan
any more gifts. Kuang An does not want you to remind him of his
help."

I said to Auntie Du, "He's modest, a good man, I know this.
But I think he's proud that I gave Hulan the earrings."

"No more gifts," said Auntie Du firmly.

"Auntie," I said, "they are only being polite in refusing."

"Maybe Hulan, not Kuang An." And then she told me how
Kuang An had come to her a month before, when I was still in jail.
He was so dumbfounded and ashamed. His schoolmate friend had
refused to talk to him, would not even come out of his office to
say hello. He was afraid to tell Hulan that his friend did not consider
him important enough to see, that he could not help her friend out
of jail.

"I'm so ashamed to tell my wife," he said to Auntie Du.

And Auntie Du told him, "Don't think about this anymore."

"He didn't help me?" I said.

Auntie Du shook her head. "He wanted to, of course. But in
the end, I went to the officials myself," she said. "It was nothing
really, it took only a little thinking for a few days. You see how
things are now in Shanghai, who is coming to take over everything.
I told the prison people you were the relation of a high-ranking
Communist leader—the name, I said, is a big secret. But I said to
them, 'If the Communists come next month and find Jiang Weili
in prison—oyo!' "

"You said this?"

Auntie Du was laughing. "You see what power is—holding someone else's fear in your hand and showing it to them! Besides, maybe
it is true. Maybe Peanut and Little Yu's Mother are now big Communists, who knows?"

Auntie Du made me promise I would not tell Hulan. You see what a good lady she was? She wanted Hulan to be proud of Kuang An. She said Kuang An's intention was there, that's what mattered. She did not need to let everyone know she was really the big hero. But I knew, and that was enough for her.

Still, there were many, many times when I had to bite my tongue. Helen would say, "Now I am asking you back for that favor." And I always knew what favor she was talking about. And Henry knew too, but in a different way. And I knew—in another different way. Sometimes she asked for a lot, like that time she wanted me to help her come to the United States in 1953 after she and Uncle Henry had run away to Formosa. She was asking your father and me to spend a lot of money. And what could I say?—"I did not really mean to give you those earrings, give them back."

In any case, most times I am glad she is here, Henry too. Their hearts are good. I get mad only when Helen acts as if she knew everything. And now you know: She doesn't.

The day after I got out of jail, I wrote a letter to Jimmy. I said I was waiting to find out what he wanted me to do. Should I come? Should I wait until he came to get me? I said I thought the Communists would be coming soon, maybe in one or two months. And then I read that letter to myself and tore it up.

I was remembering how his letters had changed over the last six months. He still called me his Little Wife. But he did not write three pages about his big love for me. It was more like two pages about his love for me, and then one page about his love for God. And a few months after that, it was one for me, two for God.

So I wrote a simple letter instead. I said I had been released from jail. I said, Things have changed in Shanghai, more than you can imagine. I said the Communists were coming, the Kuomintang were already leaving. Who knows if things would be better or worse.

That was the letter I sent. And then I decided I would wait. I told Auntie Du what I had done. Right away she said, "What? You are going to do nothing but wait? What happened to you in that jail? Did you learn only to keep your feet planted on the concrete floor? Anyone who even thinks she has a chance to leave is fighting for that chance now."

She pulled me up from my chair. "We are going to the telegraph office," she said. "Otherwise, your letter will take six months to reach him. And then what will it matter what he answers back? All your chances will be gone."

At the telegraph office, Auntie Du and I had to fight to keep our place in line. Everyone, it seemed, had an urgent message, some kind of terrible emergency. After three or four hours, we were at the front of the line. I had Jimmy's address already written down, along with my message: "Released from jail. Ready to come. Please advise. Your wife, Jiang Weili."

I handed this paper to the telegraph clerk. She read it, then said, "No, this won't do. It's not urgent enough. You must say, Hurry, soon we are *taonan*."

I thought, What kind of person tells me I need to put more words in a telegram? And then I looked more carefully at this smiling clerk. Guess who it was? Wan Betty! Beautiful Betty!

She had not died in Nanking. She explained that the day after I left, my four hundred dollars came. She could not send it back, so she used that money instead to run away to Shanghai. And now she had a son, already eleven years old, both smart and handsome.

We could not talk long in that crowded office. She told me she would send my telegram—adding the words she suggested, to make Jimmy send back his answer right away.

"As soon as his answer comes, I will bring it to your house," she said.

Two nights later, she came. I took the envelope into the bedroom and closed the door. I was shaking. And then my shakiness disappeared. Something was telling me I did not even need to open the envelope to know the answer. I knew my destiny, my fate, God's will.

The telegram said: "Praise God. Application complete for Jiang Weili Winnie Louie, wife of James Louie, U.S. citizen. Papers and seven hundred U.S. dollars coming. Leave immediately."

The next day we cashed the gold and some of my jewelry on the black market. And then Auntie Du and I went to find a visa. That place was worse than the telegraph office! People were crushed together, everyone shouting, arms waving money, people rushing forward to hear one rumor grow then disappear. The rules kept changing on how you could leave. You needed to have three countries say they guaranteed you could come if you could not return to China. I had the United States, of course, but I needed two more. That day someone said there were some openings, maybe it was for France, I don't remember. Anyway, I paid two hundred U.S. dollars for my second country. Now I would need to find only one more. The next day I came back for my paper. The man told me, "That second country was just a rumor. Sorry, now the rumor is gone." So was my two hundred dollars.

I can't remember how long I had to wait before I found another second country, and then a third, maybe two weeks all together. During that time, I was so nervous I broke out in a rash all over my body, then the muscles up and down my legs started to jump, as if little spiders were trying to get out. Beautiful Betty had to send many telegrams to Jimmy, explaining why I was delayed. Finally, my paperwork was complete. But I still needed a way to get out.

I bought three tickets. The first was a black-market airplane ticket, leaving for San Francisco in ten days, on May 15. The second and third were legal tickets, one leaving for Hong Kong on May 27, the other for Singapore on June 3. I had three chances.

I told Auntie Du that whatever tickets were left over she could have to sell or use. Auntie Du said she would decide later. Hulan had already said she did not want to leave. She wanted her baby to be born in China. Maybe you think this was a foolish idea, but I knew other people who thought the same way: To be born or buried in China, that was important. In any case, Hulan thought she could have her baby and still have time to decide if she should leave or not, no problem. She was wrong, of course. She had a lot of trouble. Why else did I have to help her?

So everything was settled, except that I did one last, foolish thing. I still wanted my divorce from Wen Fu. This was my pride, and I do not know why I could not let it go. Why couldn't I just come to America and forget everything else? But at the time, I convinced myself I could never have peace in my heart until I finished this one last thing.

I did not think I was being reckless. I had my paper saying I had been in prison by mistake. I had a visa and a telegram saying I was the wife of James Louie. And I had a plan, a careful plan. This is how it went.

Wan Betty sent an urgent telegram to Wen Fu. "Valuable package arrived for Mr. and Mrs. Wen Fu. Requires both signatures. Please claim May tenth, at two P.M. Bring telegram and name seal to Collections, Telegraph Office, Guanshi Road."

You think that greedy man could resist such a notice? At two o'clock, there he was, with his new woman, both of them pushing their way through the line. Hulan, Auntie Du, and I stood in a back office, watching. Wan Betty took the slip of paper and went to get the box in back, winking at me as she did. She put the box on the counter and asked Wen Fu and his wife to mark the receipt with their name seals. But just before he could do that, she pulled back the receipt and stared at the name. "Wen Fu?" she said in a puzzled voice. "Didn't I know you in Nanking many years ago? Aren't you married to Jiang Weili?"

Wen Fu had his eyes on the box. "No longer," he said.

"Is this your wife, then?" asked Wan Betty, looking at the large, bossy-looking woman standing next to Wen Fu. "I cannot release this package to anyone except Wen Fu and his legal wife."

"This is my wife," he said impatiently. "I divorced the other."

"Of course I am his wife!" said the bossy woman. "Who are you to question us about this?"

That's when I leaped out, Auntie Du and Hulan following right behind. "You admit this!" I shouted. "Now we have our witnesses." And everyone in that crowded office was looking.

Wen Fu stared at me as if I were a ghost.

I handed him the divorce paper to sign. Everything was already written. It stated I had been divorced from Wen Fu since 1941, that this had happened in Kunming. It said he had no more claims on me as his wife, I had no more claims on him as a husband. At the bottom were three signatures with name seals: mine, Hulan's, and Auntie Du's.

"You sign here," I said.

The bossy woman was not happy to see me, I could tell. "What kind of tricks are you playing on us?" she said.

"No tricks," I said. "If he doesn't sign, I don't care. I have a paper saying my jail sentence was a mistake. And in another week, I am leaving for America as the wife of someone else. But without this paper, you have no position in China. You will always be nothing but his low-class concubine."

People in the telegraph office were laughing. That woman was so mad!

"Sign it and be done with her," she said to Wen Fu. He did not move. He had said nothing to me yet. He was still staring in an evil way. But then he smiled, his smile growing bigger and uglier. He laughed, then signed his name and marked his seal.

He threw up his hands. "There," he said. "All done." He handed the paper back. And then he turned around, laughing to himself. The woman grabbed the package on the counter with a big huff, and they left. You see how stupid his new wife was? She took that package, a box I had filled that morning with dry cakes of donkey dung.

So I had my divorce. Can you blame me for wanting it? Can you blame me for what happened after that?

He must have been watching our place for many hours, maybe even days, because he waited until I was alone. I heard a knock at the door. I was not thinking, Oh, I should be careful. I answered it. He was there, pushing open the door, pushing me down on the floor, holding a gun to my head.

He cursed me and said I would never be rid of him, never, even if I ran away to the farthest corners of the moon. He saw the suitcase I had been packing. He threw it across the room, and all my clothes, my tickets, and my important papers flew out. He picked up a sheet of paper rolled into a narrow tube and pulled the ribbon holding it together. It was my divorce paper, the one that had humiliated him. He tore it into little pieces, telling me, "Now you are the same whore you always were."

He picked up another paper. It was the telegram from your father. He read it in a mocking voice. He tore that up too and said Jimmy's promises were as empty as the air they now floated in.

And then he found the visa and my airplane tickets, including the one for leaving the next day. And I screamed. I begged him not to tear up my tickets. He bounced them up and down in his hand as if he were weighing gold. "Why should I tear them? I could sell these for a fortune."

I was crying, begging him to let me go. He put the visa and tickets on the table next to us. He yanked my head up by my hair and said, "Beg me, beg me to let you be my wife." He waved his gun. Next to me, on the table, I saw all my chances for life, the tickets. In front of me, I saw the gun, my life soon leaving me. I knew he might be lying. If I obeyed, he might still take my tickets, he might still take my life.

What could I do? I was weak. I was strong. I had hope. I had hope. I couldn't give up my hope. And so I begged him.

And in the end, I was right. He lied. He said he was taking my tickets away. He put them in his pants pocket. And then he went into the bathroom, left me on the floor crying. But then I saw the gun on the table. I reached for it, held it between my hands, and shouted for him to come back.

When he saw me with the gun, his eyes widened; then he frowned. "You don't know how to fire a gun," he sneered.

"I will learn killing you," I said.

"I was only bluffing," he said. "There are no bullets in the gun. I just wanted to scare you."

"Then why are you the one who is scared?" I said, still pointing the gun, panting with a terrible rage. I truly wanted to kill him. I was not thinking of alibis, or jail, or ways to escape. I wanted only to kill him. And maybe I would have done this, if Hulan had not walked in the door, breaking my spell.

"Ai-ya!" she cried. "What is going on?"

"He stole my airplane tickets," I said. I did not say anything about the rape, although any smart person could have seen this: my hair, my torn dress, Wen Fu fastening his pants.

"Where are they?" said Hulan.

"In his pants pocket," I said. And then I had an idea. I waved the gun at Wen Fu. "Take your pants off and give them to Hulan."

Wen Fu stared at me. I pulled the trigger, thinking to hit the floor and scare him a little. But the gun exploded so fast it yanked my hand back, and a bullet flew past Wen Fu's head and landed in the wall behind him.

"Are you crazy?" he and Hulan shouted together.

"Yes," I shouted. "Take off your pants."

I pulled the trigger again, this time hitting the floor. He scrambled out of his pants, then threw them to Hulan. Hulan found the tickets and held them up to me, triumphant.

"Now throw the pants out the window," I said to Hulan. She waited only a second, and then, perhaps thinking I might shoot her too, she quickly walked to the window behind me, opened it, and dropped the pants outside.

"Now go chase your dirty pants!" I said to Wen Fu, and he ran out the door cursing, claiming I would never be through with him. As soon as he was gone, Hulan burst into laughter.

Helen used to talk about that day with me, until I told her not to remind me anymore. Why should I want to remember? Why should I listen to her talk about that day as if it were only a funny story?

"Oh," she would say. "Remember how Wen Fu tried to steal your plane tickets? Remember how you pointed a gun and made him give the tickets back? But the gun went off, an accident! Scared him to pieces. Oh, I can still see his face—he almost jumped out the window with his pants! And the next morning, you were on an airplane. Lucky for you."

And this was true. Lucky for me. Six days later I was in America with your father. Five days after that, the Communist flags went up in Shanghai, no more planes or boats could leave. So you see, those other two tickets would have been no use. I left before it was almost too late.

In America, I saw your father and I had both changed, and yet we had not. Our love was the same, but he now had his love for God. He could always speak English, I still could not.

At night, he held me the same way he had in Shanghai, so grateful we would never be separated. Yet I would often cry out in my dreams, "He's found me, he's caught me!"

And your father would say, "Baby-ah, shh-shh, don't think about this anymore, you are in America now."

So I never told him. I never told anyone. And nine months later, maybe a little less, I had a baby. I had you.

# 25

# BAO-BAO'S WEDDING

I just about fell off my chair. She had said it so matter-of-factly, "I had a baby. I had you."

"And?" I said, waiting for her to tell me the dreaded news—that Wen Fu was my father.

"And," she said, searching, "now that man is dead." She nodded to herself, apparently satisfied. "Now I don't have to worry. For so many years I thought he was going to fly out of a closet, or jump out from underneath my bed." Her hands flew, her legs jumped, the instincts still there. "But Beautiful Betty told me in a letter. See? No worries, she said, he's dead. Died on Christmas Day. Can you imagine? Christmas! Dead and he still finds a way to make me mad."

"That's not what I meant," I started to say. And then, perhaps because I didn't know what I meant, I started to laugh, only I was also on the brink of crying.

"What a terrible life you've had," I found myself saying. "And you thought you had to keep it a secret from everyone?" She was nodding. "Even me?" I whispered.

She nodded again. And there was no holding back my tears. "Now you know why," she said, sighing. And I thought, Then it's true. Wen Fu was my father, that awful man, the one she hated. His blood is running through mine. I shivered at the thought. I hugged my knees.

"Cold?" she asked. "Heater can be turned up."

I shook my head. I was trying to do a quick inventory of myself. I had always thought I looked mostly like my mother: my eyes, my nose, my chin, my cheekbones, my small teeth, and later on, the white hairs that sprouted out of the crown of my head when I reached my thirties. As for my height, the length of my hands and feet, those I had attributed to my father—at least, the one I thought of as my father.

"Tell me again," I finally said, "why you had to keep it a secret."

She looked away, considered the question. "Because then you would know," she said at last. "You would know how weak I was. You would think I was a bad mother."

"I wouldn't have thought that," I said.

"Yes you would," she insisted. "I didn't tell you about my past, and still you thought I was a bad mother. If I had told you—then it would be even worse!"

"I never thought you were a bad mother," I said.

"You did."

"I didn't."

"You *did.*"

And I thought, What are we arguing about? What is she saying? And then it occurred to me: Maybe she was not telling me that Wen Fu was my father, after all. She had kept it a secret only so I would not think bad things about her.

"Wait a minute. Who are you saying was my father?"

"Your father?" she asked, blinking, as if she had not considered this before. "Daddy was your *father.*"

I let out a huge sigh.

"Of course," she added quickly. "I would never let that bad man claim you for his daughter. He would never have that from me." Her mouth was set tight, determined.

And now I was more confused than ever. I thought of ways to rephrase my question to make myself absolutely clear: about blood relations, biological heritage, genetics, blood type, paternity tests, the past that can never be changed.

My mother patted my hand. "Oh, I know what you are thinking," she said quietly. "Of course, every baby is born with *yin* and *yang*. The *yin* comes from the woman. The *yang* comes from the man.

When you were born I tried to see whose *yang* you had. I tried to see your daddy. I would say, Look, she has Jimmy Louie's smile. I tried to forget everything else. But inside my heart I saw something else."

She touched my cheek, tucked a loose strand of hair around my ear. "You looked like Mochou. You looked like Yiku. You looked like Danru, Danru especially. All of them together. All the children I could not keep but could never forget."

My mother was in the kitchen putting more water on for tea. I was cracking watermelon seeds between my teeth. I've always thought the pleasure of eating watermelon seeds lies in extracting the thin slivers without breaking them, rather than in their taste.

"So you never once thought I looked like Wen Fu," I mused aloud.

My mother came back with a steaming pot. "Well, if I am honest, maybe I thought this one time."

I cracked the seed in half. "What?"

"Maybe two times, all together," she said on reconsideration.

I held my breath. She poured the tea, not missing a beat.

"This was right after Daddy died," she said. "Your temper became so bad."

Oh, this was terrible. My character—like Wen Fu's!

My mother frowned at me, as if I were fourteen years old again. "At the funeral," she said, "you would not cry, could not cry. You said Daddy was not your father. Ai! I never wanted to hear this!" She sounded as if this was not simply a memory, but the same heartache all over again. "That's why I slapped you," she said. "I couldn't stop myself. I couldn't tell you why."

"But I didn't mean it the way you were thinking," I said. "It was because—"

"I know why," my mother said softly. "Now I know you didn't mean it the way I was thinking." Then she frowned again. "But that other time! No excuse! Remember when you wanted to go to the oceanside?"

I shook my head. I honestly did not know what she was talking about.

"You were like a wild person," she said. "You stamped your

feet, yelled at me, shouting, 'Beach! beach!' I said to myself, Where does this temper come from? And then I thought, Ai-ya! Wen Fu!" Her face was contorted with misery.

"I couldn't blame you, I blamed him. All your worst faults I blamed on that bad man. So I didn't punish you, I let you go to the beach. But then, soon after that, your brother acted the same way. Wild! He shouted the same words, only this time I knew he was not talking about the oceanside. That's how I found out. Samuel and you both—calling me 'bitch, bitch.' "

"No!" I said, amazed that I had done that. "I didn't say that."

"Yes!" my mother said. "You did, he did too." She was smiling, glad to prove she was right after all these years. "And I was so glad I could no longer blame this on Wen Fu. This came from you— all by yourself! You thought I never figured this out? And I knew the other bad word you used, the one you say when you raise your fist with one finger sticking out. We have the same expression in Chinese, and others—even worse than you probably have in English. You think Grand Auntie was just an old lady? When somebody treated her bad—oyo!—all those expressions popped right out. Go do this! Go do that! I think that's what she was saying at her funeral when that banner fell down on top of her."

And now my mother and I were both laughing. "Auntie Du was so strong!" she said. "Oh, what a good lady! Oh, what good times we had together!" And then my mother smiled at me like a young schoolgirl, the way I imagined she must have looked when she and Peanut shared a greenhouse secret. "Maybe you should say you're sorry."

"To Grand Auntie? For what?"

"Not to Grand Auntie, to me. For saying that bad word." She was still smiling.

"But that was over twenty-five years ago!"

"No excuse."

"Maybe we should keep blaming those things on Wen Fu."

"Going to the ocean, that was Wen Fu's fault, too? Everything bad was his fault?"

And we started laughing again. I was giddy. Here my mother had told me the tragedy of her life. Here I had just been told that Wen Fu might well be the other half of my genetic makeup. Yet we were laughing.

And that's how I knew it was the right moment to tell her.

I took a deep breath and said it as casually as I could: "Maybe we have something else we can blame on that bad man." And then I told her about my illness.

For all those years I had imagined how it would be to have my mother know: She would be upset that this had happened to me. She would be angry that I had not told her sooner. She would try to find reasons why this illness had struck me. She would be vigilant in her pursuit of a cure.

I had imagined all this, and I was wrong. It was worse. She was the Furies unbound.

"Why did you go to Doug first? He's not a real doctor—a sports doctor! How do you know his friend is the best doctor? Why do you believe what other people tell you? Why do you believe them when they say there's no cure? Why do you believe them when they say 'mild case'? If you are tired so easily, this is not mild! This is serious! Why is your husband not more worried about this?"

The pitch of her voice rose higher and higher. I was watching her arms flailing at an enemy she could not see but was determined to find. I was hearing her rant about everything I had tried to hide about my illness. And I was helpless. All I could do was say, "I know, I know."

"Ai-ya! Wen Fu gave you this disease!" she cried. "He caused this to happen. And the microwave oven. I told you to check if it is leaking. Did you check?"

"Ma, stop," I pleaded. "It's not genetic. It's not the microwave. That's the way it is. It's nobody's fault. There's nothing you can do about it."

But there was no stopping her. She glared at me. "How can you say this! 'Nothing you can do'! Who told you this? How can you think this way? What do you call this disease again? Write it down. Tomorrow I am going to Auntie Du's herb doctor. And after that, I will think of a way." She was rummaging through her junk drawer for a pencil, a piece of paper.

I was going to protest, to tell her she was working herself up into a frenzy for nothing. But all of a sudden I realized: I didn't want her to stop. I was relieved in a strange way. Or perhaps relief was not the feeling. Because the pain was still there. She was tearing it away—my protective shell, my anger, my deepest fears, my despair. She was putting all this into her own heart, so that I could finally see what was left. Hope.

On the way into Bao-bao and Mimi's reception, Cleo tried to hold onto one end of the wedding present. And Tessa insisted she could carry it herself. So now, what used to be a martini set sounds like a glass jigsaw puzzle. Both girls were stricken speechless, each unable even to accuse the other.

Phil sighs, then points to a table and tells them to sit down. He shakes the box again and grins, and gingerly places it at the very end of the gift table. "We'll just let Bao-bao and Mimi exchange it for something they like better," he whispers mischievously.

I laugh and slap his arm. "You can't do that." And then I see my mother coming over with her present in hand. She stands on her tiptoes and puts her square box on top of another present, so that it is the highest one on the table. The gift is encased in shiny red foil, with the telltale creases showing that it was the same wrapping we used on our Christmas gift to her.

"Ma," I say, and shake my finger at her.

"Red is a good color for Chinese weddings," she insists, as if that's what I was scolding her for. "Anyway, inside is what counts. What did you get them?"

"A martini set," says Phil.

"What's that?" she asks.

"Six glasses, shaker, and stir stick. It comes in eight pieces, comes apart in eight hundred."

My mother seems satisfied with Phil's answer. "I almost got a six-piece cook set. I saw it in the paper, Emporium Capwell. Such a good deal, I thought, only forty-nine dollars. Then I went to see it. You know what it was? Three things, three lids. They consider three lids are already three pieces! The rest was just one fry pan, two little pots. I got salt and pepper shakers instead. Real crystal."

And now we are in a line, trudging slowly into the banquet area of the restaurant. My mother looks at me, frowning. "Ai-ya! This dress is too thin." She pinches the fabric. "Too cold is not good for you. I already told you this. You have to listen to me." She pulls Phil's sleeve. "Take this off. Give her your jacket. You have to be a better husband to her. If you don't pay attention, how will you help her pay attention too?"

I nudge him. "Yeah, Phil," I say. And he sighs, resigned—and yet pleased, it seems to me, that this is his fate, always to be reminded of his duty to me.

My mother pokes Phil's arm. "You should get her one of these," she says, nodding toward the back of a woman's full-length mink coat.

"It's not politically correct," says Phil with a grin.

"She would be warm," says my mother.

"She would be in trouble."

"She would be warm," insists my mother.

During the reception dinner, we have to shout to one another in the cavernous din of the restaurant. For the fourth time already, one of Bao-bao's five "co-best buddies," as he calls his ushers, taps into the microphone and booms, "Ladies and gentlemen, can I have your attention?"

The microphone screeches and goes dead, everyone groans and resumes talking. And then we hear the co-best buddy boom into the microphone again with a nasal voice.

"Is this on? Ladies and gentlemen, as you know, I'm Gary. When I first met Roger at college, I was just a young kid from Brooklyn. There we were, college roommates, thrown together by chance, not choice. I introduced Roger to the food of the gods, lox and bagels. Roger introduced me to—guess what?—chicken feet and *jook*."

As the best buddy continues with a barrage of ethnic comparisons, Bao-bao beams happily, content with the abuse being heaped upon him. It reminds me of the way he looked when he was a little boy, delighted that Mary and I let him play doctor with us, unaware that we had just made him the patient who dies in the first five minutes.

Phil rolls his eyes and mutters a bit too loudly, "Get the hook." I notice my mother is laughing, although perhaps it's because everyone else is chuckling politely. Or maybe they're not being polite. They actually like the jokes.

"Just pretend," I say to Phil. "The agenda tonight is to be nice."

"What? Me, not nice?" He blinks back at me, the wrongly accused husband.

"It's a wedding," I reason, although I am also aware of a curious urge to protect Bao-bao.

"And then I introduced Roger to 'oy vay,' " we hear Gary saying. "And he introduced me to—'ai ya.' Well, let me tell you, folks, Roger owes me one. Because I also introduced him to the lovely lady who is now his lucky bride. Ladies and gentlemen, may I introduce you to Mimi Wong Kwong!"

Mimi stands up with a wobble, her face already rosy from too much champagne. Her wedding dress looks like a costume from *Les Misérables*, torn sheafs of custom-faded ivory silk gauze. Bao-bao looks at her with adoring eyes.

"Ha-bu?" I hear Tessa calling to my mother. "What happened to that lady up there?" She points to Mimi.

"She got married," my mother shouts back.

"No, not *that*," Tessa says. "I mean why is she wearing a ring in her nose? She's *weird*."

My mother looks at the bride with a new critical eye. "Oh, this," she says. She thinks awhile, then gives her conclusion: "She is weird because she did not listen to her mother."

"It's true," says Phil. "Look at your mother. She listened to Ha-bu. Now she's not so weird." Tessa regards me with new respect.

The co—best buddy is back on the microphone. "And now we want to introduce you to the immediate family. On Mimi's side, we have the father of the bride, Mr. Thomas C. Y. Wong of Friendly Adventures Travel, and his lovely wife, Maggie." The crowd claps.

"So young-looking," my mother says.

We are now listening to an endless buzz of names, clapping politely for each of Mimi's scores of aunts and uncles, most of whom, it seems, hail from Arizona, land of cactus, a place about as far removed from China as I can imagine. And then Gary moves on to Roger's side of the family, patting Uncle Henry's shoulder in emcee fashion.

Uncle Henry, looking stiff in his rented tuxedo, bows and waves, then quickly sits down. Auntie Helen smiles broadly, does a half-curtsy, and throws a kiss to the right, then to the left. She is happily swirling in a pale green chiffon dress with tiny seed pearls sewn in curlicue patterns around the bodice. I notice she has on the imperial jade earrings my mother told me about.

And now Frank, and Mary, Doug, and their children jump up, smile and wave. I clap and clap, wondering when this torture will end, knowing what will come next.

And suddenly, the co-best buddy is saying, "Will the groom's aunt stand up—Winnie Louie! I heard she's responsible for all the lovely floral arrangements on the tables tonight."

My mother stands, nods shyly. She had been complaining loudly this morning about all the extra work she had to do in the flower shop to get ready for tonight's reception. "Helen wanted roses! Pink and yellow and white," she had fumed. "Why not just yellow, I asked her. Why not carnations?"

"Thanks, Auntie!" Bao-bao shouts, and my mother waves back to him. She actually looks proud.

"And Roger's favorite cousin is also here tonight—" And we're starting to stand up. I'm thinking this is about as corny as it gets, when my left heel catches on the carpet and Phil grabs me just before I fall. A big whoop goes up in the crowd, so loud that if this had been measured on a laugh meter, I would have surely won. I sit back down, embarrassed.

"Are you all right?" It's Mary, breathless, already at my side. And at that moment I realize: I had forgotten.

"I'm fine," I say. She stares at me with unspoken concern. "Really," I say. "And it's not the MS. It was my high heel. See?" I show her my shoe.

"Oh, right." She smiles uncomfortably.

"Mary," I say, with as much patience as I can muster, "just because I have MS doesn't mean I'm not entitled to the usual quota of klutziness."

She laughs. "Oh, I know. I was just, you know, checking." She keeps smiling. "Come to think of it, I just about broke my neck the other day, coming down some stairs in the mall—"

I put my hand up and stop her. "Mary, it's okay. Stop trying so hard."

"What do you mean?"

And then I see my mother looking at me. And I can't stop myself. "In this matter," I say in a mock formal voice, "you should not concern yourself for my sake." My mother shakes her finger at me

And Mary is still smiling, wondering why I'm giggling. I do feel mean, so I apologize.

"I'm sorry," I tell her. "Maybe we can talk about this later."

At that moment I hear the rustle of chiffon and satin. Auntie Helen claps her hand on my back.

"Enough to eat?" she says, surveying the disaster on our table. There are mounds of food still sitting in serving dishes. A napkin lies draped over the duck's head, something Cleo insisted my mother do.

"Too much food," my mother complains. "Wasted."

Auntie Helen beams, taking this as a compliment. "Mimi's parents, this is their fault. They insisted we have twelve courses. Plus soup! Plus cake! I said, Too much, too much. They said, We are doing this the American way, girl's side pays. So what could I do? Ai! Who didn't eat this last scallop? This is too good to leave behind. Winnie-ah, you take this."

"Too full," my mother says. She is now busy retying a bow in Cleo's hair.

"Don't be polite." Auntie Helen grabs Cleo's unused chopsticks, picks up the scallop, and holds it above my mother's plate.

"I don't want it."

"Take it," Auntie Helen insists again.

My mother makes a face at the scallop. "Not fresh!" she declares.

Auntie Helen frowns, then pops the condemned scallop into her mouth.

"You see," my mother says as she watches Auntie Helen eating. "No flavor. Am I right?"

Auntie Helen continues to chew thoughtfully.

"Too chewy!" my mother calls back.

Auntie Helen turns to me. "Your mother is a good cook," she whispers. "That's why it is hard for her to appreciate other good things. I already told her, When we go to China, maybe the food will not be like you remember. Everything is changed."

"You're going to China? Ma, you didn't tell me this."

"Ahh! We were only talking," my mother says. "I said only maybe. This is not for sure that we are going."

Auntie Helen continues talking to me. "I asked your mother to go with me—to do this one last favor. You know." Auntie Helen gives me a stoic look, then sighs. "Anyway, Mimi's parents, they own a travel business. So if we go, maybe we can also get a discount."

She picks up an oily pea with her chopsticks and rolls it back and forth with the tips. "Then I can see the place where I was born," she says. "I can give a banquet in my village. I heard you can treat fifty people, twelve courses, the best food—only two hundred dollars. Cheap to show off." She laughs to herself.

"Tst! Three hundred!" my mother says. "Prices went up."

"Three hundred, then!" Auntie Helen says in an exasperated voice. "Still a bargain." And then she turns to me. "Besides, that is not the only reason why we are going." She waits for me to ask.

"So why are you going?" I say.

"We are going to buy Chinese medicine," explains Auntie Helen, "rare things you cannot buy here."

"Medicine for what?"

"Auntie Helen wants to see if they have something for her brain," my mother reminds me with a deadpan face.

"Oh, right."

"Chinese medicine can cure anything," declares Auntie Helen. "I knew a lady, she had some kind of woman cancer. She went to the doctors here, nothing could be done. She went to the church and prayed, nothing. She went to China, drank some medicine every day—the cancer went away. The next time, she got lung cancer, same thing happened, cured."

"What did she take?"

"Oh, this I don't know. She only told me it was very bad-tasting. And now it is too late to ask her. She died of a stroke."

Auntie Helen stands up suddenly. "Pearl," she says sternly. "Come help me cut the cake." And before I can protest, she has her hand cupped around my elbow.

So there I find myself with Auntie Helen, standing in front of a plastic bride and groom perched on top of white frosting. And she says the inevitable: "Now I have to tell you a secret."

"No, Auntie Helen, no more secrets," I say, laughing. "I made a Chinese New Year's resolution. No more secrets."

She frowns. "We don't make resolutions on Chinese New Year," she says. "That's an American custom." And then she smiles coyly. "Anyway, this is a good secret, about my brain tumor."

How can I say I don't want to listen?

"I only wanted to tell you that your mother and I are not going to China for my brain tumor."

"You're not going?"

"No, no. I mean we are not going for me, we are going for *you*." She sees my puzzled face. "It's like this. Your mother wanted to go to China to find medicine for you. She thinks she gave you your sickness. She thinks the sickness came from an imbalance in her nature. She thinks the imbalance started in China. But she did not want to go alone. So I said I needed to go for my brain tumor, and she said, Yes, yes, your brain tumor. I said she should go, for my sake, for my last peace of mind. And how could she refuse? But guess what?"

"What?"

"I don't really have a brain tumor." She threw her hands up, empty.

"What?"

"That's right. I made it up! Oh, I was worried at one time. I saw the X rays, everything B nine. But that time I thought I was going to die, that made me think, What if I die, what if I die? I was thinking, What have I forgotten to do? And you know what? I forgot to thank your mother, all those years. What a good friend your mother is."

"I don't understand. What does this have to do with thanking my mother?"

"Well, you had a secret, your mother had a secret. I said I was going to die so you would both tell each other your secrets. Isn't this true? You believed me, hanh?" She giggles to herself like a naughty girl.

I nodded, still not understanding what this was leading to.

"And now you are closer, mother and daughter, I can already see this. This is my way to thank your mother. You know how she is, very hard to thank, very hard to give advice to."

Now it begins to sink in. "Does my mother know this, that you never really thought you had a brain tumor?"

Auntie Helen smiles and shakes her head, glad her lie is still intact. "Of course, when we go to China, you must pretend it was the magic spring that cured me, the same one that can cure you. Otherwise she would be mad I made her come."

"What do you mean, *I* must pretend?"

"You are coming, of course! Why would your mother go to China without you? She is going for you, not for me! I already told you this. I am only pretending to be her excuse. And you must pretend to go for my sake. But really you should go for hers. You owe this to her for all the worry you have caused her. Only you should never tell her this. This will still be our secret."

I am laughing, confused, caught in endless circles of lies. Or perhaps they are not lies but their own form of loyalty, a devotion beyond anything that can ever be spoken, anything that I will ever understand.

"It's a good secret, hanh," says Auntie Helen. "You think so?"

I shake my finger at her. "I think so," I say finally. And I don't know what I'm agreeing to, but it feels right.

Phil has already taken the girls to my mother's house. And Auntie Helen will drop me and my mother off. We are scooping wedding-banquet leftovers into take-home cartons.

"The fish you can leave behind," my mother tells me. "Steamed fish doesn't taste good the next day."

"Take it, take it," says Auntie Helen. "We can decide tomorrow if it doesn't taste good the next day."

"It's steamed," my mother protests.

"The outside is fried," says Auntie Helen, ignoring my mother.

I avoid the strafing. I take care of the chicken and pork leftovers. And in between I pour myself a cup of the chrysanthemum tea before the waiters take it away. "This sure is good, this tea," I say, trying to move my mother and Auntie Helen into neutral terrain.

"Oh, you haven't tasted tea until you go to Hangchow," says my mother. "The best tea in all the world."

"Oh," says Auntie Helen, her eyes lighting up. "We should go to that magic spring we once visited. Winnie-ah, you remember, that time we lived in Hangchow." She turns to me to explain. "The water coming out was heavy as gold. Your mother tasted it too."

"Very sweet," my mother says. "They put too much sugar inside."

"Not sugar," says Auntie Helen. "It was some kind of flower seeds, a very rare flower. It bloomed once every nine years, something like that. You crushed the seeds and put them in the water."

"Very expensive, too," my mother says. "Only this much"—she indicated a thimbleful—"and you had to pay lots of money."

"That's all you needed," adds Auntie Helen. "You swallowed that little amount. It went down inside you, changing everything—your stomach, your heart, your mind. Everything sweet."

"Peaceful," my mother says. "Everything inside you is peaceful, no worries, no sorrows."

"Your mother is going to buy some for you."

"If we go," my mother reminds her.

Auntie Helen laughs. "If we can go. Also if we can still find it. Maybe I won't remember where it is anymore."

"I remember," my mother says.

"You remember?" Auntie Helen says, frowning.

"Of course, I know exactly."

"How can this be? I was the one who took you there."

"I can find it," my mother says.

I watch them continue to argue, although perhaps it is not arguing. They are remembering together, dreaming together. They can already see it, the walk up the mountain, that time they were so young, when they believed their lives lay ahead of them and all good things were still possible. And the water is just as they imagined, heavy as gold, sweet as rare flower seeds.

I can taste it too. I can feel it. Only a little amount and it is enough to remember—all the things you thought you had forgotten but were never forgotten, all the hopes that can still be found.

# 26

# SORROWFREE

Today a new customer came into the flower shop, and she bought expensive things, big bouquets, many tangerine plants for a restaurant grand opening. Today Pearl's husband called me from work and asked if I can baby-sit next weekend, it is their second honeymoon. Today Helen and I were eating leftovers from Bao-bao's wedding dinner, and she told me, "You were right. That fish—no good taste the day after."

I was thinking, Today is my lucky day.

And then Helen said, "Now I have to admit something. The something is this: I have said many wrong things." I thought I was luckier yet.

She said, "I always told you Wen Fu was not a bad man, not as bad as you said. But all along I knew. He was bad. He was awful!" She waved her hand under her nose, chasing away a big stink.

So now Helen was confessing everything. Thinks she's going to die, so at last she tells me the truth!

"I tried to make you think he was a nice man," she said. "I told you it was only the accident, that's what made him mean. Do you know why?"

"You couldn't see clearly!" I answered. "You didn't know how much I suffered, how I could never forget. Finally you can see!"

"I said this so you would not blame Pearl."

"What are you saying?" I asked, suddenly scared. "Why should I blame Pearl?"

"Because if you thought Wen Fu was born bad, then you might think Pearl was born bad. But now I see this could never be the case. You always hated him. You always loved her. And she is nothing like him. So now I don't have to worry anymore. Now I can be frank. He was mean, a very bad man."

"You always knew this?" I asked. "That maybe Wen Fu was Pearl's—"

"Of course I knew!" Helen frowned. "How could I not know? I'm not so stupid. I come into the room, he's there, you have a gun in your hand, a crazy look on your face. And later, all those years—I saw how much you fought to make Pearl yours, just in case. You were never that way with Samuel. Daughters are different, of course. But still, I knew."

"And Auntie Du knew?"

Helen nodded.

"Ai, how could you both know and not say anything?"

And Helen patted my arm. "Eh, little person, who are you to ask such a question?"

After lunch, I told Helen I was going shopping. She said, "Where? Maybe I'll come."

I said, "I don't know where yet."

And she said, "Good, that's where I want to go too."

So then we went next door, to Sam Fook Trading Company. Right away, Mrs. Hong opened up her cash register, thinking we were coming in to trade twenty-dollar bills.

"No, no," I said. "This time I've come here to shop, something for my daughter." Mrs. Hong smiled big. So did Helen. I was standing in front of the porcelain statues: Buddha, Goddess of Mercy, God of Money, God of War, all kinds of luck.

"Do you want something for decoration or something for worship?" Mrs. Hong asked. "For worship, I can give you thirty-percent discount. For decoration, I have to charge the same price."

"This is for worship," said Helen right away.

"Not just for decoration," I said. And then I turned to Helen.

"This is true. This is for Pearl. I'm finding something to put inside the little red altar temple. I promised Auntie Du. For a long time already I have been thinking about this, before Pearl told me about her sickness."

And then I was thinking to myself once again—about that time she told me about the MS. Oh, I was angry, I was sad. I was blaming myself. I blamed Wen Fu. After Pearl went home, I cried. And then I saw that picture of Kitchen God, watching me, smiling, so happy to see me unhappy. I took his picture out of the frame. I put it over my stove. "You go see Wen Fu! You go to hell down below!" I watched his smiling face being eaten up by the fire. Right then my smoke detector went off. Wanh! Wanh! Wanh! Oh, I was scared. Wen Fu—coming back to get me. That's what I thought.

But then I listened again. And I knew: This was not Wen Fu's ghost. This was like a bingo blackout. This was like a Reno jackpot. This was Kitchen God's wife, shouting, Yes! Yes! Yes!

"What does your daughter do?" Mrs. Hong was now asking me.

"Oh, she has an important job, working in a school," I said.

"A very high-level position," adds Helen. "Very smart."

"This one is good for her then, Wen Ch'ang, god of literature. Very popular with school."

I shook my head. Why pick a name like Wen Fu's? "I am thinking of something she can use for many reasons," I explained.

"Goddess of Mercy, then." Mrs. Hong was patting the heads of all her goddesses. "Good luck, good children, all kinds of things. We have many, all different sizes. This one is nice, this one is thirty dollars. This one is very nice, this one is two hundred sixty-five dollars. You decide."

"I am not thinking of the Goddess of Mercy," I said. "I am looking for something else."

"Something to bring her money luck," Mrs. Hong suggested.

"No, not just that, not just money, not just luck," says Helen. We look at each other. But she cannot find the words. And I cannot say them.

"Perhaps one of the Eight Immortals," said Mrs. Hong. "Maybe all eight, then she has everything."

"No," I said. "I am looking for a goddess that nobody knows. Maybe she does not yet exist."

Mrs. Hong sighed. "I'm sorry, this we do not have." She was disappointed. I was disappointed. Helen was disappointed.

Suddenly Mrs. Hong clapped her hands together. "Where is my head today?" She walked to the back of the store, calling to me. "It is back here. The factory made a mistake. Of course, it is a very nice statue, no chips, no cracks. But they forgot to write down her name on the bottom of her chair. My husband was so mad. He said, 'What are we going to do with this? Who wants to buy a mistake?' "

So I bought that mistake. I fixed it. I used my gold paints and wrote her name on the bottom. And Helen bought good incense, not the cheap brand, but the best. I could see this lady statue in her new house, the red temple altar with two candlesticks lighting up her face from both sides. She would live there, but no one would call her Mrs. Kitchen God. Why would she want to be called that, now that she and her husband are divorced?

When Pearl came to drop off the children at my house this weekend, I said to her husband, "Go watch TV with the children. I have to give my daughter some medicine I found."

I took her upstairs to my bedroom. Pearl-ah, I said. Here is some Chinese medicine. You put this pad on your arms and legs, the herbs sink into your skin. And every day you should drink hot water three or four times a day. Your energy is too cold. Just hot water, no tea or coffee inside. Are you listening?

What are you looking at? Oh, that statue. You never saw that before. Yes, that's true, very fancy, fine porcelain. And the style is good too. See how nicely she sits in her chair, so comfortable-looking in her manner. Look at her hair, how black it is, no worries. Although maybe she used to worry. I heard she once had many hardships in her life. So maybe her hair is dyed.

But her smile is genuine, wise and innocent at the same time. And her hand, see how she just raised it? That means she is about to speak, or maybe she is telling you to speak. She is ready to listen. She understands English. You should tell her everything.

Yes, yes, of course this is for you! Why would I buy such a thing for myself? Don't cry, don't cry. I didn't pay too much.

But sometimes, when you are afraid, you can talk to her. She will listen. She will wash away everything sad with her tears. She will use her stick to chase away everything bad. See her name: Lady Sorrowfree, happiness winning over bitterness, no regrets in this world.

Now help me light three sticks of incense. The smoke will take our wishes to heaven. Of course, it's only superstition, just for fun. But see how fast the smoke rises—oh, even faster when we laugh, lifting our hopes, higher and higher.

# Amy Tan

# The Hundred Secret Senses

Olivia Yee is only five years old when Kwan, her older sister from China, comes to live with the family and turns her life upside down, bombarding her day and night with ghostly stories of strange ancestors from the world of Yin. Olivia just wants to lead a normal American life.

For the next thirty years, Olivia endures visits from Kwan and her ghosts, who appear in the living world to offer advice on everything from restaurants to Olivia's failed marriage. But just when she cannot bear it any more, the revelations of a tragic family secret finally open her mind to the startling truths hidden in Kwan's unorthodox vision of the world.

'Kwan emerges as a splendidly vital comic character…and her sensibility – call it superstitious and crazy, or call it colourfully imaginative and indicative of a proper respect for the past – pervades every part of this highly enjoyable novel.'
LUCY HUGHES HALLETT, *Sunday Times*

'The story works like a dream…and the novel is most compelling and alive when the two sisters are sparring and squabbling. Tan has a great ear for feminine chitchat, its spikiness and hilarity, its mockery and teasing.'
MICHELE ROBERTS, *Independent*

'Resist the temptation to feast on this latest offering from Amy Tan in one voracious sitting – instead, savour it, slow time. Tan's writing rolls along effortlessly, like the best-told folklore – it's simply mesmerising.'
*Elle*

🔥 *f l a m i n g o*

**P.S.**

Ideas,
interviews
& features ...

## About the author

2   Profile of Amy Tan

6   Q & A

8   Life at a Glance

9   My Favourite Books

## About the book

10   Extract from *The Opposite of Fate*

## Read on

13   If You Liked This, Why Not Try More
     From *The Perennial Collection*

# Profile of Amy Tan

*Fanny Blake*

A PERIPATETIC CHILDHOOD meant that Amy Tan frequently felt alienated and alone when she moved into another new neighbourhood and school. 'I was a child who was anxious to please adults so I'd observe teachers, how they were and who they responded to. I think this gave me an observational eye and memories that would become important to me as a writer.' When she was six she had an IQ test administered by a psychologist who was to continue tracking her until she was twelve. The first year she told Tan's parents that she had what it took to be a doctor. On the basis of that, they saw her course for life set, the only refinement being that she should be a neurosurgeon because they deemed this the best kind of doctor and the brain the most important and difficult organ. They aimed high for their daughter, and she grew up believing she had to fulfil the charge.

After a dear friend was murdered in 1976, Tan left her doctoral programme and worked for four years as a language development consultant, evaluating children with developmental difficulties and then programming objectives with their teachers and parents. 'Working with parents who'd just had the news their children weren't going to be quite perfect was the most humanizing experience I've had,' she remembers. She went on to become a project director of a federally funded demonstration project for teachers training to work with children with learning disabilities, writing the grant proposals. She then went on to work in a medical publishing company, but, discovering she was not a partner in the business, as she had believed, she decided to leave and work as a freelance business writer. Her employer's parting shot rang in her ears: 'Good luck. Writing is your worst skill. You'll be lucky if you make a dime.'

Her response was determined. 'I realize I'm someone who responds quite well to adversity. I take a dire prediction and then fight my way to turn it into something better. That's part of my notion of the opposite of fate.' As a freelance writer, Tan became increasingly successful until she was working a ninety-hour billable week, existing on cigarettes and coffee. She sought the help of a Jungian psychiatrist who dozed off during three of their sessions, confirming to Tan that she should try some self-help behaviour modification. She started to play jazz piano and attended a writers' workshop. She also turned to a number of writers for advice. Eventually she started using her own experiences and something close to her own voice to produce 'Endgame' (later 'Rules of the Game'), a short story that she took to a workshop where Molly Giles (her editor today) helped her refine it. 'She suggested I took one of the voices and made it into one story.' When it was accepted by a literary journal, *FM5*, Tan's ambitions were on the road to realization.

Her fortunes were to take another turn when an Italian magazine reprinted the ▶

❛ Her employer's parting shot rang in her ears: "Good luck. Writing is your worst skill. You'll be lucky if you make a dime." ❜

## Profile *(continued)*

◄ story without permission. Tan contacted an agent, who became a lasting influence on her life. The agent badgered her to write another story and a proposal for a book. 'I sat down for two or three hours,' remembers Tan, 'and dashed off some ideas, naming it *Wind and Water*. My agent felt it was too obtuse and wanted to call it *The Joy Luck Club* after the title of the first chapter. It seemed rather prosaic to me but I agreed because I knew she wasn't going to sell it anyway.'

At the time her mother almost died and Tan decided to take her to China and write some stories about her. When they returned, her agent broke the news that she had six offers for the book. Tan was astonished and agreed to accept the offer from the most sympathetic editor, Faith Sale. 'I sent her the stories in threes. She was very low key and kept telling me to carry on writing. Afterwards she told me she was very happy but hadn't wanted me to stop and analyse what I was doing. Eventually I packed the completed book in red paper tied with gold ribbon for luck and met her. As a result of her advice, I wrote an additional story and four introductory pieces. I did it all in a week because I was so scared they would change their mind.'

The book's success came as a complete surprise to Tan. 'I don't think anyone except my agent had thought it would hit the bestseller list. It wasn't something I'd dreamed of so I was completely unprepared for it and was scared it would change my life.'

❛ My agent felt it was too obtuse and wanted to call it *The Joy Luck Club*. It seemed rather prosaic to me but I agreed because I knew she wasn't going to sell it anyway. ❜

Change her life it did. The book was nominated for the National Book Award and the National Book Critics Circle Award and subsequently adapted into a feature film in 1994. Since then Tan has continued to draw on her family's experiences to create her bestselling novels, including *The Kitchen God's Wife*, *The Hundred Secret Senses* and *The Bonesetter's Daughter*. ■

❜ I don't think anyone except my agent had thought it would hit the bestseller list. It wasn't something I'd dreamed of so I was completely unprepared. ❜

# Q & A

**What is your idea of perfect happiness?**
It's the rare moment I finish my book and it
feels complete and safely nestled where it
belongs. Cuddling with my two Yorkies and
my husband on a rainy day at home with
newspapers all around, as well as fresh fruit
and coffee, counts as perfect happiness as
well, and easy to come by.

**What is your greatest fear?**
Losing anyone I love. I also fear the loss of my
intellect through disease.

**Which living person do you most admire?**
I can't say there is any one person. It depends
on the situation at hand. I admire some
people because they are geniuses at what they
do. I admire others because they are selfless
and favourably affect the lives of many. I
admire my husband because he has to live
with me.

**What objects do you always carry with you?**
The objects of my affection, of course, my
two Yorkshire Terriers, Bubba and Lilli. They
are only two and three pounds each, and fit
into a special bag with vented windows. Now
that England allows pets via the PETS
passports, we'll probably visit there more
often.

**What is the most important lesson life has
taught you?**
Your family can teach you both the limits of
your endurance and the limitlessness of your
love and hopes.

**Which writer has had the greatest influence on your work?**
Molly Giles, who is both a gifted writer and now my American editor, the one who reads all my rough drafts.

**Do you have a favourite book?**
*Lolita* by Nabokov is a favourite for many reasons, but especially language. *Jane Eyre* is a sentimental favourite from childhood.

**Where do you go for inspiration?**
China, especially, but other countries as well. Reading a powerful work of fiction by others also inspires me to want to write.

**Which book do you wish you had written?**
To be honest, I have never wished I had written someone else's books.

**What do you think of literary prizes?**
Many are highly political, more suited to the particular agenda of a panel of judges rather than to specific literary merit. Some are given to help raise awareness of smaller literary books, and that, I think, is a worthy thing to do. Some are concocted categories to lure famous writers (in America) to give free talks at boring meetings in exchange for a plaque made of fake wood. Very few these days are truly meaningful. But, of those that are, I do find that I have enjoyed almost every Man Booker prize-winner.

**What are you writing at the moment?**
I'm at work on a new untitled novel. ∎

> ❝ I do find that I have enjoyed almost every Man Booker prize-winner. ❞

# Life at a Glance

© *Robert Foothorap*

**BORN**

19 February 1952 in Oakland, California

**EDUCATION**

High School: Monte Rosa, Montreux, Switzerland. Colleges: Linfield, San Jose City College, San Jose State University, University of California Santa Cruz, University of California Berkeley. BA in English and Linguistics, San Jose State University; MA in Linguistics, San Jose State University.

**MARRIAGE**

1974 to Lou DeMattei

**CAREER**

Pizza slinger in college. Language development consultant for programmes for young children with developmental disabilities, 1976–80; project administrator, 1980–3; freelance business writer, 1983–8.

**BOOKS**

*The Joy Luck Club*, 1989; *The Kitchen God's Wife*, 1991; *The Hundred Secret Senses*, 1998; *The Bonesetter's Daughter*, 2001; *The Opposite of Fate*, 2003; *Saving Fish from Drowning*, 2005. Also two children's books: *The Moon Lady* and *The Chinese Siamese Cat*. Co-writer of screenplay for *The Joy Luck Club*.

Nominated for National Book Award, National Book Critics Circle Award, Orange Prize, *Los Angeles Times* Award. Received Commonwealth Gold Award, Bay Area Book Reviewers Award, Torgi Award, *New York Times* Notable Books. BAFTA nomination for best screenplay (*The Joy Luck Club*). ■

## MY FAVOURITE BOOKS

1. Lolita
   *Vladimir Nabokov*

2. Jane Eyre
   *Charlotte Brontë*

3. Love Medicine
   *Louise Erdrich*

4. Annie John
   *Jamaica Kincaid*

5. Love in the Time of Cholera
   *Gabriel García Márquez*

6. Canterbury Tales
   *Chaucer*

7. Alice in Wonderland
   *Lewis Carroll*

8. Psychopathia Sexualis
   *Krafft-Ebing*

9. Speak, Memory
   *Vladimir Nabokov*

# Extract from *The Opposite of Fate*

... FOR THE first ten years of my life, I did not know of my mother's first marriage. She kept it a secret from my brothers and me, from her closest friends. When she finally did tell me, I did not ask her any questions. In part, I did not want to think she could have once loved a man other than my father. And when I grew older, I still did not ask her about her early life in China. Why bring up the pains of her past? Of course, the questions were still there. I wondered, I imagined, I assumed what the answers might have been.

When I set out to write my second book, I remembered that conversation with my mother, about her marriage to a man she grew to despise. I decided to write about a woman and her secret regrets, and used my American assumptions to shape the story: that this woman's first marriage, while ending in hate, surely must have been born out of love. Why else would she have stayed in her marriage for twelve years?

That's what I started out writing. Fortunately, writing has a way of showing me how false my assumptions can be. My character rebelled against this fiction I had imposed on her. 'No,' she protested. 'This was not love. This was hope, hope for myself.' She refused to go along with the plot, and I found the story at a dead end.

And so I began again. I began by asking myself about hope. How does it change, transform, endure according to life's quirky circumstances? And what of the circumstances themselves: Do we believe they are simply a matter of fate? Or do we view them as the Chinese concept of luck, the Christian concept of God's will, the American concept of choice? And depending on what we believe, how can we find balance in our lives? What do we accept? What do we feel we can still change?

Eventually I wrote a book in which a mother poses these questions as she tells her daughter the secrets of her past. Since the story takes place during wartime, before my birth, I had to do quite a bit of research. I read scholarly texts and revisionist versions of the various roles of the Kuomintang, the Communists, the Japanese, and the Americans. I read wartime accounts published in popular periodicals – with different perspectives on these same groups. And of course, I needed a personal account of the war years to fact-check some of the mundane details of my story: How long did it take to travel from Shanghai to Yangchow? What was a typical dowry for a bride from a well-to-do family? For those answers, I went to my mother, who in response gave me more than I asked for. The question of the dowry alone led to a three-hour remembrance of things past – not simply about wedding gifts, but about family gossip and Shanghai manners, about a gangster who showed up at her wedding, about her innocence – her stupidity! – in marrying a man she hardly knew ...

So, indeed, some of the events in ▶

### *The Opposite of Fate* *(continued)*

◄ *The Kitchen God's Wife* are based on my
mother's life; her marriage to 'that bad man',
the death of her children, her fortuitous
encounter with my father. But, with
apologies to my mother, I confess that I
changed her story. I invented characters
who never existed in her life: Auntie Du,
Helen, Jiaguo, Old Aunt and New Aunt,
Peanut, Beautiful Betty, Bao-Bao Roger. I
took her to places that do not exist: to a
tea-growing monastery in Hangchow, to a
mountaintop village called Heaven's Breath,
to a scissors-making shop in Kunming, to
an American dance that in real life she
decided not to attend. With those imaginary
details in place, I can honestly say the story
is fiction, not true.

And yet it is as close to the truth as I can
imagine. It is my mother's story in the most
important of ways to me: her passion, her
will, her hope, the innocence she never really
lost. It is the reason why she told me, 'I was
not affected,' why I can finally understand
what she truly meant. ■

# If You Liked This, Why Not Try More From *The Perennial Collection*

*A Thousand Acres*
Jane Smiley

WINNER OF THE PULITZER PRIZE

Larry Cook's farm is the largest in his county in Iowa, a tribute to his hard work and single-mindedness. Proud and possessive, his sudden decision to retire and hand over the farm to his three daughters is disarmingly uncharacteristic. When the youngest has misgivings he cuts her out – a decision that causes chaos.

'Powerful, poignant, intimate and involving'
*New York Times*

.........................................................

*The Stone Diaries*
Carol Shields

WINNER OF THE PULITZER PRIZE

This is the poignant story of Daisy Goodwill, twentieth-century pilgrim, from her calamitous birth in Canada to her death in a Florida nursing home nearly ninety years later. Struggling to find her place in the world, she listens and observes, becoming a witness to her own life and death in this rich tale that reflects and illuminates our own unsettled era.

'I can think of few novels containing so much that is resonant and unforgettable, or that invite the reader to participate so fully and rewardingly'
*Sunday Telegraph*

## If You Liked This . . . *(continued)*

### *The Hours*
Michael Cunningham

WINNER OF THE PULITZER PRIZE AND THE
PEN/FAULKNER AWARD

From 1920s London to 1940s Los Angeles
and 1990s New York, *The Hours* recasts the
classic story of Virginia Woolf's *Mrs Dalloway*
in startling new light. Moving effortlessly
across the decades, this exquisite novel
intertwines the worlds of three unforgettable
women.

'Extremely moving, original and memorable'
HERMIONE LEE, *TLS*

### *We Were the Mulvaneys*
Joyce Carol Oates

The Mulvaney family, who live together on
picture-perfect High Point Farm, is seemingly
blessed by everything that makes life sweet.
Yet something happens on Valentine's Day,
1976 – something involving Marianne, the
pretty 16-year-old daughter. The events of
that night, hushed up in the town and never
discussed within the family, rend the fabric of
their life with tragic consequences.

'A book which will break your heart, heal it,
then break it again'                  *LA Times*

*Eve Green*
Susan Fletcher

WINNER OF THE WHITBREAD FIRST NOVEL
AWARD

Following the death of her mother, eight-year-old Evie is sent to a new life in rural Wales. With a sense of being lied to she sets out to discover her family's dark secret – unaware that when a local girl vanishes there is yet more darkness to come. Years later she remembers that first Welsh summer: her lies, her anger, her reckless search for Rosie's abductor and the lessons she learnt – about trust, identity, guilt and how to survive when love is gone.

'A passionate, intensely observed novel'

JULIE MYERSON

---

*Purple Hibiscus*
Chimamanda Ngozi Adichie

SHORTLISTED FOR THE ORANGE PRIZE FOR
FICTION

Fifteen-year-old Kambili lives in fear of her father, a charismatic yet violent Catholic patriarch, who is generous in the community but repressive at home. When Nigeria is shaken by a military coup, Kambili and her brother go to live at their aunt's home, a noisy place full of laughter. The visit will lift the silence from her world and unlock the terrible, bruising secret at the heart of her family life.

'An intoxicating story that is at once distinctly feminine, African and universal'

*Observer*

15